COLLECTIVE MARKS

COLLECTIVE MARKS

Nancy N. Feldman

iUniverse, Inc.
New York Lincoln Shanghai

Collective Marks

iUniverse books may be ordered through booksellers or by contacting:

iUniverse
2021 Pine Lake Road, Suite 100
Lincoln, NE 68512
www.iuniverse.com
1-800-Authors (1-800-288-4677)

This is a work of fiction. All of the names, characters, events, and places are either the product of the author's imagination or are used fictitiously. Any resemblance to actual persons, living or dead, events, or locales is entirely coincidental.

Front cover image: **Whistlejacket,** Oil on canvas, 292 x 246.4 cm, by George Stubbs, 1724-1806

ISBN-13: 978-0-595-37547-9 (pbk)
ISBN-13: 978-0-595-67526-5 (cloth)
ISBN-13: 978-0-595-81941-6 (ebk)
ISBN-10: 0-595-37547-2 (pbk)
ISBN-10: 0-595-67526-3 (cloth)
ISBN-10: 0-595-81941-9 (ebk)

Printed in the United States of America

To Joan Koponen

PREFACE

▼

In the 1960s, when this novel takes place, not very many horsemen in the United States had heard of dressage. Although the discipline was developed in Europe and has been practiced there from the time of the Renaissance, it came to the attention of many in the United States after the Second World War by way of the United States Military.

The French term "dressage" means, literally "schooling". In equestrian literature, it refers to the schooling (or training) of the riding horse through a gradual, progressive series of exercises aimed at developing the athleticism, balance and obedience of the horse so that he will become his rider's willing and able partner. Dressage shows, unlike most horse shows, are in the form of tests, ridden at various levels of expertise before a judge. A ride is judged not against others, but against an absolute standard, which measures the horse's training and the rider's skill in communicating with him. Both the horse and his rider must learn from each other, since they are judged as one, and even the most talented horse cannot perform without an educated rider. At the end of the show the rider receives his test sheet, scored and annotated by the judge. It reflects the judge's expert evaluation of each required movement, and includes at the end a summation of his general impression of the ride, called the Collective Marks.

The fascination that the horse holds for man derives not only from his use over the centuries as an invaluable source of transportation, work, and military prowess, but from his aesthetic appeal as a creature of grace, strength, and sensitivity and, not least, from his ability to adapt to man's needs.

It's this dichotomy between the artistic and practical aspects of dressage training that has been reflected in the growth and development of dressage in the 20th century. There is an uneasy relationship between the increasing interest in competitive dressage and that of the dressage purists in applying the principles of classical dressage. What one side sees as "circus tricks" is countered by the other side's accusations of "shortcuts" in training.

In this novel there are echoes of both points of view. I haven't bothered to define some of the terms, which I hope will be explained by the action as the young protagonist struggles along with the reader, to understand a subject in which he has a passionate interest, but practically no experience.

Readers who have come lately to dressage may notice differences between conditions, which were common half a century ago, and those they are apt to find now. Instructors, judges and competitions in dressage were few and far between at that time and out of the reach of many. Dressage horses were drawn from the hunt field, the show circuit, the racecourse and riders' own back yards. They represented the many breeds of horses in the United States, many bred for quite different uses. Although most of the relatively few instructors and licensed judges came from a European background, almost none of the horses did. Competitions were attended both by riders who simply wanted help in riding and training their horse and by those who were climbing the ladder of competitive dressage.

Enormous changes have occurred since that time, both in the quality of the horses—many of them warmbloods bred for their dressage potential and imported from Europe—and in the sophistication and skill of the average rider. Because the education and development of the rider are integral to the training of the horse, the emphasis on equitation and horse management has increased. Dressage shows are now as common as hunter-jumper shows, and talented horses and riders will often go to Europe for a season of competition before entering the International circuit. A successful Grand Prix horse may easily be worth six figures. Saddlery and riding equipment has also become specialized. Less noticeable, perhaps, but equally dramatic, is the general understanding and acceptance of basic dressage training as an invaluable asset to both the art and science of riding, not only in the gradual improvement of rider and horse but in a greater awareness of their interdependence.

CHAPTER 1

▼

It was after three when Annie finally got away from her office at the County Mental Health Clinic to start the long drive to the farm. She found the turn-off a mile or so past Northwood only because she was looking for it. The small green sign that identified it by number as a county road was half concealed by a thicket of weeds and scarred and dented by buckshot.

The narrow dirt road wound gradually upward through the dense New England woods. At the top as the land fell away, she emerged into open country, a sweeping expanse of spring grass spotted with wild flowers. In the distance fence lines followed the contours of the hilly terrain. They were the first sign of civilization she had seen since she turned off the tarred road.

Her attention was drawn to the rail fence, which bordered the road. Although it was weather-beaten, the grass under the rails and around the posts was neatly cut. In the distance she saw a figure turn two horses into a field and stand watching for a minute as they lifted their tails and trotted away together.

The farmhouse stood to her right, set back from the road and shaded by several tall trees. It was a modest, two-story frame house with a wide porch and an ell in back. The lane before her divided shortly after the house, the left fork leading down to a large barn, dwarfed by an even larger building behind it, and the right winding down the hill toward the woods and out of sight.

Annie stopped the car by the house and made her way across the grass to the front door. As she waited for an answer to her knock, she glanced through the glass panes. The hall seemed severely plain with whitewashed walls and a bare floor. A single table and a tall, ladder-backed chair were the only furniture.

She waited indecisively on the porch, listening for some sound to indicate a presence inside. All she heard were the random sounds of summer, the wind in the trees, a birdcall, the sound of locusts, and finally she turned and started on foot down the road to the barn. When she reached it, she became aware of sounds inside and saw some of the stall doors standing open. The atmosphere was redolent of hay and horses.

A horse appeared suddenly, silhouetted against the rear doorway as he emerged from his stall. As he turned toward her, Annie saw a figure at his shoulder. Man and horse came down the aisle and stopped a few feet away. The horse's ears were pricked, and he tossed his head impatiently, pushing at his handler with his nose. The man gave a gentle jerk on the leadshank and reached across with his left hand to lay a restraining hand on the horse's nose. He met Annie's eye and smiled. She thought he must be in his twenties. He had fair hair and was dressed in jeans, a faded plaid shirt with the sleeves rolled up, and work boots.

"Can I help you?" he asked. Absently he stroked the horse's nose and leaned back slightly against the shank.

"I've come to see Mr. Sarmento," Annie said, watching them uneasily. "Is he here?"

The young man glanced over his shoulder, and suddenly the horse lifted his head and gave a ringing neigh. Annie stepped back inadvertently.

"He's in the tackroom, I think. Excuse me, I have to get this horse out."

She watched him lead the horse from the barn past where she was standing. His right elbow was braced against its shoulder, so that his weight kept the animal from pulling him along. She stepped again over the threshold and heard sounds of someone moving about in one of the stalls.

"Mr. Sarmento?"

The figure inside the stall straightened, and she saw she had made a mistake. It was another young man. In his hand he held a manure fork, and he looked at her across a battered wheelbarrow that stood in the doorway.

"He's back there."

Following his gesture, she saw still another man emerge from a doorway halfway down the aisle. Later, as she drove home, she couldn't recall his face clearly but remembered only the impression he made on her: a lean man of medium height, probably in his early forties, wearing riding breeches, worn boots and a white shirt, open at the neck. His expression was hard, his dark brows drawn down in something close to a scowl. Whether he didn't see her or was too preoccupied to notice her, he ignored her utterly.

"Ivan," he said.

"Yes, sir?" The formal, almost military response sounded odd to Annie. Ivan stood almost at attention beside her, the manure fork in his hand.

"You are late. Why are there three stalls left to be done at this hour?"

He advanced down the aisle toward them, and Annie retreated a few steps.

"I just got back from town, sir—with the grain," Ivan said. He glanced over at Annie and added, "This lady wants to see you."

Sarmento gave her a cursory glance. "Yes?" he said without enthusiasm and stared past her out the barn door. It was hard to tell if the question was a response to Ivan's comment or to her.

"Erik Sarmento? How do you do?" she said. "I'm Annie Trowbridge, from the Mental Health Clinic in Reed. I wonder if I might talk—"

He seemed to be paying no attention, and, disconcerted, she floundered to a stop. The blond young man appeared again in the doorway.

"Peter, see that the water buckets are cleaned," Sarmento said.

"I was planning to do that in the morning, since we're running a bit late—"

"Whose fault is that?" Sarmento demanded. "Do them now."

"Yes, sir." Peter walked quickly away toward the back of the barn.

Annie watched the interplay between the three with curiosity, and now as Sarmento turned finally toward her still unsmiling, she started again. "My name is Annie Trowbridge—"

"You have already told me that. What do you want?"

"I'd like to talk to you, if I may. Is there somewhere—?"

"We can talk here."

"Very well. I've come on behalf of a client of mine, a young man named Michael Ross. I've tried to reach you several times by phone and gotten no answer, so I drove out hoping to find you. I hoped you might be willing to hire him."

Sarmento raised an eyebrow. "He requires a woman to find work for him?"

Annie wondered why she felt as if she were locked in combat with this man. Despite her training, she found herself wanting to take him off balance. "No," she heard herself say calmly, "he's unable to come himself. He's in jail."

She paused for a fraction of a second to measure the effect of her words, but he seemed not to have heard her. "I've been his caseworker for several years—he's just turned eighteen—since his parents' death," she went on. "They died in an accident when he was about ten. He's had some trouble with the police—minor trouble," she added quickly.

"Does it look as if I am running a reform school?"

"Of course not," Annie said appeasingly. "You were suggested because of the horses. Michael has a consuming interest in horses. He rode a lot as a child when his parents were living, and he always seems to turn up near horse facilities. He found himself a job at the racetrack most recently, but it didn't work out—"

He turned from her to watch Ivan, who was working in another stall. "I take it you have unloaded the truck?"

"No, sir, not yet. It was time to feed when I got—"

"See that the grain is put away this evening."

Ivan didn't answer, but continued to work until the center of the stall, like the others, was bare, the clean straw banked against the walls.

In her embarrassment at being a captive audience to this encounter, Annie said quickly, "I'm afraid I've come at a bad time. Perhaps I should wait until the work is finished," and she left the barn. She wasn't anxious to delay the long drive home, but she felt she must make the best of a bad situation. She wondered if Sarmento had even been listening to her.

The sun, down in the sky, hovered over the forest through which she had just driven, and the windows of the farmhouse caught the orange light. The house looked as if it were on fire, consumed from within by flames. At the bottom of the pasture the horses grazed calmly, and Annie noticed the contrast and was struck by a sense of profound isolation. Already in the fading sunlight, the air was turning chill. She turned to find Sarmento watching her.

"I'm sorry to have come when you're so busy," she began, but he said nothing.

"Is there any point in discussing this further?" Annie asked. She could hear the edge in her voice, and for the first time, he smiled.

"You wish me to take on an eighteen-year-old delinquent," he said dryly, "a social misfit who cannot hold a job—or seek one, apparently—simply because he likes horses. Have I understood you correctly?"

In spite of herself, she laughed. "You do make it sound ridiculous," she said, "but I don't know what else to do with him. It's not good for him to drift from place to place doing whatever he feels like. Now that he's turned eighteen, he's legally an adult. By all rights he should be supporting himself, but he isn't, and Reed is a small town. On Thursday he lost his job at the racetrack. He went into town, got into a fight in the local bar and was arrested. I work closely with the police in my business, and they know I've been responsible for Michael since he was a child. So they've told me essentially that if I can't find some solution for him, they'll be forced to do what they're paid to do."

"Which is?"

"Put him away, I suppose, if they catch him causing trouble again. He hasn't done anything really terrible, but he gets into fights, loses his temper—that kind of thing. I know it sounds unlikely, but he's really a very hard worker."

"I am not in the business of running a foster home," Sarmento said after a few moments of silence. "Nor do I have any interest in social work. I hope that is not too insulting?"

Annie shrugged.

"However, I can always use a strong back."

Before she could think of an answer, he continued, "Should I take him on, it would not be for any of the reasons that seem to cause you so much concern. I have not the slightest interest in the tragedies and traumas of his life, or whether people have allowed him to take advantage of them. Nor," he added as she made a move to interrupt, "do I care if he is fond of horses." He gestured toward the pasture. "The value of those animals is nearly a hundred thousand dollars. The worst of them is worth infinitely more than this individual you appear to value so highly."

Annie found herself mesmerized by the tone of his voice and his sarcastic self-assurance. There was an air of implicit challenge in his attitude, she felt, watching him. He stood, his feet only slightly apart, his posture erect and extraordinarily still, making her the object of his wintry, unwelcoming gaze. He had none of the unspoken but eloquent signs of communication that she was skilled at interpreting—the slight change in facial expression, the shifting of stance, the hand movements that signaled that a comment was self-deprecating or humorously meant. Always ready to respond in kind to such silent discourse, she found this barrier intensely disconcerting, and she listened with unnatural concentration to his words, which were delivered with an inflection she couldn't place. It sounded almost foreign, although she detected no accent in his speech, and it had the effect of weighting his remarks with an ironic significance so that she wondered if she was understanding him at all.

"Maybe I should think this over a little more," she said finally, but he made no move to indicate the interview was over. "These young men you have working for you—what do you pay them?"

"You wonder if your—client, did you say?—will find this a lucrative position? I'm afraid I must disappoint you again. I do not pay my help."

Annie stared at him. "Then why on earth do they stay?"

"Some don't. Those two," he nodded toward the barn, "have been here two and three years respectively. As to why, you would have to ask them that question. I have no interest in their motives. I'm interested in the work they accomplish."

Peter reappeared in the barn doorway, and Sarmento gave him an appraising look.

"Well?"

"We're about done, sir. Is there anything else?"

"The buckets have been cleaned?"

"Yes, and we've put away the grain."

"The stalls need to be limed."

"Ivan's doing that now."

"The tack?"

"It's done."

"Then you may start the supper." And with that he turned and walked up the lane to the house without even glancing in her direction.

Annie shook her head and gave a short, self-conscious laugh. "Well," she said sheepishly to Peter, "I guess that means I'm to be on my way."

"I'll walk you to your car," Peter said quickly. She knew he was embarrassed for her and felt both grateful and amused.

"If you don't mind my asking," she said as they walked, "why do you work here? I understand you're not even paid."

"Not in money," he said, "although my horse is here. That's money, in a way. I work off her board and mine. And then—the lessons—" He slowed to a stop. "Look, I'm sorry he was rude to you. He's like that sometimes—but he's a genius. You can't judge him like other people."

She regarded him with surprise. "A genius? Somehow I never found that a satisfactory excuse for bad manners."

"You should see him with the horses," he said, and suddenly his face lit up.

She was touched by his concern for her and by his paradoxical defense of his employer. Partly because of him and partly because she had few options, she decided at that moment to urge Michael to accept the position.

As she drove through the increasing twilight down the hillside into the woods, Annie noticed the cold. She turned the heater on and began thinking about Michael. Her position as his caseworker had not been typical. She had found herself over the years serving as both warden and advocate, and she was uncertain even now which of these roles she was playing and which she should play.

She had first seen Michael when his aunt brought him to the Family Service agency where she had then worked, shortly after the car accident that took the lives of both his parents. The aunt's story was brief and unequivocal. She was the boy's sole living relative, although she was only a half sister to Michael's father and had been fifteen years his senior. She hadn't been close to her half brother, who had lived almost a thousand miles away in Virginia, had met his wife only once, at his wedding, and had never seen the child until he arrived in Reed a few days before. "You will think me unfeeling," she told Annie, "but I am unequipped to care for a child. I have my own business to run, and I live alone."

The interview was not productive. Miss Ross had a flat, unemotional manner, and her description of Michael's family was vague and undetailed. Her brother was not wealthy, although she believed the family had lived comfortably enough in a rented farmhouse outside of Charlottesville. He had a position at the University, she said, but her tone implied that she did not consider teaching a useful profession. She herself, she added, was self taught and had never been to college.

In answer to Annie's further questioning, Miss Ross gave her a letter from her brother's lawyer which indicated that a modest trust had been set up for the boy's care and that the family's possessions were being sold, the monies to be included in the trust. Miss Ross remarked parenthetically that she had not been included in her brother's will. Michael had arrived on her doorstep with a large suitcase and no other possessions.

Turning her attention to the boy, Annie noted that he was small for his age, a solemn, sandy-haired child with watchful eyes. He spoke little during the interview and only in response to direct questions, his eyes moving from one to the other as they talked.

Annie arranged a foster home placement for him on an emergency basis, since his aunt was unwilling to keep him for even a few weeks. It was only the first of many foster homes and the beginning of one of Annie's most frustrating long-term cases. Her search for a permanent home was dogged from the start by perverse bad luck. Divorce and illness forced his removal from the first two foster families. Another placement was terminated when Annie discovered that the foster parents were making him work beyond his capacity on their farm. Three families agreed to keep him on a temporary basis only.

Although not all the problems were Michael's fault, too often his behavior was disruptive and tried the patience of even the most experienced foster parents. He was a reluctant student and did poorly in school. He was solitary and defensive and formed only one or two close friendships, and those with boys on the edge of delinquency. When he was twelve he began to run away from home periodically and often played hooky from school. At times he would be found miles away, having hitchhiked with anyone who offered him a ride.

In addition to her real concern for his physical safety, there was an aimless quality in his behavior that Annie found troubling. As the only stable figure in his life, she had received permission from the Family Service to maintain the case when she moved to the Mental Health Clinic. But despite her best efforts and the considerable resources at her disposal, she had only limited success in getting him to confide in her or to cooperate with the many good people who tried to help him. He couldn't explain his actions but responded to whatever impulse seized him with a complete disregard for the consequences.

She had concentrated on his one consistent strength, his skill in athletics, and helped him join several local teams. But Michael was not a team player. Although he was competitive and energetic, he was also self-absorbed and undependable and prone to tantrums when he felt ill treated. His coaches, like his teachers, accepted him with reluctance.

Annie had never thought he was incorrigible, only drawn by some strong inner drive she could never quite identify. He didn't seem to run away from life as much as toward some hazy goal of his own. His misadventures were reactive rather than sought out. With all of this background, Annie had known it was only a matter of time before he ended up in trouble again, but somehow she hadn't been prepared to find him in jail.

She had been called at her office that morning by Captain Nordstrom of the Reed police to say that Michael was in custody for assault and battery, the consequence of a fight at a roadside tavern the night before. She walked to the police station in her lunch hour. As she climbed the stone steps, she tried to rehearse what she would say to Michael. It was a long time since she had seen him, and over the past year or so she had known that despite her efforts he was withdrawing from her.

Captain Nordstrom showed her to a small room furnished with three wooden chairs and a table. There was wire grillwork across the curtainless window and a single ceiling light. She stared out the window through the wire mesh until she heard sounds in the hall and Michael's voice.

"I can walk for Christ's sake. Get your hands off me," she heard him say. He appeared abruptly, shoved into the room by unseen hands, and the door was shut behind him.

He looked older than Annie remembered. There was a fine growth of stubble on his face, and his brown hair was disheveled and fell over his forehead and shirt collar. He was dressed, as always, in a faded work shirt, jeans and a denim jacket. His sneakers had no laces.

Just inside the door he stopped, his eyes fixed on her with the wary watchfulness she knew so well.

"Hello, Michael," she said and waited for some signal from him. When he answered her in a neutral voice, she knew he, too, was waiting—for her. She smiled. "Here we are again," she said. "Sit down, why don't you?"

"I've been sitting all day."

She pulled a chair to the small table and sat down herself. "How've you been? We haven't seen each other for some time."

"I've been all right."

"I heard you were working at the racetrack."

"Yes."

"As a groom?"

"Sort of." He wandered toward the window and looked out.

"Michael," Annie said, "sit down."

He came obediently to the table, pulled out a chair and sat with his arms crossed and resting on the surface, watching her.

"Tell me about your job at the track."

Michael sighed. "I got a job with one of the trainers, hot walking."

"Hot walking?"

"Walking the horses after they've run. Sometimes walking others who aren't being run, after leg injuries and things like that."

"Then you were riding?"

He glanced up and gave the ghost of a smile. "Not bloody likely," he said, and she wondered where he had picked up the Anglicism. "You walk them on foot."

"I see." She waited, but he appeared to be finished. She leaned back in her chair. "And?"

"Nothing—that's it. I mucked stalls some. Wiped horses. Did some bandaging."

"Did you like the job?"

He looked at her suspiciously and gave a noncommittal shrug. He won't tell me, she thought. It's too important to him.

"What happened?" she asked gently.

"Oh, Gurney—that's the trainer—fired me," and half to himself, frowning, "was that yesterday?"

"Why?"

He shrugged. "Disagreement."

"Come on, Michael, You know I need more than that. Tell me what happened yesterday."

"He ran one of my horses. We each have a certain number of horses assigned to us, and this one was lame. He was on and off lame all the time I was there, loaded up on Bute—they all are—and he came in on three legs. That's all."

"And you said something, right? What did you say?"

"Said he was a stupid bastard." He gave her a challenging look, but when she smiled, he smiled as well. "I told him not to run him in the first place," he added.

Annie raised her eyebrows. "Did you now? I wonder why a trainer wouldn't listen to his groom's advice?"

"I'm not that dumb," Michael said defensively.

"Well, to be truthful, Michael, I'd say that was pretty dumb. He's had a lot more experience than you—"

"Yeah, making a fast buck. The hell with it. It's all over, so who gives a damn?"

"OK," Annie said. "What happened then?"

"I left."

"And went to Northwood?"

"Yes."

"And then?"

Michael pushed his chair back, got up and began pacing. Annie watched him. His back to her, he said, "Didn't Nordstrom tell you?"

"He told me his version."

"I got in a fight. Is that what you want to hear?"

"I want you to tell me what happened."

"All right," he capitulated after a moment. "I was with a girl."

"A girl you picked up?"

"Is that illegal?"

"No—"

"This guy made a couple of smart-ass remarks, and I hit him. He hit me back, and we got into a fight. I knocked him down. The bartender got in the way, so I hit him, too. He's the one pressing charges, I think. The other guy had it coming. Anyway, a bunch of furniture got knocked over, some drinks were spilled, and the girl called the cops."

"Were you drunk?"

"I'd had a couple of beers."

"Did you resist arrest?"

"There were two cops with guns and nightsticks—how could I resist?"

"It's a separate charge, you know that. Did you resist?"

"Of course I did." He hesitated a minute and then turned to her and said desperately, "What are they going to do to me?"

Annie said, "I don't know. I think it depends on you—"

Michael snorted. "On me? If it depended on me, I'd walk out of here right now. Damn cops like to throw their weight around—"

"They're only doing their job. You can't blame them for that—" She sighed, watching him close up before her eyes. Another teacher lecturing him, she thought, another foster parent making rules. She changed the subject. "I've been thinking about this all day. Maybe I can arrange something."

"Arrange something? You're always arranging something. That's *your* job, isn't it? Well, I'm sick of everyone arranging my life. I'd like to arrange myself out of this damned town. I'd like to go to San Francisco."

"At this point, I don't think many people care what you'd like to do. You're really in trouble. Can't you understand that? You're eighteen, it's not the same—"

"Yeah, yeah," he interrupted her. "I got that speech from Nordstrom already. Suddenly I'm an adult, so I should put on a shirt and tie and sell washing machines or fix cars or something. Shit, I can't do that—I won't."

"Would you rather go to prison?"

"They aren't going to send me to prison for getting into a fight. People get in fights all the time."

"No, they don't," Annie said. "If you hit someone, no matter for what reason, and he decides to press charges, you can go to jail. You'd better get that through your head. It's a real possibility, not next time but *now*, today. I want you to listen to me for a minute. You like horses—"

Michael started to interrupt, but Annie raised her voice and spoke over him. "You don't need to be defensive, it's nothing to be ashamed of. A lot of people make a living working with horses, and there's no reason you can't too. You've already done it a few times."

"Some living, mucking out stalls."

"You chose it," Annie said tartly, "I didn't. But you can't expect an employer to let you ride when he doesn't know anything about you. We've talked before about being realistic."

"I can ride."

"Maybe that's true. I don't know anything about it—"

"I do," he said sullenly, and she laughed.

"Even so, it doesn't change what you can expect. There are few jobs in this world where you start at the top. There's a possibility I can find work for you on a horse farm." She didn't look at Michael, but she heard him sit down again. "There's a man up in the hills past Northwood who has horses. I'm going to try to see him this afternoon."

"What kind of horses?"

"I have no idea," she said, exasperated, "but we're not in a position to choose, are we? Captain Nordstrom's given you the only choice you've got: find a job and stick with it, or he'll take you to court. He's told me very clearly that if he arrests you again, he'll throw the book at you. You have no other choice."

Michael said nothing.

"You have no choice," Annie repeated. "He's been very good about this. He didn't have to call me, you know. He doesn't want to send you to jail. You may not have much use for him at this point, but I've known him for a number of years. He's a decent man, and he's not kidding."

"OK," Michael said, capitulating.

She had never gotten used to his mercurial switches in mood. But now, pleased, she went on. "I've got to have your word that you'll control yourself over the weekend and give me a chance to see what I can do. I don't even know if this man hires hands or if he'd hire you. It's a really slim chance, you understand that?" He nodded. "OK," she said in her turn, "I'm going to call the Kellys and see if they'll let you stay there this weekend."

"The *Kellys!*" he said. "I'd rather stay here."

"Of course you would," Annie said, "but you can't. You lived with the Kellys for six months. I'm sure you can stand it for two more days. And unless you're not as smart as I think you are, you'll go and keep quiet about it. Please try to be kind to them and help out as much as you can."

"Why can't I stay here?"

"In jail? Because Captain Nordstrom needs the space, and because I don't want you getting too used to it. You may have a long time to accustom yourself to a cell. You don't need to start now." He said nothing.

She got to her feet and went to the door. "We're ready," she said to the policeman who was standing outside. Later as they stood at the desk, she watched Captain Nordstrom take out a manila envelope, tear it open, and pour the contents out. Michael's worldly possessions, Annie thought and wondered if he had any others: some coins, twenty-one dollars in bills, a jackknife, three nails, a piece of baling twine, a worn leather belt and two shoelaces. She watched him crouch and thread the laces through his sneakers, then stand up and put on his belt. As he gathered the other things and put them in his pockets, he asked sarcastically, "What'd you do with my duffel bag? You keeping that for a souvenir?"

Nordstrom picked up the duffel from the floor behind the desk. As Michael reached for it, Annie saw him meet the captain's gaze angrily, and she quickly put her hand on his arm. "Come on, Michael," she said. "Thank you, Andy. I appreciate this very much."

Michael started out the door and cast a last glance over his shoulder. "Take a good look, kid," Nordstrom said. "You don't want to come back here again. 'Bye, Annie. Good Luck."

Now, as she turned onto the paved road in Northwood and headed home in the increasing darkness, she thought again of Nordstrom's words. It would take more than luck to get Michael to agree to a job without pay.

CHAPTER 2

▼

In the end, Michael agreed to go to the farm without much persuasion from Annie. He apparently accepted her conviction that the only alternative was to find some menial job in town, for he had no transportation, and even the most unskilled jobs were scarce as summer came on and high school students were competing for them. He reserved the right, however, to make a final decision after he had seen the farm.

After she had spoken to Michael, Annie had called to let Sarmento know she would be bringing him there on Sunday. He showed no surprise and little interest. To her question as to whether Michael should bring any special clothing, he replied contemptuously, "Unless he wishes to go naked, I suggest he bring clothing." When she could think of nothing to say to this, he hung up the phone.

Michael said little during the ride. He sat slumped in his seat and stared out the passenger window, giving only monosyllabic responses to Annie's occasional comments. Once, after he had stared moodily at the woods for several miles, he said, "What is this guy, some kind of hillbilly?" and Annie laughed.

"No, I don't think you could call him that."

When at last they emerged from the woods, Michael sat up and looked around. As they rounded the turn by the house and started down the hill, they could see the barn and outbuildings and the massive structure behind them that was twice the size of the barn.

"That looks like an indoor riding arena," Michael said. "Lets you ride all year round. I've never seen a real one, only pictures. This guy rich?"

"I haven't any idea."

Annie stopped the car some distance from a truck and horse trailer that was parked in front of the barn and got out. Michael rolled his window down, leaned his right arm on the sill and watched the scene before him.

Peter and Ivan were standing by the trailer, talking to two women. One of them, about their age, had honey-colored hair and was dressed in immaculate riding breeches, black boots and a light blue polo shirt. The older woman wore blue jeans and a tailored, long-sleeved blouse.

Annie heard them laughing and was suddenly cheered. In many ways it seemed a good placement for Michael, with the isolation, the horses, and the other young men. She saw Peter look over at her and detach himself a few steps from the others, and she moved forward to greet him.

"You're back again," he said, smiling.

"Yes, I've brought Michael."

"Michael?"

"Yes. To work here."

He seemed puzzled. Yet she had called, and Sarmento knew they were coming. "He didn't tell you?"

"No—" Peter hesitated, and then he said vaguely, "Erik hasn't been in a very good mood. But it's OK," he added quickly. "He doesn't tell us everything. I guess he forgot."

As quickly as it had risen, Annie felt her optimism fade. She glanced at Michael, who was still sitting in the car, and when she turned again, Peter had rejoined the group.

"You know," the girl was saying. "I hope this is the right place for Calypso. Can you tell me something about your boss? Is he good? I thought I knew most dressage trainers in the east—after all, there aren't that many—but I'd never heard of him. I've never seen his name at shows or clinics, and I was a bit worried. I mean, the horse is doing so well. I don't want him to regress. It's true I'm having some problems with him now, but I guess you have to expect that occasionally with every horse. I'm showing Third Level. I came here from a show we were in yesterday, as a matter of fact. He didn't place—blew up on me in the ring. Sometimes he's really temperamental."

She turned to the trailer. The escape door in the front was open, and the horse had put his head out and was looking around with interest. "I love you anyway, even if you are a rogue," she said to him, smiling.

"Have you trained him yourself?" Ivan asked.

"Not exactly. He was started when we got him. I don't have time, what with college and all. I just ride in the summers and on weekends. But my coach is abroad, and someone told us about Mr. Sarmento. They said he worked with dressage horses."

Annie was aware that Sarmento had appeared in the doorway of the barn. He stood there silently, and the older woman stepped forward to greet him.

"You must be Erik. How do you do? I'm Ellen Bartlett. My daughter refused to unload Calypso until you were here—"

Erik's eye swung over to the young woman, who was standing with Ivan beside the horse.

"This is Pat, sir," Ivan said. "She owns the horse."

Erik gave a single nod of his head and gestured to the trailer. Ivan went around to the back, let down the ramp and waited for Pat to untie the horse. Then he released the tail chain and stepped aside. The horse came rapidly backwards down the ramp, dragging Pat with him. She held a leadshank with a length of chain across his nose, and Ivan reached to take it from her.

Peter was staring at the horse, wide-eyed, and Annie saw Ivan turn toward him and grin. Even Sarmento's expression seemed to have softened, or was it her imagination? She retreated a step toward her car.

"He's just seven," Mrs. Bartlett said. "Pat's schooled him herself to Third Level, and we've shown him extensively on the east coast. We think he has great potential. I can't tell you how many people have offered to buy him. Colonel Raeford—I'm sure you know him, he's an International judge—feels he could even go so far as the Olympics, and Pat was hoping to try—"

"Remove the bandages," Erik said.

Ivan came forward and squatted in the dirt to remove the shipping bandages. Michael opened the passenger door of Annie's car and got out. As he did so, Sarmento glanced over at him, and Annie saw their eyes meet. She turned quickly to Michael, surprised by some fleeting, protective instinct and saw his expression, for once open and filled with admiration for the horse, turn suddenly stony. He returned Erik's level gaze with his own, motionless, the passenger door still open beside him. Erik's eyebrow lifted, he gave an almost imperceptible smile, and turned to Ivan.

"Roll the bandages and put them away."

Ivan gathered the leg wraps and cottons. The horse had four white stockings, evenly matched, and a narrow, symmetrical stripe down his nose.

"You may remember what I wrote you about Calypso," Mrs. Bartlett said to Erik. "He's been very erratic and we're anxious to correct the problem. Pat's instructor, John Henderson, is competing in Europe this summer. She's taken a clinic with Emil Franck, but his barn's full at the moment—"

It was clear to everyone but Mrs. Bartlett that Erik wasn't listening, but absorbed in her own dissertation, she went on. "We hope it won't take much time to get him over this. We'd like to have him ready for the fall shows. Pat's in college, but she can get home on weekends."

Erik approached the horse and laid a hand on his neck. Calypso's nostril's widened, and he sighed and laid his ears at a neutral angle. "Perhaps you would be good enough to ride him for me," he said to Pat.

"Of course. I'll get my saddle—"

"Peter will do that." He glanced at Peter.

When the horse was saddled, Peter handed Pat the reins, and at Erik's direction she led the horse through the barn and into the large building beyond. The others followed, Annie and Michael in their wake.

As Michael had guessed, it was an indoor riding arena. The vast roof, criss-crossed with wooden supports, spanned a large, rectangle. In each of the four sides was an open double door, closed off to a height of four feet with a low plywood interior wall, hinged at each doorway. Translucent panels in the roof provided light, and Annie was amused to see that a number of small birds had nested in the rafters and flew in and out of the doors. Large mirrors were attached to the walls in several places, together with a few random letters of the alphabet painted in black on white placards evenly spaced around the walls.

Pat mounted Calypso, gathered the reins and started out to the track around the edge. She was slim and graceful, and the horse was, if anything, more elegant under saddle than he had appeared before. He trotted forward with an easy, springing stride, neck arched, face vertical, ears forward. After a few minutes of warming up, she performed a shoulder-in down one long side, haunches-in down the other. Calypso, moving in slow motion, rounded the corner and came across the diagonal in half-pass.

Expressionless, Erik watched from his position a few feet inside the arena. The horse began to canter in an effortless, rocking horse gait, circled on command, and did a simple change of lead through the center of the ring. He picked up the other lead faultlessly after two steps of trot. At length Pat brought him to the center again and halted. She was flushed with pleasure and smiling.

"He hasn't done that well in weeks," she said happily, and leaned forward to pat his neck.

"Let me see the extended trot," Erik said.

Pat's smile vanished. "I'm having some trouble with that," she admitted but obediently started out once more.

As he rounded the corner to cross the diagonal, Calypso started to canter. Pat pulled him down and started over. He cantered again, and again she brought him down. Annie watched her face, now serious, and noticed that there was a touch of anxiety in it. The third time the horse blew up. His nose came up, and he halted in midstride and reared. Beside her, Annie heard Mrs. Bartlett gasp and saw her start forward. Erik didn't move from where he stood and said nothing to help Pat as, shaken, she rode toward him at the walk.

"I'm having that trouble with his extensions," she said, shaking her head. "That's what I'm hoping you can fix."

"Fix," Erik repeated sarcastically. He gestured for her to dismount, holding the bridle, and turned to Ivan. "Fetch my whip," he said.

Mrs. Bartlett, it seemed to Annie, was ambivalent in her concern for both Pat and the horse. She said quickly, "Please be careful with him. He's a valuable horse, and we don't want to ruin what we've achieved."

Annie glanced at Erik. She saw the anger in his face and then saw him turn his eye on the waiting horse with a curious look, almost of hunger.

Ivan held the dressage whip in his hand. It was a long, slender riding whip over three feet long with a two-inch lash at the end. He moved to the off side, lengthened the stirrup several holes and returned to hold the horse while Erik mounted. He handed him the whip and stepped back.

Annie felt Michael stir restlessly behind her. When she turned, he said aloud to her, "I don't like him." She sighed. What could she say to him? Dropping the rein on the horse's neck, Erik adjusted the stirrups and allowed him to walk off. Calypso appeared completely relaxed. At length Erik gathered the reins, still with almost no tension, and started to trot. There began an odd interplay between horse and rider. The easy, springing trot shortened, the ears went back. Erik dropped the rein again and rode a circle. The handsome arched neck and vertical head carriage remained, and Mrs. Bartlett, awed, turned to the rest of the group.

"Look at that! Isn't that wonderful? That's true self-carriage, isn't it! He doesn't even need the rein!"

Erik's riding appeared effortless, his posture erect, his arms and legs relaxed and still. Only his intent face betrayed him. His expression varied from grave to amused, and now and then a fleeting look of comprehension would cross it. But his slow, mesmerizing progress around the ring continued, and although the rider appeared relaxed and motionless, the horse began to resist in small ways. Both Ivan and Peter were aware of the tension, the silent contest between horse and rider. Calypso's steps shortened, his head came up and he stiffened his back. He swung his croup inward, and Erik caught him with his leg and straightened him.

His pace became irregular, his hind legs moving together in successive small hops. He tried to canter and was checked before he had gone half a stride. Again he started to trot, and suddenly Erik took the reins in his left hand and with his whip struck the horse twice behind the girth with all his force, first on the right and then, turning his body in the saddle, on the left.

The reins slack, Calypso responded with a grunt and a series of frantic bounds before breaking into a frenzied gallop to charge headlong around the ring. Erik made no attempt to slow the horse down. He sat calmly upright, the reins loose in his left hand. His right rested on his thigh, with the whip held parallel to the horse's side.

Pat began to cry, silently, and Ivan reluctantly took his eyes from the horse and shook his head.

"Don't—" he said to her in a low voice. "He's OK."

"All that work," she said in a choked voice, "and look what he's done!"

Annie was concerned and repelled by the scene before her and glanced over at Michael. He was watching with open interest and said aloud, "What's he doing?" No one answered him.

When Calypso had gone three times around the arena, he slowed and came to a sudden halt. The reins still dangled on his neck. He was lathered and nervous, and his ears moved rapidly back and forth. As they watched, he started to trot again, his steps quick and disorganized, and again he halted. They saw him leap forward into a canter transition, and the canter was fast, almost a gallop. At last he halted again, and Erik dismounted. He reached into his pocket, fed the horse something, and led him back to the group.

"Cool him out," he said to Peter and watched him lead the horse away.

Pat's mother, who had been temporarily immobilized, was scarcely able to contain her anger. "Mr. Sarmento," she said coldly, "you are supposed to be a horseman. How dare you put on a display like that? Do you know what that horse is worth?"

"At the moment he is worth nothing," Erik said. He didn't bother to look at her as he spoke but turned instead to Pat. Annie saw her make a quick brushing motion at her eyes.

"You have learned to sit on a horse," Erik said to her, "but there your education seems to have stopped. You have effectively butchered this horse. You have turned him into a mechanical toy, and he has removed himself from you. You are riding a machine."

The shock on Pat's face made Annie's heart contract. She was surprised to see Ivan suddenly assert himself and come to her defense. "That's not fair—" he started, and Erik turned on him with a cold smile.

"Oh?" he said. "Or is it that your own judgment falters under the influence of an attractive young lady?" He turned to Pat again. "You may not be able to train a horse effectively," he said, "but I must compliment you on your ability to affect my stable help."

Ivan's face turned red, and his eyes seemed to narrow as if he had sustained an unexpected blow. He started to retort, thought better of it, and looked down at his feet. After a few seconds, he turned on his heel and walked away. Mrs. Bartlett put a protective arm around her daughter's shoulders. "I should bring suit against you," she said furiously. "You ruin a valuable animal, tell my daughter, who's trained him, that she has no ability—"

"I have not said your daughter has no ability," Erik observed calmly. "She sits the horse well, she is built to ride. She does not, however, understand her horse and has done him a great injustice. As for the horse—yes, your judges and trainers are quite right, he has enormous talent. Physically, he is built to excel, and, in addition, he is very intelligent. He is also, despite your daughter's efforts, generous to a fault to have allowed her to continue. But even a saint can be driven too far, and if your daughter continues to ignore this horse—"

"*Ignore* the horse!"

"—he will hurt her. That display he put on for her is only the beginning. Rearing is a dangerous habit. A horse rears only to rid himself of his rider or to fight to defend himself. It is a short step from rearing to going over backwards or throwing himself down on his rider."

Mrs. Bartlett eyed him angrily but evidently the last message got through to her. "Is that why you felt it necessary to beat him?" she said. "You've terrified him. You've probably set him back three years with that outlandish display."

"I assure you, Mrs. Bartlett, it is not me he fears, it is your daughter. I will tell you something about your horse. Somewhere in his background he has been well schooled. I don't know who started this horse, but I know he was a good trainer—perhaps you can enlighten me?"

Only slightly mollified, Mrs. Bartlett said, "We bought him from Karyl Svenson as a four-year-old."

"Yes," Erik said. "Well, Mr. Svenson knew this horse. He taught him to understand the rider's leg and to trust the rider's hand. Your daughter has since taught him to fear the hand, and now he refuses to obey the leg because he dreads the consequences of the hand. He is intelligent, this horse. He has learned that if he appears as a peacock and behaves as a rocking horse he will not be hurt. Ask anything beyond that and he will learn other ways to protect himself."

"Nonsense! The horse is already at Third Level—"

Erik gave a wry smile. "On the contrary. He could not even perform an adequate First Level test."

"Many judges disagree with you."

"Many judges are fools."

Annie watched Michael covertly. His eyes were on Erik with their characteristic intensity. She sensed his ambivalence and had seen him glance at Pat in a way that was clearly more than sympathetic.

It was Pat herself who finally broke the silence. "Can you do anything with him?" she asked. "I'm very fond of him. I never meant to hurt him."

Erik stared past her out the doorway and across the intervening distance to the barn aisle where Ivan stood, helping to remove the tack from Calypso. "If that is your wish," he answered her and added, "and if your mother will permit it."

"But do you think I might set him back again?"

"It is always possible. That is up to you."

"Do you think I can learn to ride him?"

"I have told you—that is up to you."

He turned abruptly, much as he had two days before, Annie thought, as if they were no longer of interest to him and his attention was elsewhere. Pat watched him walk away and turned to her mother.

"Pat," Mrs. Bartlett said quickly, "we don't have to leave him here."

"But he's right, Mom. I think I knew it all along."

"That's not what John—"

"I know," Pat said. "John's a wonderful rider, but he's a competitor. He thinks about the judges all the time. He was always telling me about showmanship— how to make the judges think they saw some lengthening if the horse wouldn't do it by shortening him still more at the end of the movement. He told me how I could cover up the horse's weak points by making a big production out of what he does well. He was in such a hurry all the time. Now that I think about it, I don't think I would have done as well as I did if it weren't that Calypso's such a beautiful horse."

Annie saw Mrs. Bartlett glance over at her, and she gave an apologetic smile. "Let's go outside, Michael," she said in an undertone.

In the barnyard, Michael looked restlessly around him. "Are you going to hang around?"

"I was really waiting for you to make a decision," Annie said. She watched him rocking back and forth on his heels, his thumbs hooked into his pockets.

"Is that girl going to work here?" he asked suddenly, and she laughed.

"Don't you wish! No, I don't think so. I think she just brought her horse here for training."

"Some training!"

Annie tilted her head and watched him, smiling. Over his shoulder she could see Pat and her mother approaching down the barn aisle. Pat went to her horse's head and patted his neck. Beside her Ivan continued brushing the horse down. Erik appeared moments later from a doorway halfway down the aisle. Mrs. Bartlett regarded him coolly, but as he passed unconcernedly by the group in the aisle, she followed him toward the door with Pat at her elbow. Erik stopped a few paces from the barn, lit a cigarette and inhaled the smoke.

"My daughter seems to think we should leave the horse with you," Mrs. Bartlett said formally. "I confess I'm not convinced it's a good idea, but he is, after all, her horse. We'd hoped it wouldn't be necessary to leave him more than a couple of weeks. What do you think?"

"I will not take him for less than three months."

"You're joking!" He shrugged but made no answer.

"Three months—" she repeated. "That's the entire summer season—" She glanced over at Pat who gave a slight nod.

"He can't go on the way he is," Pat said. Michael half turned and leaned back casually against Annie's car without looking at Erik.

"What will you do with him for all that time?" Mrs. Bartlett said. She looked from Pat to Erik indecisively.

"He will be turned out for two weeks and then brought up again to work. He will be ridden out for two more weeks and then started gradually back into training."

"Now, wait just a minute," Mrs. Bartlett said, suddenly reasserting her authority. "Calypso is never turned out like that. You don't even seem to have turnout paddocks, and we can't afford to risk his being hurt. He cost us a great deal of money—"

"He may have cost you a king's ransom," Erik said, "but he is, after all, only a horse. I will treat him no differently than any other horse."

"Have you an area where he can be kept by himself? Away from the others?"

Erik smoked his cigarette unhurriedly and then dropped it on the ground and stepped on it. "This is not a zoo, Mrs. Bartlett. The horses are turned out together, as nature intended."

Annie saw Pat smile. Michael was watching her with frank admiration.

"I have work to attend to," Erik said. "Be kind enough to make up your mind, and either remove your horse from the premises or allow me to get on with my business."

Mrs. Bartlett gave him a sidelong glance. "If I may say so, Mr. Sarmento, you don't allow much room for discussion."

"There is nothing further to discuss."

Mrs. Bartlett turned to Pat, and it seemed to Annie that she was searching hopelessly for the right answer, an echo of Annie's own uncertainty. "Very well," she said finally, "three months. But I will hold you responsible if he is injured."

There was no answer from Erik. He turned without a word and reentered the barn, and it was Peter who came to help close the trailer and to say goodbye. When the truck and trailer had disappeared around the curve at the top of the hill, Annie turned to Michael.

"Well? It's your decision, Michael. I told you what to expect."

"I don't like him."

"You could talk to Ivan and Peter."

"What for?"

"They might be able to tell you what it's like."

"I know what it's like."

"They seem to get some satisfaction from working—"

"Yeah," he interrupted her. "It's a trade-off, isn't it? They get to ride if they can stand the crap he hands out."

"Maybe." She refused to reassure him. She felt him teetering on the edge.

He said, "You think it's true what he said about that horse?"

"I have no idea." He was looking down at the ground and aimlessly pushed the dirt around with the toe of his sneaker.

"OK," he said finally, "I'll try it."

"It'll have to be a good try, Michael. You know that."

"I know." He walked to the car and dragged his duffel bag from the back seat. "You don't need to stay," he said, not very tactfully, and she smiled at him.

"OK." She slid in behind the wheel and started the engine. "Michael—" she said suddenly. "You know I'm concerned about you. Please try to get along, and let me know if you need anything. You will remember to write? You do have the stamped envelopes I gave you, don't you?"

He made an impatient gesture. "Yeah, yeah," he said, "I know. Write every week or go to jail."

"That's not the point. You know what Captain Nordstrom said. He's put you on a kind of probation. I'm sure you don't want me coming up to check on you, and Mr. Sarmento seems to have some feelings about the telephone."

Michael gazed at her gravely for a long moment and then smiled. The smile changed his whole expression. "Right," he said.

Annie looked away quickly over her shoulder, backed up, and turned the car around. With a last wave she started the long drive home. She found herself thinking of the scene in the barn and Erik's cruelty to the horse. What had Calypso done to warrant such treatment? And what had she herself done to Michael to have abandoned him there outside the barn in his ragged jeans and faded denim jacket, his duffel bag beside him in the dust? She knew little about Sarmento, and what she did know depressed her and made her uneasy. Perhaps it was true he was a genius with horses. But he was also cruel, and Michael was not a horse.

CHAPTER 3

▼

Michael leaned his elbows on the fence and gazed down across the pasture. He was relieved that Annie was gone because she embarrassed him, and yet against his will he was protective of her and didn't want to hurt her feelings. He was trying to decide what to do next when he heard Erik's voice behind him.

"You—come over here."

Michael turned his head.

"Me?" He turned around and moved warily forward a few steps.

"I take it you are Michael Ross?"

He nodded. "That's me."

"And you wish to work here, is that correct?"

"Yes."

"Would you care to explain why you wish to do so?"

Michael moved restlessly. "I have to do *something*," he said. Erik regarded him for several moments in silence.

"Indeed," he said finally. "I understand you had a minor disagreement with the local police?"

"Who told you that?"

"Your nursemaid and job seeker, Mrs. Trowbridge."

Michael stirred and cast Erik a quick, angry look. "She's not—"

"She tells me you have worked with horses before?"

"Yes, I have," Michael said more confidently.

Erik reached casually into his shirt pocket for a cigarette, his eyes on Michael's face. Michael watched him resentfully and tried to think of something to say that would indicate his own independence. Erik seemed to be trying purposely to elicit his anger and combativeness, never far from the surface. He looked down at the ground and concentrated his attention on a small anthill by his left sneaker.

"In your spare time between brawling in taverns and sleeping with whores?"

Michael was stunned. "What—" he started to protest, and words failed him. He felt himself blushing.

Erik turned his head and stared out across the field. There was a painful silence until Michael said impatiently, "Well? Do you want me to work for you or not?"

He saw Erik turn back toward him with an eyebrow raised and the hint of a smile, "What did you say?"

"I said, do you want me here or not?"

"Apparently one of us has been misled. I understood it was *you* who wished to be here. I cannot recall asking for help." He looked questioningly at Michael.

His face rigid, Michael said through his teeth, "I don't have to stay here."

"Of course not," Erik said. "You are quite free to leave." Michael glared at him in disbelief. How had it happened that from a reluctant agreement to take on a job that had been arranged without his consent, he was suddenly in the position of asking for it? But even without reflection he knew he had no choice. He had spent two sleepless nights trying to think of alternatives. He yearned to retaliate, but he was afraid of Erik and uncertain what to expect.

"No," he said at last. "I need the job." His own voice sounded thin and beseeching, and he hated himself for having spoken.

"In that case," Erik said, "I imagine I can find one or two things for you to do." He went on to outline the daily chores, and Michael, struggling with his own resentment, couldn't keep up with him. He was aware that Erik's gaze never wavered and that he couldn't control his own. His eyes moved uncertainly from one detail of his surroundings to another.

"—household chores as well as farm work," Erik was saying. "Should you fall short of my expectations at any task, you will do it over under my supervision until I am satisfied. The horses' needs will come first and take precedence over yours. You will eat only after they have been fed and sleep only after they have been made comfortable for the night. I do not care to have my orders questioned, and I expect to be treated respectfully at all times. You will call me 'sir' when you have reason to speak to me and will acknowledge it when I address you. Is that clear?"

Michael nodded grudgingly.

"Perhaps among your other shortcomings you are hard of hearing?"

Michael was trapped. Desperately he cast about for an answer. "No, *sir*," he said as insultingly as he dared, but he found Erik unmoved by his tone. "Do I get to ride?"

"Perhaps—when you have learned how."

"I know how."

"I will be the judge of that. In the meantime, there are more important things for you to do than play cowboy."

Michael felt a familiar stirring within himself, a seething fury that had paralyzed him as a child in the face of teachers and foster parents, trying to force him to do what they wished, so disinterested in what *he* wanted, and always in control while he himself was helpless.

"You don't want a hired hand—you want a slave, don't you?" he said bitterly.

The remark appeared to catch Erik by surprise, for he didn't answer immediately. Outwardly his expression was unchanged, and his gaze with its peculiar force still anchored Michael in his place. At length he gave a slight nod. "You consider yourself a slave?"

"The hell I do," Michael said with conviction, and he added, "I don't have to stay here."

Erik shrugged and walked back to the barn, leaving Michael consumed by an anger he could neither express nor control. He stood where he was for a long time, around him a vast silence broken only by the monotonous sound of cicadas and random noises from the barn. Only very slowly did he become aware that the next move was his. Erik had said all he was going to. He went to the barn and stood hesitantly in the doorway. Near him, where Calypso had so recently stood, Ivan was grooming another horse, and some distance behind him, Peter was saddling still another.

"Do you know what I'm supposed to be doing?" he asked Ivan.

Ivan straightened. He drew the brush he was holding idly across the rubber currycomb in his other hand and then tapped the currycomb on the sole of his boot. He looked seriously at Michael with dark, appraising eyes.

"No, I don't. You coming to work here?"

"Yeah."

Ivan turned back to the horse. After a moment he said, "You could ask Erik," and made a vague gesture to his rear. Michael said nothing. He stood on the threshold and watched Ivan from under his brows.

Finally, Ivan loosed the horse from the crossties and led him back to his stall. He said, "Hang on. I'll find out for you."

Later, he took Michael to the house and watched him stow his duffel in the austere room on the ground floor he would share with the other two. It was a large room, only sparsely furnished. Michael looked around uncritically. He paid little attention to his surroundings and never considered any part of them his. Only his identity and the clothes he wore were his own.

He followed Ivan back down the road to where a small lane led off to the right. Infrequently driven, it curved downhill into the woods. Grass and weeds, stunted and sparse, grew down its center. As they walked, Michael watched Ivan covertly and tried to read his face. Ivan was taller than he and moved with the graceful economy of motion that Michael had seen in Erik when he rode. He felt a sudden stab of loneliness, magnified by what seemed a wilderness around them.

"Where are we going?" he asked finally. He thought he heard a horse nearby but saw only underbrush and trees.

"To the woodlot."

"What for?"

"That's where you're going to be working."

"Yeah? Doing what?"

"Splitting stove wood."

Surprised, Michael laughed. "What's that got to do with horses?"

"Who said it did?"

In the clearing where they stood there were logs, neatly stacked, row upon row of them. "What is this?" Michael demanded. "There's wood enough here to last a year."

"That's right, and all of it's got to be split."

Ivan picked up an axe that was imbedded in a stump, upended a small log and split it in half with a stroke. Then, shortening his grip on the handle, he split each of the pieces in half.

"This size is about right," he said as he bent and tossed the pieces aside. "You done this before?" His voice was neutral, but it made Michael stiffen.

"Of course I have." He had never lifted an axe in his life.

"OK," Ivan said. "I've got to go back now. We usually have lunch some time around noon when it's convenient. You can join us, if you want, or just make yourself a sandwich. Supper's around six-thirty. If you get tired of splitting wood, you can take a few loads up. There's a cart in the woodshed behind the house. Stack the wood neatly and be sure you put the cart away. He's a stickler about things being left out."

"How long am I supposed to do this?"

"Can't say. Best thing is just do it. If you complain, he could keep you doing this kind of scutwork for weeks. You'll find he always wins in the end."

Ivan had started back up the lane when he came to a stop and turned back to Michael. "Look," he said. "I'll give you some advice. Take it easy with Erik. He's not ever someone you can mess with, and right now he's ready to take us all apart."

Michael was left to work in the woods for a week. He saw little of Erik who, despite Ivan's warning, seemed to pay no attention to Michael's work. It didn't seem to matter if it was raining or the heat was oppressive. In the woods the black flies tormented him, raising welts on his neck and wrists, although he wore his shirtsleeves down and his collar buttoned. At lunchtime, when he saw the others, he would trudge up to the house pulling the heavy cart along, and eat with them in silence. He didn't trust himself to speak, but nursed a growing anger at Erik.

He found he was expected, in fact compelled, to do a wide assortment of household chores, some of which he felt were unnecessary, and others demeaning. It was only because he observed Peter and Ivan—and even Erik himself—engaged in similar tasks, that he said nothing.

"Why should you give a damn if I make my bed, for Christ's sake?" he had demanded of Ivan the first morning.

"Don't make it then. I'm only trying to save your neck. Erik wants the beds made, we make the beds. He wants the floors swept and the john cleaned, we sweep the floor and clean the john. Make sense?"

Michael didn't answer. He disliked Ivan and felt a similar antipathy in him. Reluctantly he did his work, following Ivan and Peter's lead, but he never did it willingly and never volunteered his help. Although the work was both repetitive and boring, by far the most difficult times for Michael came when the day's work was done. When his time was his own, he chose not to share it.

The day after he arrived, Peter and Ivan drove to town but, although he wanted desperately to get away, he refused to go with them, and they didn't bother to urge him. It was Monday, their day off, and the time hung heavily on his hands. With Erik down at the barn, the house was his haven, and he didn't leave it.

In a room directly across the hall from their quarters, he discovered an old black and white television set, turned it on, and spent the long day staring at the faded picture, although he could barely make out the figures, and his thoughts lay elsewhere. The room was almost bare, furnished with two wooden chairs and a scarred table for the set. There were no rugs on the floor, no pictures on the walls. Two built-in bookshelves framed the unused fireplace, but they were empty. The television set was old, its rabbit-ear antenna broken off. Nothing he could do improved the picture or the sound, which echoed hollowly in the stark room.

Evenings were much the same, although he drew some comfort from the proximity of the others. Some evenings Ivan was absent. He drove Peter's truck into town on some errand of his own, and once or twice Peter went with him. Although Ivan maintained a distant reserve toward Michael, which he countered with his own, Peter tried persistently to include him. He steadfastly rejected the overtures, and soon they both ignored him. Even then his feelings were hurt, although he could not have said why. In a strange kind of limbo, he was marking time.

His contact with Erik that first week was limited almost exclusively to mealtime. Usually Erik ate dinner with them, although sometimes Ivan or Peter would take a tray to his room. He ate lunch, like the others, when time allowed if he bothered to eat it at all. When he was with them he was self-contained and usually said little. Remarks addressed to him were often met with a sarcastic comment, a disparaging stare, or, worst of all, utter silence. Michael was relieved when, after a meal, Erik retreated to his quarters upstairs, but the faint sound of music from his radio was constant and intrusive, and occasionally he heard him pacing back and forth after they were in bed, his light burning into the early hours of the morning.

Michael didn't know what went on in the barn, hidden as he was in the woods, but he saw trailers come and go across the crest of the road where the two lanes met, and now and then Peter, Ivan, or Erik himself would pass on horseback in the distance.

One day, tired and increasingly restless, he drove the ax blade into a stump with all his strength and left the clearing at a run. He found another pasture below the woodlot and let himself in through the gate. Four horses dozing idly in the shade regarded him with mild curiosity. He moved among them and ran his hand down the neck of one, letting the mane slip through his fingers with sensuous delight.

The familiar scent of horse filled his nostrils, and suddenly there was a lump in his throat, and he was overcome with a wave of yearning that was intangible and without focus. Bits of memories fretted at him, out of his grasp. He saw himself lying on a large lawn, cushioned in cool, fragrant grass while giant horses grazed around him. One of them pushed at him insistently, nibbling at the grass beneath him and tickling him while he rolled and wriggled. He put his hand on its hoof and tried to grasp its ankle, but it pulled away. In his mind's eye he looked upward through the horse's legs and saw his mother's face. Abruptly the scene vanished.

He leaned against the horse before him until it moved away in protest. He wondered if he could climb on its back and imagined trotting across the field and into the woods beyond. He pictured Erik coming down to find him missing from his work, the horse gone from the field, and the thought made him happy. But even in the solitude of the pasture he felt Erik's presence, and the impression was so strong that his pleasure paled, and he went back to his work, watchful and on guard.

Toward the end of the week, he came to terms with his indecision. "Do you mean for me to split wood forever?" he asked Erik at breakfast, more angrily than he had intended.

Erik regarded him with mild surprise, as if he had forgotten he was there. Michael wondered if he even remembered his name.

"Already you tire of your work?"

"You don't need any more stove wood," Michael said, skirting the question. "There's enough in the shed to last all year."

"Yes," Erik said agreeably. "Perhaps it is time for other things."

Michael couldn't believe how easily the confrontation had gone. He had rehearsed it in his mind for days, and even now he felt his heart quicken in Erik's presence. He found his stare unnerving and could never meet it, but the act of looking away seemed a signal of submission that he resisted with all his force. He compromised by looking determinedly into the middle distance, and even there occasionally the line of his vision would intersect with Erik's, and the invisible impact would seem infinitely dangerous, so that he felt Erik, too, must have noticed the encounter. He shifted his gaze to the breakfast table and began to gather the dishes and carry them to the sink.

"When you have finished here, you may come down to the barn," Erik said and left the room.

When he had completed his kitchen chores, Michael ran the distance to the barn filled with energy and anticipation. He had survived the initiation; now he'd be admitted to the inner circle. Peter and Ivan were already at work grooming horses, and he yearned to join them. There was no sign of Erik. He stroked one of the horses on the neck and ran his hand over its shoulder.

Peter smiled at him. "You've been freed?"

Michael grinned. "About time, too. What should I do?"

"Let's see—why not start on the stalls? The wheelbarrow's over there, and the forks are in the feed room."

He was still working on the first stall when Erik came into the barn. He was leading a heavily muscled bay horse with a massive neck and a large, bony, roman-nosed head. He turned him into a stall at the back and returned down the aisle with the leadshank coiled in his hand.

"What are you doing?" he asked Michael, stopping by the stall.

"Picking up this stall."

"By whose order?"

"Well—Peter suggested—"

Erik turned on Peter who was saddling a horse in the crossties. "You have impressed a servant to do your chores?"

"He was looking for something to do. I thought—"

"You thought you would ride your horse while others did your work?"

"No, sir—"

"Put the mare away. You will not have time to ride her today."

Michael, frozen, saw Peter hesitate for a fraction of a second and then start undoing the girth on the saddle.

"I asked him," Michael said quickly. "He was only—"

"Be quiet, I haven't asked for your opinion."

With the manure fork still in his hand, Michael stood foolishly amidst the straw. The wheelbarrow, nearly empty, was in the aisle. Only the sounds of the horses eating their hay and snorting the dust from their nostrils broke the silence. From the corner of his eye he saw Ivan adjust the bridle on his horse, turn it quietly, and head out toward the indoor school.

Peter returned from putting the mare away and without a word entered the stall and took the manure fork from him. Michael stepped into the aisleway, painfully aware of himself, awkward and ungraceful. Erik made a peremptory gesture toward the doorway of the barn and led him out into the sunlight. He walked without a word to one of the outbuildings, Michael at his heels like a dog.

Erik unlatched the door and stepped inside. He handed Michael a posthole digger, an iron digging bar with a flattened end, and a large ball of baling twine. He crossed the barnyard to the pasture. "This field is to be cross-fenced," he said. "The line will go from this post to the gate at the other end. Set your line with the twine. Leave space for two gates, one at each end. Peter will be here when he has finished his barn work to show you how to proceed, since he yearns to be your teacher." Without waiting for an answer, he turned and walked away.

"Jesus, I'm sorry—" Michael said when at last Peter came to join him.

Peter made a gesture of dismissal. "My fault. I should have known better."

"Does it mean no one will ride that horse today?"

"She's my horse. No one else rides her." He took an end of the twine, tied it to the base of the fencepost and started across the field.

"*Your* horse?" Michael said, walking beside him. "Are you kidding?"

"No. I brought her here when I came. She was just four. I've started eventing her, and she's going Preliminary now. I have a horse trial next weekend, but I should be riding her every day so she stays fit. He knows that. It's OK," he added, seeing something in Michael's expression, "Tomorrow she had off anyway. I'll ride her then, instead."

"That's *our* day off."

"I know."

Although Michael understood only part of what Peter was saying, it was hard to miss the significance of Erik's action. "What a bastard," he said with disgust. "Why the hell do you stay here?"

For a moment Peter seemed about to answer, then he shook his head and walked on, suddenly distant. "I can't explain," he said. "It's too hard, and you wouldn't believe me anyway. You'll find out if you stick around." He didn't speak again until it was time to set the first post. "You know how to use a post-hole digger?"

"Yes."

"OK." He paced off ten feet and indicated a spot. "Start digging here, and be careful not to break the string. I'll go up and get some posts and rails."

When he returned, driving a pickup truck down into the field, Michael had dug down barely six inches. His face was red. He had shucked off his shirt and was wrestling with the posthole digger, striking stone.

"No good," Peter said, watching him, and picked up the digging bar.

They took turns prying loose the stones from the sides and bottom of the hole and bringing them out with the posthole digger and sometimes with their bare hands. Larger rocks required a shovel to enlarge the hole, a logging chain and the digging bar to lever them to the surface. It took an hour to set the first post. Tired, Michael watched Peter insert the rail in the lowest hole and gauge the placement of the second post.

"Jesus," he said, "this'll take a month."

Peter glanced at him, and finally he smiled. "At least," he said. "Makes you realize why they build stone walls. You can't dig without hitting rock, and then you still have to do something with the stones." But even as he spoke he kept on working.

Michael picked up a small stone and flung it with all his might down across the field. "What the hell's the point?" he said furiously.

Peter straightened and wiped his face on his sleeve. "One thing I've learned since I've been here—that you do it or you don't do it, but you don't complain about it."

"*You* don't complain about it," Michael retorted. "I'll complain as much as I want. Why should I break my ass for the son of a bitch, anyway? What good's it doing *me*? He knows I came to work with the horses, but he's not going to let me, is he? He wants to make me crawl first, doesn't he? Well, you know what he can do?"

Peter said nothing. Michael seized the posthole digger from him, slammed it into the ground and brought it up filled with dirt. As though his abrasive anger was suddenly harnessed and directed, he attacked the work with a single minded-ness that seemed to block out his surroundings. The second post was set and Michael had started on the third when Peter heard Erik call him from the gate.

"I have to go," he said to Michael, but there was no answer. Intently absorbed, Michael had almost forgotten he was there.

By evening, Michael had set ten posts. He was stretched full length on the ground, half-asleep with fatigue, when Erik came. He opened his eyes to find him standing a few feet away. His heart gave a convulsive leap, and he pushed himself to a sitting position.

"Good." Erik's tone was noncommittal, and Michael got slowly to his feet. "You may put the tools away and go up to the house. You will work this week on the fence until it is done." He sighted down the row of posts and added, "Make sure your line remains straight, and when you have completed the work, see that all these stones," he gestured to the rocks that Michael had labored to bring to the surface, "are disposed of in the woods."

Michael saw in Erik's eyes that his resentment was not lost on his employer. Erik gave a slight smile, and the corner of his eyebrow lifted. As he walked away, Michael glared angrily at his back.

"You can take your fucking stones and shove them up your ass," he said under his breath and was appalled to see Erik stop and turn back to him.

"What did you say?"

"Nothing."

"It appears you've spent much of your life in the gutter," Erik said. "Or was it your parents who taught you to be so eloquent?"

"My parents are dead!" Michael said bitterly, hurling his misfortune at Erik like a weapon.

"Indeed?" Erik said. "How fortunate—"

"*What?*" Michael's voice was shaking.

"—for them," Erik finished. "I imagine they would have been disappointed to find your vocabulary so impoverished that you can express yourself only in clichés and words of one syllable." Michael was poised on the edge of assaulting him, crouched and ashen, his fists clenched at his sides. But Erik merely turned his back again and walked away. His action insulted Michael and rendered him helpless.

In his frustration, Michael seized the posthole digger and started to dig again with all his force. His mind reeled with fantasies of revenge, and he stopped only long enough to watch the horses, turned out for the night, come down into the field to join him. They approached the new fencing with both curiosity and suspicion and performed a charade of flight and hesitant return until, bored, they wound their way down toward the woods to graze. They comforted him with their presence, and talking to them, he felt his rage die down.

Finally, when the sun had set and he could no longer see what he was doing, he started wearily back, dragging the posthole digger and the bar, the shovel and logging chain. He replaced them in the shed and headed toward the house. Erik's light was on. Michael was both hungry and physically exhausted, and his fatigue extended even to his mind, numb from his own violence.

Both Peter and Ivan looked up when he came in, but neither spoke. They had mentioned his absence to Erik at supper. "Where's Michael?" Peter asked.

"Michael?" Erik had said frowning slightly. "Oh, yes. I believe he is having a tantrum down in the pasture." And he began eating his dinner without further comment.

Peter and Ivan exchanged glances, and later Ivan said, "I'll lay you odds he's gone before the week's out."

Peter laughed. "That's what I thought about you, and you're still here."

When Michael finally appeared, he gave them no room for words but lay down on his cot, fully dressed and supperless and almost instantly fell asleep.

He awoke the next morning in a kind of despair, stiff and sore, almost crippled by the abuse to which he had subjected himself. His hands were blistered and torn, both his arms and legs hurt, and his back ached. Even the muscles in his neck were sore, and his entire back, shoulders and arms were sunburned. He regarded himself in the small bathroom mirror with a sour distaste, his eyes still bloodshot from fatigue, and faced within himself a reflection far more fearful than his physical weakness. He discovered there, in the pale, cold light of early morning, that his concept of himself had changed as well. His self-confidence was as bruised and battered as his physical being, and he didn't know what to do next. He heard the others moving about, heard the door slam as they started down to feed and, far more ominous, heard the sounds of Erik rising for the day on the floor above.

His duffel bag was under his bed. He had never unpacked it, as if by doing so he would have tacitly accepted his position here and somehow surrendered to Erik's domination a part of himself that he still fought to protect. He had washed his clothes when they were dirty and returned them to the duffel bag, so that apart from his rumpled bed, there was no sign that he had ever been there.

Now he showered, painfully, dragged fresh clothing from the duffel and savagely stuffed his clothing of the day before into the bag. He was completely alone, and he walked without destination around the room. When he stopped by the front window to stare bleakly out, the pasture and unfinished fence across the road silently confronted him.

He decided to leave. He would go without a word, his duffel bag on his back, and Erik, finding him gone, would smile without surprise, for he had known all along that Michael was weak, that the work was too hard, and he couldn't take it. He would nod to Peter or Ivan and gesture to the fence, and they would plod down across the damp grass with the heavy tools and finish his work without a word of complaint, for reasons that Michael couldn't understand. He was tortured by their compliance, their calm acceptance of Erik's tyranny that never seemed to shame them or take from them their serene self-assurance as it did his own.

He thought he might stay a little longer. He wouldn't allow Erik his moral victory. He would finish the fence and then collect his belongings and walk away. A seductive daydream of self-sacrifice and heroism infused him. He saw himself as strong and silent, stoic and righteous, walking away unhurriedly up the road with a contemptuous disregard for the hardships he had been forced to endure.

The sight of his ravaged hands on the windowsill before him made him wonder if physically he could do it, but it was the only solution he could abide. He made his own breakfast, hurrying so as not to meet Erik, and was at work again by the time Peter and Ivan had returned.

For five more days he worked, solitary and uncommunicative. He ignored the half-holiday, and on Saturday he placed the last post, fitted the rails and tamped it in. When he sighted back up the line, it was with a sense of wonder that he had finished. Leaning on the post, he was aware that this visible work was the first he had ever completed voluntarily in his life, and still he wasn't certain why he had done so.

He gathered the stones in a wheelbarrow and took them into the woods, and when it was all done and he had put the tools away, he walked to the barn.

Behind the indoor school, Erik was riding in the outdoor ring. Michael leaned on the fence and watched him.

The horse trotted calmly around the track. Unlike Calypso with his elegant carriage and cadenced stride, this horse moved with lowered neck and head extended. The reins, though taut, were long, lightly in contact with his mouth. Every so often he circled, sometimes continuing around the ring, sometimes returning to the track after half a circle to change direction. Michael had the impression that Erik was only a passenger, for he never seemed to move in the saddle; the horse seemed to perform of his own accord, never hurrying, never slowing down.

He watched the horse come down to a walk at last and, following a loosened rein, drop his head so that it was almost touching the ground and then raise it and start first to trot and then to canter. He didn't know what Erik was trying to achieve, but as he stood there in the sunlight, he had a sudden sense of euphoria and peace. The rhythm of the horse as he cantered quietly around produced a responsive sense of relaxation in Michael so that he almost felt hypnotized.

Suddenly he was aware that Erik had dismounted and was loosening the nose-band on the bridle. He saw him speak to the horse and feed him something from his hand. Then, before he had prepared himself, Erik was coming toward him, leading the horse. Without thinking, he opened the gate to let them pass, and Erik stopped and looked questioningly at him.

"Yes?"

"It's done." He searched Erik's face for a sign of challenge or derision.

"Good," Erik said. "Put the horse away." And before he was aware of it, he was standing with the reins in his hand and the horse at his elbow, and Erik was already half way to the barn. He put his hand on the horse's neck and watched through the open doors of the indoor arena as Erik vanished into the barn. Then he did as he was told.

CHAPTER 4

▼

Late Saturday afternoon Erik left the farm, leaving Ivan and Peter to do the evening chores. After he had cooled out the horse and put him away, Michael hadn't seen Erik again, and he was left in the barn without a specific assignment. With his duffel already packed, he was relieved by Erik's departure and delayed his own, silently joining the others in the evening stable routine. When the horses were out and the stalls stripped for the night, all three walked together up the road to the house.

They sat around the old wooden table in the kitchen and ate a cold supper. With Erik away, no one bothered to cook. Michael felt an indolent contentment as if a weight had been lifted from him.

"You going out tonight?" he heard Peter ask Ivan, and for the first time waited with interest for Ivan's answer. To have both Erik and Ivan gone was more than he could have wished.

"Thought I would, if it's OK with you."

"Sure. I've got things to do for tomorrow anyway. You could do me a favor and fill the truck with gas and hitch up when you get back."

Ivan nodded. Michael said nothing. He didn't understand what they were talking about, but he didn't want to reveal his ignorance. He had been at the farm for two weeks, so absorbed in his own experience that he had had no curiosity about anyone else's.

Ivan yawned and poured himself a cup of coffee. "Erik gone to sale?"

Peter nodded. "I think so."

"What sale is that?" Michael asked.

"Livestock auction in North Fairborough."

"What's he doing there?"

"Buying horses," Ivan said.

"At *auction*? Is he going in the dog meat business?"

"You can find some good horses at sale if you know what you're doing," Peter said mildly. "I'm riding a horse right now that he bought there. You know Tangent? The bay mare on the right, halfway down the aisle? Nothing the matter with her except she wouldn't let anyone catch her and was scared half out of her mind. She's herd-bound. You still can't lay a hand on her if she's alone in a field. Guy who sold her told Erik he'd got so mad when he couldn't catch her that he shot her."

"*Shot* her?"

"That's what he said. Took a shotgun and just let her have it. I dug a piece of buckshot out of her just the other day, and she has bumps under the skin of her flank that I think are more. Probably work their way out one day."

Michael shook his head. "Erik tell you that?"

"Jan told me. He was there with Erik."

"Who's Jan?"

"Friend of Erik's."

Michael laughed. "You mean he's got friends?"

"One or two."

"This friend a horse dealer?"

"No, he's a journalist. He worked on the *Reed Courier*. His last name's Karras. He and his sister have known Erik for years. I think they were neighbors once."

"Jan Karras," Michael said. "Never heard of him."

"Maybe that's because you don't read the paper," Ivan said in a level tone that roused Michael immediately.

"I don't see *you* reading the paper," he retorted, but Ivan didn't bother to answer.

After supper, when Ivan had gone, Michael followed Peter down to the barn. He had volunteered to help him get ready for the competition he was to enter the next day, but it was an offer motivated not by altruism but by a growing curiosity. Erik had made no reference to the event other than an oblique reminder to Peter during the afternoon that until the barn work was completed and the horses turned out for the night, his time was not his own.

Michael held the horse while Peter washed her. They stood in front of the barn in the dim light from the aisle. The mare hunched her back against the hose, her tail clamped down. Water ran down her legs and pooled on the ground beneath her fetlocks. She stamped restlessly and raised her head, and Michael put his hand on her neck.

"How'd you get him to let you off on Sunday?" he asked as he watched Peter dry the horse with long energetic strokes and snap the rivulets of water off the scraper.

"He lets me do it—I don't know why. He sort of ignores the whole thing. I tell him the days I want to compete, and I always wonder if maybe he'll say no, but he never has."

"Does he give you a hard time if you don't place?"

"He never asks how I've done. I don't think he cares."

"Ivan go with you?"

"No, Erik won't let him."

Peter took the leadshank from Michael's hand and led the mare back to her stall. The barn was empty, the mare its only occupant this night. When he had closed the stall door, he leaned on it for a moment and watched her sniff at her bedding and then heave a deep sigh and start eating her hay.

"Pig!" he said affectionately. "I'm always afraid she'll try to roll in her stall when she's wet like that, but she's too greedy." He watched her for a moment longer and then went into the tackroom.

"Ivan has to stick around to teach," he went on as if there had been no interruption. "A lot of people come on weekends for lessons, and there's all the barn work."

"I thought *he* did the teaching," Michael said. For some reason it was hard for him to call Erik by name.

"He does. He's got his regular students, but a lot of the time we do it. He gets impatient with some people."

Michael made a derisive sound.

Peter said, "Sometimes I think he'd just like to yank the rider off the horse and ride it himself. Not everyone understands him. He has a funny way of explaining things."

"Not my idea of funny," Michael said sourly. He watched Peter, on his knees by a large wooden trunk, unearth bits of equipment and pile them together on the tackroom floor.

"What are those?" he asked, pointing.

"Galloping boots."

"Why do you need all that stuff?"

"You know anything about Combined Training?"

"What?"

"Combined Training—it's a sport."

"Like a horse show?"

"No, more like tests of how well you've trained your horse."

"Trained him to do what?"

"To be an all-around good riding horse, obedient and safe, to jump well, to be a good athlete. You ride three tests at the lower levels, and it gets more complicated later—"

"What kind of tests?"

"Well—dressage, for one."

"What's that?"

Peter laughed. "It's what we do here—didn't you know that?"

"How the hell should I know? No one tells me anything."

"Yeah—well, it means schooling a horse on the flat. In a dressage test you ride a set pattern of movements in a rectangular arena with sides only about a foot high." He looked up to find Michael staring at him and laughed again. "You show that your horse can move straight and keep his balance, that he's supple and that he moves on well—walk, trot, canter, stop—it's hard to explain."

"Walk, trot and canter," Michael repeated. "I guess you can manage that."

"It sounds easy, but it's not, really. She can do a pretty good test, if I can keep her in the ring."

Michael made a face. He was irritated by Peter's modesty. He had seen both Peter and Ivan ride past him on the road each day as he toiled in the pasture, and he envied them their easy skill, turned strong, swift and free by the animals beneath them, while he was bound invisibly to a world of earth and stone.

"It's not the same as here," Peter went on. "She's so fit, you see. She's jumping out of her skin early in the day in a strange place. It's like sitting on a volcano."

"What's the second test?"

"Cross country. You gallop a couple of miles across country over natural obstacles at a given rate of speed. There are all kinds of jumps and obstacles that you might find anywhere, like banks and ditches, jumps into and over water, up and down hill. And they're solid; they don't fall down if you hit them. You get to walk around the course first to figure out how to ride it, but the horse hasn't seen any of it before. You get points off for refusals or falls or taking too much time."

Michael gestured to the growing pile on the tackroom floor. "What's all that for?"

"Breastplate, running martingale, and my jumping saddle. I use the martingale in cross-country and stadium—that's the third test, stadium jumping—it seems to help me control her and still use a snaffle bit. She gets very strong cross country."

"And this stuff?"

"Studs for her shoes for traction, linament, my vet kit, bandages, cooler and blanket, my dressage saddle, helmet and jumping bat, cross country shirt, dressage whip, longeline, longeing whip and side reins." He touched each item as he spoke.

"Jesus!" Michael said, impressed. "Do you really need all that?"

"That's only half of it. There are the buckets, water, grooming stuff, my jacket, boots and hardhat, hay—I have a list in the trailer. Once I went to one of these things and actually forgot my stirrups. I'd had the whole saddle apart, and I stuck the stirrups in the dishwasher at home and clean forgot them."

"What'd you do? Ride without them?"

"No, that's not allowed in dressage, and you'd have to be nuts to try it cross country. Borrowed some. People are pretty nice, usually. I'm not the only one who's forgotten things."

"How about the third test?"

"Stadium? That's jumping a regular course like you might do in a stadium jumping class at a horse show. That's my horse's best phase, usually, but sometimes she gets away from me, takes off, and just goes through all the fences."

"Ever win?"

"Haven't won yet, but she's beginning to place more often."

Michael said nothing for a moment. "Do you think the horse likes it?" he asked suddenly.

"I think she does. I think that's why it's such a great feeling."

"What's her name?"

"Kestrel."

"What?"

"Kestrel. It's a kind of bird."

Michael helped him pack his gear into one of the trailers stored in the tractor shed. "Your trailer?"

"Yes, such as it is."

"You must be rich," Michael said.

"I worked to buy it. It's all second hand, and I still had to put a new floor in the trailer and rewire it. Luckily the truck had a hitch on it when I bought it."

"And the mare?"

"My parents gave her to me."

Michael was silent. Finally he said, "I had a horse once. He could do all those things you said."

"No kidding—what happened to him?"

"He was sold," Michael said abruptly, and even to him it sounded rude. "I was just a kid. I didn't know what was going on. I saw some guy drive up with a trailer, and they took him out of the stable, loaded him on and drove away. I remember I had a real screaming fit. I really loved him. I kept looking for him for years—I still do sometimes."

"How old were you?"

"Ten."

"Why'd they sell the horse?"

"Why does anyone do anything?" Michael said defensively. He remembered his parents' death only vaguely. The image of his pony walking onto the trailer still haunted him.

"My parents were killed in an accident," he said more gently. "I guess everything got sold after that."

Peter said nothing. Michael said, "I almost left today."

"Why didn't you?"

"I don't know. I still might."

"You finished the fence?"

"Yeah."

"And he's got you working in the barn now?"

"He hasn't got me doing anything. God knows what he'll make me do next."

Peter stood up. He walked out to the trailer again and stowed a bulging hay net in the front. Michael followed him.

"How far away is this thing?"

"Ninety miles. I figure two and a half hours. My dressage is at 10:07. That means I'll have to be there by nine at the latest, so I'll have time to warm up. If I'm a minute late in any phase, I'm eliminated, so I guess I'll leave around six."

Michael stared thoughtfully at the trailer and half-heartedly kicked one of the tires. "Ivan's got a nerve running off with the truck when you're trying to pack all that stuff," he said.

"What you got against Ivan?"

"Nothing. But I should think *you* would. He's always running off with your truck as if he owned it."

It was an enormous relief to have aired his resentment, and he hoped it would strike a responsive chord in Peter. Instead, Peter said, "Well, just lay off him. I know you've got problems with Erik, but you don't seem to realize that Ivan's got his, too. It's not easy working here for nothing. I don't know what you plan to do when you want to get a haircut or buy a new pair of jeans. I'm lucky because I get a few dollars from some stocks my parents gave me—not enough to live on, but enough for a few things like entering Horse Trials and buying what extras I need. Ivan's got nothing. So he picks up work at a gas station a couple of nights a week, and I let him take the truck."

Instead of sympathy, Michael felt only envy. Peter had never offered him the truck. He was beginning to feel a certain kinship with Peter, and Ivan threatened it. As Peter started back to the barn, he followed him. "Maybe I'll go with you tomorrow," he said casually. "I'd like to see one of those things."

Peter turned around. "I don't mind," he said carefully. "I'd be glad of the help. But you'd better not plan to come back with me."

"Why not?"

"Because Erik'd send you right down the road the minute you got out of the truck."

Michael considered this. "He can't tell me what to do," he said at last. "I'll leave whenever I damned well want to."

Peter gave him an exasperated look. "I'm going to bed," he said and turned out the lights in the barn. He stopped by Kestrel's stall on the way out. "Be good tomorrow," he told her. They walked in silence back to the house, and Michael could feel Peter's withdrawal. He knew he was responsible but stubbornly refused to say anything to ease the situation.

He worked in the barn all the next day. He was amazed at the amount of work to be done, although he was no stranger to stable chores. During the morning three people arrived, two to ride horses Erik had in training and one who brought her own horse for a lesson. Erik appeared to treat all of them with the same glacial disinterest, although he did work with the two whose horses were boarded there. The woman who had brought her own horse was given over to Ivan.

Michael was told to pick up the stalls. Complete mucking out was done in the evening when the horses were turned out and the stalls were left banked and limed over night. They were rebedded before the horses came in and picked up twice, in midmorning and midafternoon. Michael had never been at a farm where so much stall cleaning was required, and he made the mistake of saying so to Erik.

"Perhaps you prefer building fence?" Erik said. "I wouldn't want you to be discontented in your work."

"I only said—"

"There is nothing wrong with my hearing. When you have completed the stalls, you may start grooming the horses." But he was clearly dissatisfied with the results. "Do you consider that horse to be groomed?"

"Yes—" Michael received an icy stare from Erik, "—sir," he added, almost inaudibly.

"Do it over."

"Again?"

There was no answer. Angrily he led the horse back into the aisle. Erik stood beside him as he worked and, when Michael had finished, ran his fingers through the horse's tail.

"The tail is not brushed sufficiently."

"I've brushed it twice."

Erik's eyebrows went up. He waited in silence until Michael again picked up the brush from the grooming box. Michael had to sweep the aisle floor after each horse was attended to, and when finally he had finished, he was set to cleaning tack, only to have Erik again discount his efforts. "Show him how to clean the tack," he said to Ivan.

"I *know* how to clean tack," Michael retorted. "I've spent half my life cleaning tack."

"I see no sign of it," Erik said.

Half an hour later he returned to the tackroom, gave a cursory glance at Michael's work and found a number of faults with it. The bridle Michael had been working on hung in pieces on the harness hook. Behind him on the counter was a bar of glycerine saddle soap, a bowl of water, a can of Neat's-foot oil and assorted rags and sponges.

"It's as clean as it's going to get," Michael said furiously, spinning around to face Erik. His arm struck the can of Neat's-foot oil, and he heard the thud as it fell on its side. The oil welled out in a viscous stream onto the counter and from there to the floor. He glanced at it over his shoulder but couldn't bring himself to right the can, as if by that menial act he would destroy himself and turn into a nonentity in an instant.

Erik leaned casually against the doorjamb. Michael saw his eyes shift from the can of oil to the growing pool on the cement floor.

"I don't believe so," he said calmly. "Kindly clean up that mess."

Michael felt imprisoned, intolerably helpless. There was a painful silence until suddenly he heard himself say in a voice he didn't recognize as his own, "That's it—I'm leaving."

He lunged for the door. It seemed desperately important to get away, to pass Erik as quickly as he could. Quite casually, Erik extended his arm to the other jamb and blocked his exit. Michael stopped in mid-flight and backed up a step.

"I don't care to have my orders ignored," Erik said calmly. Michael turned his back, righted the can, now almost empty, and slammed it down on the counter. He swept the pile of rags onto the floor, kicked them angrily into the pool of oil and bent quickly to pick them up and drop them in the sink. Then he started again toward the door, his face rigid with fury, to find Erik still blocking his way.

"I'm leaving," he said tightly.

"Not as yet."

"I can leave if I want—"

"What you want is irrelevant. Finish your work."

"I did."

"To your satisfaction, perhaps. Not to mine. When the bridle has been reassembled and put away, there are still the floor and counter to be washed and the cleaning supplies to be put away. I suggest you start immediately if you want to leave while there is still daylight."

Michael hurled himself at his work, impelled by a rage that staggered him. He felt himself shaking. He didn't look at Erik again, didn't trust himself, and he couldn't acknowledge his fear of Erik even to himself.

He finished at last and with an effort of will turned, only to find the doorway empty. He started down the aisle, bitterly aware that his choice to leave was just another surrender for Erik to savor. In spite of himself, he rehearsed in painful detail Erik's amusement at his plight, and he couldn't convince himself it made no difference.

In front of him Erik strolled down the aisle, and Michael was reluctant to pass. He could see still another car and trailer in the barnyard and Ivan, his hand on the car window, stooping to speak to the driver. Michael stopped in front of Kestrel's empty stall. The car door opened and the driver got out. He was a man perhaps in his sixties, tall and slender. The hair under his cap was a snowy white.

Later, Michael remembered the scene that followed with a peculiar clarity. Erik had stepped across the threshold, and now he stood framed in the doorway. The visitor stopped a distance from him and bowed formally. "It is Erik, isn't it?" he said.

He spoke with a foreign accent, and Michael saw Erik stiffen.

"Yes." Erik's voice was guarded. The other man smiled and said something in a foreign language.

"I do not speak German," Erik said. "If you are looking for him, you are a number of years too late. He is dead."

"But of course," the visitor said easily. "I was aware of the tragedy—so unhappy for you. I remember so well watching you as a boy, so dutiful, so talented—"

"What do you want?" Erik asked.

The visitor gestured vaguely behind him. "Surely you received my letter? I have taken the liberty of bringing an animal for you to see. Your father was a friend of mine—a dear friend. He had a way with horses, did he not? A disciplinarian, yes, but I do not have to tell you so, I think." He laughed. His pale eyes twinkled in a face that, though deeply seamed and weathered, was almost patrician.

Erik turned suddenly on Ivan. "You have something better to do, I think, than to stand idly about while the horses await their feed. Bring Calypso from the lower field and attend to your work."

"Yes, sir," Ivan turned away. Michael, forgotten, stood in the shadows of the barn.

"I have been these many years in Germany," the old man was saying. "It is only recently I have returned, and, you know, I hear of you right away. You are known in your field as your father was before you. But of course that is only to be expected. A talent like that is carried in the genes, and, too, he was a careful teacher." He looked expectantly at Erik, who remained silent. "That young man is your son, perhaps?" the old man added, looking after Ivan as he walked away.

"I have no son," Erik said. "What is your business here?"

"I happened, quite by chance, to visit a livery stable some miles from here. I do still ride a little, you know, and this animal caught my eye. I prevailed upon the owner to part with him. Shall I take him off the trailer?"

"What for? Are you trying to sell him? To have him trained?"

"Ah, you are not changed, Erik. Always you were impatient and headstrong. So many times I have heard your father say—"

"Take him off," Erik interrupted. He turned impatiently and saw Michael in the aisleway behind him. "Get the horse off the trailer," he said curtly.

Curious, Michael lowered the tailgate of the trailer as the old man untied the horse. He could see only the massive hindquarters, dark bay. He unsnapped the tail chain. When the horse came slowly backward down the ramp, Michael stared at him in amazement. He was a big-boned horse and unusually tall, over seventeen hands at the withers, but very thin. His hipbones and ribs were prominent, and his backbone was visible along the length of his back. Around his withers and around a faded scar on his hindquarters there was a scattering of white hair, and the rest of his coat was dull and dusty. He was swaybacked, with large, deep depressions above his eyes. Large and splayed, his feet badly needed trimming. His mane fell from his wasted crest in long, rope-like strands on both sides of his neck, and his forelock, long and tangled, reached half way down his nose. He looked like a workhorse.

Michael waited with interest for Erik's acid response to his visitor, but he stood where he was, motionless. The old man watched him, smiling. For a long moment Erik said nothing, and then in a low voice almost without inflection, he uttered a single word.

"Wotan."

"I knew you would remember!" the old man said with delight. "So many times I have seen you ride him—so many years ago. Of course, he is not quite the same animal—they have gelded him, as you can see—but I knew you would be interested. A part of the past, yes?"

Erik's jaw was set, and he glared at his visitor. "What do you intend to do with him?" he asked finally and turned his gaze again to the horse. "He must be thirty years old."

"Yes, an old man like me, like your father would be were he alive today. Would you like him? He is yours."

He led the horse forward and Erik slowly reached out and took the leadshank. He put his left hand on the horse's neck and said something Michael couldn't hear. The horse's ears twitched. Michael saw Erik bend to run his hand down the horse's leg and pick up his foot.

"How much did you pay for him?"

"A pittance, I assure you."

"How much?" Erik insisted.

"One hundred dollars."

Erik moved suddenly past Michael and led the horse to the pasture gate where he removed the halter and turned him out. The horse lowered his head and began to graze. Erik walked back up the road toward the house. As he passed the trailer, he tossed the halter and leadshank into the interior. The old man looked after him without surprise and turned to Michael. "What is your name?"

"Michael."

"You are his student?"

"I work here."

"Ah," the old man said thoughtfully. "He is a harsh master, yes?" When Michael didn't answer, he smiled. "Yes," he went on, "I see it in your face. And yet he has talent, isn't it so? I saw it when he was still a child. He rides like the centaur, and that animal," he gestured to the pasture, "was his teacher. One owes a great debt to one's teacher, and I believe Erik knows that. Perhaps you, too, are aware of it?"

"I don't know," Michael mumbled, embarrassed.

He was almost relieved to see Erik returning. He watched him hand his visitor a check and heard the old man protest. "It is a gift, Erik—a gift to the son of my old friend. He would be so pleased—"

"I do not accept gifts," Erik said. "Now, if you will excuse me, I have work to do." He turned and walked into the barn.

The old man said to Michael, "He is not so different. Always he had his pride, even as a child." He nodded formally to Michael. "Please give him my farewells. And perhaps you will be kind enough to raise the tailgate on the trailer for me. I am an old man—like the horse." Michael lifted and secured the tailgate. He watched as the visitor started the car and made his way slowly up the drive.

Turning to look again at the old horse grazing near the pasture gate, Michael felt calmer, although he was not fully aware of it. Somehow the overpowering threat of Erik's personality had been diffused. He no longer seemed larger than life, no longer seemed to have sprung into being, all-powerful and mysterious, on top of this lonely mountain. Now it was his own experience here that seemed like a dream, shifting in quality from threatening to exciting. He had lost his ability to measure what was real and what was not, and in his ambivalence he felt thrown from reckless, impulsive action into a paralysis of indecision.

He watched Ivan lead Calypso up the road from the lower pasture. Coppery and gleaming in the light of the afternoon sun, ears pricked and alert, the horse walked in long, fluid strides beside him. Without conscious thought, Michael followed them to the barn and began helping Ivan with the evening chores.

CHAPTER 5

▼

The County Mental Health Clinic offices were in a century-old house on a shaded side street in Reed. It was set back from the street with a neat lawn in front and was freshly painted white, although its wide veranda was no longer level, and its dark green shutters slanted downward. Inside, the wide-planked floors sloped, and there were hairline cracks in the plaster.

Annie's office on the second floor was a large, square room overlooking the street. A small sofa stood against one wall, facing two armchairs, and there was a large, hooked rug on the floor. Beneath the windows, where the morning sun shone in, were a table and two wooden chairs and beside them, on the sill, a glass bottle, deep red, and the figure of a rearing horse, crudely sculpted in clay.

A few days after Annie had driven Michael to Sarmento's farm, she was catching up on her paperwork when she looked up to see Bill Freeman, the clinic's psychologist, in her doorway. They were old friends and had worked together since the clinic had opened several years before. It was Bill who had given her Sarmento's name as a resource for Michael, a lead that had come from a chance conversation with his young daughter's riding instructor.

Now he said without preamble, "I've got some more background on Sarmento in case you're still interested. Apparently his father was a German horse trainer."

Annie moved a pile of file folders to one side and leaned back in her chair. "Really? That makes sense," she commented. "He has a funny way of talking— not an accent exactly, but rather a too-perfect English. Perhaps it's the inflection. How did you find that out? From Sandy's teacher again?"

He nodded. "I asked her what more she could tell me when I picked Sandy up on Friday. She said Sarmento's father was a sort of star in his field. His name was Von Tauber. He came to this country before the war, poor as a church mouse, and settled up county with his common-law wife and son. There was a small German community up around North Fairborough, remember?"

Annie nodded.

"There seem to be a lot of different kinds of horseback riding," Bill continued. "Sandy's instructor, Connie, teaches something called Hunter Seat Equitation, and her students go to horse shows and jump over fences. Von Tauber specialized in dressage, which is a bit like gymnastics and involves training horses to do specific movements, like those famous white horses from Vienna. Recently they've begun to have their own horse shows, too.

"Sandy doesn't think much of dressage people. She says they're snobs and afraid to jump fences, but Connie's a little more tolerant and, I suspect, better informed. She told me dressage is widely respected in Europe—an art form of sorts with a long history. But not many people here ever heard of it.

"Von Tauber took his horses around to fairs and circuses and so on before they had formal competitions. Sarmento rode for him when he was old enough. Connie said she saw him ride in one of the exhibitions when she was a little kid, and it made a great impression on her. I guess he wasn't much older than she was."

Annie smiled. "I appreciate your help, Bill. I could never have put this all together for Michael without you. It may not make Sarmento much more sympathetic, but at least I guess he's a legitimate trainer. Thanks."

"Forget it. You worry too much. I'm on my way to lunch—want to join me?"

"No thanks. I have a meeting in a few minutes."

But it was only a few days later that she met him on the stairs and asked if he had a few minutes. He sat down at the table in her office and lit his pipe.

"Do you believe in coincidence?" Annie said, and she told him about her interview with Kristen Karras. "She walked in yesterday morning without an appointment, and I had a free hour," Annie told him. She looked thoughtfully down at the yellow pad on the table before her. "The thing is," she said after a moment, "she wasn't asking for help. She only wanted information—about child abuse. In the end, I think I got more information than she did."

Kristen was a slender young woman, casually dressed in a cotton skirt, blouse and sandals. Although she wasn't conventionally pretty, her face was open and expressive, with wide, high cheekbones and a healthy, clear complexion. Annie judged her to be in her mid-twenties. She wore no makeup, and her straight blond hair was pulled back from her face and secured at the nape of her neck with a clip. Her eyes were large and vividly blue, her gaze direct.

When she had shaken hands and introduced herself and Annie had invited her to sit down, she said, "I'm hoping you can answer some questions for me."

"I'll do my best."

Kristen looked curiously around and touched the small statue on the window-sill beside her. She glanced at Annie and gave a quick smile. Then she said unexpectedly, "If a person was mistreated during childhood, could he do the same thing to his own kids?"

For a moment Annie was silent. She tilted her head and looked thoughtfully at Kristen. "Do you have children?" she asked.

"No," Kristen said. "I'm not married and I don't have kids. This isn't about me."

When she said nothing further, Annie said, "I'm not sure I can be very helpful if I don't have a little more background."

"It's a friend of mine. I've known him for a long time, or at least I've known *about* him for a long time. I've only known him well for a year or two. He had a terrible childhood, and sometimes I've felt—that is, it seems like he has the same—" she cast about for a word, "the same kind of anger his father had."

"I see. Does *he* have children?"

"Not exactly."

"Then may I ask why you're concerned?"

Kristen sighed and looked down at her hands which lay folded in her lap. "The fact is, I've been living with him since last fall. I just left a couple of weeks ago after we'd had an awful row, or maybe you'd call it a disagreement—about having kids."

"Maybe you should start at the beginning," Annie had said.

Now, looking across the table at Bill, she said, "That's when she identified him as Erik Sarmento. I can't say what she told me was a surprise, but the fact of it was. It was too coincidental. I've lived in this county all my life, and I know lots of people, but I'd never heard of Sarmento until Michael went up there, and now Kristen drops in with all this."

Kristen told Annie that she and her brother, Jan, had grown up in North Fairborough on their family's farm. Their father was an extension agent, their mother a schoolteacher. The barn that once had housed their grandfather's dairy herd was now home only to the family's single cow, a few laying hens and the children's old pony. The land, almost two hundred acres, was used to grow hay as a cash crop. Kristen described her childhood as happy and basically uneventful.

Much of the time after she had started school and her mother had returned to work she had spent in the care of her brother, who was seven years her senior.

"Jan was my closest friend when I was little," Kristen told Annie. "I've often wondered how it must have been for him to have to cope with a baby sister when he was a young teenager, but if I was a bother, he never let me know it. He invented exciting games, protected and entertained me, and I'd help him with his chores."

When Kristen was five years old, the small house and barn that lay on the other side of the farm were leased to the last of a succession of tenants, a horse trainer named Von Tauber, who moved in with his wife and son and a few horses. The boy, twelve or thirteen, was Erik.

"It didn't take long for Jan to find him," Kristen told Annie, "His Dad sent him over to help my Dad and Jan with the haying, and right away they became friends. But I had almost no contact with the family. I have only a vague memory of Mr. Von Tauber as a huge man who frightened me, and I didn't really know Erik, either. What I do remember is that he never smiled and would only talk to Jan.

"Mr. Von Tauber was well-educated and spoke several languages. But he was a cruel, bad-tempered man, and he beat and humiliated Erik and forced him to work all the time. Erik was often absent from school for one reason or another, and never fit in with the other kids. Jan said that when he first came he was nearly illiterate. He did most of the work at home with the horses because his father had some physical problem and could no longer ride."

Kristen went on in her matter-of-fact tone to recite the details of Erik's bleak, tormented childhood, her brother's friendship with him, and her own reintroduction to Erik a few years before. Later Annie found herself remembering the details of her story. They would come to her unexpectedly as did the details of so many of her cases, even when the case had been closed for months.

She watched Bill tilt comfortably back in his chair, resting his hand on the windowsill for balance. He was a good listener, attentive and thoughtful, and now he smiled at her.

"Perhaps I was a little dishonest," she admitted. "I didn't tell her about Michael's being up there, or even that I'd heard of Erik. It really had nothing to do with what she was asking, and I confess I was most interested in what she had to say. It had occurred to me by then that perhaps she could be more helpful to me than I to her."

She looked down and began absently to trace over the letters of a word she had written on her pad and then, more to focus her thoughts than to emphasize the word, she underlined it and put her pencil down.

Bill said, "What did you tell her?"

"I told her the truth. I said the evidence was very strong that abused children often grow up to repeat the behavior with their own children and even with others with whom they have close relationships."

"But Erik hated his father," Kristen had said. "Why would he want to be like him?"

"We aren't always aware of why we do things," Annie said. "I don't suppose he wants to be like him, but parents are role models, no matter how ambivalent one's feelings are about them. Sometimes abusive relationships are the only ones children have known. They don't know how to form other kinds."

Kristen made an abrupt movement, almost a shudder. She frowned and as Annie watched, her expression suddenly changed. "What about the horses?" she asked.

"The horses?" Annie repeated, casting about for the connection.

"Yes. He's closer to them than he is to most people. I never saw him abuse a horse."

Annie sat quietly, considering the irony of her own experience at the farm. "I'm afraid I can't tell you much about people's relationships with horses," she said and glanced down at her watch.

"It was a mistake," she said now to Bill, "the act of a novice, or, in my case, a social worker who's uncomfortable with the subject matter. And of course it had exactly the effect you'd expect. She immediately apologized for taking up my time and got up to leave. The best I could do then was to offer to see her another time and to assure her of my interest. She said she might be in again, but I think it's unlikely."

Annie toyed absently with her pencil and sighed. "This morning, in the wake of Kristen's story about child abuse, I called Family Service to see if there was any record of the Von Tauber family. They have some old records that indicate there were complaints about Von Tauber, never fully verified, that he kept his son out of school a good deal of the time to work, but nothing of any more substance than that. They took no action. There was a notation that the mother had left the household when Erik was about fourteen, and later there was some question about foster-home placement for him after his father died in a fire that destroyed the home. He was seventeen then, and no placement was ever arranged. Apparently he took one of the horses and ran away."

Bill said nothing for a few moments, and Annie, too, was silent. She looked up to find him watching her with a half smile. The crow's feet deepened around his eyes. "You're worried about Michael, aren't you?" he said. "That's what all this is about, isn't it?"

"Yes," Annie confessed, "it's Michael. It's been over two weeks and I haven't heard a single word from him. I even wrote him a note on Friday. And then all this. It made me realize how little I know about Sarmento. The more I learn, the more misgivings I have."

Bill reached for his briefcase and stood up. "Don't worry about Michael. He's tough, and he's old enough to take care of himself. I doubt you'll see much of him any more unless he gets himself fired again. For your sake as well as his, I hope that doesn't happen. But keep me posted, will you?"

Annie nodded. When Bill had left, she gazed thoughtfully out the window. A pair of sparrows had made their nest behind one of the shutters, and now she watched one disappear behind it. Despite Bill's reassurance, she couldn't forget Erik's behavior with the horse, Calypso, and her own misgivings. Michael had accused her bitterly of not trusting him, and indeed it was partly true. He had never refused to do as she asked, and yet she had a certain knowledge that he would do almost anything without regard for the consequences if he felt challenged.

She reached over and picked up the little clay horse from the windowsill. A gift from Michael, it suddenly seemed in its primitive outlines to be a distillation of explosive temper, frozen forever inside the hardened clay. Holding it in her hands, she thought of Michael and Sarmento, and she wondered if she had done the right thing in taking him up to the farm.

CHAPTER 6

▼

With Annie's note before him on the kitchen table, Michael was trying to write a letter. He hadn't forgotten he was required to report to her, but it was a chore he resented, and so he hadn't done it. Writing was hard for him. His handwriting was uneven and ragged, his spelling capricious, but worse than the physical effort of writing was its threat to his self-esteem. He didn't want to commit himself.

He stared unhappily at Annie's note, which was neat and to the point.

> Dear Michael,
>   Maybe you've forgotten that I've been expecting to hear from you, and it's been over two weeks. I know you're busy, but I'm sure you can find a few minutes to let me know how you're doing. I don't believe you want me checking up on you, but I'm afraid I'll have to make the trip if I don't hear from you this week.

From upstairs came the faint, obtrusive sound of music from Erik's radio and in irritating counterpoint the sporadic noise of the old television in the front room. Peter had come home from his Horse Trials a short time before, unreasonably happy, it seemed to Michael, considering that he hadn't placed. When he started telling Ivan about the Trials, Michael withdrew. He turned his attention back to Annie's note:

> I'm still looking for other work for you but without much luck. Now that school is over, full-time jobs are hard to find, although in haying season farm-

ers are always looking for part-time help. Since you need a place to live as well as work, I don't think that a realistic alternative to what you're doing now.

Several people I've talked to at farms I've visited have heard of Mr. Sarmento. Apparently he grew up in the area, for some of them remember his father as a trainer who lived in North Fairborough. Some people said they've heard he's a gifted trainer. Others aren't so complimentary. No one seems to know much about him.

Please let me hear from you soon. Affectionately, Annie.

Michael stared at the window over the kitchen sink. The room was reflected in the black mirror of the glass. Apart from the stove, it seemed dingy and antiquated. The floor and counter tops were unadorned wood, the sink enameled cast iron. There was no sign of tile or linoleum. The old cabinets were painted white. He edged the pad of paper fractionally closer and wrote,

"Dear Annie, I'm OK" and tried to think what else to add. It was almost impossible for him to describe what had happened to him or even to think coherently about it. "I built a fence," he wrote but could not express its significance. "The work is hard. I chopped wood for a week. I work in the barn now, but I don't ever get to ride."

He couldn't think how to end the letter, and finally simply wrote his name. Accustomed as he was to protecting himself, he hadn't told her he was planning to leave. He was waiting for the right time, his duffel still packed under his cot. He needed only a small victory to send him on his way, but Erik gave him no such victory. Like a master chess player, he drove him back to his side of the board and checked him again and again.

The following day Ivan and Peter drove off in Peter's truck after the morning chores were done. They didn't invite him to go along, and Michael asserted what slight independence he still retained and didn't ask. When they had gone he walked into the woods, which were criss-crossed by trails marked with the prints of horses. They wound up and down hill, some narrow, overgrown and seldom traveled, others wide, deeply rutted logging trails leading to overgrown clearings where the slash was still evident through the sparse new growth of trees.

He daydreamed of riding these trails, cantering effortlessly up the hills and soaring over logs and deep ravines. His horse would look like Calypso and be his friend, mute and uncritical. He would water him in the streams and let him graze in the clearings, and when it was time to move on, the horse would come to him of its own accord.

He wondered why Erik never seemed to go anywhere. He had left the farm only once since Michael had come. He never seemed to take time off and, with the exception of people who came on business, never seemed to have visitors. Questions tormented Michael, but he couldn't bring himself to ask them and thus seem to care about the answers. Where was Erik's friend whom Ivan and Peter had mentioned? Were there no women in his life? The parallel between Erik's situation and his own made him uncomfortable. Aimlessly he wandered through the endless day and returned early to make himself supper and lie on his cot, staring at the ceiling and listening with irritation to Erik's radio upstairs.

But on Tuesday morning when he least expected it, Michael was allowed to ride a horse for the first time. He was washing out feed tubs in the tackroom when Erik came in from the indoor ring and handed the horse he had been working over to Ivan. The sounds came to Michael from the aisleway, the clopping of hooves, Erik's voice, and he didn't turn around.

"You brought Lyrik up?" he heard Erik say.

"Yes, sir. She's in the first stall." There was a pause, and Ivan said, "Are we going to put her back in work?"

"Do you think she is here just for your amusement? Of course she's going back to work. Why, may I ask, would you think otherwise?"

"I thought maybe Kristen was coming to ride—" Ivan's voice trailed off. There was a dead silence, and Michael turned around. He could see nothing from where he stood but the empty aisle outside the tackroom, but he could visualize Erik's stare.

"Sorry," Ivan said weakly.

Michael knew he would be turning quickly away to his work, cursing his error in speaking out of turn, but Erik hadn't finished with him. "You enjoyed yourself yesterday on your day off?"

"Yes—" Ivan's voice was guarded.

"And you are not too tired from your activities to do the required work today?"

"No, sir," Ivan spoke almost in a monotone.

"I am delighted to hear it. You have a new student."

"A new student—"

"That is what I said. A young woman, I believe. That pleases you?"

"If that's what you want me to—"

"I?" said Erik. "It is the young lady who wants you as her instructor. She called yesterday while you were away. She tells me she spoke to you at a show some weeks back. I'm sure you recall the conversation."

"No—I can't remember—"

"Can't remember? A young woman admires you and you can't remember?" Ivan said nothing, and Michael heard Erik laugh. "Evidently she admired the way you rode. It was not clear to me whether it was you or the horse she was most taken with or what exactly she wished to learn from you. I assumed she wished you to teach her to ride her horse, but of course, I could be mistaken—perhaps it is some other activity she had in mind."

Ivan absorbed the insult silently.

"She is coming this afternoon—three o'clock I believe I told her. Of course, if she comes without her horse, I will have to ask that you teach her what she wants to know on your own time—elsewhere."

Michael stepped from the feed room into the aisle, and Erik turned his attention from Ivan to him.

"It is time, I think, that you showed us what you know," he said to Michael. "Ivan, saddle The Phoenix and bring him to the indoor school."

The horse Ivan led from the stall was the one Michael had seen Erik bring up from the lower field some days before. A little under sixteen hands in height, he was heavily muscled and had large eyes and ears and a Roman nose. Michael looked at him suspiciously. It seemed to him that Erik had chosen this horse, so different from the others, for a particular reason.

Michael stood idle while Ivan groomed and saddled the horse. He saw Ivan glance at him and then look away and wondered if he should be helping, but something in Ivan's manner stopped him. "Am I going to ride, then?" he asked Erik.

"That is what I had in mind."

Ivan led the horse into the arena and stood at its head. Michael glanced toward Erik and saw him gesture to the horse. He felt suddenly self-conscious. He was convinced Erik was trying to trap him.

"I suppose I'm going to get on and he'll buck me off—is that right?" he asked defensively.

"Do you take me for the Lone Ranger that I should teach a horse such tricks?" Erik said. "You are the rider at the moment. You will tell him what you wish."

Nervously, Michael adjusted the stirrups and mounted. It was years since he had ridden. The Phoenix stood quietly as he found the stirrups and picked up the rein. He wished Erik would leave and let him get used to the horse, but he continued to stand in the arena and watch, his face impassive.

Finally, after he had looked questioningly at Erik for directions and received none, Michael tapped the horse with his heels and The Phoenix walked obediently, if lazily, around the edge of the arena. Michael felt his pleasure at riding again diffused by his self-awareness. What was Erik looking for?

"Trot," Erik said at length, and to Michael's surprise, the horse anticipated him and began to trot without waiting for his signal. He found himself rising easily, as if it were only yesterday he had ridden last. The Phoenix had a comfortable, springy gait, cadenced and regular. Erik gestured for him to cross the diagonal and change direction. He sat a beat and began to rise on the other diagonal, watching Erik from the corner of his eye.

"Halt," Erik said suddenly, and in confusion Michael pulled the horse down.

"Dismount." He did so, feeling weakly that he had failed the test.

"There is something amiss with the saddle?" Erik asked.

"The saddle? No, I don't think—"

"You don't care for its design?"

"I don't know—it looks all right."

"It sits level on the horse's back?"

Michael looked critically at the saddle. It looked like any other saddle to him. "I think it does."

"Then why do you find it necessary to sit upon the cantle? The deepest part of the saddle is designed for the seat, I believe, or have you, perhaps, some different idea?"

"I thought I was—"

"Then you must rearrange your thinking. Get on the horse, and kindly do not kick him in the ribs when you mount. He is not a football."

Michael remounted, found the right stirrup with his foot and gathered the rein. He tried to feel if, as Erik had said, he was sitting on the cantle.

"When you are ready, you may canter."

Michael leaned forward slightly, gave the horse a kick and saw his ears go back and forth. Finally The Phoenix broke into a ragged trot, but Michael couldn't make him canter. In his humiliation he slowly grew angry at the horse, who continued to trot around the ring with determination.

"Canter," Erik repeated quietly, and The Phoenix obediently did so. He rocked in long, easy strides around the track with neither increase nor decrease in speed. Michael stared straight ahead of him. He wished heartily that the ride were over.

"Come into the center and halt," Erik said.

He did so, thrown off balance by the abruptness of the horse's halt. In the rafters swallows darted. He could hear their wings and see in the edge of his vision the rapid arc of their flight.

"Well?" Erik said. "What have you to tell me?"

Michael was taken aback. "I don't know. I thought you were going to make the comments."

Erik stared at him in apparent disbelief. "You don't know? A rider who cannot analyze his ride is no rider at all. Perhaps you are merely a passenger. Very well, as a passenger how did you find your ride?"

Stung, Michael said rashly, "It was all right, I suppose, considering the horse is lazy and won't go."

"Lazy? You found him disobedient and stupid?"

"I didn't say he was stupid. He's just not trained." When Erik didn't answer him, he added more confidently, "What did you do, give me a cart horse to make a fool out of me?"

Erik regarded him with a thin smile. Both Ivan and Peter were watching. Neither of them met Michael's eye, but he saw Ivan wince and exchange glances with Peter. He wondered if they felt sorry for him and felt his temper rise. Irritably he shifted in the saddle, and The Phoenix stirred restlessly.

"An untrained cart horse," Erik repeated. "You may dismount from your cart horse."

Michael jumped off and stood defensively holding the horse while Erik slipped the stirrup leathers from the saddle. "Tie a knot in the rein, if you will," Erik said, and when Michael looked puzzled, did it himself. "Close the door," he said to Peter.

Peter closed the lower half of the double door at the entrance to the arena. Erik led The Phoenix to the rail, turned him loose and came back to the center where Michael stood. He said again, "Trot," and The Phoenix started again to trot around the ring.

"Be kind enough to mount the horse," Erik said.

Michael stared at him. "What are you talking about?"

"I asked you to get on the horse."

"He's trotting!"

Erik took a step backward and regarded him with mock astonishment. "How remarkably astute of you to notice that!" he said.

Michael clenched his jaw.

"Well?" Erik said.

"I can't," Michael said between his teeth.

"You can't. Perhaps you would like a demonstration?"

"Yeah, I would," Michael challenged him.

"Ivan, show him how to mount."

Ivan walked to the center of the ring, waited until the horse came by, and began to run along beside him, in step with his forelegs. He put his right hand on the pommel of the saddle, grasped the front of the flap with his left, and, bending at the waist, sprang up and landed lightly astride the horse.

Erik gave Michael a penetrating look. "That is how one mounts a trotting cart horse," he said. "Halt, if you please."

Ivan brought the horse back to where Erik was standing. Erik took the rein in one hand and placed the other on the horse's neck. He looked inquiringly at Ivan.

"I am told the horse is lazy. Do you find him so?"

"No, sir."

"Then perhaps, green as he is, he has yet to learn the aids. Ask the horse to canter, and we will see."

He stepped back. The Phoenix went from halt to canter with no perceptible signal from Ivan.

"He appears to have learned that, at least," Erik commented. "Take back the rein."

Ivan unknotted the rein. "Return to the track at trot and on the left rein, collect the horse."

The whole frame of the horse appeared to contract. His head and neck came up, his speed slowed, his strides shortened. His weight was shifted back on his hocks, and his rounded hindquarters swelled with muscle. He held his tail out from his quarters and the long hairs cascaded down. The end of his tail switched gracefully back and forth with each step.

"Extend the trot."

Like a powerful projectile shot down the side of the arena, The Phoenix moved in giant strides that scarcely seemed to touch the ground. Michael, watching intently, said in spite of himself, "My God!"

"Half-pass left," Erik said and watched with a smile as the horse moved diagonally across the arena from right to left, his right legs rhythmically crossing his left ones as he moved sideways at every stride. The moments passed, punctuated by quiet commands from Erik. At length he said, "Passage," and Michael watched the Phoenix float past him in slow motion and forgot that Erik stood beside him.

"How does he do that?" he said aloud, but he was speaking to himself.

"Canter," Erik said and later, "Counter canter" and "Change of leg." Ivan sat quietly on the horse, his expression grave. "Across the diagonal," Erik said and stepped out of the way. Then he added, "Change of leg every three strides," and

Michael watched the horse effortlessly change his leading leg every three strides, as if he were skipping.

"That is enough," Erik said to Ivan. "The horse is not straight in the changes." As Ivan dismounted, Erik appraised him thoughtfully. "Yes," he said. "Good."

He held out the stirrup leathers with the irons attached, and Ivan took them. He appeared to have been thrown off balance by the compliment, and his face reddened. Abruptly he turned to the horse, patted him on his neck, and busied himself replacing the leathers on the saddle. Michael, his unwilling audience, felt a stab of envy.

In his own good time, Erik turned to Michael. "I regret," he said, "I am unable to show you how well he draws a cart. That is one thing I neglected to teach him."

Michael said nothing. He had no way to absorb what he had just seen. He yearned to do what Ivan had. His inadequacy was more than he could bear, far worse than the quick temper that evaded his control or his restless sensitivity to the others. He turned his head and tried to block out his physical awareness of Erik's contempt. The silence was excruciating. The Phoenix still stood, Ivan at his head, in the center of the ring.

"Well?" Erik said at last. "The horse waits—perhaps you would like to ride him again?"

"For Christ's sake, what do you want?" Michael said, turning on him. "You know I can't—"

"You can't? Did I not understand you to tell me you knew how to ride?"

Michael glared at him and then dropped his gaze.

"In that case, I would say you have two choices. Either you learn how to ride, if that is your desire, or you take up some other line of work. Perhaps prize-fighting is more to your taste."

Michael felt himself growing hot. "I do not intend to stand here all day waiting for you to make up your mind," Erik said.

"You know what I want."

"You imagine I can read your mind?"

"Yes!" Michael said, beside himself.

Erik laughed. "Remount the horse."

Michael went hesitantly to The Phoenix's side and remounted. The horse, once transformed, now stood like a lump of clay. Erik stepped back and regarded Michael critically.

"You have no seat," he said. "You sit upon the cantle of the saddle as if you were in an armchair in front of the fire. Your legs are out in front of you and useless. Perhaps you think you are driving an automobile. And what is the horse to think of that? He does not know how to be an automobile. When you rise to the trot, you are behind the movement of the horse and are asking him to become slower. Your hands on the reins tell the horse nothing. You are conducting an orchestra, perhaps? Unfortunately the horse's brain is small. He doesn't know how to be an orchestra, either." He paused. "That is not to say that you couldn't learn. You have a certain natural ability. You could become a passable rider if you wished to do so, if you could bring yourself to submit—to the horse," he added with emphasis.

Michael started to retort, and Erik raised his hand.

"I am speaking," he said warningly, "and I do not care to be interrupted, even by an expert rider such as you. What I have told you I will not trouble to say again. Riding a horse is a privilege. If you do not believe that, you may dismount now and leave here. It is also an art that will take your whole lifetime to learn. Should you wish to begin, I will help you. That is all."

For a long moment Michael was silent. Finally he said unwillingly, "Yes—I'd like to."

Erik turned to Ivan. "You will teach him, starting now."

Michael made a face and looked over at Ivan. Ivan glanced at Erik.

"A good instructor learns from his teaching," Erik observed. "A good student learns from his instructor." He stood for a few seconds looking from one to the other and then turned and went back to the barn.

Still astride the horse, Michael waited until he was gone and then said to Ivan in a voice filled with sarcasm, "Now what? You going to show me how to do all that fancy stuff?"

"You might as well dismount, and we'll start with vaulting," Ivan said.

"*Vaulting*? Who cares about vaulting?"

"Get off." Michael sat stubbornly where he was. "Get off, I said."

"I told you, I don't give a damn about vaulting."

"I didn't ask if you did, and I don't care. Just get off the horse." There was no answer. Michael stared at him belligerently.

"You want to spend the next hour sitting there? OK—sit there."

Ivan turned his back, but he still held the rein firmly in his hand. Michael sat indecisively astride The Phoenix and finally dismounted. Ivan turned on him. "Let's get something straight. I didn't ask to ride the horse this morning or to give you lessons. It was Erik's idea, in case you don't remember. You think *I* enjoy this? I'd walk out in three seconds if I could rather than stand here and take a lot of shit from you. But who'd be the loser then? Me, that's who. So you can be the one to walk out if you want, but if you're fool enough to think you'll get a second chance, you can forget it."

Michael appraised him sullenly and said nothing.

"The idea behind vaulting," Ivan went on, "is to get as much weight as possible off of your legs so you can spring higher. To do that, you bend at the waist and get your torso down low. Keep your head down below your shoulders. Face forward, grasp the pommel and flap, and hop off your left leg. You can practice at a standstill by holding the saddle and swinging your leg back. Each time your leg goes back, you bend at the waist until your upper body and your right leg are parallel to the ground. You hop on your left leg each time your right leg goes back. Try it."

"You make all your students do this?" Michael asked.

"What I do with my other students is none of your damned business. Try it."

Michael allowed several seconds to pass before he made a desultory effort.

"No, that's wrong. Face forward and keep your head down. Keep your head *down*. Keep your left leg stiffer when you hop. Like this." He demonstrated.

Michael could not coordinate the actions. "So you can hop on one foot and I can't—so what? Maybe you should be a ballet dancer."

Ivan ignored him, and Michael felt his face grow red. The first few times he tried to vault, he barely left the ground and turned involuntarily toward the horse to try and pull himself up with his arms.

"Forget that," Ivan said. "That's the wrong way to mount, since you end up dragging your weight onto the horse, and when he's moving, you're apt to end up underneath him. If you vault correctly, the motion of the horse lifts you onto his back. The faster he goes, the easier it is. Try again."

Finally Michael got his right ankle over the saddle and struggled silently to gain his seat.

"Again."

He dismounted and did it again.

"Again."

Ivan kept him vaulting and dismounting until he was able to get on each time, and then he made him do it from the off side. Although Michael was gasping for breath and his legs were weak from fatigue, he kept doggedly on, and Ivan, with a grim satisfaction that sprang from the same source, allowed him to do so.

"Now try it at trot." Ivan removed the stirrups and leathers as Erik had done and sent the horse to the rail to circle left at the trot.

"You know I can't do that," Michael said angrily.

"Yes, you can. Get in step with his front legs, hold the saddle and bend over and do exactly what you've been doing. The motion of the horse will throw you up."

By the time half an hour had passed, Michael had mastered mounting without stirrups. It was simply a knack, he found, and once mastered, like swimming or bicycling, it was not forgotten. He found it considerably more difficult to stay on the horse after he had mounted, without stirrups to help him sit the springy trot. Several times he slipped sideways and had to clutch the horse around the neck to pull himself back into the saddle. Ivan refused to stop the horse when this occurred, and once he fell off to land on his back almost under the horse's feet.

"OK," Ivan said at last. "Now we'll do a few dismounts so you won't kill yourself when you get in trouble."

"When he's *trotting?*"

"Yes, to start with. The trick is to land facing forward and running. Don't stop and don't land facing the horse as if you were standing still or you're apt to land under his feet the way you did a while back. If you lose your balance, somersault."

Before the lesson was over, Michael was able to dismount from either side at trot and canter, but he still had trouble riding the trot and was sore and bruised from his occasional errors.

"That's enough," Ivan said finally. "You'll do some vaulting every day until you can get on and off from either side at a moment's notice. I'll show you some standard vaulting exercises. You do them in rhythm with the horse's stride. It does a lot for your timing and balance."

"Did you do all this stuff?" Secretly proud of himself, Michael was still not certain these tricks weren't designed to make a fool of him.

"Of course I did. How'd you think I got on this afternoon? Peter taught me. Erik taught him."

"You mean Erik does this?"

"I've never seen him, but I'm sure he can."

Still astride the horse, Michael toyed with The Phoenix's mane. He watched Ivan thoughtfully as he stood at the horse's head and undid the noseband on the bridle. He was suddenly overwhelmed by an urgent curiosity, a need to understand the secrecy that seemed to surround him, mysteries he had ignored in his preoccupation and for fear the answers would be withheld.

He chose a neutral question. "What's a phoenix?"

"Some kind of bird, I think. I don't know where he got the name, but Erik's owned him a long time. The horse is about twenty years old. You can get off, if you want."

Michael dismounted slowly. His legs felt weak and boneless, and the soles of his feet stung when they hit the ground. "Did Erik train him to do all those things?"

"Yes." Ivan put the leathers back on the saddle and ran the stirrup irons up them. He loosened the girth and prepared to take the horse back to the barn.

"Who's Kristen?" Michael said suddenly.

Startled, Ivan turned his head. "Kristen—" he repeated. "Why do you ask?"

"Heard you talking about her. Who is she?"

Ivan looked uncertainly at Michael. "She's Jan Karras's sister. She left here just before you came."

"She worked here?"

"Not exactly. She lived here—with Erik."

Taken by surprise, Michael laughed. "No kidding?" he said. "I'll be damned!"

He noticed that Ivan wasn't smiling. The subject seemed to make him uncomfortable, but to Michael it was as if he had suddenly gained an advantage in his uneven struggle with Erik. He grinned. "So that's why he's such a son of a bitch—his girlfriend ran off with someone else."

Ivan made no attempt to hide his reaction. "Don't be an asshole," he said. "You don't know a thing about Erik, and you better not assume things. He calls the shots around here. I should think you'd know that by now. If you don't, you'd better start learning it in a hurry or you'll find yourself in over your head, and I guarantee you won't find it much fun."

"Bullshit," Michael said. "I can take care of myself—I've done it all my life."

Ivan led the Phoenix into the barn without answering him.

"Is that why his friend never comes around?" Michael persisted. "Because Erik was screwing his sister?"

He knew he had struck a nerve and was grimly pleased. Ivan went deliberately through the motions of putting The Phoenix away without saying a word. Stubbornly, Michael stood outside the stall waiting for an answer.

"Jan's in Europe," Ivan said finally. "He's been there for a year. I've got work to do."

He pushed past Michael on the way to the tackroom. Michael absently rubbed the back of his neck and watched him go. So that's it, he thought. You had your eye on her yourself.

He turned to look at The Phoenix and reached over the door to stroke his nose. This extraordinary horse was his now, and soon he would be doing what Ivan had done. He turned to his work with the first optimism he had felt since he had arrived.

CHAPTER 7

▼

Starting the next morning, Michael rode twice a day, in the morning right after breakfast and again in the afternoon just before the horses were fed. He found Ivan a demanding teacher, and the lessons exhausted him, only partly because they made him stiff and sore. The years of riding his own pony many years before were useless to him, except as a bittersweet memory, and it took as much energy for him to combat what he saw as Ivan's studied assaults on his pride as it did to ride the horse.

There was also Erik, who seemed to observe their silent struggle with amused satisfaction and even to foster it. Despite the hours taken up with riding, neither Michael nor Ivan was excused from their other chores. In addition to the regular barn work there was hay to be brought in; cut and baled by a local farmer, it was left in the field for loading. They led horses back and forth from pasture to barn, held them for the vet, and tended their occasional injuries. Fences had to be repaired, and the grass grew tall around the house. Erik insisted it be mowed, and the job fell most often to Michael since Peter and Ivan had lessons to teach and horses to ride.

In self-defense, Michael learned to work hard and economically. Erik was meticulous and unforgiving in his attention to detail. He worked himself as unstintingly as he did the others and rode Calypso and Lyrik every day as well as teaching lessons and schooling several other horses. The horses he rode he groomed himself.

With increasing restlessness under the relentless workload, Michael began studying Erik, but he never seemed able to predict his actions and reactions.

Instead, he found more and more contradictions. Erik might spend hours with a horse and achieve nothing that Michael could see, or go through a long preparation fitting equipment to another only to work him for a few minutes before putting him away. A horse who seemed to be progressing nicely might be turned out for a week, while another was schooled every day to no apparent purpose.

The old horse Erik had been given received more than his share of attention. Erik groomed him twice a day and personally oversaw his feeding. His feet were trimmed, his teeth floated, his ragged mane painstakingly combed out. Erik turned him out and brought him up to the barn in a way that was totally random to Michael, who was often responsible for cleaning his stall and keeping his water buckets filled as well as seeing to it that hay was always available to him. It was in Michael's mind to ask Erik the reasons for what he did, but it always seemed as if the time was wrong, Erik was in a bad mood, he was busy, or Michael himself was supposed to be working, or so he excused his reluctance.

He turned to Peter one day when he had been made to bring a horse up from the lower pasture only to have Erik glance at it and send it back down again.

Peter shrugged. "Don't ask me," he said. "Erik does lots of things I don't always understand."

"Then why don't you ask?"

Peter laughed. "Why don't you?"

"Are you kidding? He's never answered me once since I've been here."

He was only partly comforted by the fact that neither Ivan nor Peter seemed to receive answers either.

He overheard Ivan describing to Peter a lesson he had received from Erik earlier in the week. He had been riding Orion, a young horse that had been assigned to him for training. Michael had watched him set off cross country many times on the horse while he himself was left to clean stalls and struggle with his bitter envy. A few times each week, Ivan worked the horse in the indoor arena, and on this particular day, he was having trouble with the canter.

"Everything was fine until I asked for the left lead," he told Peter. "Even though he's green, he's real willing, and I'd never had trouble with that lead before. I was getting impatient, and I took him deep into the corner and gave him a strong left rein and a hard squeeze with my legs. He careened through the corner, all disunited, and broke out in a sweat, and I suddenly heard Erik ask me what I was doing. I don't know how long he'd been standing there, but I thought he sounded disgusted, although that may be only because I was disgusted with myself."

Michael pretended disinterest, listening avidly. He tried to picture the scene Ivan described.

"He's fine on the right," Ivan had told Erik in an effort to justify himself, "but he won't pick up the left at all. I can't get him to pay attention."

"You ask, and he doesn't listen?"

"That's right, and he's getting more and more resistant."

"Yet he speaks to you, and *you* do not listen. Which of you is the more inattentive?"

"What do you mean?" Ivan said, but he knew the answer was implicit in the question.

Erik made a gesture with the dressage whip he held in his right hand. "With which leg must he start the left canter?" he said, advancing a few steps into the arena.

"Right hind."

"When you pull him to the left, do you help him engage the right hind leg?"

Ivan had been silent for a moment. "But he'll be bent incorrectly," he said at last.

"Oh? You bend the horse with the inside rein?"

"Well, I thought—"

"What are you asking him?"

"For the left lead canter."

"You would pull him off balance to assist him?"

"Of course not. I thought he'd be *more* balanced if I—"

"How is the horse balanced in the turn?"

"With the outside rein—I know that. But I thought I'd position—"

"You thought you'd put him in a vise perhaps?"

"A vise?"

"The horse is learning. You are impatient. You wish him to learn everything at once?"

"No," Ivan said, chastened. He started back to the track, picked up the sitting trot, and took a gentle contact on both reins"

"Drop the left."

"*Drop* it?"

"Yes."

"And I did," he said now to Peter, "and of course it worked. I wasn't even surprised, really. I asked him outright why Orion had done it before for me and not today, and he asked me if I'd been working him to the right the day before. Of course I had, and he said the horse was stiff in the right hind leg and I had ignored it. The fact is, I hadn't noticed it. He said the horse was more generous than I was, and he asked me why I should expect him to do as I asked when I wouldn't do the same for him. That's all he'd tell me, and I still don't know why he wanted me to drop the left rein altogether. I decided maybe Orion was expecting the left rein aid and was prepared to resist it again, and I was setting up a battle."

"Could be," Peter said. "Funny—I asked him for some help with Kestrel today and he did just the opposite—*made* me fight with her."

Michael sat up. Unnoticed, he had witnessed Peter's lesson on Kestrel that morning from just outside the arena. Erik, in the main doorway, had paused in passing, and Peter had stopped his horse and turned to him. "What do you think, sir?"

"What do *I* think? You are riding the horse, what is *your* opinion? Are you satisfied that she makes progress?"

"Not completely. She does what I ask, but she doesn't seem to improve much."

"She has trained you well."

Peter stared soberly at him. "What does that mean?"

"You treat her as a virgin—yes? But she is not a virgin. She is a courtesan, I think. She is your mistress, and you her slave."

"I'm not sure what you—"

"You make love to the horse, but it is she who gives the orders."

"If I start demanding more of her, she fights back."

"Yes, that is her nature. And it is your nature, I'm afraid, to avoid the confrontation. Am I wrong?"

Peter gave an embarrassed smile, and Michael saw to his astonishment that Erik, too, was smiling and regarded Peter with an amusement that seemed to hold none of his habitual scorn.

"I guess maybe that's true," Peter had said. "Will you help me with her?"

Without answering, Erik turned and disappeared into the barn. He reappeared with a pair of spurs in his hand and gestured for Peter to dismount.

"I've never ridden her with spurs," Peter said as he put them on. "It never seemed necessary—she's so responsive."

"She responds when she chooses, and you allow her to escape your direction. Remount and do as I say. The horse will fight you—you must be prepared for that. Do you understand?"

"Yes, sir."

"You must not punish, but you must insist, and you must not give in to her. Do I make myself clear?"

"I think so."

"Then make your seat secure. Take up the contact and do not allow it to change. You will begin to drive the horse into the hand. When she resists you, use the spur. Ask only a little, but insist upon it. She will try you out, possibly by running away from you. You must be prepared to deal with each evasion as it occurs, and there may be many. Do not be misled into thinking she does not understand what you are asking. She understands you very well—too well."

Michael had watched the ensuing scene with all his attention. Erik had moved to the center of the arena. Kestrel started to trot around the track.

"More impulsion," Erik said. Kestrel's ears went back. She increased her stride and leaned on the rein.

"Again," Erik said. "And now you put her to the spur."

Kestrel gave a great leap forward and began to fight, leaning on the bit, shaking her head. She made an effort to buck but couldn't get her head down.

"Do not take the spur from her side," Erik said quietly, "and do not freeze the hand."

Kestrel flung her head up and leaped forward in a series of jarring bounds. Erik smiled. "Take the inside rein to the inside," he said, "Drop the outside rein." Kestrel, led to the inside, careened in a tight circle. "Sit like a statue and stay on the circle."

Around and around Kestrel went, and when at last she showed signs of flagging, Erik said, "Return to the track and pick up the contact with both reins."

On the long side, Kestrel plunged ahead again, and Peter repeated Erik's instruction, using a soft but exaggerated leading rein to the inside and dropping the contact with the outside rein. Again she spun around and slackened her speed, and again he brought her back to the track.

"And now she will attempt to stop," Erik said after a time, "and you must use your spur with conviction."

Kestrel, her ears pinned, gave another leap up and forward and landed stiff-legged, shaking her head. She had lost all forward momentum and looked as if she might rear. Michael heard Peter grunt from the shock of the landing and saw him clamp his spur into her side. His face was red and it was obvious he was losing his temper.

"Correct," Erik said enigmatically. "Be careful you do not pull on the horse. You have told her to move forward, and you must allow her to do so, but at the same time you must not drop the contact, as she demands. Change the rein."

Peter brought the mare across the diagonal and changed direction. He continued his battle around the ring the other way, bringing the horse in a tight circle with a soft leading rein when she began to lean on his hand. Michael could see the effects of his exertion and the amount of strength and concentration that was demanded of him, his legs tight on the horse's sides, his shoulders back and his seat well down as if glued to the saddle. Only his arms moved, strangely independent, intricately following Erik's direction. Kestrel, by contrast, appeared to Michael tireless, powerful, radiating a fearful energy.

Suddenly Erik said, "Now you remove the spur and ride her forward."

Light as a feather in Peter's hand, Kestrel moved actively around the track. There was a graceful arch to her neck and she mouthed the bit gently, her ears now forward. "She's floating!" Peter said in his delight.

"Change the rein again. And now you need only touch her with the spur when she flags or leans on you, and touch the inside rein if she becomes strong. Resume your contact with the outside rein and ride her into it with the inside leg. She has yielded to you. Do not let her forget the lesson."

Peter brought the horse to a halt. Her coat was dark with sweat and her sides heaved. Peter, too, was winded. "Thanks!" he said, smiling and elated. Erik bowed in his direction.

"She is headstrong, your courtesan," he said. "You must work further on transitions if you are to control her in the open. Don't forget what I have told you. You must not let her enslave you, but always you must listen to her if you are to become as one." He turned and left the arena.

"So what's all that stuff supposed to mean, anyhow?" Michael said now. He made no attempt to hide the scorn in his voice. "You trying to say you understood him?"

"I don't know if I understood him exactly, but I understood Kestrel. Isn't that the point?"

Michael shook his head. "You're always making excuses for him whatever he does." But despite his bravado, he felt a reluctant admiration for Peter's success with his volatile mare and a nagging suspicion that he had witnessed something beyond his own understanding.

Michael had The Phoenix in cross ties the next afternoon when he heard the sound of a car outside the barn. Strolling down the aisle, mildly curious, he was taken aback to find himself face to face with Bill Gurney, the trainer he had worked for at the racetrack. Gurney was as surprised as he.

"Well, I'll be goddamned," he said.

For a moment Michael was speechless. He stared dumbly at Gurney in a vain attempt to make sense of his presence here and then felt himself blushing and turned quickly to retreat the way he had come. He almost collided with Erik.

"Evening, Erik," Gurney said. "Scraping the bottom, are you?" He gestured to Michael. "Where'd you find *him*?"

Erik looked from one to the other. "I'm afraid I don't understand you."

"The kid—is he working for you?" Michael stirred uncomfortably and glanced toward the back of the barn.

"In a sense," Erik answered with his characteristic half smile.

"He was working for me a month ago. You should have called me. I'd have warned you off." Michael, his temper rising, headed toward the back of the barn.

"Just a moment—" Erik raised his hand. "Perhaps we should hear what this gentleman has to say."

"What gentleman?" Michael said angrily. Erik gave him a warning look.

"Yeah," Gurney said nodding, "he hasn't changed much. He's still a hot-tempered son of a bitch. I fired him, and if you're smart, you'll do the same. Smartass kids think they know it all, and not one of them can tell his ass from a hole in the ground."

Erik regarded his visitor in silence.

"Can't trust 'em to follow an order," Gurney went on. "Steal you blind. Lazy, that's what."

"You have problems controlling your help?" Erik said.

"Oh, I control 'em all right. I fire 'em. You'll do the same soon enough, I dare say."

Erik turned slowly around to include Michael in his gaze. "Perhaps," he said.

"Well, he ain't worth what you pay him, take my word for it. He tried to tell me how to run my business. He done that for you yet?"

"You ran my horse when he was dead lame—" Michael interrupted. "Someone ought to tell—"

"Not as yet," Erik said to Gurney. He turned to Michael and added, "You have work to do, I believe?"

"Work's done," Michael said. He was treading a precarious line so as not to lose face in front of Gurney. "I'm getting ready to ride," he added and glanced smugly at the trainer.

"You will not have time to ride this afternoon. Put the horse away," Erik said. "I have noticed that the manure pile is too close to the barn. When you have finished here, you will move it."

"*Move* it?"

"Ten feet should be sufficient."

"You want me to move that whole pile ten feet?" Michael repeated, incredulous.

Gurney laughed and slapped his leg. Erik's eyes had not left Michael's face. "Perhaps you think it of little importance that a horse be left tied without supervision in the aisle. I do not share that attitude. Put him away. Then fetch Ivan."

Michael cast Gurney a look of pure hatred but he avoided meeting Erik's eye. "Yes, *sir*," he said rudely. Erik reached into his shirt pocket, withdrew a cigarette and lit it.

Gurney was leaning weakly against his car, laughing. "By Christ," he said, wiping his forearm across his eyes, "you can work for me any time! Move the manure pile—eh? I'll have to give that one a try myself!" He pulled himself together with an effort and gestured to the trailer. "Here he is, then. Took me and my brother and his oldest kid two hours to get the bastard on."

For a moment he glanced from Erik to the faded trailer. Then he sighed and shook his head. "It sure beats hell how things work out," he said. "That kid, for instance. He wasn't a bad worker to start—no worse than the rest. Did what had to be done and shut up about it. I had a couple lame horses—that's what got to him. I ran one on Bute one day, and he shattered an ankle. Bad luck, no question about it. The kid was his groom, and he took it kind of hard and gave me some lip. Hell, I know how he felt—felt bad about it myself, but I don't take that from the kids, you know. They'll be lucky if they don't end up doing a lot worse than that if they stay in this game long as I have.

"I told him to hit the road and damned if I didn't run into him in a bar that same night, and the son of a bitch took a swing at me. Damned fool's suicidal—ruins his own chances. Not a trainer in North Fairborough would hire him now. Reminds me of this horse I got here." He sighed, and stared thoughtfully out across the pasture.

"Get the horse off the trailer," Erik said to Ivan, who had appeared in the doorway.

"Watch yourself," Gurney said, and turning to Erik began to tell him about the horse. "He's got good breeding, this horse—Native Dancer and a good-producing stakes mare. I picked him up at a yearling sale some years back. Started him at two and couldn't train him to the gate. Damned fool had a fit—wouldn't break out and wouldn't load. Went up and over on the jock a couple of times. We tried about everything, sweet talk, blindfolds, chains, cattle prod—you name it. There are some like that, damn their souls, and he was a lulu, I'll tell you that.

But by damn, he was a good-looking colt and sound as a dollar. I didn't want to sell him—know what I mean?

"I shipped him off to my brother's farm and thought maybe he'd wise up in a year or so. But no dice, he was as crazy as ever. So I had him cut. I thought maybe he'd settle a bit, and I sure couldn't use him for breeding with no track record. I thought maybe I could sell him to the horse show crowd, good-looking horse like that. But he near killed my brother's kid trying to train him. So I figured let Erik fool with him and go from there. If you can do anything with him, I'll let you have him for cheap or I'll pay you flat out and turn around and resell him myself. I'm afraid he's dog meat, but you've got a good record with some of these ding-bats."

Ivan opened the escape door on the trailer and stared silently in at the horse. He turned to Erik. "You might want to see this, sir."

Erik walked over and glanced in. The horse, a steel grey, wore a surcingle and breastplate with an arrangement of straps that anchored him to two rings on the trailer floor. Two lead shanks secured his head. He wore a padded head protector on his halter. Drenched with sweat, he stood trembling.

"He goes up in the trailer," Gurney explained. "Gets his feet over the bar and pitches a real fit. Watch it when you unload."

Erik called Michael back to assist, and Ivan, watching Michael's expression, saw his own shock reflected in his face.

"Undo his head first," Gurney said. "The straps unsnap from the floor. Watch his front feet—he'll strike at you. Take one of the shanks off and throw the other over his neck. Your boss can catch it when he comes off."

The horse, his head released, lunged upward against the restraining harness, and although his shoulders were still anchored to the floor, his head nearly struck the ceiling.

"Easy—easy—it's OK—" Ivan said soothingly.

Michael climbed into the trailer through the escape door on the off side and squatted to undo the snap. The horse threw himself back against the restraints in panic, and Michael felt his heart lurch in sympathy. He glanced at Erik, standing by the ramp, but couldn't read his face. Erik waited until, for a fraction of a second, the horse's weight came off the tail chain and then unsnapped it.

"Right," Gurney said to no one in particular, and then to Ivan and Michael, "Undo your snaps on three: One—two—three."

Released, the horse plunged backward. Erik seized the shank and followed him rapidly backward for thirty or forty feet. He made no effort to stop him, but when the horse halted and gave a frenzied leap forward, he threw all his weight to the side, and the horse went to his knees. Erik watched him scramble to his feet and let the shank loose. The grey, confused, was still shaking.

"Will he lead?" Erik asked.

"Oh, sure. He's learned that much. But don't try to tie him—he'll go up on you. He's broken a dozen halters and about hung himself a couple of times."

"Hold him," Erik handed Ivan the shank. To Michael he said simply, "Do as you have been told," and indicated the barn. Michael had no choice but to go.

Ivan took the lead rope. The grey was still shaking, and sweat trickled down his legs. Erik laid his hand momentarily on the horse's neck and set about removing the harness. Then he went slowly to his heels to remove the leg wraps.

"Watch his feet—" Gurney said, but the horse, at least temporarily, was still. His head drooped.

"He is tranquilized?" Erik asked.

"Hell, yes. I shot him so full of Ace he should be walking on his knees. Damned stuff makes some horses go nuts, but I figured what the hell? He's nuts anyway—what have I got to lose?"

When the bandages were off, Erik got to his feet and began rolling them absently, watching the horse. He was strikingly handsome, still a dark grey, although the color was beginning to lighten on his barrel and around the stripe on his nose. His legs were black, like his mane and most of his tail. His hindquarters were clearly dappled.

"I sure like the look of that horse," Gurney said wistfully. "I wish you luck with him."

Erik gave a noncommittal grunt. "Yes," he said. "You have handed me a problem. It may come to nothing, but we will see. He has a great deal to unlearn before much can be done with him."

"He don't know shit, that horse," Gurney said. "Ain't nothing for him to unlearn. He's just like that kid there—all fireworks and no brains—useless."

Erik indicated the horse and said to Ivan, "Take him to the outside ring and cool him out in there. No water." He turned to the trainer, "What is his name?"

"Blue Tango—by Native Dancer out of Mood Indigo."

"How old is he?"

"Five." Gurney began to close the trailer. "Got to hit the road," he said. "Got another horse coming in tonight. Glad I bumped into you at sale, Erik—it's been a while. I've given you some real losers over the years, haven't I?" Erik smiled.

Gurney climbed into the car and rested his left arm on the windowsill. "Let me know how you make out," he said before he drove away.

Erik walked to the outside ring and leaned on the fence. For a long time he watched as Ivan led Blue Tango around and around. When finally the horse was cool and dry, he sent Ivan for a brush and some grain and, handing him the lead-shank, started brushing the horse down with firm, long strokes.

The grey accepted the grooming with ears back and skin quivering. When it was over Erik offered him a bite of grain and then left the paddock, taking the bucket with him. He filled it with water and offered it to the horse. Blue Tango was thirsty and emptied it.

Ivan said, "Are you going to leave him out here?"

"Yes."

"Shall I rig up a trough for him?"

"No water," Erik said. He removed the halter and let the horse go. The grey began to trot up and down the fence line. Occasionally he would slow and, putting his nose to the ground like a dog, move restlessly around the ring, returning to trot the fence line once more.

Ivan hesitated before he asked, "Why would you leave him without water?" He was surprised that Erik answered him.

"He has decided to do without mankind—one can hardly blame him. It is my intention to try to change his mind, to make myself and then, I hope, others indispensable to him. He will not eat or drink unless he takes it from my hand. Many horses will reject feed—few reject water for long, although he may lose weight and become to a certain extent dehydrated. We have been told this horse will not tolerate restriction. He fears the stall and the trailer, and he will not be tied. I regret I haven't a larger area to turn him out, but this will have to suffice. The pastures have grass and water available. This doesn't."

"But won't you have to spend hours here? Will you feed him his hay by hand, too?"

"He will take nothing except from my hand," Erik said. "Yes, it will be very time consuming, and it may well all be for nothing. It is possible the horse will not survive it. If he doesn't eat when I feed him, I will remove the excess. That is unnatural for a horse. Left to himself he would spend sixteen to eighteen hours a day grazing or picking at his hay. I must also spend considerable time grooming him, a process he seems to tolerate at the moment but does not enjoy."

"To get him used to being handled?" Ivan asked.

"No, because he *is* used to being handled. I will do what the horse has learned to accept, and I will reward him frequently for that acceptance. I will do nothing I know he will not tolerate and thus I need not punish him."

He looked thoughtfully at Blue Tango. Ivan was gratified by Erik's unaccustomed confidence and anxious to prolong it. He asked, "And then what? What will you do with him next?"

"I will have to wait and see what he tells me," Erik said. "At some point, when he has accepted me as important to him, I will have to have a few words with him about the direction of his life—but that is still in the future."

Blue Tango stopped by the gate and nickered, staring with ears forward over the fence toward the barn. Abruptly, he started pacing the fence line again.

"He'll be lonely down here all by himself," Ivan said.

"Of course. That is what I intend. He will miss the other horses, and I will be but a poor substitute. I will be, however, the only substitute he has."

He looked over at Ivan as if suddenly aware that he was there. "You have the evening feed to attend to. It is late," he said and started back to the barn.

CHAPTER 8

▼

On Sunday morning Kristen stepped out onto the front porch of her brother's house, leaned on the railing and looked out over the rosebushes into the yard. It was warm, and she was barefoot in a pair of faded jeans and a short-sleeved shirt. When Jan had left for Europe the previous summer, he had left his house in Northwood in her care. Small and manageable, it was located on a back road where there was little traffic and only a few neighbors close by. She had given up her rented room in Reed, and with the exception of the months she had spent with Erik, it had been her home and she had been happy there.

It was in this house three years ago that Jan had introduced her to Erik, and she thought of that evening now. She had just graduated from the University, and was spending the summer helping her mother prepare the family farm for sale. Her father had died two years before, and her mother planned to remarry in the fall and move to Florida. Neither Kristen nor her brother could afford to keep the farm. Jan had declared his independence some years before when he bought his house, and although Kristen was saddened to see the farm sold, she was philosophical.

At that time her own plans for the future were vague. She was a talented painter, had studied art in college and had even sold a few watercolors, but it seemed unlikely she could support herself with art. She had been offered a job in the County 4-H program by the extension service, and planned to accept it in the fall. In the meantime she was enjoying the unscheduled days and even had time to record some of her favorite places in ink and watercolor when she and her mother weren't busy.

Jan had called to ask her to supper one Friday as he sometimes did, and she had arrived at around seven, still dressed in her paint-spattered jeans and an oversized shirt of her father's. Her hair was hastily done in a single braid down her back, and under her arm she carried some watercolors to show him. To her surprise and embarrassment she discovered that Jan had another guest that evening.

She hadn't recognized him. She had believed that the strange, alien boy who had lived next door was dead, and she couldn't resurrect him. Now, in retrospect, she wondered why she hadn't made the connection. Although she had been barely ten at the time of the fire, she remembered the boy's brooding, gaunt and stoic figure, the features framed by dark hair and bold, angular eyebrows, the direct, unsmiling gaze, and none of these characteristics were much changed by time.

"I'm so terribly sorry—about your father—about the fire," she said impulsively when Jan had introduced them.

Erik laughed. He put the glass he had been holding on the coffee table and lit a cigarette. He was watching her with a clinical, unwavering stare.

"Don't waste your sympathy," he replied. "It was many years ago."

"Still, it was terrible. And we thought you were dead as well—at least I did." And she looked at her brother and realized that he had known the truth all along.

At dinner she asked, "Whatever happened to your father's horses?"

He gave her a guarded look. "I wouldn't know."

"But Wotan? Wasn't that his name—Wotan? Your horse?"

"Wotan was sold."

"You sold him?" she repeated in astonishment. There was an imperceptible pause, and Kristen felt an odd discomfort. She glanced over at Jan, but he didn't meet her eye.

"He was sold by his owner," Erik said.

"But you were his—"

"I rode the horse. Von Tauber owned him."

"Oh," Kristen said lamely, "I see." She busied herself with her meal for a little while in silence, but before long she asked, "How did you get out of the fire that night?" and it was her brother who answered.

"He got out before the fire went out of control. He was worried about the horses. When he found they were safe, he took Nightingale—remember her?" Kristen shook her head. "Well, he took her and rode away. He worked at various jobs until he had enough money to buy a place outside of town. So here he is."

It didn't seem reasonable. She could tell from Jan's tone that she wasn't to question him, and listening, she turned her head to look inquiringly at Erik. He was looking at his plate, finishing his meal.

"What happened to Nightingale?" she asked.

"I left her in the care of the blacksmith," Erik said. "She was in foal to Wotan. She dropped a colt the following spring. The mare is gone now, but I still have the colt. He is fifteen years old now."

"Fifteen! What's his name?"

"I call him The Phoenix," Erik said. "A new life from the ashes of the old."

Kristen smiled at him, and suddenly he responded. He gave her a smile of such intensity that she blushed and looked away. Jan, too, was smiling.

She turned back to Erik, still somewhat ill at ease, but fascinated. "What do you do now?"

"Do?"

"I mean, for a living. What kind of work do you do?"

Again there was no immediate answer and again Jan spoke for him. "Rides horses, buys them, trains them, and sells them."

Kristen gave him an irritated glance and then ignored him. The atmosphere was uncomfortable. Jan was falsely offhand and unnaturally cheerful. She herself seemed to be babbling.

"What did you do when you went away?" she went on insistently in her anxiety to translate Erik into something familiar.

"I worked."

"Doing what?"

Erik said to Jan, "Your sister is like you, Jan—persistent." He pushed his chair back from the table and lit a cigarette. "One works," he said to her, "at whatever one has to."

"What did you work at?"

"A number of things—"

"What things?" Consumed by her curiosity, she wondered if she were being rude. But he still smiled at her, and she met his eye for as long as she could.

"At first I worked on farms. I did whatever I was told. I took care of cows, chickens and sheep. I cleaned out pigpens and cow barns and brought in hay. I fixed machinery, dug ditches, drove horses and tractors and built fence. You should be familiar with what is required on farms."

"But you were taught to train horses—"

"The world does not clamor for boys who train horses. Occasionally, if I was fortunate, I was hired to clean stalls and, rarely, to exercise horses."

"Exercise horses? At race tracks?"

"Sometimes."

"Around here?"

"No."

"Where?"

Again she felt him hesitate. He put his cigarette out in the ashtray. "I was in Canada much of the time," he said at last.

"Canada?"

"Yes."

"But why? Everyone around here knew your Dad. I'm sure you could have—"

"Yes, well, I didn't," Erik said with sudden vehemence. "I should be glad," he added only slightly less harshly, "if we might allow what is past to remain there."

"I'm sorry," she said immediately, her face burning. "I'm so sorry. I didn't mean—"

"Don't apologize to me. I have never had much use for apologies, and they do not become you."

With this he turned to Jan, dismissing her from his attention, and began to talk about his plans for the weekend. Kristen felt her face flaming, but her distress at the rebuff was eclipsed by her curiosity, which was so strong she could barely contain it. Some of what he had said, like Jan's breezy answers, didn't make sense. He must have been living in this area for years, she thought, and yet I've never seen him or heard anyone mention him.

Erik left right after supper. He said he had to get up early, and Kristen noticed that Jan didn't seem surprised. When he had gone she was almost relieved, and Jan was apologetic.

As they stood together in the kitchen washing the dishes, she said, "You've known all along he was alive, haven't you?"

He acknowledged that he had. "The next day, when I heard Nightingale was gone, I was pretty sure. And he waylaid me a few days later outside of school. He said he'd been caught trying to steal feed for the horse, and they were trying to make arrangements for the courts to put him in a foster home. He told me the mare was at the blacksmith's, and he was going to run away."

"Didn't you try to stop him?"

"No, I didn't. It wouldn't have done any good. Besides, I thought he was right. I couldn't imagine him in a foster home. He would only have run away again and maybe gotten in worse trouble."

Kristen watched him. His face was grave, and there was concern reflected in his gaze. In her memory, Erik's face seemed just the opposite.

"But what about his father? How could he have left that night without knowing if his father was safe and just leave him to die? Why didn't you tell us? Why did you wait so long? I don't understand it."

She ran a sponge around the sink automatically, and when he didn't answer, turned to face him. He was leaning back against the counter, and she studied his lean, athletic figure and saw him for an instant not as her brother, but as Erik's friend. She grappled with the sudden knowledge that there was a part of Jan she didn't know.

He sighed. "I think I just didn't want to have to answer all these questions," he said.

But later, as they sat on the porch protected by the darkness, he had spoken of their childhood. "You were just a little kid, Kris. I couldn't tell you everything. Von Tauber was an evil man, if I can say that without sounding melodramatic. He was talented all right, and he knew his business. He'd grown up in Germany and apprenticed for years and years—in the military, I think, under the best of their riding masters, but something in him had soured. He treated Erik and his mother as his servants or worse, and Erik hated him. I tell you the man was a sadist, and he made Erik's life miserable. It's a wonder Erik survived. So don't ask why he left him there. It served the son of a bitch right. It was the first time Erik had been free since he was born."

Kristen watched him, her eyes wide in the dim light. She could think of nothing to say. Jan went on more quietly, "He asked me not to tell. He didn't trust anyone. I think Mom and Dad would have taken him in, but he wouldn't let me tell them. He went to Canada, as he told you. I helped him in that part—he didn't even know where Canada was. I loaned him as much money as I had and he took a bus north and crossed the border on foot, somewhere in the wilderness. He did just what he told you, and he was there for four years. He told me no one asked questions up there. There were a lot of farms miles from anywhere. They were glad to have the help. Even at that age Erik was pretty resourceful, considering what kind of life he'd had. He practically never got to school, particularly after his mother left. His father made him work." Jan paused and then added, "He asked me to teach him to read."

"He did? And did you?"

"I did. He actually knew the basics, but it was hard work for him and he didn't have books to read. In the beginning I filched some of your first grade readers and tried to tutor him when we had time, and later I leant him some of mine. He didn't have much time to read, but he was a fast learner. Later he stole some of his father's books on riding, but I couldn't help him with them. They were very technical and some of them were in French and German." He looked off into the darkness, and after a moment added, "His father made him learn the author's names and quote passages from their writings to his friends, and then he would ridicule Erik in front of them. 'See,' he would say, 'how a child has the conceit to believe he knows more than the Masters.' Erik can reel off those names even today—Pluvinel, Baucher, Fillis, de la Gueriniere, and, Steinbrecht. Even I can recite them, their names, at least."

Jan leaned back in his chair and stretched. He laughed. "I'll tell you a story. In tenth grade we were in the same class in Social Studies—which is to say I was in the class, but Erik rarely came. That bastard, Gillette, was the teacher, and one day he was going on about the French Renaissance and it was one of the few days that Erik was there. We were sitting together in the back of the class, and Gillette spotted Eric and began to pick on him because he hadn't been there and hadn't read the assignment. I kept trying to pass him answers, but he just sat there never looking at the notes, just staring back at Gillette without a word, and finally, exasperated, Gillette said sarcastically, 'Mr. Sarmento, can you name even *one* prominent Frenchman of the eighteenth century?' and without missing a beat Erik said, 'De la Gueriniere.' Just like that. It's the only time I ever heard him say anything in class."

"What did the teacher say?"

"Well, he looked like he'd been hit over the head. 'What did you say? Who?' he said, and Erik repeated it and the whole class turned around and began laughing. I asked Erik the other day if he remembered that, and he said he didn't remember what he said, only that they laughed and he didn't think it was funny and didn't understand the joke. What he did remember was that I lost my temper and got us both in a fight and we were sent to the office."

Jan sighed. He tried to describe his feelings to Kristen. School was for him a bittersweet memory, for he had loved school, an uncharacteristic feeling for a boy his age and one that had set him apart even then. He had thrown himself with all his heart into both his schoolwork and as many extracurricular activities as he could fit into his schedule. But even as he loved the experience, he had known even then that Erik hated it, and he felt himself responsible on those rare days when Erik appeared. In his ill-fitting clothes, haphazardly gathered from thrift shops and second-hand stores, Erik was an alien figure. His erect bearing, his impassive immobility and the hint of potential aggression in his eyes made the other students wary, and they treated him as animals might an unknown prey, carefully, curiously, trying to assess his nature and their own roles in relation to him. Erik set himself apart by choice, defensive, suspicious and unresponsive, and it was only Jan who knew from his own experience the effort it cost him.

Kristen said, "When he went away, did you hear from him?"

"Not a word."

"Didn't you worry about him?"

"Sometimes. But you have to realize that as kids days and weeks would go by when I never saw him at all. Dad forbade me to go over there because he thought Von Tauber would take it out on Erik, I think, and his father wouldn't let him leave the place. When he came back from Canada, he acted like he'd never been away except that he was older and in charge of his own life, and so was I. The Phoenix was already three years old. Estep—you remember—the smith who used to trim Molly? He had raised The Phoenix like his own pet, but until Erik came back, the horse had never been ridden. Estep let Erik live in his barn loft. And he lived there for years, going out to give lessons and train horses."

"But I've never heard anyone mention him. I've never seen him anywhere—"

"Why should you have? He's always been a loner. The only people who know him are horse people. In some ways I think he found the work he did with horses in those early years worse than working for his father. He told me once that he was forced to do things he knew were wrong because he had to have the money. When he made enough he bought his own horses, one or two at a time, to train and sell, and it's only very recently he's had enough to buy his own place."

Standing now on the porch, Kristen sighed. In the short time she had been standing there, the peaceful, sunny morning seemed almost to have changed color and to have become tarnished and ordinary. The monotonous sound of the cicadas was so loud it drowned out the birdcalls.

It was then it occurred to her that she might drive up to see Erik. It need not be anything more than a courteous attempt to explain her abrupt departure, an apology for the suddenness of it, an explanation of her decision to put some distance between them. After all, it was not simply her fault. It was he who had stormed out of the argument and had not returned that night. And he had made no attempt to contact her although he must know where she was.

Having decided, she gave herself no chance to change her mind, but paused only long enough to put on her shoes and socks before running down the steps to the car. When she had turned onto the narrow dirt road, she found herself following a horse trailer that crept up the long hills in low gear, but she was not impatient. Instead she gave in to a long reverie.

She couldn't remember exactly when Erik had become so central to her life, only the heady, carefree days she had spent with him. Her first visit to the farm had been with Jan, just a few days after he had reintroduced them. She had been surprised at how isolated it was and how poor. Erik had bought an old abandoned farm overrun with weeds and scrub, and almost single-handedly he was bringing it back to life.

The old house, weather-beaten and sagging, had had neither central heating nor running water. There was an old, stone-lined well with a hand pump by the back door and an outhouse at the rear. Much of the roofing was gone on the barn, and rain had rotted some of the rafters. A few outbuildings, in various stages of disrepair, were scattered around the house and barn, and what fences still stood were low, half buried stone walls or were made of ancient, rusted barbed wire. Not a single neighboring farm was still in existence. Their owners had abandoned the rugged, inhospitable land, and only occasional loggers and deer hunters were left to share it with Erik.

By the time of Kristen's first visit, the barn was already under reconstruction, with an ample loft and a new roof. A few horses were temporarily housed in some of the outbuildings. The pastures, which over the years had gone to scrub, were newly cleared, and temporary fencing enclosed a large area. The house, still primitive and shabby, at least had running water, although it was still dependent on its fireplaces and the wood stove in the kitchen for heat.

Kristen had entered Erik's world with enthusiasm. She loved animals and had a natural way with them herself. At his invitation she rode with him, and at his direction she began to work seriously on her riding skills. To this task she brought a naive confidence and a natural relaxation, for she had ridden often and informally in childhood. From Erik she learned a classical balanced seat and the range of aids that allowed her to affect the horse. The lessons were a joy to both of them, a kind of communication in code, and he was clearly delighted with her progress. One afternoon in the fall, on a freezing, overcast day, she went with him to see a trainer at the track, and Erik bought a young black filly and spontaneously presented her to Kristen.

Her bond to Lyrik was immediate. Lyrik's to her was gained over the months—almost three years—she had ridden her. From the beginning she was Lyrik's only rider, but for the first year she never rode except under Erik's exacting supervision. She managed both her work schedule and her riding by careful organization, and her days were full and happy. Lyrik had a sweet and accepting nature; she was naturally social and responded well and positively to reward and with great chagrin to punishment. Only rarely did she show her temper and even then was soon coaxed back to equanimity.

At the crest of the hill Kristen watched the trailer in front of her move slowly down toward the barn while she slowed and stopped her car in front of the house. She sat with her hands still gripping the wheel and looked at the house, trying to control her anxiety, which was half anticipation and half dread. Her car was like a cocoon, and the house was the single place on the farm where Erik was not likely to be at this hour.

Erik had made the second floor his living quarters. The original master bedroom with its fireplace became his living room, a small back room his bedroom. None of the upstairs rooms connected directly with any others, and going from one to another required passing through the wide hall at the top of the stairs.

When first she had seen them, his quarters were nothing short of stark, items of furniture garnered from second-hand stores, no rugs on the floors, no curtains at the windows or pictures on the walls. Yet the rooms had been spotlessly clean and neat, the bed made, nothing littering the surfaces. It was Von Tauber's relentless discipline, Jan had said, a legacy Erik was unable to reject and which reached down even now to affect the living quarters downstairs. Looking up at the windows, she could see the curtains she had herself made and wondered for a moment if her other touches were still in evidence. Were her paintings still on the walls, her treasured sketch of Erik on horseback still standing on the bookshelf? And had anyone bothered to fill the copper vase with flowers since she had left? She got out of the car and started down the road to the barn.

There was no one there except the owner of the trailer she had followed. The trailer was parked outside the barn and a horse under tack was tied to it. Kristen heard the owner moving around inside the trailer and didn't stop to say hello. From the corner of her eye she saw the movement of a horse and rider in the indoor arena, but when she glanced inside she saw that it wasn't Erik. At the back she found a grey horse loose in the outside ring but still no sign of Erik. In a way she was relieved. Over the woods a hawk was soaring. It was profoundly still, and the air smelled of pine and wood smoke.

Kristen walked to the back of the indoor school. The rear door was only open a crack, and she looked through it to see Ivan teaching a lesson. Maybe nothing has changed, she thought, her heart lifting as she recognized The Phoenix but not his rider, a young man riding without reins.

"OK, Michael," she heard Ivan say quietly, "Now, halt." She smiled in recognition. She had practiced the same lesson herself when she was first learning. She saw the rider take hold of the pommel of the saddle and pulled himself down against it

"I can't," he said.

"Close your legs and brace your back."

The Phoenix began to trot. Michael, bouncing in the saddle, clung to the pommel.

"Walk," Ivan said. "Now, do it again. Get your leg back and sit more to the front of the saddle. And—halt."

Kristen saw the rider again try to brace himself. Again The Phoenix trotted. Michael, red in the face, reached for the rein that was knotted on the horse's neck.

"Whoa," Ivan said, and the horse stopped instantly. "No rein. I want you to use your back. Try again."

As the horse came past the doorway, Kristen heard Ivan say, "No. Bring your legs back."

"They *are* back," Michael said in a defensive tone.

"No, they're not. Swing them back from the hip."

"God damn it—they're back as far as they'll go!"

"Take your stirrups back and look at the leathers. They're not perpendicular to the ground. You're sitting back on the cantle again with your feet forward. That's why you can't use your back. Only your leg aids are affecting the horse, and that's why he keeps trotting."

Michael looked down at his legs and made an effort to draw them back.

"That's it," Ivan said. "Now try it again."

Kristen saw the door across from her darken, and Erik's familiar figure came into the ring. She watched him close the lower part of the door behind him and walk over to where Ivan was standing. Feeling her heart quicken, she wanted to call out to him but was silent.

"Your student advances?" Erik asked Ivan.

"Not exactly. I can't get him to keep his legs back. I've been trying to correct his position at the walk so he can use his seat to stop the horse. He can't seem to get it. The horse trots each time." At Erik's appearance, Michael straightened and did his best to follow Ivan's directions.

"Now—halt," Ivan said. Again The Phoenix plunged determinedly ahead and again Michael, completely out of balance, bounced perilously in the saddle. In self-defense he started rising to the trot.

"Sit," Erik said.

Suddenly Michael snatched the rein from the horse's neck and with his feet braced forward again in the stirrups, made a furious attempt to yank the horse down. The Phoenix flung his head up, thrown off stride, and Erik appeared to explode across the ring. He reached The Phoenix's side, grasped Michael by the arm, and jerked him ruthlessly from the saddle. Michael made a desperate effort to pull away but lost his balance and fell from the horse. Erik stepped away, released him and watched him land heavily on the ground on his back.

Kristen raised both hands to her face and gasped. She made a strangled sound, almost a groan. Unaware of her presence, Erik took The Phoenix's rein, spoke a word or two to him and handed him over to Ivan.

Michael lay stunned on the ground. He drew his knees toward his chest and tried weakly to rise. The wind had been knocked out of him, and he struggled helplessly. He seemed to Kristen like a wounded animal that, at the feet of the hunter, instinctively tries to flee without the means to do so. He never looked at Erik, but at last he managed to rise, and with one arm still clutched to his stomach, he drew his other wrist across his face.

"Remove the reins from the bridle," Erik said to Ivan, "and leave the arena."

Kristen could feel Ivan's apprehension as he obeyed. As he fumbled with the buckles she saw the comprehension come to Michael. His face, at first pale, was now suffused with color. Erik gave an impatient gesture, and Ivan walked away toward the barn with the reins in his hand. Michael glanced after him and made a move to follow. The Phoenix stood untethered in the ring.

"Where are you going?"

For a moment Michael said nothing. He came to a hesitant stop and turned back. His face was bleak, filled with dread and humiliation. "I thought—" Michael said weakly and subsided. He was still staring at the ground, perhaps willing it to open and receive him. Swallows swooped in the rafters, unheeding, undeterred, and Erik faced him in silence.

"I didn't think you'd want me to ride any more," Michael said at last. "I'm sorry. I was only trying to stop him." He finished almost in a whisper.

"The reins were knotted on the horse's neck?"

"Yes."

"Why?"

"So I wouldn't use them, I guess—"

"You guess?"

"I know they were."

"You were told specifically they were not to be used?"

"I guess so—"

"Yes or no?"

"Yes."

"And deliberately disobeyed your instructor?"

"I couldn't stop the horse."

"Answer me."

"I guess I did."

"You guess at your own behavior?"

"No—I did."

"And took out your own incompetence upon the horse?"

After a brief silence, Michael surrendered. "Yes—sir."

"Get on the horse."

"Now?" There was no answer. He turned and mounted The Phoenix.

"You have been told, I believe, to bring your leg into the correct position?"

"Yes, sir, but I—"

"And again you choose to ignore your instructor?"

"No, I just can't seem to do it."

"Why?"

"I don't *know* why."

"Upon what do you sit?"

"On what—? The saddle?"

"Naturally one sits on the saddle. On what part of your anatomy?"

"On my seat."

"What part of your seat?"

"My *seat*."

"Wrong."

"I don't know, then."

"You are sitting on the end of your spine. Your back is bowed. You have two seat bones, do you not? Or must we assume you are unique among men?"

"I don't know."

"You don't know? Then I suggest you find out. Place your hand on the saddle beneath your seat. Adjust your position until you feel your seat bones."

Michael put his right hand under his seat, squirmed in the saddle and straightened slightly.

"Like most people you also have a crotch—is that correct?"

"Yes," Michael said. A note of suspicion had crept into his voice.

"The correct seat puts equal weight on the two seat bones and on the crotch. You seem unable to accept that for one reason or another. Perhaps you are afraid you will castrate yourself on the pommel?"

Michael flushed. "I don't think—"

"I assure you, men have ridden horses for centuries. I doubt they would continue to do so in the face of such a consequence." Michael looked down silently at the horse's withers. "Now adjust your position until it is correct. You feel both your crotch and your seat bones in the saddle?"

"Yes."

"See that they remain there. Now bring your legs back from the hip. It becomes possible now, yes?"

"Yes."

"And was not possible before?"

"No."

"Then perhaps," Erik said dryly, "you have finally learned something. Dismount."

When Michael was standing on the ground again, Erik said, "Assume a sitting position as if you were on a chair." Michael tried to do so, crouching.

"No. Keep the torso erect, the thigh parallel to the ground, and the lower leg perpendicular to it."

"I can't."

"Why not?"

"Because I'll fall over backwards."

"Because there is no chair to support you?"

"Yes."

"And you think the horse is a chair to support you in that position?" Silence. "Riding is not an activity where one sits idly on a chair. One stays always in a standing position, with the knees and ankles flexed and the weight in the saddle, so that should the horse vanish from beneath him, he would land on his feet. The ankle is always beneath the hip. Is that clear?"

"Yes, sir."

"Remount. You sit correctly?" Michael nodded. "Ask the horse to walk—not, as seems your preference, with the heel, but with the lower leg." The Phoenix moved off placidly.

"Fortunately for the horse," Erik said bitingly, "he cannot feel your hand at the moment. What can he feel?"

"My legs."

"And?"

"My weight?"

"And?"

Silence. After a moment Michael said, "I don't know."

"Dismount."

Michael vaulted off. The Phoenix continued to walk around the arena.

"Whoa," Erik said quietly. Michael looked at him expectantly.

"You may leave the arena."

"What?"

"You have lost your hearing as a result of your fall?"

"But why?"

"Because it is apparent you cannot think for yourself. When you are able to do so, you will answer my question. Until then, return to your work. Or—" Erik paused, "perhaps you would prefer to take your leave?"

He watched Michael walk away and when he had almost reached the doorway, said, "You abandon your mount, still saddled, because you have not the skill to ride him?"

Michael stopped. For a moment he was motionless, his back to Erik, and then he turned silently toward The Phoenix and, grasping the cheek piece of the bridle, led him away. He was visibly angry, but he said nothing. Erik stood for a moment looking after him and then followed him out.

Kristen stood where she was, her heartbeat so rapid that she could hear the sound of her pulse in her ears. Instead of her anticipation at seeing Erik again, now she was afraid she wouldn't be able to avoid him. Behind her the grey horse stood by the paddock gate, his ears pricked, waiting for company. She, on the other hand, wanted only to be alone, unseen, and like a guilty child she crept around the other side of the barn and tractor shed until she reached the woods bordering the lane that led to the woodlot and lower pasture. She made a long detour through the trees, around the back of the house and eventually to her car.

On the way home she tried not to think about the scene she had witnessed, although she felt Michael's humiliation as acutely as if it were her own. She had seen Erik do it before and she knew now with hopeless certainty he would do it again. Against her will her eyes were filled with tears. She remembered suddenly that she had forgotten to speak to Lyrik and felt a sudden pang. Erik would never be guilty of that, she thought sadly. Erik would never forget a horse. She drove all the way home without encountering a single car.

CHAPTER 9

▼

It was raining on Monday morning when the Mental Health Clinic opened. Eleanor, the administrative secretary, was the first to arrive. It was still a few minutes before eight-thirty, and she was surprised to see a figure sitting on the steps. For a moment she hesitated, her hand on the low, wrought iron gate.

The young man was disheveled and unsmiling. Eleanor glanced up and down the street to see if anyone else was around, half ashamed of her apprehension. It was only when he stood up at her approach that she recognized him as one of Annie's clients although she had seen him only a few times over the years.

"Michael, isn't it?" she said. "You're an early bird. Are you here to see Mrs. Trowbridge?" He nodded.

Eleanor rummaged in her purse for the key. She felt a fleeting hesitation about opening the door, alone with this young man, and regarded him from the corner of her eye. He had followed her up the steps and now stood beside her, his thumbs hooked into the pockets of his jeans. He looked as if he might have slept in his clothes.

"Come in," she said finally and opened the door. "What time is your appointment?"

"I don't have an appointment."

"Oh, I see," Eleanor said. "Mrs. Trowbridge should be in soon, but if she doesn't have a nine o'clock appointment, she sometimes does errands on the way. Let me look up her schedule for you."

She heard the door close and Bill Freeman and Dee Spellman, the other social worker, came in. They stopped in the doorway of her office to say good morning.

"She's free until ten," Eleanor said to Michael, "but I can't guarantee she'll be in much before then."

"Is there a problem?" Dee said. "Oh, it's Michael Ross. How are you, Michael?"

"OK," Michael said shortly. He glanced at the door.

"I have a few minutes," she went on, "Can I help you?"

"No thanks," Michael said. "Maybe I'll wait outside."

Eleanor said, "Do sit down. You can wait in here. I know Mrs. Trowbridge will be glad to see you."

He sat down wordlessly, hunched forward with his elbows on his knees, looking from under his brows at the room around him. Dee shrugged, smiled at Eleanor and excused herself.

"Cream and sugar?" Eleanor poured two mugs of coffee and handed one to Michael.

"Yeah—thanks."

For the next half hour Michael watched clients come in and staff members meet them and later escort them out. From his seat by the window, he stared out into the rain and willed Annie to arrive. When she finally appeared in the doorway, he got instantly to his feet and watched her expression turn from shock to pleasure. Impulsively she stepped toward him as if to embrace him, and in answer he gave a slight smile and raised his hands in front of him in a gesture half of response, half of rejection.

"Michael—I'm so glad to see you! How are you?" She moved back a step and smiled at him to mask her sudden fear that something had happened. "Come upstairs. Eleanor, hold my calls, would you please? My ten o'clock—who is it?"

"Mrs. Edsall—"

"Oh, dear," Annie said. "Do you think it's too late to reach her now?" She looked at her watch. "Try, would you please?"

She led Michael up the stairs to her office and closed the door behind them. "Now," she said, "sit down and tell me about yourself."

She watched him look around the room and saw his eye linger on the little statue on the windowsill.

He said, "You still have my horse."

"Of course I do."

"I was real proud of that horse when I made it. I liked it being wild like that— rearing and carrying on."

He turned to face her, and against the bright light of the windows she found herself squinting slightly to make out his features.

"It's Monday," she said. "What's happened? What are you doing in town?"

"Nothing's happened," he said irritably. "It's my day off."

He was silent for a few seconds and regarded her from under his brows. Then he added bitterly, "You always think I've done something, don't you?"

Annie was thoughtful. What he said was true.

"I guess you're right," she acknowledged, "but you must admit I didn't usually get called except in a crisis, did I? Anyway, I'm glad there's nothing wrong this time. Tell me about your job—how's it going?"

"It's all right, I guess." Michael began to move restlessly around the room.

"Please," Annie said, "sit down."

Obediently, he took hold of one of the wooden chairs by the table and swung it around to face her. He sat near the edge of the seat, his hands on his knees and waited for her to speak.

"And Mr. Sarmento? Are you getting along with him?"

"He's a son of a bitch," Michael said evenly. "He's just like what I told you—makes you do all kind of crap if you want to ride—" He frowned and looked away from her. "I can't stand him," he said without conviction and then, more strongly, "He doesn't like me, either."

"I'm sorry," Annie said. "I hoped this could be a real chance for you, that maybe you could even ride once in a—"

"I *do* ride," Michael said. "Twice a day."

"Oh," Annie said, "I'm glad. Does he give you lessons? Peter said he was a very good teacher."

Michael made a face. "It's hard as hell. He won't let you make a mistake—he expects you to know things I never even heard of, and he won't answer questions—" He seemed embarrassed by his own vehemence. "Actually, Ivan gives me lessons usually," he said more calmly. "I don't like him much, either."

Annie sighed. The phone buzzed, and she picked it up.

"Oh, that's fine." She glanced at Michael and met his eye. "Thanks so much, Eleanor." She hung up and made a note on her calendar. "My next appointment's been canceled, so we have some time. You've been there over a month, Michael. You're not thinking of leaving, are you? I want you to remember—"

"I'm not leaving," he said quickly. He looked down at his feet, and again it seemed to her he was struggling with himself.

"What's the matter?" she asked gently. He glanced at her for an instant, and his face looked almost hunted. "Is this really your day off?" she said with a sinking feeling.

"You think I'm lying?"

"No, but it's nine in the morning, and you live twenty-five miles away. How did you get here so early?"

The silence that followed confirmed her misgivings. "Tell me," she said firmly.

He rose to his feet and walked over to the table. He always seemed to keep his back to her when he had something he didn't want to have to tell her. He made a muffled sound like a groan and, as she leaned forward to hear him, said, "Yeah, I lied to you—sort of." He spun around. "It *is* my day off, that's true. But I'm in a hell of a mess, Annie."

He used her first name without thought, but it was the first time in her memory he had ever done so. She waited, aware of how difficult it was for him to translate his feelings into words.

Michael sighed and finally began to talk. His eyes, characteristically vigilant, rested without wavering on her face.

"He let us off last night, after chores were done. We went to Northwood in Peter's truck. Why the hell do I always end up in Northwood? Rotten cow town—there's only about two places to go in Northwood. Anyway, Peter and Ivan both know a lot of people there. Peter went to find his girlfriend, and Ivan called up some girl he knows, and she was supposed to come down to the Alehouse to meet him. I just tagged along with him to the bar—same damned bar I had that trouble in before, but what the hell? There's no other place to go."

He leaned back with his hands on the table behind him for support and paused. When she said nothing, he went on. "The track's outside of Northwood—the racetrack. All the grooms, hot walkers and exercise boys hang out there, particularly Sunday nights after they race on weekends.

"It was the first time I'd been off the farm since I went up there, and I was feeling good, you know? I was sick to death of having to deal with Erik. He's been giving me a lot of shit lately, and I was glad as hell to get away.

"We don't usually get off Sunday night. We're supposed to do chores Monday morning and get off after that. Don't have to work again 'til Tuesday morning. But somehow Peter got him to let us leave Sunday evening and not have to work until tonight instead. We were glad. Monday nights are dead in town—everyone has to work Tuesday. The idea was that we'd go back late last night and sleep in today." He stopped and turned again to the window.

"But you didn't go back?" Annie prompted.

"I got into another mess. That damned bar's jinxed for me. It was jammed when we got there, but we found a table. I didn't want to wait at the bar, on account of the bartender, you know. I was sure he'd give me a lot of crap about hitting him, and I didn't need that—I didn't want to get into that. I had an argument with Ivan about it. He wanted to be at the bar so he could see his girlfriend when she came in the door. But anyway, we found a table and ordered a couple of beers. The waitress was new on the job, and I knew her. I used to go to school with her. I didn't think I'd give a damn if I ever saw anyone from school again or not, but I always kind of liked her. We got to kidding around, telling stories, and Ivan's girlfriend finally came. We were sitting around waiting for Peter to show—he had the truck—and more and more people kept coming in. Some were guys I knew from the track, some Ivan knew. We shoved a couple of tables together—" He turned to face Annie and, on impulse, came back and sat down.

"We were really having a good time, just kidding around, everyone bitching about their jobs, their bosses. Actually, Ivan wasn't. He was too wound up with his girlfriend, and I wasn't saying too much, just kind of listening and kidding around with Mary Lou—the waitress—we were keeping her busy. Everyone was feeling pretty cheerful after a while, and Peter and his girlfriend came in. We'd begun scrounging some more chairs, when a guy showed up I used to work with at the track. The guy's a real asshole—sorry—he's a real—" He cast about help-lessly for a moment, and then he said vehemently, "I hate his guts.

"He began showing off by getting on my case every time Mary Lou came by—lots of crap about how I'd done a rotten job at the track—gotten fired—how he'd had to teach me everything I knew and all like that—bunch of lies. I got a little hot, told him to get back to what he did best, shoveling manure, and one thing led to another, and he started telling everyone what his boss had told him about what Erik made me do—oh, hell, it's a long story. Ivan and Peter got into it and told him to buzz off and leave us alone, and his buddies began to support him, and first thing you know things got loud and the girls got nervous. Peter and Ivan wanted to leave." He gave a helpless gesture with his hands.

"How the hell could I leave?" he asked rhetorically. "Peter and Ivan and the girls were already on their feet when the bartender came over to see what was going on." He gave Annie a look of outrage.

"He took one look at me—I swear to God—one look, and hightailed it over to the phone and called the cops again. I hadn't done a damned thing—I swear I hadn't—except give this asshole a hard time. I knew I was in for it. Peter and Ivan said they were going to split before the cops came—I guess I don't blame them—and they wanted me to go, too. But I couldn't go then and listen to that son of a bitch laugh in my face about running home, could I?"

"Of course you could. You could ignore it when people make fun of you—"

"Maybe *you* could," he said. "I didn't. I figured I'd get the last word in and then cut out. Figured they'd take their girlfriends home and come back for me at some point." He sighed.

"The cops came, all right, and the bartender just stood behind the bar and pointed at me, and this cop came swaggering over with his nightstick and all, acting like he was God's gift to the world, one of the same damned cops that roughed me up before. He said, 'You Michael Ross?' He knew damned well I was. And everyone was sitting around like it was a funeral or something. Even the guys at the bar were watching. So I said, 'No, I'm George Washington.' A few guys laughed, and he got pissed off and grabbed me by the arm." He leaned over with his elbows on his knees, clasping his hands between his legs, and groaned.

"I hit him," he said.

Guiltily he looked up at Annie to see her reaction and, when she said nothing, he looked away again and added, "I wasn't too careful, and I hurt him. I just didn't think—I was scared of what I'd done—I didn't mean to do it. I knew there'd be trouble, so I took off out the back while the going was good. But I couldn't hang around and wait for Ivan and Peter, could I? I knew there'd be another cop waiting in the car. So I hitched down here to Reed and figured I'd go to your house, but I changed my mind when I got there—it was two o'clock in the morning. I didn't want to wake you up."

Annie had been steeled to the events Michael recounted, but she was disarmed by the simple conclusion.

"You can always wake me, any time," she said. "You know that. I'd have been glad to give you a bed."

The phone buzzed in the middle of her thought, and distractedly she picked up the receiver. "Yes? What? Oh, I see—yes. Would you ask him to wait just a few more minutes, Eleanor? She saw Michael glance at his watch. "I'll call down when I'm ready—yes. Thank you." She hung up and turned again to Michael. "Well, Michael? What do you intend to do now?"

"I don't know. What should I do? I have to be back at work by four."

"How did you think you'd get there?"

"Hitchhike."

"Michael—how many cars go up that road in a day, and particularly if it's a day off?"

"Well, then I'll walk up from the road."

"Seven miles? Uphill?"

"I'm not crippled."

"Perhaps you could call and explain."

He gave an incredulous snort in answer. "Explain? Are you kidding? He'd tell me to take a walk. He doesn't listen to excuses. He doesn't *accept* excuses, especially from me."

"Do you *want* to go back?" she asked.

He shrugged and gave her a wry smile. "Yeah," he said, "I might as well. Beats selling washing machines."

Annie considered him for a moment. "Yes, I imagine it does," she said. "But it's hard work, isn't it?"

"Yeah, in a way. At least the way *he* runs things, it is. But I don't mind the work—it's not the *work*. I mean, I've mucked stalls before, groomed horses and all that stuff. I like horses. I just like being around them. He's got some nice ones up there. The one I'm riding—you remember that stuff that horse, Calypso, did when we went up there? Well this horse can do *all* that stuff and other things too. You should see him."

Suddenly his expression turned grim, and he looked at the floor. "Oh, hell," he said bleakly, "I don't know what to do next. I don't even know what I *want* to do next."

Annie changed the subject. "Have you any money?"

He nodded. "I got my check. There's nothing to spend it on up there. What about the cop?"

She picked up the phone. "All right, Eleanor, would you ask him to come up?"

Michael's expression turned wary. He stood up, and Annie rose with him, walked to the office door and turned to face him. "Captain Nordstrom is downstairs, Michael. He's asked to see me. I want you to stay here until we straighten this out."

"I'm getting the hell out," he said and added reproachfully, "You could have told me."

"Where will you go? You can't keep running away."

"You can't stop me—"

"Then you'll have to make me move, because I'm not moving away from this door on my own."

He stopped, glared at her, and turned abruptly away. When Captain Nordstrom knocked on the door and Annie opened it, he was staring out the window and refused to turn around.

"Good morning, Andy."

Nordstrom replied formally with a nod. His eyes went to Michael's back.

"Sit down," Annie said to him. "Michael, come and sit down."

"I'd rather stand up," Michael said.

Annie stared thoughtfully at him and then walked over and touched his arm. "Please, Michael," she said. "Come and sit down." Unwillingly, he did so.

"Now," Annie said. "Andy, would you tell us what you plan to do?"

Captain Nordstrom sat erect in his chair. "I thought I'd straightened you out, kid," he said calmly. "Now you're in a world of trouble."

"Andy," Annie said. "Michael's told me what happened last night. Are there charges placed?"

"There will be," Nordstrom said. "Fighting in bars is one thing. Assaulting an officer's another. He tell you about that?"

"Yes, he did." Annie saw Michael stir restlessly and said, "Michael—wait a minute." To Nordstrom she added, "He said the officer laid hands on him, and he struck him without thinking."

"Yeah?" Nordstrom said. "Well, my man doesn't tell it quite like that."

"Well, it's true!" Michael said. "I've got witnesses—"

Annie raised her hand. "Wait a minute," she said again. "What did the officer say, Andy?"

"He said the kid gave him some lip, assaulted him and took off. Nothing about laying hands on him,"

"Well, he did," Michael broke in. "He grabbed me. I didn't do a damned thing to him. I was sitting down at a table when he came at me."

Captain Nordstrom regarded him appraisingly. "Where'd you learn to fight like that?" he said stonily. "In the gutter?"

To Annie's surprise, she saw Michael redden. He looked at the floor. "I'm sorry about that," he said finally. "It was an accident."

"An accident?" Nordstrom said. "Funny kind of accident." He turned to Annie. "Struck the officer in the groin with his knee."

Annie looked startled. She turned to Michael, feeling momentarily helpless.

"He grabbed me," Michael said again, his voice rising. "I swear he did. You can ask anyone there—they all saw it. He didn't say I was under arrest or anything. He just asked if I was me and grabbed me by the arm. What was I supposed to do? Are cops supposed to grab people for no reason? I didn't do a goddamn thing to make him do that. I *wouldn't* have done anything. It was just—I just reacted—"

Nordstrom shook his head and turned to Annie. "I thought we'd got this all straight, Annie. I told you I wasn't going to fool with this kid any more. He was supposed to get a job and stay out of trouble, and here he is right back in hot water again—"

"He did," Annie said quickly. "He has a job. He's been working steadily since you saw him last."

"Then what's he doing here?"

"It's my day off," Michael said.

"That doesn't excuse your fighting in bars."

"I wasn't fighting."

"Where you working?"

"On a farm."

"That right? Who's your boss?"

Michael hesitated. He glanced at Annie. "Erik Sarmento," he said at last, reluctant for some reason he didn't understand. He was startled to hear Nordstrom laugh.

"No kidding?"

"Do you know him?" Annie said, surprised.

"I've heard of him. I know a friend of his pretty well, a reporter on the Courier who used to cover the station. Good man and a good friend of Sarmento's. But I expect I'll get to know him better before long."

Michael straightened in his chair and gave him a suspicious glance. "Why?"

"'Cause I think I'll drive on up to his place and talk to him about his help."

"You can't do that—" Michael said, suddenly both angry and apprehensive.

"Why can't I?"

"He doesn't know about this. He doesn't need to know about it. It's none of his business."

"Really? Well, I'm about to make it his business."

"Andy," said Annie, "I don't think you need—"

"I have a lot of respect for you, Annie," Nordstrom said. "You've been this kid's social worker for a long time. But the way I figure it, if he's working up there now, this guy Sarmento's taken over your job. I've heard he's a tough cookie. Maybe he can do more than you or me."

"You *want* to get me fired?" Michael asked bitterly.

"Fired? Why should he fire you? You didn't hit *him*, did you?"

Michael stared resentfully at him. "It's none of his goddamned business," he said again. He turned desperately to Annie. "Can he do that?"

"I'm afraid he can, Michael. What about the charges, Andy?"

"If the kid's right and the officer was out of line, we won't worry about it," Nordstrom told her. "But I don't like what the kid did, Annie. I don't like it at all. I tell you straight, kid, I see you spit in the gutter or cross a street against the light from now on—you'll end up in court so fast it'll make your head spin. You hear what I'm saying?"

"Yes."

Nordstrom gave him a contemptuous look and glanced at his watch. "I'll be on my way, then," he said. With a gesture to Annie not to get up, he rose and made his way out.

Michael stared after him. "You think he'll really go up there?" he asked Annie.

"I think he might."

"Oh, Christ," Michael said. "He'll kill me."

"It may not be so bad," Annie said without conviction. "I'll drive you up, Michael, if you like."

"No," he said almost rudely. "I'll get there myself."

He walked out the front door of the Mental Health Clinic in his shirtsleeves, as he had arrived. It had started to rain again lightly, and Annie stood at the window and watched him walk away, his head down. She had been impressed by how healthy he had looked, young and strong, deeply tanned and fit, but now he only looked young and, since his visit here, forlorn.

CHAPTER 10

▼

Michael started walking about a mile before the dirt road turned off from the highway. He had had trouble getting rides. There was little traffic going out of town in the late morning, and the thick, grey mist and occasional pelting rain obscured him as he stood by the side of the road.

He was quickly drenched and soon cold, trudging along with his shoulders hunched against the rain. The water ran down his face and into his eyes, so that he had to run his fingers through his hair and shake his head like a dog. His clothes clung to him like some alien, chilly skin, and the cuffs of his jeans where they hit his ankles began to chafe uncomfortably. With his sneakers saturated, his feet squelched in water. They seemed swollen, foreign entities attached to his legs, which he had to guide at each step to their proper place.

He was very nervous about the time, although he thought he could get back by four. He had turned his watch on his wrist to protect it from the rain and consulted it constantly. As he walked doggedly onward beneath the dripping trees, he began to think of the previous night and to brood about Erik.

The incident with The Phoenix still hurt him, not only physically where Erik had hurled him to the ground, and not just because he suffered from Erik's anger and disdain. In the short time he had been riding The Phoenix, he had grown fond of him, his rhythmic, springing gaits, his cheerful and tolerant disposition, and his incredible talent and training. Although Michael had neither the knowledge nor the skill to tap this talent, Ivan's performance remained in his mind, and he was determined to learn. He felt terribly guilty over his treatment of the horse and burned at the memory of Erik's scorn.

Even now his mind skirted reluctantly around the thought of Erik, for he didn't want to acknowledge to himself how much he feared him, and how much his fear was tied to a fierce yearning for Erik's approval and concern. He felt as if his own independence was at stake, an independence he had nourished and protected all his life, from his foster parents, his teachers, his would-be friends, and even from Annie. But he had no protection from Erik, no defense against his tyranny, no wall he could erect around himself. Like an irresistible force, Erik breached his defenses with ease, armored against the weapons he tried to use, amused by his resistance, impervious to his hostility.

It had been Peter's idea that they be excused from chores on Monday morning, and when to their surprise Erik assented, he and Ivan made plans to leave right after supper. Michael, who had refused to accompany them before, now found himself desperate to get away from the farm, from the feeling of being slowly crushed and slowly brought to heel.

"Does that mean me, too?" he asked suddenly, and Erik glanced over at him.

"What did you say?"

"I said, can I go, too?" He was braced for a brusque refusal.

"What you do on your own time is a matter of complete indifference to me," Erik had said. But what would he think now if Captain Nordstrom drove up and told him what he had actually done on his own time?

His thoughts turned again to The Phoenix, torturing him with the memory of the horse's head flung up as Michael jerked on him, his nose out, the look of alarm as the whites of his eyes showed, the faltering in the confident trot. He felt bathed in guilt, a lump in his throat. How could he ever apologize to the horse? How would Erik ever know how desperately he regretted it—or would he even care? He was afraid he would never be allowed to ride the horse again.

And yet, he thought, Erik's done things just as bad to horses. What about the grey horse in the paddock behind the riding arena? Why did students come voluntarily to Erik to be abused, castigated and ridiculed? And why, having found out what he was like did they come back again? He thought of an incident a few days before that he had witnessed for himself. A young man had come for his weekly lesson. Michael had seen him there before and paid little attention, but this day, when he had finished what he was doing, he was drawn by curiosity to the indoor arena to watch. The lesson was half over.

Erik stood in the arena, slightly off center. The horse was cantering, and every now and then Erik stepped away from his place to allow him to move through the area where he had been standing. When he was least expecting it, Erik looked over at the door, saw him, and turned back to the rider. To Michael's amazement he paid him no attention, nor did he look back at him again.

"It is better," he said to the rider, "but still you drive too much with the seat. Bring the shoulders back and concentrate upon the rhythm. Allow the angle of the hip to open if necessary, but do not make extra work for yourself and your horse. You must have the sensation that you lift him before you with the leg."

Michael leaned his arms on the half-door, watching the horse and rider pass before him in a serpentine now at true canter, now at counter. Erik followed their progress with his eyes.

"No—*no!*" he said sharply at one point. "Where has the impulsion gone? The horse labors to stay in canter. You daydream perhaps? If you have other things on your mind, it is better that you dismount and leave the horse to his own concerns."

"Sorry," the rider mumbled, coming down to trot and then to walk, "I guess I'm getting a bit tired."

"Indeed? And yet I cannot see that you have done much of significance except to drive the horse's back into the ground. It is he, I think, who struggles to keep you in balance while your mind is elsewhere."

The rider stopped his horse, took the reins in his left hand and ran his right wrist back and forth across his forehead. He looked expectantly at Erik, who allowed a long silence to ensue and then impatiently grasped the dressage whip he held by its tip, raising it in front of him until its handle with the flattened knob on top was pointed at the rafters above him.

"Thus you appear on the animal's back," Erik said as the handle of the whip bent first in one direction and then the other, the end imprisoned in his fist. "The horse's best efforts—" he moved his hand and thus the erratic swaying of the whip, "—only increase the problem. It is far easier, I believe, to achieve the balance as nature has designed, like so." And he allowed the whip to slide through his hand until he held the handle and raised the slender end uppermost. "Thus the rider's seat and the horse's back dictate the position of the upper body." He moved his hand to and fro, the whip still vertical, and then carelessly gestured with it to the end of the arena. Obediently, the rider started out to the track. Erik leaned down and absently picked up a small stone that had worked its way to the surface of the tanbark. "Yes, good. Walk," Michael heard him say. The horse, allowed off the bit at last, turned into the center and walked inward to where Erik stood. The rider was smiling. He jumped lightly off the horse's back.

Michael sighed. He came within sight of the crest of the hill and could see the road curve gently toward the house. To his left the pasture sloped away. It was ten minutes to four. He broke into a jog. His wet clothes chafed, and he was very cold. Peter and Ivan were both in the barn, but he didn't speak to them.

"You are late," he heard Erik say from the tackroom doorway.

"No, I'm not. It's four o'clock."

"It is ten minutes past four."

Oh, shit, Michael thought. Aloud he said, "I'm sorry," and added, "sir" for good measure.

"That is irrelevant. I believe I have told you before it is the work that concerns me, not the state of your emotions."

Michael clenched his teeth, self-conscious under Erik's critical eye and aware that a puddle was forming where he stood in the aisle. He hadn't slept since six o'clock the previous morning, and now he found himself shivering uncontrollably.

"Go up to the house," he heard Erik say to Ivan and Peter. "Michael will do the chores this evening."

Michael turned away and started into the feed room. Over his shoulder he said, "What about the horses in the lower pasture?"

"What about them?"

"Am I supposed to feed them, too?"

"Do you imagine they will feed themselves?"

Michael sighed. "Can I change my clothes first?" he asked hopelessly.

"I have told you the horses' welfare takes precedence over yours. If you wish to play in the rain on your day off, that is your affair, but the horses will not suffer the consequences."

When Michael reached The Phoenix's stall, he unlatched it, went in and stood beside him for a moment while he ate. He put his hand on the horse's neck. The Phoenix's coat was glossy and soft, his muscles hard. At eighteen he appeared to be only half his age. How old had Erik himself been when he trained this horse? Scarcely older than Michael himself.

It was seven o'clock before he finished his work. He watched the horses disperse through the field, unconcerned by the rain, which had turned to a steady drizzle, and turned gratefully toward the house only to find Erik in the hall.

"The work is finished?"

"I think so."

"The indoor school has been picked up?"

Michael hesitated, and his heart sank. He considered lying in the hope that he might complete the work in the morning before Erik rose. "No," he said finally, "I forgot."

"See to it."

Michael let the screen door slam and headed out again into the rain. When he returned, he found he had missed supper. Peter and Ivan were sitting at the kitchen table, playing cards. He headed into the shower and gratefully stripped off his soaking clothes. He felt depressed, physically uncomfortable and tired, and he dreaded the following day. The Phoenix was still denied to him, and the implications of Captain Nordstrom's threat weighed on his mind.

When he had stepped from the shower and was dressed again in dry clothes, he gathered up his dirty laundry and made his way to the washing machine.

"What happened?" Ivan asked as he returned through the kitchen. "We waited for almost an hour. They said you'd left-"

"Yeah, I went to Reed."

"To Reed?" Peter said. "Why'd you do that?"

"Reasons."

"They said you hit the cop—is that true?"

"Yeah, it's true."

Peter regarded him for a long moment. "We saved you some supper, but you'll have to heat it up. There's coffee, too, if you want some."

"I'm not hungry," he said untruthfully. "I was up all night, but I'm not sleepy, either."

"Did the cop arrest you?"

"Not then—I split. He may place charges, I don't know. The police captain's mad as hell. He said he was going to come up here and talk to Erik, the son of a bitch."

"Jesus!" Ivan said, "I hope he doesn't."

"Erik's already mad at me," Michael said, "for just about everything." He sighed.

"It's your own fault," Ivan said.

"You're a fine one to talk," Peter said before Michael could retort. "He's been in hot water himself a few times," he added to Michael. "He ran off one day when he got mad at Erik. He hadn't finished chores, and Erik went after him on horseback."

"You're kidding!" Michael regarded Ivan with new interest. "What happened?"

"He came back," Peter said, and he punched Ivan lightly on the arm. "Didn't you?"

Ivan made a face and smiled sheepishly. "Yeah. He told me I couldn't leave until the chores were done and that if I didn't get back in a hurry he'd tie my hands to the saddle and drag me back. So I came back. It seemed the lesser of two evils, somehow."

Michael laughed. He felt suddenly happy. In the weeks he had been there he had never before felt one with Ivan and Peter. He had been excluded as much by his own self-absorption as by them, and although he had seen them put down by Erik innumerable times, he had never felt that it was as intolerable to them as it was to him.

The next morning the rain had stopped, and it was sunny and cool. Still tired, Michael could barely make himself get up and was late again to his work. There was no sign of Erik, and when he appeared at breakfast, he seemed unconcerned. Peter was talking about the behavior of the horses in the lower pasture. It was his job to feed them each day, and at every feeding he struggled to open the gate into the field and to make his way to the loafing-shed feed room through a throng of impatient horses.

"What I can't figure out," he was saying, "is why they don't have sense enough to realize that they get in my way and make it twice as long before they get fed. I can't even open the gate without a shoving match—"

Erik glanced up. He was smiling. He said, "Sense? How can they be sure that if they did not crowd the gate you would feed them at all?"

Peter stared at him. "You mean, they think that what *they* do affects *me*?"

"One does not know what a horse thinks," Erik said dryly, "but what man thinks is always open to question. It is not always easy to know what is cause and what is effect. You have rewarded the horses for crowding the gate morning and night."

"It's the last thing I wanted them to do—"

"Then you have discovered a pitfall in training. Too frequently one teaches horses bad habits as well as good ones."

"That's true with Tangent, I think," Peter said suddenly after a moment of silence. "I think I've scared her. Lately I've been riding her on a fairly loose rein, and she's much more relaxed. It's as if when I kept her in check because she was so apt to shy, she assumed there was something dangerous around to shy at. She still shies sometimes, but I can usually feel it before she does it, and sometimes I can deflect it by moving her on." Erik nodded, but said nothing. "I thought maybe I should start her in some ring work. Do you think so, sir?"

"I will ride her today," Erik said. "You may ride The Phoenix."

Michael saw Peter glance at him and then back to Erik. He shoved his plate away and rose to his feet, stung by the change in atmosphere. The conversation had shifted somehow to include him. Erik did not look up. Carrying his dishes to the sink, Michael turned suddenly in his tracks, and said without thinking, "If you can feel what the horse is doing, then he can feel what you're doing—isn't that true? I mean, if Peter can tell Tangent's going to shy, then she must be able to tell he's expecting it by the way he feels to her—"

Erik stopped eating and looked at him. "Yes?" he said.

"Is that true?"

"Do you think it is true?"

"Then the horse can feel the position of your seat and back if you can feel the movement of his back with your seat. That's right, isn't it?"

"Is it?"

"Yes," Michael said, all at once struck by the simplicity of his idea.

Erik laughed. "The rider begins to think," he said.

"Can I ride then?" Michael asked, barely keeping his temper in check. He put the dishes down on the counter.

"Yes,"

"This morning?"

"No. Peter will ride the horse this morning."

"Why? He's got other horses to ride."

"I don't care what other horses he has to ride. My concern is with the horse. Do you imagine your efforts will keep him in training? It is quite the opposite. Your work must be undone periodically, and today is such a time."

He watched with satisfaction as Michael grew red under his eye. "Clean up the kitchen," he said as he rose from his chair. "Peter, come with me. We will see how effective you have been with Tangent."

Later when Michael got to the barn, Erik said, "Take a sickle and trim the fence line."

Michael said resentfully, "What's that for?" He was certain that Erik was merely seeking to make him feel the edge of his authority.

"To control the weeds."

For a moment Michael stood indecisively where he was. He was stuck. Even when his mind told him there was no choice, his pride kept him frozen where he stood. With something between horror and elation, he found himself reaching to take hold of the manure fork, which leaned against the stall door beside him.

"I'm not going to do that," he said, his voice like an alien echo in his ears. But he had not the conviction to back up his statement, and in two strides Erik had reached him, torn the fork from his grasp and hurled him backward until he staggered against the open stall door and grasped it for support.

"Exactly what did you intend to do with this?" Erik demanded, and Michael was suddenly aware that for the moment Erik's violence was no better controlled than his own.

"Nothing—I don't know—I just—I didn't think—" he stammered.

"That is apparently a permanent condition with you. I have given you an order. Do as you are told."

"Yes, sir," Michael said, hating Erik, hating himself.

He was still nursing his frustration at noontime when he saw a car drive over the hill. It stopped where he was working and he recognized the driver, the girl who owned Calypso. In his relief at the interruption, he smiled and said, "Hi. You looking for someone?"

"Mr. Sarmento. Is he here?"

"Out riding—your horse, as a matter of fact. He should be back soon."

Even as he spoke he could hear the hoof beats and looked across the road. Erik was galloping the horse at speed around the perimeter of the hay field. Calypso was flattened out like a racehorse, and Erik, stirrups shortened, rode with his back almost parallel to the horse's. He scarcely moved, his seat slightly out of the saddle, his arms extended, following the motion of Calypso's head and neck.

"Jesus," Michael said in admiration, "look at—"

"What's he doing?" Pat said simultaneously. "What does he think he's doing?"

Michael felt a perverse pleasure at her shock; her distrust of Erik reflected his own. But in spite of himself, some part of him identified with Erik. His confidence in Erik's horsemanship was complete.

As they watched, Erik straightened slightly and sat down in the saddle, and the horse slowed and collected himself. Erik rode across the road at a canter and set him directly at the pasture fence. Calypso cleared it with an easy, graceful bound and cantered down into the pasture. When Erik dropped the rein, he slowed and came down to a walk, the rein loose on his neck, his sides heaving. Erik rode casually around the field at a walk and let the horse saunter at his own speed to recover.

"Come on— I'll go with you," Michael said to Pat and they walked to the barn to wait. "She came to see her horse," he said when at last Erik appeared with Calypso.

"That hardly explains why you are here," Erik said. "Take the horse. When you have rinsed his legs and brushed him off, return to your work."

Michael took Calypso's rein, removed the bridle, haltered him and tied him in the aisle. He loosened the girth on the saddle, fetched a bucket of water and a sponge, and did as he was told.

"Miss Bartlett," Erik said without enthusiasm, "you are here for what reason?"

"I was up this way. I thought I'd check with you on Calypso's progress."

"As you can see, he is in one piece."

"Will you explain to me why you are galloping and jumping him? He's not a jumper, he's a dressage horse." She drew a deep breath and added, "I sent him to you for schooling in dressage."

"I do not need to be told why the horse was brought here," Erik said. "That was self-evident. If you are unhappy with my methods, you are free to take him away. As your mother was careful to point out, he is your horse. I will remind you, however, that I expect to be paid for the three months you contracted for."

"No—please—that's not what I meant. I only wondered why you are doing that to him. Won't it make him difficult to control—all that galloping?"

"Did you think he looked difficult to control?"

"No, but you're a man, and I'm—"

"A woman," said Erik. "That is also self-evident. If it were not, my stable hands would not find it necessary to accompany you wherever you go."

Pat blushed, and Michael, rinsing off Calypso, felt a protective, angry reaction, but he didn't look up. There was a painful silence until Pat finally said, "I just wondered what your reasoning was."

"I have taught the horse to gallop," Erik said. "He did not know how to do so when he first arrived. In fact he has only just learned in the past week. I have also taught him to jump small obstacles out in the open, and I have taken him swimming. The horse is learning to be a horse, a lesson long overdue, since you persist in treating him like a clockwork toy." He walked over to Calypso and gestured at him.

"You may notice he is beginning to gain muscle. He has been climbing hills. He starts now to stride out with economy, a more effective way of covering ground than bobbing up and down like a jack-in-the-box. For the present he carries his head lower than he did. I have encouraged that to develop the muscles in his back, which will allow him to swing his back when he moves. In sum, the horse is learning to go forward. He is enjoying the opportunity, I assure you."

"Yes, I see. That's what you were trying to teach him when we were here before, isn't it? To go forward when you gave him the aid?"

Erik gave a formal, ironic bow.

"He won't forget the dressage movements, will he?"

"Why should he? He has never heard of what you call dressage, but he has learned the aids, he has the gymnastic ability. It is you who must learn them, not he."

"Will you help me?"

"If you wish, but not until his term here is completed." He put his hand absently on Calypso's neck. "The horse is a pleasure to ride," he said more gently. "He has enormous talent, and he is very kind."

Pat smiled. She toyed with Calypso's forelock and stroked his nose. "I know he has," she said quietly. "More than I have, I'm afraid."

Michael led Calypso into his stall. He yearned to ride him and knew he never would. When he started back to work, Pat walked with him to her car.

"Why is he so hostile?" she asked. "I'm almost afraid to say anything."

"Don't ask me, ask him."

"I wouldn't dare," she said and then curiously, "Do you like working here?"

"Not much, but I like riding the horses."

"Yes," she agreed, "I can see why. But I can't help wondering about the things he does with Calypso. I've never heard of a trainer doing things like that. Every other trainer I've ever seen would take the horse, work him in the ring for a few weeks and straighten out the problem. And here's your boss galloping around, jumping fences—Calypso never jumped in his life that I know of."

"Well, he has now."

"Yes, that's the point. I just hope I can manage him when I get him back. When I was here last, he had the horse in such a state I was afraid he was ruined. I was afraid Mr. Sarmento had frightened him so he'd never trust anyone again, so he'd be afraid of his rider. I don't think that's the way to train a horse."

"You saw him," Michael said, suddenly to his own surprise defending Erik. "Calypso's not afraid of anything. I never saw one of his horses that seemed afraid of him. Even when he gets after them, they seem to understand what he's doing." He was silent for a moment. "I can't say the same for people." He sighed and leaned his hands on the windowsill of her car. "You live near here?"

"No—a long way off. That's why I came up today, because I was in the area." She smiled at him.

He shrugged.

"Michael," came Erik's warning voice from the barn, "return to your work."

"I have to go." Michael turned away reluctantly, and went back up the road. She waved at him as she drove past, and he raised his hand in a half-hearted gesture and watched her out of sight. Angrily, he began hacking at the weeds.

He was still working along the road when the police car came in sight in the late afternoon. His work had been interrupted only to allow him to ride, and he had been elated to find himself at last able to correct his position on the horse and even to begin to sit the trot. He knew immediately now that it was Captain Nordstrom and was at once both apprehensive and bitterly angry. One hand on the fence and the sickle still held in the other, he glared at the white car that glided slowly up the road. He could see Nordstrom's arm in slate blue shirtsleeves resting on the open windowsill and the Police Department's insignia emblazoned on the door.

"Bastard," he muttered to himself.

The car slowed to a stop beside him. Nordstrom spent a moment looking him up and down. He was shirtless, his shirt thrown carelessly over the fence. His jeans were dirty. He hiked them up and reached for his shirt.

"Never mind," Nordstrom said. "It's not you I came to see, it's your boss. Where is he?"

"He's not here," Michael lied. "He's gone into town." He saw Nordstrom's face tighten. It had been a long drive for nothing.

"When do you expect him back?" Nordstrom asked without much hope.

"I don't know. After dinner sometime."

"I see," Nordstrom said, and Michael saw that he was looking for a place to turn around. He had a sudden fear that he might drive down to the barn.

"You can turn around right here," he said, gesturing to the hayfield, and knew it sounded strange the minute he said it. Nordstrom appraised him silently.

"Where does this road go?"

"To the barn. There's a lane that goes off to the right just ahead. You can turn around there, if you want."

"No, I think I'll have a look around the barn, since I'm already here."

"No one's supposed to be down there when he's not here except us."

"Then get in," Nordstrom said, and he reached across the passenger's seat and opened the door. "You can come with me and keep an eye out for your boss's welfare."

"I can't," Michael said quickly. "I'm supposed to work here—"

"Get in."

When the car pulled up to the barn, he jumped out, appalled at the thought of Erik's seeing him in a police car. Both Peter and Ivan were stripping stalls. Erik was not in sight.

"He doesn't like people in the barn," Michael said again. "He's not here, I told you."

"Then why're you so jumpy, kid?" Nordstrom asked. He looked over at the others. "Your boss here?"

"I told you he wasn't," Michael said, hoping Peter and Ivan would support him if only with silence.

"He's out back," Ivan said.

Captain Nordstrom nodded without surprise. "I thought he might be. Mind telling him I'd like to talk to him? Not you," he said to Michael, who made a move to return to his work.

"I have to go back," Michael muttered without hope. "He told me—"

"Well, I'm telling you to stay right here. I'll explain to your boss."

Michael turned away abruptly and went over to where Peter was working.

"You lied to him?" Peter asked in a low voice.

"What else could I do?"

Peter shook his head. "That was a mistake. Brace yourself and take it, because that's what's coming. And for God's sake, don't start another fight. He's already in a bad mood."

Captain Nordstrom looked incuriously around the barn. The stalls were empty, the horses turned out. He watched Ivan returning from the back of the barn. "He's busy now," Ivan said, avoiding Michael's eye. "He said he'll come in when he's finished."

"How long's that apt to be?"

"Can't say. Ten minutes, twenty minutes—maybe half an hour."

"I'll wait. I'm not going to make this drive again."

"Good," Michael said rudely and received a calculating stare.

"Look," Nordstrom said evenly, "I'll tell you this once and only once. You get over there where I can keep an eye on you, and keep your mouth shut. I hear another peep out of you and you're getting in that car and going back to town with me. You got that straight?"

Michael turned his back, slouched over to where Nordstrom had indicated and was silent. Erik came in carrying a halter and leadshank and a bucket, and with a glance in their direction disappeared into the tack room. Captain Nordstrom had started forward and then, as Erik vanished from sight, he turned resignedly to wait for him.

When he reappeared he was stony-faced. There was no hint of curiosity or amusement in his eye but rather a certain wariness, as if he readied himself for what was to come.

Nordstrom regarded him with open interest. Little was known of Erik in the community, and as he approached, Nordstrom recognized in him a particular force and authority not so different from his own. He was used to the reactions he produced in many people, the uncomfortable self-consciousness, the contrite apology, and the occasional hostility exemplified today in Michael's behavior.

"I'm Andrew Nordstrom, Mr. Sarmento," he said, extending his hand. Erik stared at his visitor with no change of expression and ignored the overture. Ivan and Peter continued their work. Neither of them looked up. Michael was staring fixedly out the door. Unwillingly, feeling Erik's eye on him, he glanced over at him and quickly looked away.

Erik walked past Nordstrom and out the door of the barn. The police chief, disconcerted, followed him. Michael moved closer to the door, compelled in spite of himself to hear what might be said, and it was to him that Erik spoke.

"You have left your work again?" Michael looked doggedly at the floor. "Go back to it."

"Hold on," Nordstrom said and raised his arm as if to block Michael's way. "I brought him down here. I want a word with you about this kid."

There was still no answer from Erik, but a strange expression crossed his face, and he turned around as Nordstrom spoke.

"You hired him a month or so ago, I understand. Were you aware he'd been in trouble with the law?"

"Yes."

"But not aware he got himself in trouble again Sunday night. I don't suppose he told you that, did he?" Michael made a restless move behind him, and Nordstrom glanced over his shoulder. "Cool it," he said.

"I told you to go back to your work," Erik said warningly, and Michael started out the door.

"Wait a minute, kid," Nordstrom put in, and Erik turned on him.

"Kindly do not interfere in my affairs," he said. "I will decide what he does as long as he works for me—unless you are here to place him under arrest?"

"No, he's not under arrest, but I have some—"

"Leave us," Erik said coldly to Michael.

"So you can talk about me behind my back?" Michael said and saw Erik's eyebrow go up and the familiar, sarcastic smile.

"Perhaps," he said. "Now go." And Michael stalked back up the lane.

"Look here," the captain said in a tight voice, "I'd as soon you don't interfere in my business, either. I want to talk to you about that kid."

"I have seen no one prevent you."

"I wanted him to hear this."

"Then you will be disappointed. Say what you came to say, I am busy."

Nordstrom took off his hat and ran his hand through his hair. He gave Erik an appraising look. "I'd hoped we could work together on this," he said. "I think we share a problem here."

"I do not share problems."

Nordstrom, silent for a moment, changed his approach. "I know a friend of yours pretty well," he said. "He told me about your operation up here." He paused to wait for Erik's acknowledgement and was met again by silence. "Jan Karras—used to cover the station for the *Courier*," he went on. There was still no answer.

"OK, about this kid," Nordstrom said with a tinge of irritation. "You gave him the day off, and he came into town and got into an argument in a local bar, struck one of my officers and ran off. I don't know what your attitude is about this kind of thing, but I don't take assaulting an officer lightly, myself. The kid's been hanging around for years with deadbeats who get along on what they lift from the local merchants. He can't seem to keep a job and to top it all, he has a big mouth. I've had it with him. He's got a real bad attitude, and one way or another I think he needs straightening out." He watched Erik expectantly and he saw him return the gaze, his eyebrows raised questioningly.

"Well?" Nordstrom said.

"I fail to see how your problem concerns me."

"He works for you, doesn't he?"

"Yes."

"Then you'd *better* be concerned. One day he'll go into town and he won't come back. I'll send him up the river, and you'll be short a hand."

Erik shrugged. Nordstrom straightened and said thoughtfully, "Can't say I understand you. You trying to tell me you don't have trouble with him?"

"Did you hear me say that?"

"Well, that's the message I get."

"The problems I have with my help I deal with myself," Erik said calmly. "I do not seek the help of the police, and I do not expect you to seek mine with your problems."

Nordstrom absorbed the comment wordlessly and finally he said, "I see." He controlled an impulse to retort.

"Well, I'll tell you. Maybe you're right and you don't need my help, but I'd appreciate it if you'd do what you can to influence him. He's scared of you for some reason—even I can see that—but he's not scared enough of me, apparently, although he ought to be. I'll be honest with you; I don't want to send him up much. A kid his age in prison doesn't have much to look forward to, and his social worker's a real nice lady. I'd like to help the kid if I can—"

Erik was staring at him in disbelief. "Why?" he said.

"Why?" Nordstrom repeated, nonplussed.

"Has he asked for your help?"

"Of course he hasn't."

"Then I suggest you let him make his own mistakes and take the consequences."

"And see him go to jail?"

Erik shrugged his shoulders. "Yes," he said.

Nordstrom shook his head. "You're a pretty hard guy," he said. "I thought *I* was pretty tough."

"If you have nothing further to say, I have other things to do."

Nordstrom shook his head again slowly and sighed. Then he made a gesture of resignation and went to his car.

CHAPTER 11

▼

Following Nordstrom's visit, Michael found himself in a familiar predicament. He was consumed by curiosity about what had taken place and infuriated by Erik's peremptory dismissal of him in front of Nordstrom, an insult that was underlined by the officer's cold appraisal as he drove away. But as he so often did, he chose ignorance over enlightenment in the superstitious hope that if he were unaware of the consequences, they would not exist. Thus he maintained his isolation as long as he could and avoided facing Erik.

As dinnertime neared he saw Erik appear in the lane. Michael threw down his sickle and vaulted the fence to disappear down into the pasture. He made his way through the field to the barn and joined Ivan and Peter, taking silent refuge in their company on the way up to supper.

He maintained a determined silence throughout the meal and rose to clear the table before the others. He stood at the sink, carelessly swiping at the plates under the tepid stream from the tap, and pretended indifference to the conversation behind him although he was listening avidly.

"I will not be here this evening," Erik was saying. "Ivan, answer the phone, if it rings."

"Yes, sir," Ivan answered him, restricted by the offhand comment to the house.

"And Michael—" Erik paused. Michael, as if he had been scalded, spun around to face him, already building within himself an arsenal of defenses. "Leave the dishes for now and return to your work. You may clean the kitchen when it becomes dark."

There were two more hours until sunset. Michael snatched a dishtowel from the towel rack and dried his hands and arms. He flung it on the counter and headed for the back door. Later, when Erik drove past him down the road, he turned his back until the truck was out of sight.

As he swung listlessly at the grass, he began to daydream. He was riding The Phoenix in the arena. He could feel the cadenced springing of the trot and became part of the rhythm, both creating it and somehow animated by it. He watched his own slow progress in his mind as he had watched Ivan. The horse's power became his own, controlled by the imperceptible tension of his calves and thighs, the reins like a delicate filament between his generous hand and the accepting mouth. He experienced the surging transition to extended trot and felt the horse return under him to ordinary trot, and then the lifting of his forehand and thrust of his hindquarters as in slow motion he floated into an airy passage. In his mind the horse flowed, endlessly supple, through serpentines, half circles and half-pass left and right.

The Phoenix broke from halt to canter effortlessly, his tail raised and cascading, ears forward, trusting Michael's hand, obedient to his seat and legs, and Michael, a centaur, gave his own physical being to the horse and was hypnotized. And then Erik came into his vision, watching intently, as Michael had seen him watch horses perform before, and almost in spite of himself he seemed to be drawn across the tanbark bed of the arena until he stood near the center. Michael, at one with his horse, circled lightly around him, still and tall, godlike.

"Halt," Erik said. His tone was almost deferential, and The Phoenix came instantly to halt at Michael's command and stood, poised, ready for whatever his rider might ask of him next.

"Yes," Erik said. "Well done."

The sun, bright orange, hung above the woods, and as Michael watched it sank inexorably behind the trees. He worked long after night had fallen, straining to see. He wondered where Erik went in the evenings and tried to picture him in the bar in Northwood. On his way to the tool shed to put the sickle away, he mused over what he had learned from Peter and Ivan and tried to imagine a woman living with Erik.

In the midst of his reverie, he was startled to see Peter emerge from the darkness of the pasture, leading a horse.

"What's the matter?" Michael asked and moved toward the gate. He watched Peter work at the chain that held it. It was his own horse, Kestrel, he had by his side.

"I don't know exactly. Something's not right with her. Turn on the light, will you?"

Michael did as he was asked and without waiting for Peter to suggest it, scaled the ladder to the loft and dropped a bale of straw down through the trapdoor. He watched it thud into the aisle, followed it, and bedded the stall in silence. Peter stood wordlessly in the aisle with Kestrel as Michael worked. When the mare was turned into the stall, she lay down almost before Peter had swung the stall door to behind her.

"Colic?" Michael asked.

"I'm afraid so. She seemed kind of stiff when I turned her out, and there wasn't much manure in her stall tonight." He tugged at the leadshank, and Kestrel raised her head but made no attempt to rise. She tried to roll, but Peter stopped her. "Come on," he said to her, "get up," and finally she did so. Peter put his ear to her side. She kept swinging her head sideways as if she were watching and suddenly turned and tried to lie down, her knees buckling.

"Damn!" Peter said. "I hate this. Get Ivan, will you?"

"He's supposed to be listening for the phone," Michael said and immediately regretted it. It sounded inane.

"Just get him, would you please?" Peter's voice was tense. He stood in the stall, watching his horse, and then, as Michael turned to leave, reopened the stall door and brought her out into the aisle.

A little later, Ivan appeared in the doorway with Michael at his heels. He said, "Can you hear any gut sounds?"

"No."

"Did you take her pulse?"

"Sixty, near as I could tell. She doesn't want to stand up. I can't decide whether to let her lie down or to try to keep her up. I'm afraid she'll get cast in the stall, and yet—" He stopped in midsentence. The mare kept swinging her head and neck around to look at her side. She moved restlessly, humping her back, and kicked at her belly.

"I'll call the vet," Ivan said. The dim, yellow barn lights rendered the surrounding darkness opaque, and Ivan, once outside, was swallowed instantly by blackness.

Michael stood in the shadows of the aisle. "She ever done this before?" he asked.

"Once, not as bad as this. I just walked her out of it. Get some mineral oil from the feedroom, would you? And a dose syringe—"

Michael helped position the horse's head while Peter filled the syringe and inserted it into the side of her mouth. But Kestrel was uncooperative. She pulled violently away and flung her head around. Absorbed in her own discomfort, she shifted uncomfortably from side to side.

"He's out," Ivan said when he reappeared. "I called two others. One's away, the other's taking his calls and is out on an emergency. I left a message."

"Damn!" Peter said again. "They're never around when you need them." He looked indecisively at Kestrel and again put his ear to her side. "Nothing," he said. He started to walk her, but again her knees began to tremble, and she went down in the aisle with a sound that was half way between a grunt and a groan. Helplessly they all stood watching.

"Did she eat supper?" Michael asked.

"Yes. She left a bit, but she often does that."

"Drink her water?"

"Yes."

The mare rolled, her shod feet lashing. She was slow to return to her side and lay incongruously on her back, her tail moving from side to side in the dust. Peter thrust the shank into Michael's hand and went himself to the feed room. He returned with a hypodermic syringe which he held uncertainly in his hand and looked down at his mare who still thrashed in the aisleway.

"Tranquilizer?" Ivan asked him, and he nodded.

"Should I, do you think?"

"Anything. She's really uncomfortable."

"Let's get her up again. Maybe I should walk her—" he paused and glanced desperately at Ivan. "I wish to hell Erik was here," he said and looked at his watch. "It's quarter to ten. Christ—he could be out for hours."

For three more hours they watched helplessly while Kestrel grew increasingly worse. They tried their best to make her comfortable, coaxed her to walk and administered two more doses of mineral oil and another injection of tranquilizer. Her pain seemed unremitting. She broke out in a patchy sweat and her breathing became rapid and irregular. Occasionally, frantic, she began to fight their restraint, and even when they held her with two lead shanks dragged them around the barn.

In self-defense they put her in her stall. She strained repeatedly without success, her back humped and tail raised, and when they took her temperature it registered a hundred and four. Her pulse, too, crept up, and soon they were unable to keep her on her feet and allowed her to sink into the deep straw.

Peter's face was grey and anguished, and all of them suffered with her as she thrashed, her eyes at first wild and then almost unseeing. By turns they jogged up the hill to the silent house to call the vet until Ivan, when the cool voice sounded once again from the answering machine, flung down the receiver, swearing. All of them knew colic was potentially lethal, and this colic didn't seem like any other they had seen.

Erik did not return until two in the morning. He appeared in the barn doorway suddenly, and for a moment they all looked at him with startled eyes. He stepped to the doorway of the stall and gazed at the horse, and then he looked over at Peter.

"How long has she been like this?"

"I noticed something wrong when I turned her out," Peter said. His voice was dull. "I can't reach a vet. We've been trying since nine o'clock."

Erik crouched beside the horse, laid his hand on her jaw and felt for her pulse. The pulse, still rapid, had seemed increasingly weak to Peter. He had tried to cover her with blankets, but in her frantic thrashing, she kept kicking them off. Her skin was damp with sweat and clammy.

Erik stood up and, turning abruptly without a word, left the barn. Peter, his heart heavy, followed him. He stopped in the barn doorway and watched Erik stride off toward the house, and he made no answer when Ivan came to stand at his elbow and spoke to him in a weak attempt at reassurance.

They were exhausted, bruised from Kestrel's desperate attempts to escape the pain that had driven her to lunge wildly around the stall. She had lifted them from the ground as they tried to restrain her, pinned them between her and the stall sides, flung them into the walls, the door, the hayrack and each other until they fled the stall and locked the door behind them. A half hour before she had sunk to the ground for the last time, groaning and weak.

Peter blocked the door when Erik returned.

"Sir, I'd like to wait for the vet. Please—he's bound to come soon."

Erik's face was expressionless, but he pushed Peter aside with something close to anger.

"Get the horse on her feet," he said to Ivan.

They struggled with her. She didn't want to rise, indeed could barely do so, but finally, with Erik's help, they forced her up, and Erik led her staggering into the aisle and out into the warm night. Peter was still standing by the door as if frozen, and Erik thrust the shank into his hand and said, "Take her around the side of the barn."

"I can't," Peter said in a whisper. "Ivan—"

"Do what I tell you," Erik snapped, and wearily, automatically, he obeyed, dragging his feet as the mare did beside him.

By the side of the barn, Kestrel staggered and went to her knees, and Peter dropped to his own beside her, his arm across her neck. Without a word Erik put his revolver to her head and shot her. Peter didn't move, but he raised his eyes to Erik's face, and his own expression was enigmatic. He watched Erik eject the cartridge and replace the gun in his pocket.

Erik met his eye for a long moment before he said, "Go to the shed and fetch the tarpaulin. Cover the horse." He said nothing when Ivan obeyed the order instead of Peter, but it was the only concession he made.

Michael, in the shadows, was grieving, less at Kestrel's death than at Erik's callous indifference to Peter's feelings and therefore to Michael's own. There was an eerie unreality to the evening. Kestrel at seven, headstrong and healthy, was suddenly dead. Not twenty-four hours ago he had watched Peter ride past him, hardly able to contain her at the walk. Her coat shone, and she radiated energy and excitement, and now her body lay sprawled, her belly swollen, her legs brazenly splayed and her neck thinly attenuated.

He watched Ivan unfold the heavy tarp and cover the horse carefully, as if he were making a bed. The day's events seemed to have happened weeks before, the peaceful darkness of the night around them to be a cruel irony. In silence, Peter watched Ivan and crouched only once beside Kestrel to lay his hand on her neck and stroke her ear. A thin line of blood and a small hole marred her face.

Erik didn't move. When she was covered, he said to Peter, "Turn out the lights in the barn. Tomorrow see that Kestrel's stall is stripped."

Peter looked up at him gravely but said nothing.

"Immediately after breakfast," Erik went on, "you will take the backhoe and dig her grave in the lower pasture. Take her down with the tractor and logging chain." Michael saw Peter swallow. He didn't answer and Erik didn't wait for him to do so but turned and went up to the house.

Peter was not allowed to mourn his loss, at least outwardly. Erik forced him to remove all traces of Kestrel's presence in the barn. Her stall was immediately assigned to another horse. Her name was struck from her stall, the chart in the feedroom, from Peter's saddle rack and from the blacksmith's schedule. No one was allowed to help Peter with the painful task of burying his mare, as he dragged her by the hind legs down the lane behind the tractor and then filled in the trench. At no time did Erik acknowledge his loss or his grief.

Like Peter's alter ego, Ivan suffered for him and silently reached to support him and to stand between him and Erik's intractable force. Erik's response was swift and devastating. He treated Ivan like an errand boy and disparaged his work. When Ivan retreated in self-defense to a morose silence, he ignored him utterly, and when, a slow and growing anger rising in him, Ivan resisted his contemptuous treatment, he seemed almost pleased.

Ironically, Michael became the beneficiary of the strange conflict, which surrounded him. Still a partial outsider, he was thrust from Erik's notice and therefore from the pressure of his authority. Erik ignored him completely, not as he so often did when Michael battled furiously against his demands, but as if he were not there at all, and, oddly, Michael seemed to lose his own self-awareness. He performed his chores in silence and reacted without thought to Erik's established routine.

Peter bent to Erik's will without a word, watching him intently in a kind of dazed puzzlement. He did as he was told without complaint, but when two days had passed, he suddenly packed his things and drove away. He didn't warn Erik he was going, and Michael, who was cleaning tack, watched him gather his belongings as he had the evening before the Horse Trials and dared not speak to him.

Erik came down the aisle of the barn to see the old truck and trailer vanish up the drive. He stepped outside, lit a cigarette, and stared after it for a long time. Then he returned to the barn and gave Ivan a long, speculative look where he stood by Kestrel's stall. Ivan returned his gaze, his hostility written on his face, and when he spoke his voice was barely under his control.

"You son of a bitch," he said. "You made him go, didn't you? You killed his horse and drove him away on purpose."

Michael stood in the doorway of the tackroom behind Erik and quailed at the words. He felt as if he himself had uttered them, and Erik would turn on him and destroy him, as swiftly and mercilessly as he had Kestrel.

Erik stirred. "The horse was dying," he said quietly. "She asked for relief, and I gave it to her. A horse has no control over its suffering, but a man must learn to control his own."

"Bullshit!" Ivan said. "Is that why you made it worse for him? Is that why you made him dig her grave and bury her and go on as if nothing had happened at all?"

"Yes," Erik said and regarded Ivan calmly.

"Jesus Christ! Don't you care about him at all? He's worked for you for three years for nothing—don't you care?"

"What has that to do with anything? Perhaps you would like to join him? If not, there is work to be done, and you may attend to it right now." He glanced over to where Michael stood frozen, absorbed in his own apprehension at Ivan's outburst.

"Feed Blue Tango," Erik said.

"Feed—" Michael repeated stupidly, for only Erik fed Blue Tango, and now he was striding away from the barn with Ivan glaring belligerently at his back. Michael found himself unable to think ahead, to imagine what would happen even a few moments from now. What would Ivan do? How could they go on without Peter? What would Peter do now—where would he go? And how could he himself endure Erik's subjugation and his own uneasy relationship with Ivan?

Blue Tango stood eagerly at the gate. When he had haltered him, Michael stood with the bucket in his arms while he ate, He watched the horse, suddenly aware of the dark eyes, the fine, pale eyelashes, the individual black and white hairs that shadowed his expressive face. Flies settled around Tango's eyes, and Michael swept at them angrily. With little shade, Tango was their natural prey. Bending down, Michael saw that the horse's belly was raw in a line from his girth to his sheath. What was Erik trying to accomplish with this imposed isolation? He felt at one with Tango, two loners forced to depend on Erik for their well-being.

Solitude was familiar and comforting to Michael, and alone with the horse he felt himself relax. He was threatened by Tango's frequent pacing of the fence line, his hopeful stance at the gate, ears pricked, yearning for company, and he was glad that for now, at least, he was still.

In the week that followed, Michael and Ivan sought uncertainly to reach an accommodation. Peter's absence had forced them into an uneasy alliance, since they shared his duties as well as their own. Ivan took Peter's students, those that Erik refused, and Michael did his barn work. But he was still not allowed to ride the horses Peter had been training. He was still limited to The Phoenix and Ivan's supervision.

After his outburst at Erik, Ivan seemed to gain a measure of self-control. Michael withdrew into himself and silently did as he was told, like a sleepwalker. Their nerves raw, neither could face the additional pain of clashing with Erik or each other.

Erik kept them relentlessly at work, and himself as well. He rode five or six horses every day and never mentioned Peter's absence. He didn't retreat from them as he had in times past when the mood seized him, but demanded their acknowledgment of his presence at every meal and frequently throughout the day. They became so sensitized to him that a raised eyebrow or a simple gesture was enough to set them to redoing a task or anticipating an errand. And there was an added burden, since now they had no way to leave the farm except by walking or accepting Erik's charity in loaning them the truck. He never refused such a request, but they bore the weight of his amused awareness of their dependence.

On Monday evening, two weeks after he had left, Peter returned in his battered truck without the trailer. The house, though lit, was silent. There was no answer when Peter hesitated in the upper hall and then knocked on Erik's door. Returning to the truck, he saw the light in the barn and walked down the lane as he had each day for the past three years.

Erik was in the tackroom, mending tack. He stitched deftly by hand with two large needles and a spool of waxed thread. The radio was on, and the sound of an English horn, hauntingly clear, echoed through the empty barn. In the doorway of the tackroom Peter stopped and was met by Erik's level stare as he looked up. Only his eyes moved, and his expression was neutral. Peter recognized the armored glance. Erik never allowed himself to show surprise, and it was only with his horses that he seemed unguarded.

As he drove up the long road, Peter had rehearsed the scene, and now he said, "I'm sorry. I'm sorry I left so suddenly. I just—" but he couldn't finish. He met Erik's eye for a brief moment and looked away, helpless and inarticulate. Erik said nothing. Moths moved erratically around the bare bulb of the ceiling light, and their shadows made the light around them tremble.

"May I come back?" Peter asked.

"You seem to have done so."

"I mean, to work. To stay and work."

Erik leaned back and regarded Peter with what seemed to be indifference. "I cannot afford to have my help abandon the horses without warning on some kind of whim."

"It wasn't a whim," Peter said quietly, "and Ivan and Michael were here. I've said I was sorry—"

"I doubt the horses would consider that a suitable alternative to dinner," Erik said. He turned back to the bridle he was mending, and Peter watched him.

"What more do you want?" he asked finally. "You shot my horse—you seem to expect me to act as if nothing had happened. Are you so heartless—"

Erik smiled. "Yes," he said.

"What's the matter with you? I've worked for you for three years now for nothing. Haven't I done my work? Have I ever complained about it or asked you for anything? And what have I got now? Nothing."

"That angers you?"

"Of course it does. What do you expect?"

"Good." Erik cut the heavy thread he was using with a pair of scissors and threw the bridle aside.

Peter, suddenly pale, stared at him wordlessly and then turned away. "Jesus Christ!" he said under his breath. "What's the use?" And yet he couldn't bring himself to walk away.

"You found me needlessly cruel in the matter of your mare," Erik said from behind him. "Perhaps it is so. I have had such losses myself, and I will tell you that sometimes one's rage is all one has to combat the pain. But anger is difficult for you—that is your weakness. Even now you seek to deny it. I have seen it in your riding. You are a pacifist, I think."

Peter turned half way around in the doorway, put his hands behind him on the jamb, and leaned his back against it. The rough wood against his hands was oddly comforting.

"You have done well with Tangent," Erik went on. "Do you know why?"

Peter stood motionless and watched Erik. He was taken aback by the words and the sudden change in atmosphere, but he answered with a kind of automatic obedience. "I like her. I feel she needs reassurance, and I kind of understand her nervousness."

"Yes. She recognizes in you a certain strength. She depends upon it, and it makes her calm. Your own mare also recognized it, but she was willful. She found it necessary to test you. She asked you to fight with her, and you could not."

For several seconds Peter said nothing. All of Erik's abuse after Kestrel's death had not hurt him as much as the quiet statement that he had failed her. And the worst of it was that he knew what Erik said was true. His throat ached, and all at once he found himself confessing, relieved to say what he had himself known but never wanted to admit.

"She should have been Ivan's horse, shouldn't she? That's the kind of horse he does well with. I know that—"

He saw Erik straighten, and the thin, sardonic smile returned, the mocking eyebrow arched. "You bathe yourself in your own inadequacy? Still you seek the easy solution. Do you think that fortune places horses on this earth to be assigned to you according to your nature? Have you learned nothing in three years? One can only change oneself. One learns to deal with a horse depending on the needs of the horse, not his own." Abruptly he reached over and turned the radio off. "You dishonor your mare if you dismiss her as unfit to be your mount. You owe her more, I think, than weakly to turn her over to Ivan in your mind because you were unwilling to do what she asked of you."

"I didn't," Peter said, for he was stung by the criticism. "I did try—"

At this remark Erik interrupted him. "Yes. And now you will try harder, I believe."

He picked up the bridle he had tossed aside on the counter and absently rearranged it and hung it in its place. Then he turned out the light, and Peter stepped back to let him pass. Erik walked to the doorway of the barn, and Peter followed him. He watched Erik reach into his pocket and light a cigarette. As he dropped the match on the ground, he said as if to himself, "I do not care for excuses. If you wish to ride well, you will not accept such weaknesses in yourself. You will change them and become stronger. Don't tell me again that a certain horse is for a certain rider. Become that rider."

"Do you think I can?"

"If you cannot, do not waste my time and your own. You may be surprised at what you can endure. You fled when you felt that your life here was intolerable, and yet you returned, and perhaps the returning was more difficult than the flight."

He changed the subject suddenly. "Kestrel was dying. Were you aware of that?"

"Yes, but I thought maybe the vet—"

"The vet would have done nothing. There was nothing to be done. The horse had a twisted gut. She was dying."

"I just hoped—"

"Then you were a fool. You were only prolonging her agony with your hope. What do you think I have been saying to you? To spend your time hoping is to waste it. You must face your own pain to combat it. You must deal with what is real, not what you wish were real."

"Yes," Peter said quietly. He was uncomfortably aware of Erik's scrutiny.

"Put your things away and kindly move your truck where it belongs."

"Yes, sir," Peter said.

He watched Erik return to the house and after a moment followed him. He moved his things into the house and put the truck in the shed. For a moment he stood at the pasture gate and stared down across the field.

Dimly he understood Erik's savagery after Kestrel died. He would have liked to treasure his loss as irrevocable and tragic, to have kept Kestrel in his mind as beautiful, beyond his reach, a free and untamed spirit horse, but Erik had denied him that. The horse was dead, and he himself had had to lay her to rest and watch her topple, rigid, into the gaping trench, lifeless and grotesque. And his own slow and awakening resentment was not simply a byproduct of his ordeal but the whole purpose behind Erik's actions.

He sighed and trudged back up the lane. His eyes rested on the yellow rectangle of Erik's window, which seemed to define the quality and direction of his life.

CHAPTER 12

▼

Michael had thought life at the farm could never be the same, even after Peter returned, so it was with disbelief that he saw Peter settle back into the daily routine as if he had never left. He said nothing to Michael about his two-week absence, and although he didn't bring up the subject of Kestrel, he made no attempt to avoid it when her name was mentioned in passing. Michael watched his interaction with Erik with fascination and found no indication from either of them that anything out of the ordinary had happened.

But if Michael noticed no change, Ivan did. The change was in Michael. His increasing proficiency on The Phoenix became both a satisfaction and a trial to Ivan. He was pleased at how quickly Michael advanced, for he was soon able not only to maintain his position, but even, at times, to put suggestions into practice. Yet he still lacked a perception of his own limitations and those of his mount, and it was only Ivan's self-discipline that kept him from losing his temper and rashly provoking another confrontation between them. There were times when he could barely contain his anger when Michael ignored his insistence on refining a movement again and again and blithely proceeded to improvise, intoxicated by his sense of power over the horse. One day, when Ivan felt his own animosity driving him to recklessness, he turned on his heel and left the arena, torn between the relief he felt and the possibility of Erik's anger.

He found Peter in front of the barn washing down a horse and told him what he had done.

"He's arrogant as hell," he said bitterly. "If he was riding any other horse, the horse would straighten him out, but The Phoenix is too honest, and he sure as hell won't listen to me. I think it's time he was put on another horse—maybe one like Tangent, but I guess that's not going to happen."

Peter straightened and began drying the horse with a sweat scraper.

"Why not tell Erik?"

"I guess because I know just what he'd say—it's my problem. If he knew I'd walked out of there just now—I hate to think." He watched the rivulets of water run down the sweat scraper onto the ground and automatically took the lead shank from Peter and held the horse for him.

"Tell him. You won't be any worse off than you are now."

"I guess so—"

In the tack room he confessed his problem to Erik. "You are telling me you have taught him all you know?"

"Not all I know, just all he's willing to learn from me."

Erik leaned back against the counter and was silent. Emboldened, Ivan said, "That's why you assigned him to me, isn't it?"

"Perhaps. Have you learned nothing from the experience?"

"Maybe," Ivan answered as ironically as he dared, "how to control my temper."

"Oh? It must have escaped my notice. There is the matter of the unsupervised student still mounted in the arena."

Ivan glanced away and said nothing. He watched Erik open one of the cupboards and withdraw an assortment of rags. He tore a long piece from an old sheet and tossed it carelessly on the counter.

"What's that for?" Ivan asked.

"To teach the blind to see. Come, we will find out how your student progresses."

Alone in the indoor arena, Michael was guiding The Phoenix in a series of circles and turns at the walk. Still without reins, he had been astonished to find he didn't need them to ride, and it gave him a sense of power even beyond what he had imagined. The horse seemed to become a powerful extension of himself, guided by telepathy. He treasured a feeling of victory at Ivan's departure as he watched himself in the large mirrors placed at the end and side of the arena. Even when Erik appeared, he wasn't daunted. He was confident he had corrected the shortcomings Eric had so scathingly pointed out on the day of his first ride. But he was still a trifle on guard when he looked over to where Erik stood and saw him nod in apparent satisfaction.

"Your position has improved," Erik said. "Perhaps now you can sit the trot without embracing your mount around the neck?"

Michael dropped his feet from the stirrups and moved The Phoenix into a trot. He sat it without difficulty. His back was naturally supple, and his relaxed figure followed the springing action of the horse. It was the result of hours of practice, for Ivan had forced him to do it at every lesson. Erik's smile gave him a dizzying sense of success.

"And canter?"

Michael asked for the canter. The Phoenix answered his aid without hesitation, and he sat erect and swung easily to the horse's stride. Erik nodded.

"When you are ready, halt." His voice was quiet, so as not to influence the horse.

Michael came at length to a ragged halt, and Erik turned on Ivan.

"Am I to understand that you have not yet succeeded in teaching him the proper use of the back?" he said.

"He seems to think he already knows it," Ivan said.

Erik stepped forward. "You are pleased with your progress?" he asked Michael.

"I guess so."

"You *guess* so? Why else would you stare like Narcissus into the glass but for your own self-admiration?"

Silence. Michael's expression turned sour. "I was watching the horse," he lied after a moment.

"You were watching the horse," Erik repeated. "Just exactly what were you watching?"

"To see that he bent through the turns."

Erik gave a short laugh. "Were you indeed?" he said. "You are satisfied that you progress, but Ivan doesn't seem to share your enthusiasm."

Michael glanced over at Ivan.

"He suggests that you ignore his direction. Is it so?"

"No," Michael said quickly and then modified his answer. "That is, only when I already know what he's saying."

"I have seen little in your performance here to indicate you already know anything. The fact that you no longer sit like a broken twig hardly qualifies you as an Olympic rider. On the left rein, canter from C to A and halt."

Michael did so.

"How would you evaluate that halt?"

"What does that mean?"

"I believe I asked for the halt at A. Why does the horse stand at the letter F?"

"I guess I gave the signal too late."

"Repeat the exercise." Michael did as he was told. "You are pleased with that effort?"

"It was all right."

"And what evidence do you have for that remark?"

"I'm at A now. That's what you asked for, isn't it?"

"I asked for the canter with halt at A. Why, exactly, did you come to trot between E and K instead of maintaining the canter to A?"

"Because it takes him a while to stop."

"Does it? Dismount." He gave a casual wave to Ivan who mounted The Phoenix and settled himself into the saddle. Michael groaned audibly.

"Canter, please, halting at B, C, E, and A in succession. Without trot, if you are capable."

With the exception of one halt at the letter E on the side of the arena, which The Phoenix overshot by a stride, the halts were abrupt and square without any sign of trot.

"Thank you," Erik said. He turned to Michael, who was scowling. "Well?"

"Well what?"

"Have you an explanation for your own inadequacy?"

"No."

"What did you say?"

"No, *sir*."

"Perhaps it is one of those mysteries of life that has no explanation?"

"Maybe."

"Or perhaps you have been carried away by what you imagine is your elegant appearance and have neglected to learn to ride the horse?"

"I haven't—"

"If you do not wish to take instruction, I may be able to find one or two tasks for you to do away from the barn." He turned to Ivan. "Teach him the correct use of the back. You can use one of Museler's methods, if you wish."

He stepped back as Ivan dismounted, but he didn't leave. Ivan turned to Michael. The Phoenix stretched his head down and sighed with resignation. He snorted audibly through his nostrils.

"When I've told you to brace your back, you've been stiffening the small of your back in the saddle," he said formally. "That's like half an aid, and The Phoenix gives you half a response. That is, he comes to trot and then to walk and halt. He doesn't understand you. Lie down on your back."

"What?"

Ivan gestured to the floor of the arena. "On *that*?" Michael said. "Why?"

"Just do it. I'm going to show you why."

Michael glanced indecisively at Erik, who was standing in the doorway. After a moment of hesitation, he did as Ivan asked. Lying in the dirt, he stared up into the rafters and felt not only the ignominy of his position but also a sense of physical helplessness, as if Ivan might attack him.

"Cross your arms and raise your hips off the ground. No—put your feet flat on the ground by bending your knees slightly. Yes, like that. Do it until you remember what it feels like. That's the correct aid." He allowed Michael to get up and made him remount the horse.

"Now try it out at the walk. Remember the aid goes all the way through to your knees. Drop your heel and use your lower leg to ask for the activity of the hindquarters and then brace."

Michael did so. He was immediately successful, but the speed of the halt threw him forward, so that he kept his seat only by bracing both hands on The Phoenix's neck. Ivan glanced over his shoulder at Erik, who again advanced toward the center and spoke a few words to him. He left the arena, and Erik turned his attention to Michael.

"Turn onto the center line and halt. Then ask the horse to canter." And when Michael had done as he asked, "You canter on which leg?"

"What?"

"Which lead does the horse take?"

Michael looked down at the horse's shoulder. "Left," he said as the horse reached the letter C and turned left.

"How do you know that?"

"I asked him for it, and I can see it."

Erik nodded. "Walk," he said. "Starting with the left hind, count aloud the footfalls of the walk as the horse's feet strike the ground."

There was a dead silence. Uncertainly, Michael looked down at The Phoenix's shoulder. "I'm not sure what you mean," he said.

"Oh? I thought it fairly simple. How many beats to the horse's walk?"

"How many beats—"

"That is what I asked you."

"He's got four legs—four, I guess."

"And the trot?"

"He's got four legs no matter what gait he goes at," Michael said sarcastically.

"They strike the ground separately at all gaits?"

"How am I supposed to know that?" Michael said. "I'm not a horse."

"Fortunately not. But since you seem rather proud of your eyesight, you may dismount and watch the horse until you are able to give an intelligent answer to the question."

Michael watched The Phoenix walk quietly around the arena. He said defensively, "Four—that's what I said."

"Four," Erik repeated, and to The Phoenix, "Trot." He regarded Michael with his eyebrows raised.

Michael frowned. "All his legs hit the ground—I said that."

"Separately?"

"No, not separately. Two at once."

"Two at once. Which two?"

"The opposite ones. Right front, left hind, and left front, right hind."

"Then perhaps now you can answer the question. How many beats in a completed stride at the trot?"

"Two?"

"I am asking the questions," Erik said. "It is for you to provide the answers."

"Two, then."

The Phoenix was told to canter. "The canter?"

There was a pause. "Four?" Erik's face was expressionless. "Three or four—" Michael added uncertainly.

"You are fortunate to have such eyesight, since you cannot seem to use your ears to equal advantage. Answer the question."

The sound of the hoof beats, although muffled by the tanbark footing, was distinct.

"Three," Michael muttered.

"Whoa," Erik said quietly to The Phoenix, and to Michael, "Remount the horse and do as you were instructed. At the walk, starting with the near hind."

There was a long silence. "I can't tell," Michael finally admitted. From the corner of his eye he saw Ivan reenter the arena.

"Because you cannot see?"

"Yes."

"A child of five could do as much. It has taken you two months to learn to use your eyes?"

"No, I already knew that."

"Then why, may I ask, are you wasting Ivan's time?"

"What do you want me to do?" His voice reflected his mounting frustration.

"I'm afraid it will be necessary to deprive you of the opportunity of watching yourself perform. Ivan will have that pleasure, since he is your instructor." He turned to Ivan. "Blindfold him," he said.

The Phoenix looked startled and suddenly began to trot.

"You think I'm crazy?" Michael said, his voice rising. "I can't ride blindfolded." He braced himself angrily in the saddle and stopped the horse.

"*Can't?*" Erik said with emphasis. "If you can't, then we all waste our time."

Michael looked indecisively at Ivan who stood, his face quite serious, with the blindfold in his hand. "Did *they* have to do that?" he asked with a gesture toward Ivan.

"No."

"Then the hell with it. I'm not going to either."

Erik looked speculatively at him. "Neither Ivan nor Peter was as skillful as you," he said. "Neither of them knew how to ride with their eyes, a rare talent you seem to have been given. Both relied on more traditional skills—a feel for the horse." He nodded to Ivan.

"Bend down," Ivan said to Michael, but Michael, his mouth pressed into a thin line, dismounted.

"Go to hell," he said to Ivan.

"Put the horse away," Erik said.

Michael turned without a word and led The Phoenix away. It was a bitter victory, for he knew Erik wouldn't let him ride again until he surrendered.

He maintained an outward calm for the next two days, although inwardly he raged and contemplated his situation with a feeling of righteous self-pity. It was only a matter of time before he would have to go to Erik and ask for what he had just refused. He put it off as long as he could and then accepted the inevitable.

"I'd like to ride again, OK?" he said one day, trying to keep the resentment from his voice.

Erik, preparing to mount a horse, said offhandedly, "No, it is not convenient at the moment."

"Then when?"

"Hand me my whip," Erik said to Peter.

"When?" He heard his voice crack and betray him. There was no answer.

"When?" he repeated.

Erik mounted the horse. "Thank you," he said to Peter as he received the whip, but his eyes were on Michael. "This horse requires an occasional reminder that the rider's aids are to be obeyed." He moved the horse suddenly forward and rode away.

Michael glanced at Peter. "Bastard," he muttered. He found himself shaking and irritably shifted his weight.

Peter laughed. "You can't win," he said. "Haven't you learned that yet?"

Michael glared angrily at him. "Why'd you come back here?" he asked.

"Because I *have,*" Peter said.

Three more days passed and Michael began to feel desperate. He watched Erik for some sign, however slight, that he was relenting, or for an indication that the time was right. In the meantime he turned his helpless fury to his work. His physical energy seemed inexhaustible, and even Erik acknowledged his efforts with a lifted eyebrow. But more and more of his assigned tasks were away from the barn. He hoed the garden, mowed the lawn, and gathered the produce. He trimmed fence lines, dug rock from the fields that had been heaved to the surface by the winter frost. Some of the time he spent on his knees, washing the kitchen floor. He was even assigned to washing the windows in the house and moved the cumbersome ladder from place to place with barely controlled impatience. Each morning he resentfully awaited the day's assignment, and each morning it was more of the same.

He chose a time when Erik was in the kitchen alone. In place of resentment, he felt only a restless longing for change. He grasped the back of one of the kitchen chairs, leaned his weight on his hands and said, "If you won't let me ride, what's the point of my working?"

Erik turned slowly around from the sink where he was washing his own breakfast dishes. "I was under the impression that it was you who chose not to ride."

Michael was surprised to find that this comment didn't produce its usual effect in him; in fact it made him laugh. "Yeah," he said. "I guess it was." He stared at the checkered oilcloth that covered the kitchen table and absentmindedly brushed a few grains of salt off the surface. "But it's you who keeps me from starting again," he said tentatively and then, resigned, asked quietly, "What do you want me to do?"

"What you are told."

Michael sighed. "That's what I've *been* doing."

"Yes, but it is not only my orders I expect you to follow. Ivan is your instructor, I believe. And, beyond that, it is your horse who will teach you. You dismiss that fact as if it did not exist."

"No, I don't—"

"On the contrary, you do. You have yet to learn his language, concerned as you are at the moment with your own skill. And you dismiss Ivan with the same contempt, although he is familiar with the language and can explain it to you."

Michael was silent. He traced the line of red squares with his finger. "OK," he said finally, "I'll do what he says. Does that mean you really expect me to ride blindfolded?" Erik didn't answer but turned back to the sink as if the conversation were ended. Michael stared at his back. "When?" he demanded.

"Later this morning when your work is completed."

So Michael submitted to being blindfolded. He felt like a fool and was truly frightened at his helplessness. Several times he clutched frantically at the saddle, fearful of losing his balance. Finally Ivan told the horse to halt. For the first time he felt sorry for Michael.

"Look," he said, "I'm not going to ask you to do anything sudden that will make you fall. You've got to trust me and you've got to trust the horse if you want to learn anything. Erik's a tough teacher, but he knows what he's doing. And I can tell you this, if you don't stop hanging onto the saddle, the next step will be that he'll tie your hands behind you so you can't."

"The hell he will."

"The hell he won't. And if you don't do it his way, you won't ride. It's as simple as that." After a pause he added, "You're as tight as can be. Relax."

"I can't relax."

"Then let's quit for a while. We'll try again this afternoon. I'll tell you exactly where you're going and what to expect."

Michael pulled the blindfold off. His face was pale and he felt shaken. He vaulted off and ran the stirrups up. "Jesus," he said, "I don't know—"

"You know what Peter did when he left here?" Ivan interrupted him. "He told me he went back home and asked for a job at some fancy training barn. When the trainer asked for references, Peter mentioned Erik, and the guy laughed. He said Erik was a crazy man who taught circus tricks to horses. He said his theories were off the wall, and no judge would give him the time of day, and that's why Erik rarely showed his horses. But he gave Peter a job mucking stalls and let him fool with a couple of the younger horses.

"Peter said the trainer got on his case about everything he did. He complained that Peter spent too much time grooming. He just wanted him to brush off the mud and do the mane and tail. When he warmed up a horse, the trainer said he wasted too much time. He said Peter didn't ride with enough contact and should be getting the horses on the bit. He didn't have time to waste, he said; he was training dressage horses and wanted them on the bit. Peter said he didn't ride a single horse that was supple enough to turn a corner properly. He said he didn't sleep for two days thinking about it. He *knew* Erik was right. He could tell by the horses he rode there."

"So he quit?"

"That's right."

"Is that why he came back?"

"Partly, I guess."

"He tell the trainer what he thought of him?" Michael asked.

"Peter? Of course not."

"Would you?"

"I doubt it."

"I would have."

"Yeah," Ivan said. "I suppose you would. You're always doing stupid things," and instantly the fragile contact between them was broken. Michael stalked away, leading The Phoenix.

For the next week, Michael rode without sight. He found it a fearful experience and therefore exhausting. In the beginning, The Phoenix seemed to have forgotten all his training and Michael to have lost control over him. The horse would trot without warning and even canter when he least expected it. He knew it was his fault, for his muscles tightened in panic against his will. Unable to stop the horse, he was at the mercy of Ivan's quiet commands.

He stared into the blackness of the blindfold, his nerves alive and jumping, his legs tight on the horse's sides, his hands hovering only inches from the pommel. Ivan's voice was his only beacon, and when each lesson ended he regarded his teacher with mingled relief and resentment.

But after a few days he did relax, and as Erik had clearly intended, he began to use his other senses to regain control. Like a mirror image of his own growing perception, The Phoenix began to respond and his response restored Michael's confidence. With Ivan's assistance, he learned to discern the beats of the horse's strides and to feel where each leg was at any given time.

"You can only see the front legs," Ivan explained, "but you must always have the feeling you're riding the hind legs, where the impulsion comes from. The hind legs start all the movements, and eventually your awareness of what the hind legs do will determine when you give an aid."

Michael began to notice qualities of movement he hadn't known before, and when finally Ivan brought a lunge whip into the arena and guided the horse without the use of his voice, and Michael was able to anticipate and stay with the movement without losing his balance, he was allowed to remove the blindfold.

The experience of blindness, even in so limited a circumstance, left an indelible brand on Michael. He hadn't known the extent of his dependence on his sight, his major source of protection, which enabled him to do his work, escape from Erik's notice or to try to interpret other's motives. His gaze had a peculiar intensity and vigilance at the best of times, for he looked out on a world that he believed might turn hostile in an instant and which seemed constantly to make demands upon him. He found himself awakening at night in a panic from nightmares of silent impotence and vague, menacing terrors, and he would sit upright in bed, his heart pounding, and look frantically through the surrounding dark until he could discern the shadowed forms around him and convince himself that he was whole again.

When he pulled the blindfold off for the last time, he found Erik standing with Ivan in the center of the arena.

"Fetch the reins for this bridle and send Peter here," Erik said to Ivan while Michael sat on The Phoenix, absently stroking the horse's neck.

While they were waiting, Erik said to Michael, "You have accomplished the first step. But before you get too carried away with yourself, I will remind you that what you have learned is within the grasp of anyone who applies himself, and most require considerably less time to master it than it has taken you. You will now learn how to handle the rein and having done so, to start communicating with the horse. You have learned some of the language—now you must learn the rest. Should I find you abusing the horse as you have done in the past, you will continue your education elsewhere. Is that clear?"

"Yes, sir," Michael said. "Is Peter going to teach me?"

"That was my intention."

"What's the matter with Ivan? Doesn't he know this stuff?"

"'This stuff' as you so casually put it, is part of any horseman's basic training. Ivan is perfectly competent to teach you but, like the horse, he needs a vacation. It was not a task he found particularly pleasant."

"Hell, I did all the work."

"On the contrary, The Phoenix did all the work. He, too, needs a vacation. You will start riding out with Peter tomorrow morning. You will ride once a day instead of twice. When I judge you competent, you may start riding other horses. Peter has a certain skill with his hands. You would do well to pay attention to him."

When Peter appeared, Erik was explicit. "Teach him," he said dryly, "that there are other uses for the hands than fighting. When you have finished this morning, send him to me."

Michael felt a sense of euphoria after Erik had gone, but he found Peter as demanding in his own way as Ivan had been.

"Take up the rein," Peter said. "You know how to lengthen and shorten the rein?"

"Of course. What do you think I—"

"Then shorten them about four inches," Peter interrupted. "Most people when they start allow the rein—"

"I'm not starting. I've—"

"—to get too long," Peter continued as if he hadn't spoken. "There are three ways to use your hands: actively, by pulling or using a direct rein to turn the horse, passively, by following his motion, or resistively, by resisting what he does without pulling, like using a supporting rein or when you ask for a rein-back. In all cases, your hands must be independent of your seat and not influenced by it. You'll use the passive rein most of the time, the resistive rein often, and the active rein only rarely, when you want to change something. Most of your attention, while you're learning, should be on legs, seat and position, which should be sec-ond-nature to you by now, but all your aids may change without your being aware of it when you start using the reins and riding over uneven ground. So think first of seat and legs. The horse must have the impulse to move forward always, even when he's standing still or reining back. Understand?"

"Sure. Clear as mud."

"On the right rein now, trot. Gradually shorten your rein until you feel the horse's mouth. You're looking for an elastic kind of feeling that shouldn't change unless you ask it to. Maintain the contact by asking the horse to move into it and yielding with your hand."

But he allowed Michael only a few minutes to ride and then told him to dismount and put the horse away. "That's all for now."

"What are you talking about? What have I done now?"

"Nothing. It's enough for today."

"Who said so?"

"The Phoenix. You get so carried away you don't pay attention—"

"I do—"

"—and he's tired. He's been working for over an hour."

Michael looked down at the horse in consternation. "He doesn't feel tired to me. He's going like he always does."

Peter sighed. "Look, do you have to argue about everything? The horse is tired. Put him away."

Michael dismounted. He was disappointed and resentful, cut down to one session of riding a day, and his irritation turned on Erik, whose direction, through Peter, he was forced to accept. It was less the specific rules he must follow that tortured him, than the quality of Erik's control, casual but exacting, turning him this way and that like a dog in training on a leash who is utterly dependent on his master's command and always threatened by the choking restraint of the collar around his neck.

"Erik can go to hell," he said to Peter's retreating back and felt better, although there was no response from Peter.

CHAPTER 13

▼

He's making me ride blindfolded. He won't even let me use the reins. How am I supposed to do that? I'll probably kill myself, and he won't give a damn. In fact, he'll be glad. I think that's why he makes me do it anyway.

Michael's note was signed with his name and under it the faintly accusing statement, "I thought you were going to find me another job."

His letter was written in pencil on a torn sheet of notebook paper, and the lines were smudged and uneven. But although they were carelessly scrawled and probably exaggerated, the words were more directly descriptive of his thinking than any Annie had received from him before, and they touched an area of anxiety in her that she had been trying to repress. On a sudden impulse, she sat down and wrote a quick note in answer:

I haven't had much luck in finding farm work for you, but there are a number of possibilities here in town that you may want to consider. I can help you look for an inexpensive room near your work. I know it's not what you might choose, but it would be a steady income for you, and it would give us time to find something better and more permanent. I'm enclosing the 'Help Wanted' column from Sunday's *Courier*. Affectionately, Annie

By the time Michael received her answer, he had forgotten what he had told her, and he only glanced at the note and stuffed it into the pocket of his jeans. It was lunchtime, and all of them, including Erik, were in the kitchen. The day was windy and cold, and it had rained steadily since before dawn. The horses had come in wet and impatient for their feed, backs hunched against the wind, and three lessons had been canceled. The blacksmith was expected in the early afternoon, but for the moment they were enjoying an unusual lull in the day. Basking in the warmth from the woodstove, Michael was starting his third sandwich when the phone rang.

"Answer it," Erik said when it had rung three times and none of them had moved. He nodded to Ivan who did as he was told.

"Mr. Sarmento?" It was a woman's voice.

"No, this is Ivan. Would you like to speak to him?" Erik gave him an irritated glance and an impatient wave.

"I'm afraid he can't come to the phone right now," Ivan said and turned so that his back was to Erik. "Is there any message?"

"This is Pat Bartlett. Do you remember me?"

"Sure I do—you own Calypso."

"That's right. Is he busy? I won't take a minute—I just want to ask him a question."

Ivan hesitated. "I'll see," he said finally. He put his hand over the mouthpiece, lowered the phone and said over his shoulder, "It's the girl who owns—"

"I am not deaf."

"She wants to ask you a question."

"What question?"

"I can't ask her that," Ivan said, turning around. "It's none of my—"

"First you assume I am deaf and now you are dumb?"

Ivan glanced from Erik to the phone. "He wants to know what the question is," he said apologetically, and she laughed.

"Would you tell him there's a dressage show in a few weeks in North Fairborough? I've had Calypso entered for some time. I was wondering what to do about it." After a pause she added, "Look, I'd really like to ask him something. Won't he talk to me for just a minute?"

Ivan sighed. "I'll ask him. She really wants to talk to you," he said to Erik.

Michael tilted back in his chair. He glanced at Erik and saw him drum his fingers impatiently on the surface of the table.

"I'm sure she has no secrets from you," Erik said pointedly.

Ivan turned grimly back to the telephone. "Can I ask him for you?" His voice had become formal, more to protect himself from Erik than from her.

"I know Calypso has a few more weeks there," Pat said. "I was wondering if I might ask him an enormous favor—if he'd ride him for me in the show." Ivan turned back to the table.

"She wants to know if you'll ride Calypso for her in the North Fairborough show. He's already entered."

"You may tell her I would be delighted," Erik said, and there was a short silence. They all stared at him. "Since I will be there anyway with three of my own horses."

Ivan appeared paralyzed. He stood by the phone with the receiver in his hand, and it was several seconds before he raised it slowly to his ear. "He said he'd be glad to. Some horses are going from here anyway."

"I really appreciate it—thanks so much. Thank him for me, would you, please?"

"Sure will. 'Bye." He hung up the phone and turned to Erik. "I thought you didn't like shows."

"Did I say that?"

"You don't usually go to them."

Erik regarded him thoughtfully. "Horses need exposure to new places and other horses," he said, "and I thought you would enjoy the opportunity to demonstrate your skill. Perhaps you will attract another student."

"Me? Am I supposed to go, too?"

"Of course you will go. All of you will go. Orion is entered—I believe you have been riding him?"

"Do you think he's ready?"

"I would hardly have entered him if I did not think so."

"Who else are you sending?" Peter asked.

"Tangent."

"Tangent? I'm not so sure about her. I don't know if she'll—"

"She will do as you ask her, if you have done your work. If you have not, it will be quite evident, and although it may hurt your pride, it will not hurt the horse."

Michael, his elbows on the table, leaned forward. "Who's the third? The Phoenix?"

Erik turned his head slowly. "The Phoenix? Why should he go to shows? He has already received his schooling."

"But you said three—"

"Yes. I am sending Lyrik."

"Lyrik?" Peter said, and before he thought, "Who's riding her?"

Erik turned on him angrily. "I am riding her. What did you suppose?"

"Sorry."

"Did you say I was going?" Michael said. "Am I going to ride?"

Erik laughed.

"Of course not. You are the groom."

Ivan and Peter exchanged glances. They had never seen Erik ride in a show, although he had sent them on occasion and sometimes went to shows with students who paid him to coach them. His attitude toward competition was a mystery to them. He often seemed unconcerned with the results of the tests they rode and scarcely glanced at the test sheets they showed him. He was more interested, apparently, in their own evaluation of their rides. But even then it was hard for them to tell if it was a real interest or simply an exercise in self-criticism. He rarely attended these shows himself, but when he did he watched their performances from the sidelines, and his comments later were often more useful to them than the judge's.

Erik was often asked to judge, though rarely at large recognized competitions. "He's too controversial," Jan had once told Peter, "and he can't get a judge's card. He won't ask for the required references. He's been a little careless in some of his comments to competitors, and many of them won't show under him. It's the business of big shows to draw riders, and riders go where they think they'll do well. There's a certain amount of point chasing in dressage shows like other shows, I gather. Erik doesn't always follow the rules."

Peter had repeated this information to Ivan and later to Michael.

"And yet," he said thoughtfully to Michael, one evening as they waited their turns in the shower, "it was because he was judging at a show I was in that I came here."

Michael looked up. "Yeah?"

"I'd had Kestrel about six months and taken her to a couple of dressage schooling shows and one Novice Horse Trials. She'd been a disaster. Dressage was her weak point, although one judge had given me a fifty-seven, which is sufficient. She'd barrel off cross-country all right, although I couldn't control her. It was a big runaway scene, and I came in about three minutes under the limit. But in the dressage arena she was like a time bomb. So I'd signed her up for this dressage schooling show, and I'd gotten there very early. I'd thought maybe I could settle her with enough warm-up. But she fought me all through it, and when I went in the arena she was a real witch. The best I could do was to hang on and steer and try to keep her from jumping out of the arena altogether.

"I hardly saw Erik, just a figure sitting there when I tried to keep her still enough to salute. All I wanted was for the damned test to be over. I'd scratched my other two classes and was ready to go home—I was feeling really down—when the steward told me to hang around until the class was finished. At the end of the class I saw there were three of us waiting there, and I knew the other two had had really nice rides. For a moment I thought there'd been some kind of mistake and maybe I'd somehow won something, though it seemed unlikely. But Erik stepped from the judging stand and called the other two in and actually rode their horses himself. I guess that's done in Europe sometimes in upper level competition, but this was Training Level Test Two! Even the steward looked amazed, but he wasn't about to argue with a judge. Then, when they had gone, he made me dismount, and he rode Kestrel."

"No kidding!" Michael said. "How'd she go for him?"

"I don't even know. I was so taken aback that for some reason I was apprehensive about letting him ride her. She was being such a bitch—I guess I thought he'd get mad at her and beat her up or something. I sort of followed him around where he rode as if to take her back. I'd started to protest when he was getting on, but he'd ignored me. When he saw me still in the arena when he was riding her, he turned on me, stopped the horse dead, and said 'Out!'" Peter laughed. He seemed delighted with the memory.

"Did you go?"

"I sure did, like a whipped dog! I didn't know what was going on or what I was supposed to do. There were a few other people watching, and I felt like a damned fool. He only rode her for a few minutes—I think he just trotted her around in a few schooling figures—and then he rode over to where I was standing by the side, dismounted and told me to get on her again. At this point the steward was getting a bit uptight, the next class was due to start. But I did get back on—I didn't have much choice. He told me to ride her around the arena.

"She felt different from the minute I got on her, much more attentive, somehow, but she began gaining speed, and Erik said, 'Put your legs on the horse's sides.' I guess I looked at him as if he were crazy. I felt as if she'd go right off into space if I used my legs. 'Do as you are told,' he said, and I did. She *slowed down*. It was incredible. She felt light as a feather, and I saw him give a sort of smile and wave me out of the ring."

"Did you win anything?"

"Are you kidding? I came in dead last. I got threes and fours on every movement. But his comments were terrific. I still have that test sheet; I've practically memorized it. On the first movement—where you enter and move down the centerline—he'd said, 'The gladiators enter the arena, already at odds.' And later, at the end of the test, he'd written, 'When two warriors contend, only one will prevail. The horse has done so in this test. A performance that should have been music was merely noise.' How about that?"

Ivan emerged from the bathroom and sat down on his bed.

"I was telling him about the first test I rode for Erik," Peter said. "There was one place, a trot circle, I think, where he'd simply said, 'If the test had called for the shape of an egg, this might have been sufficient', and at a disastrous transition to canter, 'The horse explodes, abandoning the rider'." He shook his head.

"He gave Kestrel a seven on 'Gaits' in the Collective Marks, and me as rider a four with the comment 'The rider remained in the saddle throughout the test'. And under 'Submission' he'd given a three and written '3 for the horse, 7 for the rider'. That stung a bit! It was funny to see all his comments on the test written in the polite, neat handwriting of his scribe, and then his own handwriting on the Collective Marks in black ink. It was only when I got home and read the test sheet again that I saw he'd written over onto the back of the sheet, 'The horse has talent and, despite this performance, so does the rider'.

"I thought about that test a lot. I'd never seen comments like that, and somehow they made a lot of sense. They sort of captured my problems with Kestrel in a nutshell. So I started asking around about Erik. No one where I lived had ever heard of him. I finally tracked down the show organizer, and she gave me his phone number and told me he lived in Northwood. I tried to call him, but I couldn't ever get an answer, so I drove over one day and asked around until someone told me how to get here."

"What happened?"

"When I came up here? Well, it was different, that's for sure. The indoor school wasn't built yet. The riding ring was just a field with a few boards on the ground to mark off the size of a dressage arena.

"I'd been working at a stable near home—lots of riders coming in and out, cars parked all over, kids hanging out, coke machine in the tackroom, people cowboying around everywhere. The horses at that place never got out to speak of; there was no pasture, only a small field of dirt and weeds. Erik's place seemed stark. No one was here, the horses were out, and Erik was mucking stalls. It was eerie.

"I walked in and said, 'Mr. Sarmento?' and he looked at me as if I were some kind of interloper who had invaded his space. I blurted out who I was and asked if he gave lessons. He said he did, and I asked how much it would cost. He named a figure that was way out of my price range. I kept Kestrel at home, and my parents paid all the expenses. We had a couple of pleasure horses—none nearly as good as Kestrel. But I'd graduated from high school, and I didn't want to ask them for money. They were nice about the horse, but they weren't real happy to have a kid who was nothing but a stall mucker and didn't want to go on to college or get what they thought was a decent job. So on the spur of the moment I asked if I could work for him. He said yes, but he wouldn't pay me a cent, just room and board for the horse and myself. So that's what I did."

Now, in the kitchen, Michael glanced covertly at Erik and saw him rise to his feet. "There is a horse arriving tomorrow afternoon," he said. "Mrs. Hughes removes her horse today after her lesson. Ivan, strip the stall and wash it down. Rebed it tomorrow morning. Wash out the water and feed tubs and replace the salt block. Michael, prepare Mrs. Hughes' horse for her to ride and see that her tack is clean. After the lesson you will assist me."

"Doing what?"

Erik ignored him and turned to Peter. "A customer is coming at three with Miss Stewart to look at her horse, Crystal. That is your responsibility. You will ride him if the owner does not wish to do so."

"*Stewart?*" Ivan said incredulously. "She's selling her horse?" But he, too, received no answer. Erik was already on his way to the barn.

The farrier had already arrived and started to work. His truck with its portable forge and anvil was backed up to the open door, the tailgate down. Orion stood cross tied in the aisle. Peter and Ivan stopped to greet him. Michael stayed in the background. The smith tossed the worn shoe he had just removed into the base of his toolbox, looked up and grinned at them. He held the horse's foot cradled in one hand and casually brushed off the surface of the sole with the other, then reached for his pincers and began to clip away the excess hoof wall.

"What do you do to this horse to wear his shoes out like this, eh?" he said with a wink at Ivan. He pointed to the old shoe. "Wore the groove clean off the shoe." He tossed the pincers aside and picked up his knife. "Hey, Pete," he said conversationally, and Michael glanced over at Peter. No one called him Pete. "Where's your mare? I was going to start with her, but you got her hidden somewhere."

"No, she's gone. She had a bad case of colic. We had to put her down." He spoke without resentment, and Michael felt an unreasonable anger at him. The smith dropped Orion's foot gently and straightened. "No kidding? Say, that's a shame. Nice mare, too."

Erik appeared from the tackroom. "Do I pay you," he said to the smith, "to waste your time in idle conversation with the stable help when there are five horses to be shod?"

The farrier bent quickly and picked up Orion's foot again.

"Ah, Erik," he said quietly, "you're a one, you are. You'll kill us all with work one of these days."

Later Michael watched Mrs. Hughes lead her horse into the indoor school, and when he saw Erik follow her, he returned to where the farrier was working. He was a stocky, cheerful man with tight curly hair and an open, freckled face. Glancing up, he caught Michael's eye and grinned. "You're new then, eh?"

"I've been here about three months."

"Must have missed you the last time I was out. How d'you like working for Erik?"

"It's a job."

The smith straightened. "Name's Will," he said. "What's yours?"

"Michael."

"He's done, then." He gave Orion a slap on the rump. "Who's next?"

"The Phoenix, I guess. I'll get him for you." Michael turned Orion into his stall and brought The Phoenix out. "How long you been shoeing for him?" he asked.

"One way or another, since I was a boy." Will smiled at the horse and put his hand on his withers for a moment. "I learned from my old man when this fellow was a baby himself." He laughed. "Yes, I been shoeing horses since I was twelve and helped my dad, and I learned a couple of things, I did." He began to remove The Phoenix's shoes. "Two things," he repeated. "Get it right the first time, and don't argue with Erik." He smiled happily at his own wit and worked quickly, talking as he did so.

"I wasn't much for schooling, but I learned those two things all right, the one from my dad and the other from your boss. I was about fifteen when Erik came to us, and I thought I knew horses pretty good. I didn't get to drive nails, just handed my dad his tools, kept the forge fired up good, and sometimes leveled a foot here or there or pulled a shoe. I figured I'd practice on The Phoenix, here. We raised him, you know. He was kind of a member of the family. Your boss had just come to live with us then, and I'd hardly spoke two words to him—not much of a talker, Erik—and he come on me that day fooling with this fellow's feet, and by God he reamed me out, he did."

Michael smiled bleakly. "Oh, yeah? What'd you do?"

"Well, I said to myself, 'Who the hell's this son of a bitch to give me orders on my dad's place?' I told him where he could go and waved my rasp at him, and before I knew what was happening he knocked me ass-backwards over the anvil and busted my arm."

He stood up straight, grinned at Michael and gave The Phoenix an affection-
ate pat on the rump. "I tell you I was right thick as a youngster. I give a yell, and
my dad come running. Know what he did?" Michael shook his head. "Hauled me
right off to the woodshed and whaled the living tar out of me, busted arm and all,
and *then* took me to the doctor. And I learned, by God, I sure did. Never argue
with Erik!" Grinning, he shook his head. "There's others," he added, "don't have
to bust an arm to learn that lesson."

Michael stirred and glanced over his shoulder. "What did he say?"

"What?"

"Erik. What did he say?"

"He never said a thing. Ain't said he was sorry yet, though I been waiting fifteen years to forgive him." He chuckled and wiped his forehead with his sleeve. "I
ain't anxious to bust another arm—" He paused to turn a shoe in the forge with
his tongs. "He's OK, Erik—long's you don't cross him."

The smith's words made Michael uncomfortable. In his mind he had often
clashed physically with Erik and had savored the release of hitting him, hurting
him, knocking him down. Sometimes in these fantasies he was on horseback, and
the horse somehow expanded his strength so that he was faster, stronger, invinci-
ble, while Erik stood unhorsed below him, weak and at his mercy. But even with
all his concentration he couldn't carry his daydream to a conclusion. The end of
the story faded to nothing before him, and like the man who rides the tiger and
cannot dismount, he saw no way to end the battle without himself becoming its
victim.

He took Mrs. Hughes' horse when she returned to the barn after her lesson
and, still half-absorbed in thought, went through the expected routine: cooled
out the horse, brushed him down, and ran a damp sponge over the tack. At the
owner's direction, he blanketed the horse, led him out past the blacksmith's truck
to her trailer, and began wrapping his legs in shipping bandages.

"—appreciate it more than I can tell you," Mrs. Hughes was saying to Erik. "I
can't thank you enough. I feel a lot more confident. There were times when I
thought I'd bitten off more than I could chew with this one."

"Yes, he is distractible. You must remind him occasionally where to turn his
attention."

"Well, at least now I have the tools to do so." She was holding the end of the
lead shank while he worked, and Michael felt her watching him and glanced at
Erik.

"You think I should continue with the longeing before I ride?" Mrs. Hughes
was asking. Skillfully, Michael wrapped the last of the four bandages down over

the horse's heels and back up the leg. He took the safety pins from between his teeth where he held them and started pinning.

Erik said, "Yes. You will reinforce your dominance over the horse from the ground. The influence will carry over when you ride. You need not keep him on the line for long—just until you have his undivided attention." There was an imperceptible pause, and he added, "Some horses, like some people, require constant repetition of that lesson."

Michael's face went white. He stood up suddenly and turned on Erik. "What the hell does that mean?"

Mrs. Hughes looked startled, and Erik's eyebrows went up. "Were you included in this conversation?" he inquired, and Michael's resolve faltered as quickly as it had flared. He turned abruptly to the trailer and began to lower the tailgate. Mrs. Hughes gave an embarrassed laugh and looked at Erik. If he understood her unspoken question, he didn't bother to answer it. "Load the horse," he said to Michael and watched him obey with an expression that seemed half amused but contained an element of aggression that only Michael recognized.

In the shadows of the barn, Michael could hear the blacksmith whistling tunelessly to himself as he worked. He took the horse from Mrs. Hughes and led him onto the trailer, tied him and secured the tailgate. When she had driven away, Michael followed Erik warily into the barn.

Lyrik stood in the aisle. She was a tall mare, almost seventeen hands, fine-boned and delicate for her size. She was bobbing her head rhythmically up and down in the crossties, but she stood without moving her feet. Michael put his hand on her nose, and she flattened her ears momentarily and then gazed innocently at him. He smiled, suddenly and inexplicably cheered.

Erik had stopped beside the horse. "Your father, is he well?" he said to the smith.

"He does right good for a man with a bad heart. He can still shoe a horse pretty good, but he tires easy—know what I mean?"

Will dropped Lyrik's foot and straightened up slowly. He rubbed his lower back absently with his right hand. "He asks after you every time I come out, and after The Phoenix. He likes that horse."

Michael saw Erik nod. "Yes," he said and turned to Michael. "Get me a leadshank, a longeline and a dressage whip."

By the outdoor ring Erik took a halter from the nail where it was hung outside the fence and opened the gate. "Come," he said to the horse, and Tango approached him and stood to be haltered.

"Did you teach him that?" Michael asked.

"It is I who care for him," Erik said. "I could speak to him in Greek, and he would come to me." He snapped the leadshank to the halter, tossed the end of the longeline over the horse's back and reached to bring it under Tango's belly like the girth on a saddle. He dropped the snap end through the hand loop to form a kind of slipknot and brought it up between the horse's front legs and through the halter ring. The excess line he held coiled in his hand.

"Lead the horse to that post," he said, indicating the gate post, "and tie him up."

"I thought he didn't tie," Michael said uncertainly.

"He is about to learn."

As Michael started to tie the horse, Erik snubbed the longeline around the post, still holding the end in his hand. Tango stood quietly, apparently unaware of the restriction.

"Put your hand on his chest and ask him to step back."

Gingerly, Michael moved the horse back. When the rope was taut against the halter, Tango suddenly panicked and flung his weight back on his haunches. Erik shortened the longeline around the post and the line tightened in a noose around his shoulders.

Michael sprang away. He watched the horse in a mixture of fascination and a painful kind of empathy. In confusion Tango leaped forward and then swung his hindquarters to the side. He hurled his head viciously from side to side, crouched, but was apparently unwilling again to test the line around his girth. Erik patted him on the neck but in the next instant raised the whip in front of his face and sent him violently backwards against the restraining line. Again he jumped forward and crouched, shaking, and again Erik put his hand on his neck and spoke quietly to him. He raised the whip again. Tango had broken a sweat, but he didn't move.

"Fetch that bucket of grain and offer it to him," Erik said, but he didn't seem surprised when Tango refused it.

Michael heard his own heart pounding in his ears and felt weak. He put the bucket down and leaned for a moment on the railing of the fence.

"Untie him, and lead him across the ring," he heard Erik say. "If he resists, yield the line immediately and ask by tugging gently. Tie him to the post over there." He walked beside the horse, the longeline still in his left hand, the other on Tango's neck.

The scene was repeated at several different places in the ring. Michael was given the whip and told to touch the horse on the legs, the belly, the back and hindquarters. Tango tried the longeline one more time and lashed out viciously at the whip with both fore and hind legs. The lesson continued until the horse succumbed and stood trembling. Erik told Michael to fetch a towel and rub him down. Tango didn't move.

Erik sent for the blacksmith and pointed to the horse. "Trim him," he said. "We will not bother with shoes for the moment."

Michael saw Tango's eyes roll. He stood with Erik's reassuring hand on his neck, his hind legs slightly under him as if he were about to back up.

"He give me a fit the last time around," Will said dubiously. "You going to stay here and help me deal with him?"

"Do your job," Erik said, but Michael thought he seemed pleased at the smith's hesitation. The blacksmith grinned sheepishly and ran his hand down Tango's front leg. "You're the boss," he said, and tugged at the leg. But the horse refused to pick up his foot.

Michael said, "What's the matter with him? He's always picked up his feet before. In fact, I never saw a race horse who wasn't completely used to farriers."

"He has learned a lesson," Erik said, "and he has learned it thoroughly. To move is to cause oneself pain, and the safest course is not to move. We must now teach him what the limitations of that lesson are."

But it was several minutes before Tango allowed his leg to be bent and raised, and then, on three legs, he again hurled himself backward. Erik spoke sharply to him and again he leaped forward. He tore his leg from the smith's grasp and almost knocked him down. Erik said a soothing word and patted him. Before long, persuaded, he raised his foreleg on command. But Will had the same trouble again with his hind leg. It seemed frozen to the ground, and he raised it finally only to kick savagely at the smith, who crowded his haunches in self-defense.

"Jesus Christ!" Michael said. "Get the hell out of the way!"

"Not on your life!" Will said in a strained voice. "Step away and you get nailed twice as hard. He can't get much force into that kick with me right next to him."

Erik had spoken sharply to the horse at his disobedience, and when again he lashed out, responded with the whip across his haunches. Will ducked as Tango leaped forward toward the fence, both lines now slack.

"Christ, Erik—have a heart!" he said and bent again to try the hind foot. The horse was not allowed to rest until by repetition, punishment and reward he had finally capitulated. Immobile, he picked up his feet without resistance. Erik untied him, removed the halter, and pushed him gently away from his position at the fence. When the horse had taken a few tentative steps on his own, he called him again. Michael was astonished to see Tango, ears forward, walk up to him.

"He's got to be nuts!" he said disparagingly. He identified himself in some way with Tango and wished he would disobey. The scene had amazed him, and yet it filled him with a vague sorrow. He was aware that he didn't want to see Tango surrender.

Erik laughed. "Hardly," he said. "The horse is clever."

"Clever! He should hate your guts, not ask for more."

"That is exactly what he does—avoids asking for more," Erik said and put the halter back on. He led the horse to the gate, tied him again to the post and offered him grain. Tango plunged his head into the bucket.

Michael watched Erik with revulsion. He hated him. "Can I go now?" he asked coldly.

"No, there is further work to be done."

Michael felt curiously weak. He was told to lead Tango from the enclosure. Erik took the longeline and ran it through the ring on one side of the halter, over the horse's head, and snapped it to the ring on the other side. He tightened the noseband of the halter and said to Michael, "Lead him into the barn."

"Into the barn? Will he go?"

"He will do as he is asked."

"How do you know that?"

"Because I will require it."

"Bullshit!" Michael said under his breath in disgust. He struggled with a rising anxiety. He heard Erik call Ivan and Peter and direct them to bring another length of rope. Michael looked from one to the other. They took up their positions behind the horse, one on either side. The rope stretched between them like a barrier. Erik, on the off side at Tango's head, held the longeline loosely folded in his right hand, the whip in his left.

Michael, on the near side with the leadshank, led the horse toward the rear entrance to the barn. His head was light, and his heart hammered in his chest. He felt he was becoming deaf. The sounds around him came from a great distance, and he had the illusion he was leading the horse to some fearful destination on a treadmill he couldn't stop. The barn seemed endless miles away and he struggled toward it, his legs leaden and reluctant. "It's only to the barn," he heard himself say in a whisper, partly to the horse, partly to himself.

Tango halted suddenly and Michael, unprepared, fell forward. He saw Tango go up, arching over him, a huge, dark shape, and for a moment caught sight of Erik's face. Michael staggered sideways away from the striking hooves, and Erik leaned against the longeline and jerked the horse down. Peter and Ivan had moved up on either side, and the rope they held creased the horse's haunches above the hocks.

Tango began to fight frantically, and Erik loosed the line and struck him on the croup. Each forward step, however reluctant, however accidental was rewarded with a loosened line and a quiet "Yes—" from Erik, and each time Tango reared he was punished uncompromisingly with the longeline pressing on his sensitive poll. Twice he stopped dead, shaking, and accepted Erik's soothing hand on his neck, only to erupt again in panic.

Michael's panic matched Tango's. He stared, paralyzed, at Erik, horrified by the horse's struggle and what seemed to be a light of combat in Erik's eyes, an almost savage elation.

Tango began grunting, great strangled, incoherent sounds that pierced Michael's heart. He heard himself echoing the horse and was suddenly sick to the very source of his being, nauseous and dizzy. He dropped the shank and doubled over and as suddenly Tango gave up and walked into the barn. Michael sagged to the ground in his wake, sick to his stomach, driven to his knees.

CHAPTER 14

▼

Kristen sat at the table in her small living room and stared at its littered surface. It was late in the evening, and she was trying to compose a letter to her brother, but couldn't seem to concentrate. His most recent letter to her lay on the table together with an assortment of books, a slender vase of flowers, an empty teacup and saucer and her writing pad.

Despite the hour it was hot, and the air was humid and still. She tilted back in her chair, put her hands behind her head and stretched. Then she dropped the chair to the floor, stood up, and, walking to the door, flung it open and stepped outside. Erik was standing on the steps.

Kristen gave a small involuntary gasp and caught the edge of the screen door with her hand. Her eyes opened wide, and her heart began racing. "Erik—" she said weakly, and felt an onslaught of conflicting emotions that ranged between sudden fear, relief, and anger at herself for being caught off guard.

Erik stood motionless halfway up the steps, clad incongruously in jeans and a ragged denim jacket. He stared moodily at her. After several seconds in which Kristen looked helplessly to either side, she let the screen door close behind her and leaned against it. Only then, feeling exposed on her own front porch, did it occur to her to wonder what he was doing there in the middle of the night.

Erik came slowly up the rest of the steps and stopped a few feet away. "Are you alone?" he asked.

"Yes," she answered weakly and then with more confidence, "Of course I'm alone—what'd you expect? It's almost midnight."

He said nothing more, and they stood looking at each other over the few feet of intervening space until Kristen relented and, reaching behind her, opened the screen door.

"Come in," she said in a low voice, and when there was no answer, "Erik? Do you want to come in?" She led the way into the house and gestured to a chair. "You scared me," she said, still feeling shaken. It was true. He still scared her with his brooding stance, his solemn, unkempt appearance, and she was relieved when he sat down.

"Erik—have you been drinking?" she asked. When he only looked back at her with his dark, somber eyes, she said, "I'm sorry. It's very late, and I didn't expect—would you like something to eat? Tea?" and she thought, why do I always apologize? Erik shook his head.

Kristen sighed. She was still standing uncertainly, her hands on the back of a chair that she kept between herself and Erik. She said, "You *are* drunk, aren't you?" But she had never seen him drunk.

"I have been drinking, yes," he said finally. "I haven't been fortunate enough to get drunk—in the sense you mean."

Kristen went into the small kitchen alcove, put the kettle on, and then turned and leaned against the doorjamb. "What's happened? Why have you come here?" she asked with misgiving.

It had been almost three months since she had left him, and with the exception of her one disastrous visit to the farm, of which he was still unaware, she had neither seen nor heard from him. She started to say so and thought better of it. She realized that her hands were trembling and slipped them into the rear pockets of her jeans.

Erik moved impatiently in his chair and looked around him. "Jan has been gone for a long time," he said as if he hadn't heard her. "I owe him a debt, and I can't repay it. I knew at the time I couldn't, but I wasn't aware that I would increase it over the years until it became intolerable for us both—"

"A debt? What debt? What are you talking about?" The kettle began to whistle maddeningly from behind her and she reached around, pulled it abruptly off the flame, and began to make tea. She glanced sideways at Erik with growing uneasiness.

"All those years since we were children—especially those years—"

"You mean because he helped you run away? After the fire?"

He made a dismissive gesture. "No, I am speaking of my survival."

"You *are* drunk," Kristen said again almost in a whisper, and she put a cup of tea beside his chair and retreated again to the doorway.

Erik went on as if he were talking to himself. He wasn't even looking at her. "With Jan's help I achieved a certain independence. I still struggle to control my life, and sometimes I feel I've succeeded. I have the horses—they are a kind of salvation. I have authority over those who work for me, and for a time I thought I had you—"

"I'm not a horse," she said stiffly and felt her eyes filling with tears in spite of herself. "You have no authority over me, and I'm certainly not part of any debt you owe Jan. He doesn't own me either."

He didn't seem to have heard her. Kristen turned away. Angrily she tried to blink away the tears. She found a Kleenex in the kitchen and blew her nose. After a moment she drew a deep breath and moved purposefully to a worn armchair where she sat down and drew her legs up under her, curled up like a cat, as if to protect herself. She looked up to find Erik watching her.

"What do you want?" she said in a choked voice.

"As I have said, I thought I had control of my life, and yet lately I have felt my control over myself eroding. I am not sure I can predict my own actions."

Kristen's heart tightened in her chest. In her mind as clearly as if she were watching a film in slow motion, she saw Erik pull Michael from The Phoenix's back onto the ground. She took a deep breath and managed to say, "What have you done?"

"Did I say I had done something?"

Kristen sighed. "Not exactly."

"Some time ago, shortly after you left, a man who claimed to be a friend of Von Tauber came to see me. He brought with him a horse, which he left with me. It was Wotan."

Involuntarily Kristen raised one hand to her face. Her eyes widened.

"The horse was very old, thirty at least, and he had been ill-used. He died today." Erik said quietly.

It was a moment before Kristen understood him, and when she did her sympathy for him was tempered by a guilty sense of relief. Her fears were groundless, and all that he had needed was someone to talk to. She said, "Oh, Erik—I'm so sorry—" but although her lips moved, she spoke soundlessly. The words refused to come out.

"I am sure it was painless, possibly a heart attack or a ruptured blood vessel," Erik went on. "I don't suffer for him, only for the years he was away from me. I doubt most horsemen ever know a horse like that. I was incredibly fortunate to have had such a teacher. I see him in The Phoenix at times, but he had something

The Phoenix does not, some kind of independence or challenge that made his performance seem to be of his own volition, and I to be privileged to share it."

He paused, gazed intently at her and leaned forward in his chair. "Wotan," he said again. "Do you remember when he came? No, of course not, it was before we lived on your farm, before I met Jan. I cannot remember where Von Tauber found him. He was a three-year-old, unbroken." He sighed and then suddenly smiled. "He was a big horse, with a big heart. And he was difficult—very. I was ten at the time. I hadn't had to deal before with such a challenge.

"The first time I rode him—despite the hours of longeing, the handling, the work in long reins—he threw me repeatedly—six, seven, eight times. And then before I could gain my feet, he charged me and bit me. He lifted me off the ground with his teeth in my shoulder, shook me and flung me aside like a terrier tosses a rat. Had I had the choice, I suspect I would have crawled to the nearest corner to lick my wounds. But Von Tauber was as relentless as the horse. We worked with him for four hours without rest. The horse was staggering with fatigue, and I could barely control my arms and legs."

Kristen was mesmerized. "What happened?" she asked.

"He gave up. I rode him each day, and each day at some point he had me off." He laughed. "He was a great deal stronger than I. It was two more years before I began to grow into him. But I was very fond of him. He was like a reflection of myself, and I understood him. I began to be aware of his potential, and he taught me to ride, that horse."

He paused, looked down at the cup in his hands, and drank his tea, now cold. Listening to him, Kristen was reminded that she had never heard Erik speak of his father except by his proper name, as if by that formal address he could distance himself and deny the relationship.

"When suddenly we understood each other," Erik went on, "there was almost nothing we couldn't do. I was forced to show him many times. You were a small child, and I suppose you don't remember. Many, many times. Those exhibitions, they were my worst nightmare. It wasn't the riding—I could forget during the performance—it was the awakening when it was over and we stood for the salute, and I had somehow to bear the applause, the people, the questions, and Von Tauber. One is very vulnerable after such an experience." He glanced up to meet Kristen's eye and added, "You understand? To have it over is like dying."

Kristen nodded. She couldn't speak for fear the tears would come again, and sat helplessly, stricken by his words.

Erik sighed. "Age and illness take horses," he said thoughtfully, "as they do men. It was the horse who was my father, not the man."

Kristen tried to remember Von Tauber, but had only a vague memory of a huge figure and couldn't remember the context in which she had seen him. Or had she ever seen him? She remembered only Jan's bitter description of Erik's wary attentiveness and stoic silence in his father's presence, of Von Tauber's silky, suggestive voice and his sudden, terrifying rages. Jan had spoken of his correct, almost archaic English. Erik's speech still echoed its inflections, he had told her, although he didn't have his father's accent. She had seen for herself the hidden scars that Erik bore to this day, and yet he had never mentioned those years to her, and she had never asked.

Now, thinking of her own carefree childhood, she said, "How old were you when your father began to treat you like that?"

There was a moment's silence before he answered her. He frowned. "I cannot remember."

"Even when you were very little?"

"Especially then. Subtler forms of torment he saved until later. I thought we had agreed to forget what is past."

"I know you said that," she answered, "but I can't."

Erik got up suddenly and walked over to the window. He leaned his hands on the sill and stood motionless with his back to her. "Very well," he said in a muffled voice, "I have observed you long enough to know you must have your questions answered. This is not my favorite topic of conversation—I don't share my life easily. But if you must, ask me your questions and we will have done with it."

He turned around and, still standing, answered her questions factually and without emotion. It was his cool dispassionate acceptance of what he related that she found the hardest to bear.

"What about your mother? Didn't she try to protect you?"

"She was not a brave woman. She was afraid of him."

"He beat her, too?"

"Sometimes. But I believe it was I he hated, not her. If he mistreated her it was to punish me. I kept away from her for just that reason. I didn't care to see my mother beaten."

Kristen stared at him. He seemed perfectly composed. "How did you survive?" she asked. "How did you learn to ride?"

"He taught me to ride. He could no longer ride himself."

"Why not?"

"He was partially crippled. A young horse he had been training had fallen on him, and he had broken his back. And after that he became grossly overweight.

But he was a more than competent horseman, although his methods of teaching were remarkably unpleasant."

He paused and reached absently into his shirt pocket for a cigarette. "Perhaps you remember my teaching you to sit the trot? One learns to relax the muscles of the loin to allow the seat to move with the horse, and there are a number of exercises to help one learn the balance. You recall? The exaggeration of the swing, the slight shift in weight from one seat bone to the other, the mental absorption of the rhythm—"

"Yes," Kristen said.

"Another method is to place a stick across the rider's back held in place by his elbows and to tie his feet beneath the horse. A few hours in such restraint on a longeline at the mercy of the trainer's whip and one learns quickly to sit the trot and not to drop the stick, even when he is only five or six years old."

Kristen stared wordlessly down at her lap. Moments passed. Finally she said, "I don't understand how you can even look at a horse now—"

"That is the irony, because with the horses he gave me the key and, in a sense, salvation. Perhaps he would turn in his grave if he knew that. It was the one thing we had in common. He was an extremely knowledgeable horseman. He could read a horse like a book and was rarely wrong in his assessment. But he could only perform through me, and I found as I rode that I could learn from the horse what was required and avoid some of the consequences of his anger. He was never brutal to them. It was me he despised, perhaps because in spite of himself he needed me."

For a moment Erik was silent, and then he said suddenly, "The horses—there is no better creature to model oneself upon. They were unconcerned with him. They didn't complain. They forgave me whatever I might do to them in my innocence, my ignorance. And they had not my weakness—they didn't weep or plead or despair. They somehow kept their independence, although we had taken much of their freedom. It was only as I became older that I understood that, as a rider, I could add to that freedom, and I could share that strength."

In spite of the heat Kristen felt cold. Still very close to tears, she got up and went into the kitchen to make herself another cup of tea. The hour was beginning to catch up with her, and she had a slight headache. She stood by the stove trying to compose herself, at the mercy of ambivalent feelings about Erik's visit.

"Erik?"

"Yes—"

"Your mother left your father, didn't she?"

"Yes."

"She left you, too. How could she leave you there?"

"She had no choice. She wanted me to go with her, and I could not."

"But why?"

"I couldn't leave the horses," he said. "She couldn't provide them for me, and I needed them more than I needed her."

"What an awful thing to say—"

"It is the truth. I was relieved to have her gone. She caused me a great deal of pain, and it was a pain I couldn't defend myself against."

"Have you seen her since?"

"No."

"You never tried to find her?"

"No."

"Why?"

"Why? For the same reason I don't believe she has looked for me. I doubt if either needs to be reminded of what each allowed the other to suffer at his hands."

"But it wasn't the fault of either of you."

He didn't answer her. She stood at the counter and sipped her tea. Without looking up she said, "I guess it must have been a relief in a way when your father died."

"Yes."

She went back to her chair and again curled up in it. Its large overstuffed arms and back embraced her. She said, "I don't remember that night—I was asleep, but Jan told me about it and how they couldn't put the fire out because the well went dry and it was the only water source. And he was frantic because he thought you had been killed too."

"Yes."

"How *did* you escape?"

The silence that followed her question was so long that she wondered if he had heard her, and she looked over at him. He seemed to be assessing her, and at length he sighed.

"I didn't escape," he said. "I set the fire."

"*What?*"

"I set the fire. It was the day Wotan was sold, a day in early October. I remember clearly how cold it was, overcast and frigid. Von Tauber sold the horse for a song, and he must have been worth a fortune. He did it to hurt me, and he didn't want to wait for a buyer. There was almost no demand for dressage horses back then. But he didn't tell me he had done it until the trailer drove into the yard. He gave me no warning, no time to prepare myself.

"He brought Wotan from the stall and ordered me to bandage him for the journey. I had wrapped the horse a hundred times before, and yet it took forever. My hands shook so that I kept dropping the bandages and having to start over. Von Tauber made me put the horse on the trailer, although he could have done it himself. In fact the horse trusted me, and he loaded himself while I stood at the ramp and could hardly release the leadshank. When I went to the side door to tie him, Von Tauber pushed me away and did it himself. He wouldn't let me say goodby to him, or even put my hand on his neck. I was never to ride him again."

Erik lapsed into silence. Glancing up, Kristen saw him staring fixedly not at her but somewhere behind her. For several seconds neither of them spoke, and then Erik straightened and in a voice that was edged with bitterness went on, "I watched the trailer drive away. I couldn't move. And when Von Tauber called me back into the barn to do the evening chores, I looked at Wotan's stall where the door stood open into the aisle, and I no longer wanted to live.

"Von Tauber told me then why he had sold the horse. He said it was to teach me humility and self-discipline. It was a weakness to form an attachment to an animal, he said, and then he laughed.

"I turned around, and I hit him. He fell like a stone onto the concrete floor of the aisle and struck his head. I knew he was dead even before I went to look. I knew he was dead because I wanted him dead. I dragged him to the house and went back to the barn to finish the chores. Later, when it was very late, I set the fire."

Kristen watched him. She said nothing for there was nothing she could say. She didn't doubt the truth of the story and if she was surprised it was at her own numb acceptance. She felt only a deep sorrow for Erik and, for reasons she didn't wholly understand, for herself.

"I have asked myself again and again if I intended to kill him when I struck him," Erik went on. "I still don't know the answer. I think probably I did, at that point. I certainly never regretted it for I had so often wished him dead. On the contrary, I felt only astonished at my good fortune, and uncertain what to do with it." Suddenly he laughed. "When I lived at Estep's, I often rode by an old house where there was a dog chained in the yard. He used to charge to the end of his chain and rage at me as I passed. One day when he was doing so the chain broke. The dog didn't know what to do with his freedom. He ran aimlessly about with no thought of attacking the horse and finally went back to his doghouse and lay down. I had something in common with that dog." Kristen stirred in her chair.

"If I feel remorse at all," Erik added, "it is that Jan was forced to be an accomplice in an act that repelled him, and now, perhaps, that I have involved you."

Kristen shook her head. "Never mind," she said quietly. "I'm glad you told me. It was a long time ago and you were just a boy. I know you didn't mean it to turn out like that." She looked up at him and smiled. A warm feeling of forgiveness suffused her. He seemed to read her mind.

"I do not need to be forgiven," he said harshly, "for that."

"What do you mean?"

"Haven't you noticed that once an act is performed, no matter how difficult, it becomes easier to perform that act? I see it every day in my horses and also in my students—"

"Don't be silly," Kristen said uncertainly. "Do you really think of yourself after all this time as a potential murderer?"

"The man is dead. He was, however, my father, although I would give a great deal to deny it, and although he is gone, I cannot kill that part of him that is within me."

Kristen put her hand out slowly as if to shield herself. In her shock she watched Erik's face and felt a tangible, empathetic pain. Although the corners of his mouth were turned down, she had the impression he was smiling.

"One faces the truth," he said, "regardless of the consequences."

He regarded her with a quizzical expression, and under his eye she began to feel a nagging anxiety, which was close to fear. "What's happened?" she asked, speaking more to herself than to him.

Erik drew a deep breath and sighed. He walked with a weary step to the kitchen and poured himself another cup of tea. "I have a grey horse that was brought to me for retraining. I have been keeping him in the outdoor ring for some time. Today I have confronted him with the assistance of Michael, my new stable hand. He refused to be tied; we tied him. He fears enclosed spaces; we brought him into the barn and put him into a stall."

"Without trouble?" Kristen asked. She remembered the horse restlessly pacing the fence line as she stood at the rear door of the arena.

"No, not without trouble. It was necessary to subdue him."

"But it was successful? He's all right?"

"The horse is fine. It is Michael, I am afraid, who suffers."

"He got hurt?"

"In a sense," Erik said obliquely. "I made him assist me. He did so, but with reluctance. He released the shank at the last moment, and it was only by good luck that the horse was unaware of it, although I still had the longeline over his head."

"Oh—Erik," Kristen said. "You didn't lose your temper—"

"I am afraid so. Had the horse won at that moment, a great deal would have been lost."

"What did you do to him?"

"When the horse was secure, I went back to find Michael. He was on the ground outside the barn. He looked quite ill. I was very angry. I ordered him to his feet."

Kristen tried to master a hopeless sense of foreboding.

"Didn't you think the horse might have injured him?"

"I didn't think so, and if I had, it would have made no difference. I was concerned only that he had jeopardized the horse." Erik looked down at the cup in his hand. He spoke quietly without emotion, but Kristen saw vividly what must have ensued.

"He did not get up at once. He said he felt ill, and I believe he did. But I was not in the mood to be ignored, and I didn't care about his illness. I told him again to rise, and when he didn't immediately do so, I pulled him to his feet and struck him."

He looked gravely at Kristen and interrupted himself. "'The one best precept, the golden rule in dealing with a horse, is never to approach him in anger. Anger is so devoid of forethought that it will drive a man to do things which in a calmer mood he will regret'. Those are Xenophon's words.

"Michael made an effort to defend himself. In fact, he seemed ready to strike me back—an error in judgment, I'm afraid." He lapsed into silence again and gazed keenly at Kristen. "Now do you understand? I could have killed him then. He was weak and unable to protect himself, and yet I might have done so had not Will Estep interfered."

Kristen said nothing. She could feel the tears coming again and could hear a dog barking in the distance.

"I was at the house when Peter called me. He feeds the horses in the lower pasture. He told me Wotan was down, and I went immediately to him. He was dead when I reached him. I dug a trench and buried him, and then I left."

Kristen swallowed and said in a broken voice, "Where were you going? What did you plan to do?"

"In the beginning I had no plan. I felt I must leave, I must remove myself for the sake of everyone, not least myself." Erik leaned back against the doorjamb and reached behind him to put his cup on the kitchen counter. "What kind of man abuses his authority in such a fashion? I have learned today what I am capable of when I can no longer control myself, and God only knows who might be the victim the next time."

For a time Kristen stared at him. Her headache had localized behind her right eye, and both her eyes stung. She could feel dampness on her cheek, and when she brushed it away she noticed a tremor in her hand. Erik's face seemed to reflect an ineffable sadness, and she was powerless to change it.

"Is that why you came here—to tell me that?"

"Yes. And to make clear that regardless of what I would wish, I cannot have you back."

Kristen got up slowly from her chair and went to him. She put her arms around his waist and laid her head against his shoulder. His arms closed around her and held her tightly, and she felt his hand on her hair. They stood for a long moment in a silent embrace, but then he released her and held her from him. "It's late," he said. His voice was thick and barely above a whisper. "I must go." He turned from her and went quickly to the door. She was left standing by the window.

This parting was irrevocable, and Kristen knew it. There was nothing she could do to drive away the fears that haunted him or, worse, her own conviction that they might be justified.

"What about Lyrik?" she asked. "Will you take her back? I have no way to keep her." It seemed almost an irrelevant question, and yet she waited with an aching heart for his answer. She felt tied to Lyrik. The horse was part of her and connected her to Erik in a way that she couldn't describe. Together they had raised and trained her, watched her gain confidence and learn. She was the child they would never have.

But he didn't answer the question, and she thought that perhaps he hadn't heard her. Instead he said from the doorway, "Are you going to the Fair?"

"I hadn't thought—"

"Sunday afternoon," he said. "There is a dressage show. Ivan and Peter are riding. I would like you to come. I have something for you."

"All right."

"There will be time enough then to discuss Lyrik," he added to her surprise.

When he had driven away, she stood by the screen door and listened to the night sounds. Heat lightning, muted by the heavy atmosphere, flashed fitfully on the horizon. The tears she had been fighting all evening ran unheeded down her cheeks.

CHAPTER 15

▼

Michael walked aimlessly down Reed's main street. His earlier determination to visit Annie had evaporated, and he was moving in the general direction of the clinic only because he could think of nowhere else to go. When he came to the edge of the park, he stopped, leaned against the low stone wall and looked at his watch. It was a little after nine, the time of day when he would ordinarily be saddling The Phoenix, settling the saddle on the horse's back, absently checking that the pad was drawn up in the gullet of the saddle before he reached under the horse to take hold of the supple girth. Even the simple act of tacking up had opened him to Erik's criticism when he had first been assigned that task.

"For what reason do you attempt to strangle the horse?"

"What?" He was struggling to tighten the girth against the horse's resistant swelling.

"Do you think yourself stronger than he?"

"Do you want me to let the saddle slide around when I ride?"

"I want you to use your mind, if you are able. Place the girth in the first hole. Bridle the horse and raise it another hole. When you prepare to mount, you can draw the girth to its proper position without difficulty. It takes two to make a battle, perhaps you will learn that eventually. Battles are sometimes necessary, but far more rarely than you would wish, I think."

Moodily, Michael watched a stray dog sniffing at a trash can. The dog approached him with its tail low and its expression appeasing. Michael shoved him away with his foot and tried to swallow to ease the ache in his throat. He felt very lonely. He picked up a stick, fished his jackknife from his pocket and began to whittle. He let his mind drift back to The Phoenix and his rides the last couple of weeks with Peter.

Release from the confines of the indoor arena and Ivan's persistent drilling had been a joy unmatched in Michael's experience. It was early autumn, and the trees were beginning to turn color against a bright blue sky. The weather was crystal clear and cold, the sun warm and exhilarating. The Phoenix, freed from his own restrictive regime, came alive beneath him. He seemed a different horse, and in the beginning Michael had difficulty controlling him. Strangely, he didn't care. He was pleased and excited by the horse's independence.

An almost electric communication passed between them as they shared their elation. The Phoenix danced beneath him and jogged sideways up the road.

"You're holding him in too much," Peter said. "Give the rein a little and try to relax your seat."

"He's doing fine."

"He's not supposed to jig like that. You want to make him walk."

Michael laughed. "*You* want me to make him walk. I don't give a damn if he jigs."

"All right, have it your way. But make him walk." And so Peter became the sole dampening influence on Michael's euphoria. Persistently Peter kept at him. "You're restricting him again. Let him go."

"I can't help it. He just goes faster."

"When he does, use your seat and check and release with the rein. You know what to do."

Another time he said, to Michael's surprise, "When you go down a steep hill like this, lean a bit forward."

"Forward? I thought you were supposed to lean back."

"Forward. He needs his hindquarters free to use as a brake. Don't zigzag. Go straight down."

"Why?"

"It's easier for him. When you zigzag he's unbalanced. Horses don't brace sideways very well." And later, "Don't let him career around corners. Get him balanced—bend him a little."

"I thought he was supposed to be trained."

"He is. He'll do what you ask."

"I don't want to ask. I just want to ride."

They pulled up one day at a stream. Peter had been silent all morning. Now he said to Michael, "Look, you're making things really hard for me, you know that?"

"Who—me?"

"Yeah, you. This isn't a holiday, whatever you may want to think. You're supposed to be learning to ride, remember?"

"You know I can ride. Have you seen me fall off yet?"

"I don't give a shit if you fall off," Peter said. "Everyone falls off now and then. But your position's gone to hell. You're starting to ride the way you did when you came, your feet stuck out in front of you with your ankles and knees stiff as boards. Your hands are bouncing around all over the place—"

"They're not either," Michael retorted. "The Phoenix's head isn't steady."

"Why do you suppose that is?"

"Who knows?"

"I know, and you can be sure Erik does. It's your hands."

Michael stared into the stream and watched the current over the flat rock ledges. "I'm sick to death of worrying about Erik," he said finally. "This is the first time I've had any fun since I came up here. You think I'm going to let him push me around out here?"

"I thought you *wanted* to learn."

"I do, I am, but not every minute. What the hell do you ride for? It's like going to school—what's the pleasure in that?" He continued to stare moodily into the stream. "He *wants* to make me hate it, do you think I don't know that? Make me into some kind of puppet jumping around when he pulls the strings."

"You think Ivan's a puppet? Or me?"

"I only know what he does to me," Michael said stubbornly. "I don't care about anything else."

"That's pretty obvious. But it's me he gets on when you don't do what you're supposed to. You're losing your ability to analyze where you're weak, and that's the whole point of taking instruction. I'm not kidding," he added. "Your larking around has already affected the horse. Why don't you think of him for a change?"

"Don't give me that," Michael said. "He likes it."

"You're bothering his mouth, and he's beginning to resist you."

"He does what I say."

"Only because you both want the same thing at the moment. I doubt he respects you enough to do so when he wants something different from you."

Michael was set back by the remark, but he was reminded of it the next day. He had allowed The Phoenix to brush past Peter's horse on the trail and to take the lead, an irritating habit he had when the trail was narrow and he didn't want to deal with the horse's fretting in the rear.

Peter had had enough. He slowed his horse, called to Michael, and turned abruptly on to another trail toward home. He set his horse into a canter. The Phoenix, still fresh, bounced eagerly along beside him, his head even with Peter's knee. Peter increased the pace, and at length he let his horse gallop headlong down the trail. The Phoenix took off under Michael and ran away.

On the narrowing trail Michael was torn between excitement and apprehension as he saw Peter's horse move out ahead of him and eventually disappear around a bend. He couldn't stop The Phoenix, and he was less alarmed by this than by the fact that he couldn't guide him, either. Pulling with all his strength, he felt no response, only the reins being drawn inexorably through his numb fingers.

He struck the ground at speed, torn from the saddle by a tree limb before he understood what had happened. He rolled over and over automatically as Ivan had taught him, and, disoriented, his eyes shut, he was aware of flickering shadows on his eyelids from the dappled sunlight and a total, eerie silence. He got shakily to his feet and began to trudge down the trail, already rehearsing the inevitable confrontation with Erik. He was overwhelmingly relieved to see Peter, some time later, riding slowly back along the trail, leading The Phoenix. Peter looked down at him and held out The Phoenix's rein without a word. Michael took it. It was broken at the buckle, and Peter had tied it. He remounted slowly.

"You did that on purpose, didn't you?" he asked finally.

"Yes, although the fall wasn't in the script. I didn't think you'd listen to me, but I thought you might to him."

"Yeah," Michael said. "I guess so." He couldn't believe The Phoenix had done this to him.

"It's not his fault," Peter said, reading his mind. "It's yours. You did all the wrong things."

"What did I do?"

"Crouched over his neck like a jockey. What happened to the seat aids you learned? Your legs were pulled up under you so you couldn't use them, your toes went down, you began to bounce, and your reins were too long again. Now, let's make a clean start. *Ride* the horse, don't be a passenger. *Think.* Use your head. In the beginning you'll have to do lots of things that feel unnatural, later they'll become automatic."

They walked the horses down the trail in silence, and after a while Peter said, "I'm sorry. I shouldn't have done that. Erik would have my head if he knew."

"Hell, he'd have done it himself."

"I don't think so. He wouldn't do that to the horse."

"Well, I'm not about to tell him," Michael said, and he smiled at Peter. But the feeling of apprehension had remained with him as he faced a dimension in The Phoenix he hadn't known existed.

Peter did nothing to allay his uneasiness but again became his teacher, and Michael strove to do what he asked. He came in from the rides exhausted and frequently almost subdued. He no longer chafed at being able to ride only once a day, he was too tired, and Erik's workload made him more than ready for bed shortly after supper.

"Jesus, I don't know what's the matter with me," he confessed one night to Peter as he collapsed yawning on his bed.

"You're trying too hard," Peter said.

"What's that mean?"

Peter laughed. "I wish you could relax a bit. First you won't do a thing I say, and now you try to do everything at once, and then you work around the barn as if there were a fire under you—"

"You *tell* me to do everything at once, what do you expect?"

"Yeah, I know. Hard as hell, isn't it?"

Ivan came onto the room, and suddenly Michael wanted to change the subject. His back to Ivan, Peter went on, "Also, I think you're still a bit scared after the fall—" Michael saw Ivan look over at him and lost his temper.

"You're full of shit!" he said. "I'm not scared. What's there to be scared of?"

"OK—OK," Peter said. "Maybe I was wrong."

The final reckoning came a few days later when they happened to meet Erik on the trail. It was only later that it occurred to Michael that Peter must have spoken to him. He was aware of Erik's appraisal as they rode in front of him across the hilly field toward home, and he sat rigidly erect. He was scowling as he listened to Peter who, as if Erik were not there, continued to correct him. They had been practicing maintaining rhythm at various gaits over uneven ground, and Michael was having trouble cantering down hill. The Phoenix kept dropping into trot.

"You're doing that," Peter told him. "You're pulling him down."

"No, I'm not. He keeps gaining speed."

"It just seems that way because you're going down hill."

Michael knew that Erik was watching, but the harder he tried, the more ragged was the horse's performance. Finally Peter said, "Let's call it a day. You're too stiff, and The Phoenix is falling apart, too."

Erik intervened. They were less than a mile from home. He dismounted and said to Peter, "Take my horse and return to the barn."

"Yes, sir. Should Michael—"

"Michael will stay here." The Phoenix looked anxiously after the departing horses and moved restlessly. Michael waited defensively for what was to come.

"You have difficulty in cantering down hill." Erik said. "Why?"

"I don't know."

"You restrict the horse, and he slows down. What is your reasoning?"

"I'm not restricting him."

"The horse does not lie. That vice belongs only to man."

Erik reached into his shirt pocket, found a cigarette and lit it. He said nothing further, but simply waited. Finally Michael was driven to break the silence.

"All right, so I restricted him. He was going too fast."

"You have already been told that was not the case. You are afraid. Is it not so?"

"No, it's not. What's there to be afraid of?" Michael's heart was sinking.

"You are afraid you will fall off or that the horse will fall with you. Correct?"

"No," Michael said. To admit fear to Erik was a subservience he couldn't abide.

"Very well. Ride across the field to the fence row."

"You want me to canter?"

"Trot will do."

He rode to the fence line and waited for Erik to join him. Parallel to the road, the fence line bordered the pasture on the rim of a steep bank, which leveled out into the pasture and sloped gently down to the woods. Erik took down the three rails, which made up a section of the fence and gestured to the bank.

"Proceed down the drop."

Michael hesitated. "Canter down that?" he asked doubtfully.

"Walk. Put the feet a little forward with the heels down and look straight ahead." The Phoenix walked up to the bank and dropped his front legs down without hesitation. His attention was still on the horses in the distance.

"Return and repeat the exercise at trot." Michael did so. "Return again and canter."

"Canter?"

"That is what I said. Are you afraid?"

"No."

"Very well, in that case we will skip that exercise and go on to the next."

Michael watched with misgiving as Erik reinserted the lowest rail in place. "You may now canter over the fence. There is a mere three foot drop on the other side." He never took his eyes off Michael.

"I can't do that," Michael said after a moment.

"Are you afraid?"

"I told you I wasn't—"

"Then we may raise the obstacle."

Erik put the second rail in place, stepped back, and indicated the fence.

"I told you I couldn't—what do you want from me?"

"The truth will do. You say you are not afraid, and yet you cannot do what is required. Why not?"

"I don't know how."

"Shall I tell you how?"

"No. I don't want—I'm not going to."

"Shall I raise the fence?"

"No—"

"You are afraid?"

"Oh, all right. Of course I'm afraid. I told you I didn't know how—what do you expect?"

"Since you are afraid," Erik said, "we must, of course, lower the obstacle." He removed the middle rail. "Now tell me if it was also fear that made you refuse to attempt the lower obstacle?"

Michael glared at him. "Yes," he said finally.

"Very well." Erik removed the lowest rail. "And to canter over the bank—that also frightens you?"

"I guess maybe." He had given up again.

"Trot over it again." And when Michael had done so, "You felt yourself insecure?"

"A little."

"Why?"

"I don't know."

"You were afraid?"

"I don't think I was—"

"What did I tell you when you walked over the bank?"

Michael frowned. "I think—you said look straight ahead and put my feet forward."

"Correct. Why?"

"I don't know."

"Trot the obstacle again. Look down where you will land and keep the lower leg on the girth."

Michael went confidently toward the drop. The next thing he knew he was lying on his back on the ground, catapulted over The Phoenix's left shoulder. He got up slowly. The Phoenix grazed calmly a few feet away, the reins around his ears.

"That is the reason," Erik said. "If the leg is back, one has only the knee to support oneself in the landing, and if the upper body loses balance or is drawn forward by the shock, the knee acts as a pivot and drops one over the horse's shoulder as you have discovered. One rides into such an obstacle looking ahead and with the leg a little forward and the heel depressed. Do it again."

Michael did.

"Now canter the obstacle. Are you still afraid?"

"A bit," Michael admitted.

"Very well. This is how you must ride it: take the horse in a circle until you have achieved a controlled and balanced canter and come straight to the bank. With the torso a little forward, look at the barn at the end of the field and don't take your eyes from it. Put the feet forward and depress the heel. Place your weight in your heels, lightening the seat, and *do not restrict the horse*. If you do as I have said, you will not fall. If you do not, you may fall, but as you have discovered, it is unlikely you will injure yourself."

Michael stared at Erik for a long moment, but he did as he was told and, to his surprise, hardly felt the landing.

"Again," Erik said with no acknowledgement of his success. In all, he cantered the bank five times. Erik did not raise the fence again as Michael had feared he might, but replaced the rails and said merely, "Enough. We ask too much of the horse. Drop fences abuse the legs. What did you feel in this exercise?"

"Feel?" Michael said hesitantly. "I guess I was surprised not to notice it more. The landing, I mean."

"What I felt—I think my ankles. I felt my heels go down."

"And your arms?"

"My arms—I don't know. I think they sort of went up?"

"Indeed. You were attempting to fly, perhaps? An appropriate posture for a bird but hardly for a rider."

"I wasn't thinking of my arms."

"Clearly. But one doesn't ride successfully without thinking. The ankles—yes, that was quite correct. You will remember that feeling. Whenever your stirrups are shortened as they have been these last two weeks, you must feel your ankles like springs beneath you. Whenever your seat leaves the saddle to rise to the trot, to gallop or to jump, the ankle must relax to allow the heel to go down. Go back to the barn and attend to the horse's legs. The Phoenix will rest tomorrow. You can resume the next day with the canter down hill. Don't lie to me again, or to

Peter, or to yourself. Fear is dangerous, for it stiffens the joints and turns the rider rigid. You must face it to prevail over it. A rider who lies to himself will hurt himself or his horse eventually. The horse always knows—you cannot deceive him. Do you understand that?"

"Yes, sir." Michael said. He felt his face burn. Erik turned away without further comment, and Michael watched him until he disappeared into the house.

Now, rootless and idle for the first time in many weeks, Michael began to dig at a knot in the stick he was whittling. The point was still imbedded in the wood when the blade snapped suddenly in half. He flung the stick away, looked angrily at the truncated jackknife, and hurled it after the stick. For a moment he stood by the wall and contemplated the perverse sequence of events that had so casually turned against him, and then he roused himself and set off toward the center of town.

He held the newspaper ad Annie had sent him crumpled in his hand when he entered the hardware store. Mr. Elkins, the owner, was busy with a customer, and Michael busied himself examining the bins of nails. When the store was empty he moved up to the counter.

Elkins glanced up. "Oh—it's you," he said guardedly. "I thought I told you not to come in here."

"I want to buy something."

Elkins eyed him with disfavor. "With what?"

"I've got money."

"D'you steal it?"

"No, I didn't steal it," Michael said in a level voice. "I've got my own money—"

"Yeah? Since when?"

"Is this stuff for sale or not?"

Mr. Elkins didn't answer. "Who you been fighting with now?" he asked instead.

"What?"

"Your face. You're a mess."

"Thanks."

"Picked someone your own size for a change, did you?"

"Get off my back," Michael said. "I ran into a door."

Elkins laughed. "I'll bet you did," he said more gently. "What do you want?"

"Jackknife."

Elkins moved over to the glass case and unlocked it. Michael chose a jackknife and paid for it. He put the crumpled newspaper clipping on the counter. "I saw your ad in *The Courier*. You still looking for help?"

Elkins gave a derisive snort. "You? You think I'm crazy?"

"I know the stock—" Michael started, but he knew it was hopeless.

"Yeah, so I found out. You also know how to open the safe. I found that out, too."

"For Christ's sake, that was a year ago. I was going to pay you back. I *did* pay you back."

"That long?" Elkins said facetiously. "Imagine that! What you been doing for the last year?"

"Working."

"Yeah? For who?"

"On a farm."

"Fired?"

"No."

"Quit?"

"Yeah," Michael answered after a moment. "I quit."

"Well, I don't make the same mistake twice, I'll tell you that. And I'll tell you another thing, quitting a job before you have another is plain stupid. You ought to know that. Now, get out of here."

For a moment Michael cast about for something to say, but his heart was no longer in it. He turned away and headed out the door. On the street he looked bleakly around him. Utterly alone, he could think of no one who was his friend, no one who needed or trusted him. He would be unable to find work and had no place to sleep. The self-confidence that had sustained him was gone—Erik had taken it from him as he had taken his work, his energy, his independence and his pride. What did he want to do? He could think of nothing. He was used up and discarded before he had had a chance to try himself.

CHAPTER 16

▼

It was there that Ivan found him, a few minutes later. He came out of the tack shop across the street and paused for a moment, unsure of his own feelings toward Michael. But something in Michael's solitary stance caught his attention, and he crossed the street.

"Michael? Are you OK?"

Michael turned his head and looked at Ivan with a blank, abstracted gaze. Then his eyes widened, and he seemed relieved. Ivan was surprised, for the strain between them was plain to them both.

"Yeah—yeah, I'm OK," Michael said slowly as if he had just awakened. "What are you doing here? Are you by yourself?"

"I was in the tack shop. I had a lot of errands." Ivan looked at his watch. "I'm supposed to be back by twelve. You want a cup of coffee? I've only got to get the grain, otherwise I'm done."

"Sure, I guess so," Michael said.

Seated in a booth in the drugstore a few minutes later, Michael sighed and rubbed his forehead. "What'd you get?" he said finally and looked pointedly at the paper bag beside Ivan.

"Gallon of Bigeloil, fly spray, some antibiotic ointment, a couple of brushes. Brought in some repairs. Bought myself a new stock—for the show."

Michael nodded bleakly. He felt Ivan's eyes on his face and tried to cover his bruised cheek with his hand.

"What are you going to do? You going to come back?" Ivan asked.

"You kidding? I can't go back."

"Why not?"

Michael watched him warily. "You've got eyes, haven't you?"

"You mean because Erik lost his temper?"

"Lost his temper hell! He'd have killed me if he'd had the chance."

The waitress appeared with their coffee. Michael put his hands around the mug and watched the steam that lay along the surface.

"Yeah," Ivan said thoughtfully. "He was pretty mad."

At this understatement, Michael roused himself. "Pretty mad? Well, can you tell me what made him so damned mad? I didn't do anything—I don't think I did anything—" But he wasn't even certain of that.

"You dropped the shank."

"I couldn't help it. I felt lousy. Besides, so what? He was controlling the horse, not me."

"I don't think you understand—"

"You're damned right I don't! I haven't understood a damned thing since I went up there. But I know this much. He doesn't have any use for me. He never has had and he's made a point of letting me know it every time he can. He's got all the cards—"

Michael stopped, embarrassed by his outburst. Ivan stirred his coffee and drank it slowly. "You're as hooked as the rest of us, aren't you?"

"Yeah." Michael couldn't describe his misery. It was an obscure area within him, and it eluded his grasp.

"You going to get pissed off if I tell you something?" Ivan asked.

"No, I'm too damned tired to get pissed off."

Ivan laughed. "I don't know *what* got into Erik yesterday. He was sort of sour all day long. But that thing with Tango—you had the leadshank, and even though Erik was the enforcer, as far as the horse was concerned you were calling the shots. You've got to start thinking like a horse in this game. When you dropped the lead rope right when the horse was fighting, it was as if you dropped it *because* he was fighting. If he'd gotten that message, we'd have had a hell of a time with him next time."

"Well, I can't see what difference it made. He went in."

"He didn't know you'd dropped it. It was sheer luck."

For a moment Michael was silent. "He could have said that without hitting me," he muttered.

"He might have, if you'd gotten up when he told you to."

"The hell with it," Michael said.

Ivan propped his elbows on the table between them. "The thing you have to understand about Erik is that you have to do what he says. It's as simple as that. When he says stand up, you'd better damned well stand up. I think that's what made him mad."

"Would you kill someone who didn't get up when you told him to?"

"No, and I don't think he would either—"

"He would have, I tell you! You think I don't know what he did? I've been in a few fights, and I know what it's like. He wasn't kidding around."

"That's something different."

"Oh, yeah?"

"You tried to hit him back. That's what set him off." Ivan risked a quick look at Michael, who was staring moodily into his coffee mug. "He doesn't dislike you," he said very casually. "You're a bit too sensitive about that. If he did, you can be damned sure he'd have packed you off the day you came, or any day he felt like it the way he did the others—"

"What others?"

"Didn't you know there'd been others there besides us?"

"There have?"

"Hell, yes, several times. He always needs people to work, and guys come up and ask for jobs now and then. Most don't get past the no-salary part. A couple that did left a few days later—couldn't take it. Didn't like splitting wood," he added significantly. "No one expects anyone like Erik. The three of us are the only ones he's ever kept, and he doesn't compromise. If we weren't there, he'd do everything himself."

Michael stared at him.

"I remember two guys at different times, and there may have been others before that—" All at once Ivan interrupted himself. "I've got to get out of here—" He dug into his pocket for change and dropped it on the table. "Want to give me a hand with the grain?"

"OK," Michael got to his feet. "I haven't anything else to do."

At the feed mill they stacked the burlap sacks into the back of the pick-up. "Why doesn't he get this stuff delivered?" Michael asked. "It's stupid to have to run down here all the time and wrestle all these bags around."

"Not so stupid. They told him they'd have to charge him extra because we live so far out, and he told them to go to hell. Why should he care? He's got us to do the work. The horses make out the same either way, and so does Erik." Ivan jumped down from the bed of the truck and looked at his watch again. "I'm in for it. I've got to hit the road in a hurry. You coming?"

He delivered the invitation in an offhand tone, but Michael knew immediately it was intended to help him save face. He kicked the rear tire of the truck in a restless attempt to put off his answer.

"What would I do?" he tried to make himself think ahead. "I mean, when I get there, what would I do?"

"Eat crow," Ivan said impatiently. He climbed into the cab of the truck and started the engine. "Get in, for Christ's sake. What have you got to lose?" He was surprised at his own relief when Michael walked around the truck without a word and climbed in beside him. As he drove out of the yard, he glanced over at Michael and grinned. "I'll drop you off at the house," he said, "and you can get cleaned up a bit."

"What did he say when I wasn't there?"

"Nothing. I don't think he even knew you'd gone—none of us did." He told Michael about Wotan. "It was a bad afternoon all around," he said. "How *did* you go?"

"Started walking and hitched a ride with the smith when he came by. Hitched another into town—some old farmer who drove about five miles an hour."

"What'd Will say?"

"Not much. Told me I shouldn't be in such a hurry. Made some stupid excuse about Erik's temper. But I think he was a bit shook up himself." Staring out the window, Michael added, "I can't believe I'm doing this. Tell me about the others who worked up there."

"The first guy came up with his horse. He was a real superstar type and thought he was God's gift to the horse world. He really was a fair rider, but like clockwork, you know? When he finally got to ride, Erik took one look at him and just crucified him. Made fun of his clothes, his tack, his mannerisms—everything that might have impressed anyone else. The poor sucker didn't know which end was up. He made the mistake of trying a little name-dropping—the famous people who'd taught him. He only wanted Erik to admire him." Ivan laughed. "Three guesses what that got him! Erik would pretend to forget his name all the time and refer to his horse in some kind of disparaging way. Once I remember him saying, 'Of course one cannot expect too much of a Standardbred—' A Standardbred! That's a trotting horse!"

"I know what it is."

"Yeah, well, the guy drew himself up. I think he thought Erik must be really ignorant. His horse was an imported Trakehner, a nice horse, and of course Erik knew it perfectly well. You had only to look at his brand. When the guy corrected him, Erik said, 'A Trakehner?'—he was in great form and having the time of his life—'I am unfamiliar with that term. Is that some kind of western horse?'

"Peter and I were standing at the gate, almost keeling over laughing, although it was kind of excruciating in a way. The poor guy in his fancy breeches and jacket—he wore a jacket to ride every day and would go all the way up to the house to change—began giving a lecture to Erik on Trakehners, bloodlines and all. Erik's father had Trakehners—Wotan was one and The Phoenix is half Trakehner. And once he started, Erik wouldn't let him stop, just kept asking more and more detailed questions until it dawned on the guy that he'd bitten off more than he could chew.

"Erik wouldn't let him work in the barn. Probably a good thing—he was a lousy worker anyway, one of those guys who can't seem to unbend enough to get his hands dirty. He was a dead loss, and Peter and I had to work twice as hard to make sure he got his stuff done. Erik put him up on all the toughest horses, and the poor guy just fell apart. I think he must have lost ten pounds. It was terribly embarrassing. He lasted less than two weeks."

Michael shook his head. "Sounds about right," he said bitterly. "Who was the other?"

"Well, that one was even worse. The guy was servile as hell, a real ass-kisser. He was always rushing to do what Erik asked, and Erik let him. He'd give him these exaggerated compliments, which were just to make Peter and me mad. I couldn't stand him, and I don't think Peter could either, though he didn't say so. I've often thought the only reason Erik let him stay five minutes was because we felt that way.

"The guy had an electric seat—you know what I mean? He made every horse he rode go crazy, even The Phoenix. Erik noticed it at once, and one day he turned to Peter and told him to bring Kestrel out for the guy to ride. Kestrel would have killed him. She was volatile as hell and always tried out her rider. Peter just sort of turned white. I still don't know who it was Erik was trying to lean on.

"I was sorry as hell for Peter. He wouldn't look at Erik, but finally he said he wouldn't do it. I think Erik was expecting that. He told the other guy he was to be gone by lunchtime and watched him practically run out of the barn. Then he turned on Peter and let him have it. He made him bring the horse out and get on her and just tore him apart. He pointed out everything she did wrong and made Peter admit it was his fault, and then he pointed out all of Peter's weaknesses and told him that as long as the horse was in his barn he would decide who was to ride her. He made me ride her and then he rode her himself, and Peter took it and said nothing. I felt rotten. I knew exactly how he felt. I asked Peter later if he thought Erik would really have made the guy ride Kestrel, and he said no, but not because of Peter or the other guy, only because it would have been bad for Kestrel.

"Peter was pretty miserable for a couple of days, and Erik knew it and was as godawful as he could possibly be to him until Peter finally lost his cool and answered him back. It scared me—I didn't know what was going to happen, but Erik just raised his eyebrow—you know how he does—and let him off. Never said another word."

Ivan fell silent. The road in front of them was almost empty. Covertly, Michael watched his face. His eyes were dark, his eyebrows almost straight across his brow, and the planes of his face, although he was clean-shaven, were accentuated by the dark shadow of his beard. His expression was serious, almost brooding, and he stared straight ahead of him down the road.

"How'd you happen to get up there?" Michael asked, and was surprised he had never thought to ask before.

"Oh, it's a long story."

"It's a long road."

"Yeah," Ivan acknowledged, and after a moment he said, "I was a city kid. My father was Russian. Came over when he was about my age. He had a little grocery store with an apartment over it where we lived. I worked there, and so did my brothers and sisters and my mom. I didn't get on too well with my dad. He was real hard on us. He expected us—the boys—to grow up and take over the store, and none of us wanted to. We just wanted like hell to get out of the damned place.

"I was the youngest and the only one to finish high school. One of my brothers ran off and joined the army. The other went to work in a gas station and so that left me. I wanted to go to the State University. My parents got into a fight over it. I would have been the first ever in my family to go to college, which my mom thought was a big deal, but my dad thought was crazy. He said I didn't need to go to college to sell groceries, and it was a whole year before I saved enough to start.

"I didn't do well. I only went to get away, and I didn't know what I wanted to do afterward. I met this girl, Edie." He sighed. "Same old story, I guess. I was really nuts about her, and I spent all my time following her around. It turned out that her old man was rich as hell, and she asked me to her house one vacation. She lived on this big estate like you see in the movies—acres and acres, servants, riding stable, the works.

"Edie was into riding. She rode the show circuit all up and down the east coast and even took time off in the winter to go to Florida. I don't think her parents knew what to make of me. I sure didn't know how to act around them. I don't really know what she thought of me—she had enough other guys around—but she introduced me to the horses and to the groom. He was a nice old guy and a natural with horses. Irish, I think he was.

"I really got hooked that week. I thought I'd died and gone to heaven. Edie rode every day, and I'd watch her, thinking she was really great, and Mac—the groom, that is—would tell me stories about how she'd ridden and hunted and shown since she was six, as if she was his own kid, he was that proud of her. He showed me how to tack up for her and a bit about grooming, and I'd help him out around the stables. I felt a whole lot more comfortable down there than up at the house."

He turned the truck onto the dirt road, and they began the slow climb to the summit. The truck bounced and rattled on the uneven surface, and Ivan shifted to a lower gear. "Anyway," he continued against the whine of the transmission, "she got her dad to give me a summer job, and I sort of became her groom. I went with her to the shows that summer to get the horse ready and to hold him for her, take him when she came out of the ring, see that there was hay and water and that the horse was bandaged for the trip. I was really nuts about her, but I don't think she ever took it as seriously as I did. She'd leave me with the horse when she went off with her friends in the show crowd for hours, and then she'd be all wide-eyed and apologetic when she came back. She could have asked me along, but she never did. I think she was ashamed of me. I was jealous as hell, but afraid she'd tell me off if I said anything."

"Did she win?" Michael asked.

"She won her share. She said her horse wasn't top of the line, but she'd been to Madison Square Garden a couple of times. She took her horse someplace or other every weekend. Anyway, I couldn't stay in school—couldn't concentrate, couldn't think. She got her parents to let me stay in a little room over the stables and pay me a bit."

"Did you sleep with her?"

"Yeah, and so did about ten other guys, I found out later. By some freak accident, she came up to Erik's one day when her coach was away. Someone must have said the horse would do better with a little help, and Erik happened to be nearby. One day she told me to load the horse and drive her up here, and I did. At that point I was pretty used to handling horses from the ground.

"When we got here, there wasn't anyone in the barn. We walked through and watched Erik teaching a lesson in the outdoor ring—the indoor arena wasn't built yet. He was teaching a young woman on a black horse. I was amazed. I don't know how many lessons and clinics I'd been to with Edie—lots—and her coach was always at the shows to school her between classes, but this was different.

"Erik had a really great dialogue with the rider. He'd watch for a while and ask a question, and she'd think about it and ride around and answer, and sometimes she'd make a comment or ask something, and sometimes they'd smile or laugh. Although it was very informal, they were so involved in what they were doing that they didn't even notice us. And you'd never have known Erik was like he is from what I saw. He was completely polite and relaxed. What I didn't know then was that the horse was Lyrik, a very young, green Thoroughbred then, and the rider was Kristen." He let a few seconds pass in silence. "Things were simpler then," he said, half to himself.

"So you asked for a job?"

"No, it didn't occur to me. I was Edie's groom. I did see that Kristen rode differently, but I didn't think about it. I didn't know enough to have an opinion. I thought Edie was the last word in everything.

"Edie sent me to tack up her horse and bring him to where she was standing by the outdoor ring. I could see her talking to Erik. Kristen was in the barn unsaddling her horse, and I remember she smiled at me as I started to take Edie's horse past her. Then I heard Erik say, 'Tell your groom one does not lead a horse past a strange animal in a barn aisle without consequence.'" Ivan gave a short laugh and a slight gesture with his head. "It sounded so foreign to me that I never forgot it. Word for word, that's what he said. I turned and took the horse around the barn to where they were standing.

"I could see immediately that Edie was turning her sex appeal on Erik, giving him the eager wide-eyed look and going on about her horse. I'd seen her do it before, and it drove me nuts, and she knew it. But when I'd get mad, she'd give me a 'what'd I do?' kind of look and pretend she didn't know what I was talking about."

"What'd Erik do?"

"Nothing. He was watching the horse. When I got there, he gave me a sort of cursory glance and said, 'Remove the martingale.'

"'He always wears—' I started to say and looked to Edie for what she wanted me to do. 'I'm not accustomed to saying things twice,' Erik said, and when Edie nodded at me, I took the martingale off.

"At this point I was getting kind of uncomfortable. I was used to being treated as a groom, but usually I found people were sort of super-kind and appreciative. I kept looking at Edie for direction, and Erik kept watching us both with a kind of nasty, knowing smile. I started to feel really resentful, because Edie began to act even more as if I were her servant, as if she were trying to prove something to Erik.

"I finally got the horse straightened out, and Erik led the way into the ring and gestured for her to mount. He didn't tell her what to do, and she didn't ask, just began riding around as if she were performing for a horse show judge. Finally she stopped—ran out of things to do, I think—and said, 'Well? What do you think?'

"'About what?'

"'About the horse. Shall I sell him and buy another? There's not much point—'

"'One can always purchase a new machine with less mileage,' Erik said, 'if that is what one wishes to do.'

"She gave him an exasperated look and said, 'I've told you what I want, either to improve the horse or get one who can do the job. What I'm asking you is whether this horse is worth it.'

"'Worth what?'

"'Well, the schooling time,' Edie said kind of angrily, and Erik said, 'You have spent time schooling this horse?' with his eyebrows up as if he were really surprised.

"'Of course I have,' she said. 'Do you think he got this way by himself?'

"And you can imagine what Erik said to that: 'Yes, entirely by himself. He shows no signs of having been schooled. He moves on the forehand, shows little flexion in his joints and little energy in his movements.'

"'I haven't the slightest idea what you're talking about,' Edie said. 'Are you saying I should get rid of him?'

"'Did I say that?'

"'You've said all my work has had no effect on him.'

"'That is your fault, not his,' Erik said. 'Take up the rein.' She did. 'Move him into trot and shorten the rein.' I watched her do as he asked. I thought she looked really elegant. "'I believe I told you to shorten the rein,' Erik said, and she said, 'I have.'

"'Then do it again.' And after a few seconds, 'More.' The horse slowed up until he was almost walking.

"'Move him forward,' Erik said. 'No, do not drop the rein contact.'

"Her poor horse didn't know which end was up. He poked his nose up and opened his mouth and began to take quick little jog steps. Edie looked disgusted. She couldn't keep the contact.

"'Don't tell me this is how you want him to go,' she said finally. 'I'd be laughed out of the ring.'

"Erik ignored her. 'Sit the trot,' he said.

"Even I could see she couldn't do it. With his nose in the air and his back stiff, he was hopping around and tossing her up and down in the saddle, and she kept leaning forward and putting her weight in her stirrups to avoid the shock.

"Erik finally stopped her. He was obviously irritated, and I found myself really mad at him because I knew Edie was. He said to her, 'Cross the stirrups over the saddle, and kindly make an effort to ride your horse. It is not your appearance we are concerned with at the moment, and so you may cease your attempts to freeze yourself into that ridiculous position and adapt yourself to your mount.'

"She turned red in the face, and I was outraged. I went into the ring and said, 'Come on, Edie. You don't have to listen to this crap!'"

Michael grinned. "What happened?"

"Not what I expected. I thought she'd be glad of an ally, but it wasn't Erik that read me out, it was Edie. I guess she was embarrassed to have me try to rescue her. She said, 'Ivan, you get out of here. This is none of your business,' and I saw Erik give me a knowing look and laugh, and suddenly I felt as if they had all at once joined forces to put me in my place. I spun around and stalked off, and I heard Erik say, 'You, the groom, come here.' I turned around, but I was damned if I'd go out there again.

"'Dismount,' Erik said to Edie, and she did. He led the horse past where I was standing to the gateway, and called Peter. Edie was left like me, standing in the ring, but she didn't speak to me.

"When Peter came, Erik said to him, 'Assist him to mount,' and gestured at me."

"You're kidding!" Michael said.

"I just gaped at him and finally stammered, 'I don't know how to ride,' furious to be put in that position. And then Edie really did me in. Smiling, she said, 'Go ahead, Ivan, do as you're told,' like I was her pet dog or something.

"The worst of it was that shit-eating grin of Erik's as he watched me react to Edie. I wanted to knock his teeth in. I clenched my jaw, and I heard Peter say, 'On three spring up,' and under his breath he added, 'Don't worry—just relax.'

"I got on somehow, but it's a wonder I didn't go right over the horse and onto the ground on the other side. It was the first time in my life I'd ever been on a horse, though I used to daydream about it a lot.

"He made Peter lead the horse around the ring, and told me to do a lot of exercises—all those warm-up exercises I had you do every day. I was trying about as hard as if I were going out for the Olympics. I was damned if I'd make a fool of myself, and the horse was just plodding around like some riding stable plug with none of the animation he'd shown with Edie.

"Peter saved me that day. He kept saying, 'Good, good, you're doing fine,' but never loud enough for Erik to hear, and smiling at me the way he does when he thinks someone's miserable. Finally Erik said, 'Dismount,' and I did, somehow or other. I felt so bow-legged I could barely walk. Erik walked out of the ring, but Edie was still standing there, smiling.

"'You looked a perfect fool,' she said to me. We went back to the trailer, and Erik came out to watch me put the horse away with Edie supervising.

"'Do you intend to charge me for that ridiculous demonstration?' she asked him.

"'On the contrary,' he said. 'I should be delighted to pay you for what I have observed today.'

"'Which is?' She was icy as hell.

"'That your groom is the superior horseman,' he said offhandedly.

"'What are you talking about?' she said in a defensive voice. I was staring at both of them, trying to figure out who was being insulted and how I should react. I was almost as mad at Edie as I was at him for making a fool out of me.

"Erik just stood there lazily watching Edie. I couldn't stand it. So I turned my back and put the horse on the trailer. I heard him say, 'You have been riding for many years?'

"'Since I was a small child,' she said.

"'Yes,' Erik said. 'It is unfortunate.' As I came out of the trailer, I could see her staring at him. 'Your groom, however, has not a similar handicap. Were he able—'" Ivan glanced over at Michael. He was struggling with a reluctance to continue the story and a compulsive need to relive the moment. He swallowed and cleared his throat. "'Were he able to turn his attention from you to the horse for a few weeks, I could teach him to transform your animal. With you, the time would be wasted.' Edie looked over at me as if she suddenly hated me, and I knew he'd done that on purpose. I started to say, 'Edie—' and heard him laugh.

"'Ivan, shut up and stay out of this,' she said, and to Erik, 'If that's your idea of a joke, it's not funny. I don't care to be compared to a beginner who sits like a sack of potatoes and doesn't know one end of a horse from another.'

"'You speak disparagingly of your own groom? Perhaps, that being the case, you would be willing to part with him?'

"At this point he did something so incredible, I could hardly believe it. He reached into his pocket and pulled out a handful of bills and began looking through them.

"'Would twenty dollars be sufficient?' he asked.

"We both stared at him, and neither of us said a word. I couldn't believe anyone could be so damned insulting. Edie turned on her heel and got into the truck, but I glared at him and finally said as sarcastically as I could, 'What do you think I am, a slave?'

"'That was my impression,' Erik said. 'Perhaps I was mistaken?' He stuffed the money back into his pocket and he added with the same damned smile, 'It may be that nature deprives the hound of his reason when the bitch is in heat.' And he just turned away and sauntered back into the barn."

"Jesus!" Michael said. "That's worse than I got!"

"Yeah," Ivan said thoughtfully. "It was pretty bad, and I was too thrown by it to do anything. I just climbed into the truck, slammed the door and drove the rig away. Edie wouldn't talk to me. I was mad at her, too. He just shot everything all to hell." He slowed the truck and stopped in front of the house. "Want to get off here?"

"So what happened? How'd you get up here?"

"Later," Ivan said. "I haven't time now."

Michael jumped down from the truck. He wondered if Erik was there or down at the barn. He walked slowly up the steps and into the front hall, his footsteps loud in the silence. The large room with the three cots in it seemed a sort of sanctuary. He saw his duffel bag under his cot where he had forgotten it and went over and sat down. Slowly he lay back for a minute and stared at the ceiling, thinking of Ivan and Erik, of Peter and Erik and of himself. The phone rang in the kitchen and rang again, over and over, and listening he fell asleep, his hands crossed over his stomach, his sneakers still on his feet.

CHAPTER 17

▼

Michael was awakened at suppertime by the sounds from the kitchen. He felt disoriented. His limbs were leaden, his mind weighted by a sense of oppressive dread. He sat on the edge of the cot, put his face in his hands, and tried to gather the fragments of his awareness into comprehension.

He made his way slowly to the bathroom and rested his hands on the edges of the sink. Leaning on them, he let his eyes close again and struggled groggily with the question of how to present himself to Erik. The problem had been with him since he had decided to come back, but he had pushed it to the edges of his mind. What would Erik do?

The sound of Peter's voice came through the wall, but he couldn't make out the words against the random sounds of dishes clattering and feet walking about the kitchen. He looked at his watch. Almost seven. That's right, he said silently to his reflection, fall asleep, you stupid bastard. Make things real easy on yourself. Now what? They'll hear the shower—what the hell difference does it make? You think he's going to walk in here and haul you out of the shower? But he went quickly to the bathroom door and locked it. Ten minutes later he stood in the doorway to the kitchen. There was no sign of Erik.

Peter was standing at the stove. "Where'd you come from?" he asked.

"I fell asleep." Michael glanced at the table where Ivan sat, tearing up lettuce for salad. It was set for three. Who was the third? "Why didn't you wake me up?" he said in an accusing tone.

"Sure," Ivan said. "Hey, Erik, OK if I go wake up Michael and do this work a little later on?" He glanced over at Peter.

"You expect the horse's routine to be changed so that you can turn yourself into an alarm clock for one who shirks his work?" Peter said to Ivan in a chilling imitation of Erik.

"Lay off!" Michael said angrily. "I don't need that from you." He paused to listen for Erik's radio upstairs, but there was only silence. He indicated the table. "Who's that place for?"

"It's for you," Peter said. "Erik's already eaten."

Michael pulled a chair from the table and sat down. He was ravenous.

"How come he ate early?"

"Why don't you ask him?" Ivan said.

Michael ignored the question. "What do you think I should do—wait till tomorrow and just show up for work?"

"Tell him you're back tonight, and get it over with," Ivan said.

There was a pause, and the weight of it seemed to Michael to be directed upon him. "Oh, shit," he said, and pushed his empty plate away with a restless motion of his hand. "What kind of life is this, anyway? You work your ass off all day and then end up cooking the meals, washing clothes, cleaning the damned house—there's nothing to do—"

"Yeah?" Ivan said. "You've made up a fair list."

"You know what I mean. The damned television only gets one channel, and you can't even see that because of the snow. It's miles to town—we live like a bunch of monks—"

"Christ, he's breaking my heart," Ivan said.

"An American tragedy," Peter added in a solemn voice, but he couldn't keep his face straight. Both of them braced for Michael's retort, but after a suspicious look at each of them, his face suddenly relaxed and he started to laugh.

"Yeah," he said at last. "I guess it is pretty funny if that kind of thing makes you laugh." He leaned back in his chair, and added, "Oh, hell—"

Peter got up and began collecting the dishes. "You know the ropes. Go find Erik, take your medicine, and get on with it."

"I can't," Michael said bitterly. "I can't stand it when he starts jerking me around—it's not worth it."

"Then why'd you come back?" Ivan asked.

"It's your fault I came back—"

"Bullshit! You're not going to pin that one on me. No one makes you do anything. It's not worth the effort."

"Look," Peter said, "Erik does that stuff on purpose. You just need to be ready for it."

"Yeah," Michael said. "Get ready for your own funeral. Guy's a goddamn sadist, that's what."

"What's that make you?" Ivan asked.

"Makes *you* a masochist," Michael retorted. "Doesn't make me anything. You don't see *me* asking for that kind of crap."

"Is that right? Looks to me like you like nothing better than getting in hot water up to your neck."

"Shut up!" Michael shoved his chair back furiously and stood up.

"Hey, cut it out!" Peter said sharply. "Sit down for a minute and cool it. Have some coffee. There's plenty of time to sort things out."

Ivan got up, turned his back and carried his dishes to the sink.

"Sit down," Peter said quietly to Michael and brought the coffee pot to the table. "Look, you've got a short fuse. Erik finds someone's weak point right off the bat, and that's what he aims for. You play right into it every time." He grinned across the table at Michael. "It's not just you. Me, he *tries* to make me lose my temper, because he knows damned well it's hard for me to do it. He makes you control yours because that's what's hardest for you. It's like it's a game with him. Ivan, you want coffee?"

Ivan came back to the table and sat down. He kept his eyes studiously away from Michael. Michael gestured at him with his head. "What about him?" he said to Peter.

"Ivan? Self-conscious. Can't stand being embarrassed in front of people. Haven't you noticed? Erik hands it to him all the time. But I'll tell you something, it's only when I was able to get really mad that I could deal with some horses, even Kestrel. I'm not good at the strong-arm stuff. I always got on with horses that needed to be handled with kid gloves, but I tended to give in to the ones who resisted me. Ivan's the opposite in some ways. If horses give him a hard time, he straightens them out in a hurry. I think you're like that, too, but you lose your cool and think of yourself more than the horse sometimes. You take everything personally. Erik'll work on you until, by God, you can stand anything and still get the work done."

For several seconds Michael was silent. Finally he said, "There's other ways of teaching people to ride. He could just *tell* us—"

"Fish could fly," Ivan commented, "if they had wings."

"He could do a lot of things," Peter said, "But he doesn't, and if you can't swallow it, you'd be better off elsewhere. Somehow, I don't think *he's* going to change."

"Where'd *he* learn to ride?"

"I don't know."

"God taught him," Ivan said facetiously, and Michael laughed.

"Yeah," he said. He regarded Ivan thoughtfully. "You never did finish the story."

"What story?"

"How *you* got up here."

"Oh, that—" Ivan said. "There's not much more to tell. Erik drove a giant wedge between Edie and me that day. She was furious at him and at me, too. She kept using that incident against me. She'd tell everyone how he had said I was so great and would invite me to ride her horse and show them. I got so I couldn't stand to be around her, but I couldn't stand anyone else around her either. She began going out with other guys. She took them riding with her. I was left to play the groom.

"She kept putting me down all the time, always too busy to see me alone, until finally I wised up. I'd sit in that damned little attic room in the barn and torture myself. I wished I could ride and show her I was as good as anyone else. And then one day I realized that the riding part was as important to me as Edie was, that I didn't give a shit if she was there or not. She'd killed all the feeling I had for her, but I still loved the work and the horses.

"I knew it was just a matter of time before she told me to leave. And even if she didn't, I couldn't take her treating me like a stable boy, even though that's what I was. I kept thinking of Erik and getting a certain amount of pleasure out of how he'd put her in her place, even though *I* couldn't do it and even though he'd put me in mine, too. One night I hitched into Northwood and got plastered. Peter was there. I'd had enough to drink that I told him the whole thing. He told me how he'd come to work for Erik and what he was learning, and I figured, what the hell? So I came up here. I swallowed my pride and asked Erik if he'd teach me in return for my working."

"He said yes?"

"Oh, he laid a lot of shit on me about Edie. He said I was a prisoner of my own passions, and if I couldn't control myself better than that, how did I think I'd have enough self-discipline to handle a horse. He was obviously enjoying the spot I was in, but he said I could work here without pay and he'd decide later whether I could ride.

"I didn't say a word. I just did what he said to do. He wouldn't let me off the place at first except on my day off. So I had no way to make money, and if I wanted to buy soap or a new pair of jeans or I needed a haircut, I had to depend on Erik, and he knew it. Every now and then I'd lose my cool and end up spending a few days down in the woods, or running errands or miles away digging up rocks or fixing fence. And then he relented and told Peter to teach me to ride."

"He was the best student I ever had," Peter said. "He was absolutely desperate to learn. And he kept asking all kinds of questions. A lot of them I couldn't answer. I kept referring him to Erik, and he wouldn't ask Erik—"

"Nerves were too raw," Ivan said to Michael. "Like you, I guess. I just didn't want to lay myself open. But it was stupid, I realize now. Erik doesn't mind your asking—it's just that often he won't give you a straight answer. Instead, he sets you up to think about it. You asked who taught him, and I think he taught himself. I think he figures out what to do from the horses."

Peter shook his head and laughed, "Well, that's a romantic theory! No, someone taught him all right. His position's too classical to be self-taught. That kind of seat—you know it yourself—it's the result of hours and hours and hours of practice."

"Did you ever ask him?"

"Yes, I did once. He made some sarcastic remark about how everything he knew he learned at his father's knee. He won't ever answer personal questions. But I think Ivan's right about one thing. Apart from his own riding skills, I think he does figure out what to do from the horses."

Michael could hear the crickets' loud, monotonous singing outside. It was getting dark. He got up suddenly and turned on the light. He would like to have frozen this moment in time, the protective nearness of the others, Erik's absence, the simple room with its bare, wide floorboards and wooden counters, the woodstove. Unlike the rest of his life it seemed unthreatening, functional and calm.

"Where's Erik?" he asked at last.

"Down at the barn, I think," Peter said. "He's begun riding Lyrik at night."

"At night? What for?"

"I don't know. He's keeping Tango in and The Phoenix. He said he'd turn Lyrik out himself later. I think he'll keep Tango in for a while, until he thinks of his stall as home."

"What about The Phoenix?" Michael said. He thought of The Phoenix as his own.

"Babysitter. To keep Tango from tearing the place down when the others go out."

"Christ," Michael said wearily, "I feel sorry as hell for that horse."

"Oh, he'll come around all right," Ivan said.

"How do you know?"

"Because that's the way things are around here. He'll shape up or end up in a can," and because he couldn't resist, he added, "just like you."

To stem his restlessness, Michael went outdoors. He climbed the fence and began to walk the fence line in the upper part of the pasture. It was very dark, and the grass was wet. Not far away he thought he made out the shapes of horses and stopped to watch. They might approach, curious or suspicious, they might allow him to come to them and to handle them, or raise their heads from their grazing with a mild interest soon spent, or use him as an excuse to spook and gallop away, but fondness or emotional attachment was absent. Even when crowding the gate in the morning, it was their feed they anticipated, not his presence. Their attitude was at best polite, even responsive, but not to his own individuality, and for some obscure reason he found that immensely comforting.

At length the light in the barn went out, and he saw Erik appear from the darkness and disappear into the house. He waited for only a few minutes after he saw the upstairs light go on before he followed and went quietly upstairs.

In the three months he had lived there, he had never had reason to go upstairs, although Peter and Ivan regularly did to keep Erik supplied with firewood or to take him an occasional meal. When he reached the top, he found himself in a wide center hall. The light from under one of the doors was the only illumination. He knocked. "Yes, come in."

Erik was seated by the fireplace where two small logs were burning. Michael was taken aback. His imagination had imbued this meeting with such ominous portent that he almost couldn't believe the prosaic surroundings. The room was nothing like he had expected. He had imagined furnishings larger than life, a certain opulence, some external sign of Erik's authority. He felt strangely disappointed.

His face near his eye was still swollen. He could feel it when he smiled or moved his jaw, and part of his cheek that he usually couldn't see impinged on his vision. He knew Erik was watching him, but he refused to look at him and stared instead around the room. Erik's desk stood just inside the door; against the wall was a bookcase filled with books. He had never seen Erik read anything.

"Shut the door," Erik said, and obediently he reached behind him and pushed the door closed. "Would you care to tell me where you have been?"

"No—" It was not what he wanted to say. It had been drawn from him without thought.

"In that case," Erik stood up, "there is nothing more to be said."

Michael felt his resolve weaken. He groped behind him for the doorknob and clutched it with all his strength, pulling frantically against himself, for it was his own weight that kept the door closed.

"Wait a minute," he said lamely. "Just wait a minute—I went into Reed."

Erik said nothing.

"Well—Jesus, what did you expect me to do?"

"I believe I have answered that question before. The answer has not changed. Since you seem to have remarkable difficulty in remembering what you don't wish to hear, I will repeat it for you. I expect you to do what you are told. Is that clear?"

Michael closed his eyes tightly for a second, swallowed, and managed to say, "I don't know if I can." He heard his admission with surprise, as if it were another person who had said it. He added, "You hit me—I don't have to take that."

"On the contrary," Erik said. "You will take whatever I decide is appropriate if you want to work here."

"What kind of bargain is that?" Michael demanded, suddenly angry. "I do all the work, break my neck—"

"Enough!" Erik raised his hand and cut Michael off in mid-sentence. "I assume you came up here for a reason. Either tell me what it is or get out."

Michael was startled into silence. What had he intended to say? "I don't know," he stammered at last. "I mean, I wondered if I still have a job—"

Erik turned his back and stared into the fire. Michael waited apprehensively for him to speak, but when the seconds dragged by in silence, his anxiety turned to irritation again.

"I've been working here since June without being paid a red cent. You've made me do all the rotten jobs that no one else wants to do, and not only that but I've been working a lot more than eight hours a day, and I never get—"

Erik spun around. He was scowling. "Silence!" he said. "I have no time for this. Sit down." He indicated a straight-backed wooden chair across from his own. "I am tired of your complaints and your self-indulgent surrender to impulse when conditions are not to your liking. I am not a substitute for your social worker, nor am I willing to tolerate a series of temper tantrums when there is work to be done."

He stared at Michael with icy contempt, and too late Michael knew that he had gone too far. There was nothing he could say to justify himself. For an agonized moment he saw himself through Erik's eyes, a whining, self-centered weakling. He had no choice but to leave, just when he had decided to stay.

"I guess you want me to go, then," he said in a monotone.

"Did I say that?"

"No—" Suddenly he was very close to tears. He stared with all his determination at the floor beneath his feet. "I wouldn't care what you made me do as long as I could—" His voice faded and he couldn't finish the sentence, which he felt would put him still more at Erik's mercy and underline his weakness.

"As long as you could what?" Erik asked relentlessly.

"Work—"

"That goes without saying."

"—with the horses. I can't—"

"Yes?"

"I can't work anywhere else."

"Why not?"

"You know why—no one will hire me."

"And the reason for that?"

"All those things you said," Michael admitted reluctantly.

Erik got to his feet. "There is a hot plate behind the desk," he said. "Heat some water for tea."

Michael watched him leave the room and stared after him in consternation. Was this small task that Erik had assigned him a reprieve? Was it a demotion? Michael put the kettle on and moved over to the bookshelf. He stared at the books. They all seemed to have something to do with horses and riding. He had never heard of the authors, and he saw that some were in a foreign language. He didn't dare take any from the shelf. He was still standing there when Erik returned, stepped over to the desk and made two mugs of tea. He took one and gestured to the other.

"Now," he said, returning to his chair, "we will discuss *you*. Sit down."

Seated stiffly on his chair, Michael balanced his mug awkwardly on his knee. "Those books," he said at last, "have you read them all?"

"I do not keep books for decoration. Yes, I have read them."

"All of them?"

"All of them."

Michael stared at him. "There are so many. How can there be that much—"

"Man has his limitations and conceits. The horse is a challenge, and men have met the challenge in a number of ways. Many think they have found the answer and are anxious to record it for those who come after them. They have been doing so since Xenophon."

"Since when?"

"Since the time of Xenophon, over two thousand years ago. Xenophon was a horse trainer as well as a warrior. Many of the teachings that are practiced today may be traced to him. However, it is not Xenophon I intend to discuss this evening."

Michael stirred restlessly.

"You have said you want to work with horses," Erik went on. "Depending upon what you want to do, you have a number of choices."

"Choices? I haven't had many so far."

"That is your fault," Erik said, "because you are a slave to your own impulses. No one has forced you into the kind of indiscretion you are so prone to." Michael looked away.

"I will tell you something about men and about horses," Erik said suddenly. "Neither can perform without the other, they are each other's prisoner. You can go anywhere to ride if all you want to do is to balance yourself upon the horse's back. The school horse is at the mercy of such riders. He seeks his freedom elsewhere, away from the rider's influence. He is simply a machine. The challenge to the rider—to all of those riders—" he waved at the bookshelf, "is to keep what is so elusive and to make it part of himself."

It seemed to Michael that Erik was talking to himself. "Each other's prisoner," Erik repeated, as if struck by the thought. "Yet each is freed with the assistance of the other. What is the aim in schooling the horse?"

The sudden question caught Michael off guard. "Uh—I don't know," he said automatically, much as he had in school when the teacher caught him daydreaming.

"You don't know? Do you mean that you have been riding twice a day for two months without listening to what your instructors are telling you, to say nothing of the horse?"

"No," Michael said quickly, "I just forgot."

"Answer the question."

"To get him to move forward freely—"

"And?"

"To do what the rider says, and to relax?"

"How would you teach a horse to relax?"

"I guess you'd get him to trust you."

"How?"

Michael felt suddenly exhausted. He stifled a yawn and tried to gather his thoughts. "I think you'd try not to scare him, try to get him to trust you and then to rely on you."

"How?"

"Be consistent. Maybe establish some kind of routine."

"You are familiar with the Collective Marks?"

Michael frowned. The term sounded familiar and he was sure he had heard it, but he was afraid to claim he had. "I don't think so," he said.

"The judge of a dressage test—any test—gives a mark for each movement of the test. At the end he sums up his general impression of the horse's training and the rider's effectiveness in what is called the Collective Marks. They include what you have just described. The horse must be taught to demonstrate relaxation, impulsion, and submission to the rider's aids. Yes. And yet it is beyond the notice of most horsemen that the rider himself cannot escape the identical training. Do you understand?"

"I guess so," Michael said slowly. "I think—"

"No, not as yet," Erik said in answer to his own question. "Perhaps the forward impulse—that is what drives one and in turn enables the horse to perform—yes, that I believe I see in you, not controlled, not efficiently directed, but there, nonetheless.

"Relaxation? Rarely. It comes and goes with your awareness of yourself, a relatively constant condition. But you are naturally coordinated, you have a good sense of timing, you have only to learn the concentration and to put in the hours necessary to use the muscles as they must be used to affect the horse. That cannot be hurried for either horse or rider. It will take months—years, perhaps, and even then, like the highly schooled horse, one must keep in condition. One cannot take a vacation from riding and expect to be the same rider when one returns."

Erik looked over at Michael with his accustomed unwavering stare. "No doubt you will have anticipated what I will say to you next. Even now I see you prepared to resist it."

He was smiling, but for once the smile seemed almost friendly, and Michael found himself smiling in return. Erik was saying more than he could absorb, yet he tried hard to remember the words.

"It is the submission that is lacking," Erik said. "I don't tell you that lightly. You are aware of it yourself, I think, if we may take your actions of the past weeks as an example."

Michael shifted uncomfortably in his chair.

"At the lowest level of training one requires submission of the horse. If one is careful he may advance in training to a certain point without much resistance. The horse, however, will resist. Every horse will resist, and one must meet those resistances and overcome them, one way or another. Resistances will occur again and again for various reasons. The horse must be taught to submit, to seek the way to submit, to be sufficiently conditioned to do so.

"And so it is with the rider. He must open himself to the demands of the horse. He must listen to what his horse requires. It is that which tells the rider when he has asked too much of his mount, or perhaps not enough. It is that which tells him what his horse can achieve, when he must ask, and when he must not interfere.

"If the rider is concerned only with himself, his appearance, the state of his emotions—" Erik watched Michael pointedly and paused. It seemed a long time before he continued. "Such a rider will never be a real horseman. He lacks the generosity that is the horse's extraordinary gift. He may apply the aids mechanically when he wishes, and the horse will respond mechanically. It will be immediately apparent."

The tea in Michael's cup was cold. He had been afraid to drink it and possibly draw attention to himself. Now as Erik watched him, he put the cup down gently on the floor beside him.

Erik moved slightly in his chair. "The horse is honest and without guile," he went on. "He cannot be expected to change his nature, nor can you change it. Man can only change himself. I have said that I do not mention this lightly. It is a quality almost totally absent in you, and I am not certain if it is within your capability to control yourself to the extent you must. It is a serious fault—more serious, perhaps, than any other, for it means you do not listen to your horse. I will not have such a rider on my horses or on my place. Do you understand that?"

Wounded to the base of his being, Michael nodded.

"I have not yet dismissed you as hopeless," Erik said. "I do not dismiss a difficult horse as hopeless without working with him, but I am not so blind as not to know there are some horses who have not the temperament to get far in training."

Michael looked up uneasily.

"I expect a great deal from my horses," Erik went on, "as I feel they do from me. The same holds true of those who work here. If you wish to remain, you will accept that without question or complaint. I warn you in advance that you will find the experience painful, for I will not tolerate resistance—perhaps you have found that out already. From now on you will find it even harder and more painful, for despite your demands that I make your life easier, I will make it harder. I intend either to turn you into a horseman or to be rid of you. Is that clear?"

"Yes," Michael said, and suddenly he awoke from his reverie. "Yes, sir." He knew it was the right answer. He felt himself redden, and he added in his own defense, "But at least you reward your horses, don't you? I've seen you do that—what do I get out of this?"

"The rider receives his rewards from his horse as the horse does from his rider. Should you become such a rider, you will find yourself well rewarded for your pains. Should you not, you will simply suffer, and your misery, I assure you, is of no concern or interest to me whatsoever." He waved toward the door. "That is enough, I think, for the present."

As he was leaving, Michael hesitated in the doorway.

"I just wanted to say that I—"

"Keep your confessions for your social worker," Erik said, "and close the door behind you."

CHAPTER 18

▼

Michael rose reluctantly the next morning to tend the woodstove in the kitchen. He had come to bed after the others were asleep, and when he heard the random, obtrusive sounds of their rising at dawn, he turned onto his stomach with his head half buried in his pillow and didn't get up until he heard them leave the house.

He was frying sausage when Ivan and Peter came back. He knew they were watching him, tactfully silent, but he was unwilling to speak. By the time Erik appeared, all three of them were seated at the table eating.

Peter got up and poured Erik a mug of coffee. In answer to a glance from him, he turned the kitchen radio off. The resulting silence made Michael acutely uncomfortable. There was nothing in Erik's appearance or behavior that was in any way different than usual, but he felt his own role had changed, although he was uncertain how. It was as if he were on trial, and although the feeling was familiar, for the first time he knew the outcome was desperately important to him and a matter of indifference to Erik.

Erik began to issue the orders for the day. He spoke first to Ivan, then to Peter. At last he said, "Michael, turn The Phoenix out in the upper pasture. Clean his stall and Blue Tango's."

"Yes, sir." His penance was starting. If The Phoenix were out, he wouldn't ride.

As if Erik had read his thoughts, he continued, "You will ride The Phoenix lightly each evening for a half hour before he is fed this week and for fifteen minutes next week. After that he will be turned out in the lower pasture. His feed is to be cut accordingly—consult the feed chart.

"When Ivan has finished with the tractor, take the spreader, remove the old manure pile and spread it on the hayfield. It is up to you to find the time to do it. You must spend at least an hour with Blue Tango each morning. I want him groomed thoroughly and his feet picked up and cleaned frequently until he allows them to be handled without hesitation. Tie him in his stall for this purpose. Later he will be cross-tied in the aisle. You will start riding him this morning under my supervision."

Michael looked at him in astonishment. "Me?" he said weakly.

"That's what I said. You will be responsible for all the routine stable work this week, since Ivan and Peter have other tasks. That includes cleaning the stalls and grooming the horses. Do you understand?"

Michael heard the words and felt a swelling, secret excitement.

"I said, do you understand?"

"Yes, sir." After Erik had left and they heard the screen door close behind him, none of them spoke for a time.

Michael turned the Phoenix out, filled with regret that the horse would so soon be lost to him. He approached his work with Blue Tango with mixed feelings. Tango was a stall walker; he paced his stall like a caged animal. It was an irritating, intractable habit almost impossible to break and, like other stable vices, sometimes spread to other horses in the barn. Tango's stall was in the corner at the back, The Phoenix next to him. Now, with the stall beside him empty, he walked restlessly around and around. His morning's hay ration, unfinished, was trampled into the soiled straw of his bedding. Already he had made a path around the edges of his stall.

Michael haltered and tied him. He wondered if Tango would fight the restraint again, and whether it might be wiser to clean the stall when he was at liberty to move around. Erik, preparing to ride, had Calypso cross-tied in the aisle. He paid no attention to Michael. Michael worked gingerly around Tango and was relieved to see the horse unconcerned by his presence. Tango, unlike himself, bore no perceptible marks of his defeat.

The morning went badly. The individual stable chores were familiar to Michael, but somehow, left to accomplish them alone, he couldn't organize his time. He had barely started to pick up the stalls before Erik reappeared. Calypso had to be cooled out, and Erik's tack, hastily placed by Michael on the saddle rack, had to be wiped off. The wheelbarrow stood in the aisle, and the manure fork leaned against a stall door. Erik's irritation was plain.

Silently Michael moved from task to task, working as quickly as he could. The hose slipped from its bracket and fell to the floor, releasing a small stream of water into the aisle. It tripped him when he hastened to coil it back on its holder.

"Why is Crystal's stall unlatched?" came Erik's voice.

"I was about—"

"Latch it." He started to comply and threw the coils of the hose over the bracket, only to watch them slip again limply to the floor.

"You have left Lyrik without water for some reason of your own?"

"I haven't had a chance—"

"Attend to it."

He hurried blindly from place to place, unable to remember what he had already accomplished and what still remained to be done. Erik called him several times to help unload horses and receive Ivan and Peter's students.

It was almost noon before Erik told him to saddle Blue Tango. He was grooming the horse in his stall, and at the words he headed quickly toward the tackroom.

"Come back here." He turned and retraced his steps. "Are you in the habit of leaving horses tied in their stalls, the doors open, while you go off about your business?"

"I was just getting the tack—"

No answer. He loosed Blue Tango and latched the door.

"Fetch Ivan and bring the horse into the aisle."

He called Ivan from his work in the tractor shed and led the horse from his stall. Tango plunged through the doorway, almost knocking him from his feet, and dragged him unwillingly beside him down the aisle. Angrily, he dug in his feet, jammed his elbow into the horse's shoulder and leaned against him, swearing silently to himself.

Erik appeared from the tackroom, a dressage whip in his hand, and Michael felt his heart sink. Whatever the nature of the connection he felt to the horse, he couldn't abide seeing him punished again. He treasured the strength and independence he felt in the animal, even if it were to be turned against himself.

"Whoa," he said under his breath and put his left hand on the horse's nose. Tango began throwing his head and snatched his nose from under Michael's hand. His ears moved back and forth, and suddenly with little warning he laid them against his head and reached savagely for Michael with his teeth.

"Son of a bitch!" Michael said. He jumped back and jerked the shank down hard against the halter ring. Tango stood beside him, all innocence, but Michael was painfully aware of the horse's power and his own comparative vulnerability.

He sensed Erik's presence behind him. His heart was pounding and his legs felt weak. Erik said nothing.

Ivan stood in the doorway of the barn. His hands and arms were black with engine grease, and he wiped them on a rag at his belt. Erik approached the horse and slipped a longeline through the halter ring. He brought it over Tango's head, snapped it to the ring on the other side, and handed the line to Ivan.

"Cross-tie him," he said to Michael.

"He ties OK in his stall," Michael said suddenly. "I could saddle him in there." It was a weak and indirect plea, and he knew it would be refused.

"Do as you're told." Erik's face was stony and impatient. He tapped the whip rhythmically against his boot, his eyes on the horse.

Reluctantly, Michael attached the first tie to the halter ring. Tango accepted the action and swung his haunches until he was facing the wall. Michael straightened him, still holding the leadshank in his hand, and attached the other tie. He stepped in front of the horse, handed the leadshank to Ivan and glanced again at Erik. Erik nodded toward the tackroom.

Uncertain in the cross ties, Tango was clearly nervous. He gathered his legs under him and began a slow and restless dance. From the tackroom as he held the saddle in his arms, Michael could hear Erik's voice, speaking now to the horse and now to Ivan.

"Be prepared to loose the ties immediately should it become necessary."

"Yes, sir." Ivan kept snapping the leadshank down against the halter, a reminder to the horse, Michael thought, of the consequences of rearing, or perhaps an attempt to get him to concentrate on something else. He was aware of Tango's ears moving nervously back and forth and the alternate hopping action of his hind and front legs, as if he were a draft horse attempting to start a heavy sledge, a scene Michael had watched with fascination several times at the county fair.

He managed to saddle the horse without too much difficulty, only to hear Erik say, when he had drawn up the girth, "You are satisfied with the fit of the saddle?"

"I hadn't thought—"

"Then do so."

Michael looked critically at the saddle. "It's a bit low on the withers."

"Well?"

"You think it's *too* low?"

"I have asked you."

Michael was silent. He didn't know the answer. "I guess I'd better change it," he said uncertainly. He undid the girth and exchanged the saddle for one with a narrower fit, watching to see that it sat properly on the horse's back before he drew up the girth.

Tentatively, he said, "Maybe I should use a saddle pad?" and when there was no answer, "Should I?"

"What for?"

"In case it doesn't fit right?"

"If your clothing doesn't fit, is your solution to stuff it with excess padding to make it do so?"

"No."

"What *is* your solution?"

"I don't buy stuff that doesn't fit."

"Why, then, should your mount be so inconvenienced? There are a number of saddles in the tackroom. There have been no horses I can recall that could not be properly fitted. You are satisfied with that saddle?"

"Yes."

"Very well. Proceed."

When the horse was ready, Erik fitted him with a longeing cavesson and took the longeline from Ivan. "Lead the horse to the indoor school," he said to Michael. "Ivan, stay behind with the whip. There may be difficulty persuading him to enter the arena—be prepared for it. Do not," he added pointedly to Michael, "choose that moment to faint or drop the line. Do you understand?"

"Yes," Michael said. "Yes, sir." But he suffered for Tango and spoke to him in an undertone as he led him. Tango was hesitant, but he followed obediently. When he had entered the arena, Ivan closed the door behind them and set the longewhip inside.

Erik stood by the horse's head and looked him over critically. He secured the reins and stirrup irons so they wouldn't slip and tightened the girth.

"Have you longed a horse before?"

"No, sir."

"Very well. There are a number of reasons to longe a horse. We are concerned with only two at the moment. The horse has been in his stall for two days. He is not accustomed to confinement. We will allow him to exercise himself for a time on the line.

"Pay particular attention to the second reason." He spoke without emotion, his eyes on Blue Tango. His hand rested lightly on the horse's neck. Tango stamped impatiently and moved his quarters sideways. "I have worked with this horse. He understands the function of the line and the whip, which will serve the same function as your leg when you ride. Is that clear?"

"I think so."

"You will not look for the quality of the movements at the moment, or the speed of the transitions, or his balance, but only for obedience, strictly for obedience."

He led the horse to the center of the arena and began looping the longeline across his palm. The longe whip was under his right arm, its handle to the front. "I stand in place," he said to Michael and, taking the whip in his right hand, made an infinitesimal gesture with it toward the horse's hindquarters. The lash hung down, trailing in the dirt. Tango began to move around him, following his leading hand.

"I allow the line to lengthen to its fullest extent, and I ask the horse to move outward until the line is taut. I keep the horse always between the whip and the hand, facing his shoulder. The tension on the line is equivalent to that on the rein."

Tango began to trot of his own accord and then to canter. He increased his speed until, with a sudden great buck, he started to gallop. His flight was interspersed with bucks and kicking, both sideways and straight behind him. Startled, Michael heard him squeal and looked over at Erik. Erik's face was impassive. He did nothing but pivot on his left foot, facing the horse.

"He plays," Erik said, watching him, "and I let him. Perhaps you can tell me why?"

"Because he's full of himself, and you want him to get the edge off?"

"Not that I want him to—I am indifferent. He needs to do so, indeed he can hardly help himself. Why, since I have told you we wish to establish his obedience, do I let him behave this way?"

"I don't think he's being *dis*obedient," Michael said, defending both himself and the horse. He saw Erik give a slight, acknowledging smile, and Michael thought tangentially, damn, that horse is beautiful.

"Quite right. Since I have told him nothing, his behavior is his own. There is no advantage in asking for a response one has little hope of receiving."

He turned slowly as Tango flashed around him. Eventually, Michael saw him lift his hand and twitch the line. "Whoa," he said quietly, but he allowed the horse several seconds to comply, repeating the order and drawing in the line with a give-and-take action of his hand.

Tango dropped into trot and soon to walk and halt. Michael could see the pink interior of his nostrils as they widened. His eyes were large and bright, his ears forward. He gave a series of snorts and shook his head, and the black mane fell on both sides of his neck, but he stood still as Erik approached.

"I have let him play," Erik said, "but only within the limits I establish. Such behavior may be allowed a young, green horse, particularly one who has been confined. But there is an element of danger in such activity. I have seen horses break a leg on the line. I have seen one kill himself. It will not be tolerated later, and even now I allow it only at the outset and only for a time I predetermine. As the horse learns, I become more demanding." He looked directly at Michael. "You are familiar with that approach, I believe?"

Michael didn't answer. Under Erik's supervision he longed the horse, this time in the opposite direction. As Tango moved around him, he could feel his powerful force through the line in his hand. "Whoa," he said at last in response to a gesture from Erik, but it was a long time before he could get Tango to stop, and then only by shortening the line and pulling with all his strength until the horse swung in to face him, the line slack. He felt a certain danger, as if Tango might come at him as he stood defenseless in the ring.

Erik watched in silence. It was only when Michael finally stood at the horse's head that he said, "Insufficient. You have allowed the horse to do as he pleased. The line was not consistently taut, and your whip was useless. Never allow a horse to turn in toward you on the longe. If you ask the horse for a response, you must be prepared to deal with his inattention. I believe we have discussed this before."

"You will not ride the Phoenix this afternoon. Instead, you will ask Ivan to supervise your longeing of him until you are better able to elicit the desired behavior." He removed the longeing cavesson and straightened the tack. "Now, you are faced with the task of riding this horse. How do you intend to go about it?"

"What's he going to do?" Michael countered.

"That is a meaningless question. I am not a soothsayer."

"Well, what's he done before? Do you know?"

"Yes, we have some information on his background. He was prepared for the track as a two-year-old but could not be persuaded to enter the gate although a number of efforts, some quite unpleasant, were used to induce him to do so. Subsequently, he was ridden by a young man of limited skill in an attempt to turn him into a show horse. What methods were used, we don't know. We know he resisted—successfully—and that he has reared and gone over with his rider."

"Great!" Michael said darkly.

Erik smiled. "Are you afraid of the horse?"

Michael reddened. "Of course I am. You think I'm stupid? You think I want him falling on *me*?"

"If you don't, see to it that he doesn't."

"How am I supposed to do that?"

"Forewarned is forearmed. It's time you began to use your mind. I have told you something about this horse's background. Have you drawn no conclusions?"

"Yeah, I've drawn a conclusion," Michael said. "I conclude some idiot's mistreated him."

Erik regarded Michael with a smile. "Excellent!" he said. "And?"

"And he's going to kill the next person who climbs on his back?"

"Why should he do that?"

"So he won't get another dose of the same medicine?"

"You think he objects to someone sitting on his back?"

"I don't know. He might."

"And if he does, how will you deal with him?"

"Am I supposed to know that?"

"Since you are to ride the horse, you'd be well advised to think about it, yes."

"I guess you'd have to show him it didn't hurt him—that you weren't going to hurt him."

"How?"

"Sitting on him without hurting him."

"How might you hurt him?"

"Well—maybe his back's sore."

"You think his back is sore?"

"How the hell do I know?"

Unperturbed, Erik said, "You have groomed and saddled him. Have you seen evidence of a sore back? Heat? Swelling? Pain?"

"No."

"Then let us make a hypothetical assumption that his back is not sore," Erik said facetiously. "What else might he have objected to?"

"You mean aside from someone sitting on him?"

"Yes."

"Being kicked suddenly, struck, yanked on—"

"Very good. I presume you will make sure such unpleasantness does not occur when you first ride him. Tell me what you will do this afternoon."

"Get on him," Michael said, "carefully so as not to hit him in the side or on the back, sit quietly down in the saddle and use almost no rein."

Erik took a step backward and gestured to the horse. Michael had only the blind hope that Erik would not have allowed him to proceed if he had given an incorrect answer. Or was he letting the horse teach him the consequences of his own mistakes? He shortened the rein on the horse's neck and prepared to mount. Instantly, Tango began to move restlessly around him. He swung his quarters away and stepped backward. With his right hand on the stirrup, Michael couldn't keep him still enough to mount. He turned hesitantly to Erik. "Will you hold him for me?"

"No. The horse is telling you something. It's up to you to answer."

"I don't know what you're talking about," Michael said.

"What does the horse's action tell you?"

"That he doesn't want me to get on."

"He doesn't *want* you to get on? You're fanciful. You ascribe human characteristics to the horse. Or is it yourself you're describing? I believe it would be more correct to say the horse is signaling to you that he will not *let* you get on. Am I right?"

"OK," Michael said with an effort to control his temper, "he won't *let* me get on."

"And so you will do what?"

"I suppose I'll make him let me get on."

"How?"

"Get my foot in the stirrup one way or another and just get on."

"What would you expect him to do under those circumstances?"

"Fight."

"How?"

"Rush forward, take off, buck, rear—how do I know?"

"You cannot know, but you have made a reasonable guess. What would you do then?"

"Try like hell to stay on, shorten the rein, try to make him stop. Hang on—"

Erik laughed. "Yes, you want to be a cowboy. What would you expect to be the result of such a scene?"

"I'd expect to fall off."

"And the horse, what would he have learned from the lesson?"

"Just what he already knew—how to get rid of his rider?"

"And?"

"Isn't that enough?"

"You would have reinforced the horse's expectation, wouldn't you, that the rider is dangerous and will hurt him?"

"What else can I do? Not get on at all?"

"That is another alternative, but hardly a useful one. Do you think I accepted this horse for training with the idea that he could not be trained?"

Michael said nothing. He could hear the swallows in the rafters and purposely concentrated on the sound.

"You have mentioned," Erik went on, "that your aim is to convince the horse that you will sit on him without hurting him, but at the same time you will insist he *allow* you to do so. Is that correct?"

"Yes."

"You have a range of behavior to deal with. Is it your intention to let minor disobedience go by so he will trust you and to punish major resistances like rearing?"

"Yes."

"Incorrect," Erik said. "If you allow minor disobedience, you teach the horse the value of resistance, and you choose a far more dangerous arena in which to do combat—one where you are very apt to lose. Isn't it so?"

"I guess maybe," Michael conceded.

"Then I suggest you ask very little of the horse, but that you insist that what you ask is obeyed. You have here an animal that will not let you mount. How does he prevent you?"

"By moving around."

"So your task is to see that that minor disobedience is discouraged and a more desirable behavior substituted. What do you do?"

"Make him stand still."

"How?"

"I don't know. Hold the reins tight?"

"How will he react to that?"

"Oh, Christ—how do I know? Stand still?"

"Do you really believe that a horse that has in all probability been punished with the rein will stand for your pulling on the rein while you mount?"

"If I could get him to stand for just a second or two even if I don't have time to get on, I could reward him," Michael said slowly.

"Ah," Erik said, nodding, "now you use your intelligence. You have been working with Peter for several weeks. Hasn't he taught you the use of the rein?"

"Yes."

"Have you learned, then, that you cannot force a horse to go with a touch of the leg or to stop with the rein—you merely give him a signal he has learned to obey?"

"Yes."

"Put a bit in the horse's mouth and apply pressure, and the horse will seek to reduce the pressure until he is taught otherwise. He will try a number of things until he finds one that works. Stopping is only one of those possibilities, and if the rider is wise, he will immediately relax the pressure when the horse happens to stop, and thus teach him that that is the correct response.

"I suspect we have here an animal who has learned that rearing will reduce the pressure in his mouth—not because the rider purposely rewards that behavior, but because the rider falls in the dirt and drops the rein. We must retrain him. We start from the ground by teaching the horse to stand. It is only if he stands that you can mount in the way you have described, gently, without frightening or hurting him. You understand?"

"Yes."

"If the horse seeks to remove the pressure from the bars of his mouth, it follows that you may not keep a constant pull on the rein—correct?"

"Yes."

"Why?"

"Because he'll begin to pull against you to get away, and he'll win because he's stronger than you."

Erik nodded. "What is the alternative?"

"To tug gently, and if he pulls back release the rein and ask again. That way he has nothing to pull against."

He saw Erik smile. "Peter has done his work."

"I've always known that," Michael said in disgust.

"Always," Erik repeated. "Proceed with the lesson."

Michael turned toward the horse. He had hardly changed his stance when the horse began to move around him again and Michael, aware of Erik's eye on him, put his hand on the horse's neck and stroked him lightly.

"What are you doing?" came Erik's critical voice from behind him.

"Trying to make him relax."

"Is that the function of this lesson?"

"Well, I can't teach him anything when he's a nervous wreck."

"Is that so? I suggest you have just taught him the benefit of disobedience."

Michael turned around. "What? I haven't even started to teach him anything."

"Then why have you rewarded him for moving?"

"I haven't—" he started to say, but his hand still rested comfortingly on the horse's neck, and he jerked it back, suddenly self-conscious. "What would you have me do, punish him? He'd just think this whole business is dangerous to him."

"Correct," Erik said. "Perhaps you know of some law that requires you always either to reward or punish your horse?"

Michael was silent for a moment. Then he gained courage and said, "Can't you let me do this without watching? I can't think—"

"In that case," Erik said, "I will stay to insure that you do."

It took Michael half an hour to get Tango to stand still while he stood beside him facing his tail, the stirrup in his hand. During this time, Erik watched silently. He said nothing as Michael tried repeatedly to reposition the horse. He was finally successful when he thought to place Tango in the corner of the arena, his hindquarters to the wall, so he could neither back up nor pivot away.

Absorbed with the problem and given a free hand with the horse, Michael forgot Erik's presence. He found himself talking to Tango in a tone that varied from warning to encouragement, and when finally Tango stood for him, he fed him sugar from his pocket and patted him enthusiastically on the neck. He moved the horse out of the corner to other areas of the ring and returned to the corner when he moved. He was finally able to put his foot up to the stirrup as Tango stood motionless, and he led him back to where Erik was standing, considerably more confident.

"Proceed," Erik said.

"You mean mount?"

"Yes."

And Michael mounted the horse for the first time, hesitantly, not quite sure of himself, but aware that Tango was also nervous. He shared with him a faint but hopeful trust that each would not be betrayed by the other. He settled into the saddle as quietly as he could, the reins loose on Tango's neck, and patted him. He was exultant. Tango stood still. Michael dismounted, and Erik raised an eyebrow.

"Well?"

"I don't think I should do any more," Michael said quickly. He was breathing hard. He was amazed to find he had been holding his breath.

"Oh? Why not?"

Was it the wrong answer? "Well," he said, staring at the ground, "because it's gone all right. I mean, he's done it all right, all I've asked—"

"Yes?"

"And if I start something else and it goes wrong, he'll think this part's wrong, too. I mean, he won't know if any part of it's right—"

Erik said nothing.

"Is that right?" Michael said.

"You are the rider."

"Then I'm going to stop for now." When there was no further word from Erik, he led the horse back to the barn.

His victory with Tango buoyed him for the rest of the day. He treasured a secret happiness. Often he wouldn't immediately recall its source, and when he did, he would glance at Tango walking the borders of his stall and think to himself, I did it—all of it.

He began to keep a surreptitious watch on Erik, not as he had done before from a defensive need to protect himself, but with a compelling curiosity. Obsessively he reviewed the lesson in the arena and tried to convince himself that Erik had in some way changed. It was impossible for him to remember, and there was certainly no evidence of it now.

Michael couldn't control his need to know. He wanted Erik to acknowledge his success. It seemed almost as important as the success itself. Finally he indicated Tango over his shoulder and said as casually as he could, "He's restless. He hasn't stopped walking since I put him away."

Erik was standing in the doorway, watching a car and trailer labor up over the hill before descending to the barn. He glanced at Michael without comment. "Prepare the horse for his lesson," he said and indicated the trailer, which had stopped in the yard.

CHAPTER 19

▼

Michael didn't remember that he was supposed to dispose of the manure pile until the day before the fair. He was seized with a moment of mindless panic, unable to remember when he was supposed to have done it and how, even now, he could find the time to get it done. He hurried through the morning stable chores and coped grimly with a series of events that seemed malevolently designed to hinder him.

When finally he had finished the barn work, he drove the tractor and spreader to the hayfield and began the tedious circling of the field. As he drove he brooded moodily on the events of the past week. True to his word, Erik had increased his demands, and Michael in his turn had made an uncharacteristic effort at self-control.

His work with Blue Tango was his greatest frustration. Contrary to his expectations, Erik made few comments but watched in silence as he tried to figure out what to do with the horse. The first few days had been limited to mounting and dismounting and walking the horse gingerly around in circles. He seemed to be getting nowhere.

Throughout the week he had sustained himself by thoughts of the coming fair as a welcome change of pace and a rare taste of freedom. The evening before a chance comment of Ivan's had threatened even this small comfort. They were sitting around the kitchen table after they had finished supper and Erik had returned to the barn. Michael had made a full pot of coffee, and already it was half gone.

"Looking forward to riding at the fair?" he said idly to Peter.

"Kind of," Peter said. "It should be interesting with Tangent as flaky as she is, but to tell you the truth what I'm really loking forward to is watching Erik ride."

Ivan glanced at him, nodded and stirred his coffee. He made a muffled sound of agreement.

"He hasn't ridden in a show since I came," Peter went on. "I never understood why. I get a kick out of it myself, and Erik's got such presence on a horse."

"You think he showed when he was a kid?" Michael asked.

"I guess he used to give exhibitions at fairs, horse shows, things like that," Peter said. "Apparently they didn't have dressage shows back then—not in this country, anyway."

Michael tipped back in his chair. "How old do you suppose he was?"

Ivan said, "Pretty young, according to Jan Karras. He was a lot younger than any of us. Just a kid."

Michael watched him pour another cup of coffee and pushed his own cup forward for a refill. "How's this all going to work?" he asked. "I mean with all the horses going back and forth and the others that are left here? When's the show start? What are we supposed to be doing?"

"There are really three shows," Ivan said. "The 4-H and Hunter-Jumper shows are during the week. The dressage show's Saturday and Sunday. Peter and I ride both days, but I think Erik's classes are on Sunday."

"Calypso goes both days," Peter corrected him. "Lyrik's on Sunday. I read in the program that he's doing some kind of demonstration after the show's over, but he never told me that."

"Nor me," Ivan said. "He only told me our schedule."

"What schedule? He never told me anything at all," Michael said.

"He said old Mr. Estep's going to keep an eye on things when we're gone," Ivan said. "You'll feed and muck out early and then the horses will be turned out. The ones that are entered in the show will go down Saturday and stay there over night. Peter and I are staying with them. You and Erik will come back in the evening to feed. You'll have to ride in the evening."

"What are you talking about?" Michael demanded of Ivan, dropping his chair to the floor. "No one told *me* that."

"Didn't Erik say you were supposed to ride every day except Mondays?"

"He's not going to make me ride when the show's going on," Michael protested.

"Don't bet on it."

"For Christ's sake, you think I'm going to miss Saturday night at the fair? Forget it!"

But he was still agitated when Erik returned from the barn and Erik noticed it at once. "You have a problem I should know about?"

Michael struggled with himself. Finally, he burst out, "What's this about my riding Tango on Saturday? Am I supposed to do that?"

"I gave you your instructions. I assume you would not wish me to repeat them?"

"Saturday's the fair—"

"I hardly need to be reminded of that."

"I thought I was supposed to be working there."

"You are."

"Then how am I supposed to ride?"

"You will be here to feed night and morning. I'm sure we can find time for you to ride in the evening."

"I'm not supposed to work at night."

"Oh? Another new rule you have made up?"

"Look—" Michael said. "I don't care if I miss a lesson—"

"Indeed?"

"I wanted to be down there Saturday evening," Michael went on doggedly. "I've already made arrangements to meet someone."

"Then I suggest you unmake them."

Michael was still for several seconds before he got suddenly to his feet and left the room. When he had gone, Peter eyed Erik with a sense of indecision and then said recklessly, "You're awfully hard on him—"

"That is my intention."

"Is he getting on all right with Tango?"

"Yes. They are much alike. They should do well together, provided I can insure that one does not kill the other." He laughed. The confrontation seemed to have cheered him.

"Do you think he has that much skill?"

"Of course not. But his basic riding is quite good when he keeps his temper and listens to the horse. Unfortunately, I'm forced to keep him under close supervision to see that he does so."

Surprised that Erik had allowed the conversation, Peter watched him thoughtfully and then said, "Would it be so unreasonable to let him off Saturday night, since he's already made plans? He could give us a hand—"

Erik made a disparaging sound. "Better an evening spent on the back of a horse than that of some woman behind the midway. You can save your concern—I understand Michael. It is he who doesn't understand himself."

"In what way?"

"He is a man of action. When he wants something he cannot immediately have, he would lay hands upon it and bring it to himself by force. He has yet to learn the value of inaction, of self-denial. Perhaps he will never learn it. That's what I intend to discover."

"I think he just wants you to approve of him."

Erik shrugged. "That is *his* problem," he said. "I don't care about it. He must learn to be independent of such weakness."

Michael had driven half way around the field before he realized that the spreader was finally empty. He disengaged the gears and drove back to the barn, wondering if he was late for his ride on Tango.

In the tackroom he found Peter preparing to clean his tack. His saddle lay on the cleaning rack, his bridle on the harness hook.

"Where's Erik?" Michael asked from the doorway. He spoke with misgiving. He was late again.

"Went off on Calypso out back somewhere."

From the corner of his eye Michael could see Tango walking in his stall. He felt a restless urge to confide in Peter and a familiar reluctance. Finally he said off-handedly, "I don't know if I can hack this much longer—"

"What?"

"I don't know—" Aimlessly he pushed a piece of straw around the cement floor with his toe. "I don't know what I'm doing with Tango, and I can't even seem to do this other stuff right, like the barn door. I knocked the damned thing right off the track this morning. I forgot to refill the grain bins last night, and this morning we had nothing to feed—it made me half an hour late. Ivan's had to bail me out twice. Erik looks like he'd like to break me in half—probably would, too, if everyone weren't so damned busy."

"That wouldn't stop him," Peter said. "Don't worry about it. He's in a bad mood, that's all."

"Why the hell should *he* be in a bad mood? *I'm* the one who should be in a bad mood. I can't satisfy him no matter what I do." He sighed and listlessly moved into the tackroom.

"How's Tango coming?" Peter asked him at length.

"Who knows? I spent the whole first day just trying to mount. Since then I've been walking him around—stopping, walking, turning, stopping—that's all. Erik stands around asking what I'm doing and why, what I'm *going* to do and why, and damned if *I* know what I'm supposed to do. He's never once said I'm doing the right thing. He only tells me when my answers are wrong, which is most of the time."

"Hand me the polish, would you?" Peter said. "Thanks. I wouldn't get discouraged. You must be doing all right—he'd tell you if you weren't. And Tango?"

"He walks, turns and stops. It'll be five years before he canters at the rate we're going."

"Well," Peter said vaguely, "it'll all come together at some point."

"What I want to know is, why am I doing it? You know, I used to wonder when I first came here why you and Ivan put up with all this shit, and now I'm doing the same goddamn thing, and I *still* don't know the answer."

Peter smiled, but he didn't answer. He put his saddle away and began to clean his reins. Absent-mindedly Michael started to help him take the bridle apart.

"I can't believe that about tomorrow night," Michael went on. "Do you think it matters a damn if Tango misses an evening of walking and stopping? I've been looking forward to tomorrow night for weeks. I had a date—there's a party after the fairgrounds close."

"I know how you feel," Peter said. I think you deserve a lot of credit for taking it the way you did. If it's any comfort to you, Ivan and I aren't going to get time off either. We have to baby-sit the horses down there."

"You can have your own party in the barn loft. I'd have settled for that."

"You like Tango a lot, don't you?"

"Yeah, I do, poor horse. I was sure amazed when he told me I'd be riding him."

"You must have done something right, or you'd never have gotten the chance. Erik's that way with horses. He says you don't ask them to do something unless you know they can. Same thing with us, I think."

They heard the sound of hooves in the aisle. Erik had returned from his ride.

"Take the horse and sweep up this mess in the aisle," he said to Peter and turned to Michael. "Why aren't you ready to ride?"

"I am ready."

Erik regarded him critically. "Change your clothes."

"What?"

"In your zeal to accomplish your work, you appear to have spread most of the manure pile on yourself."

Later Michael mounted Tango without a word and started him walking, the rein loose on the horse's neck. Unlike The Phoenix, Tango did not follow the bit with his head and neck but moved tentatively, his neck raised, his nose forward, the reins dangling. His steps were short. Michael, careful to sit as still as he could, felt the horse might explode into violence at any moment.

When he braced in the saddle and spoke, Tango stopped, but it was as if he himself braced for a further demand. Michael touched him gingerly with his legs and, when he started forward again, picked up the left rein and brought it carefully to the inside. Only the weight of the rein provided contact. Tango veered inward toward the center. Facing Erik, Michael stopped him.

"What's the point of this?" he asked. "I don't even know what I'm doing."

"What?" Erik said. "The expert is at a loss? What are you *trying* to do?"

"I thought you told me to walk around and stop."

"That is what you suggested. I don't recall telling you to do anything."

"Well, for God's sake! *I* don't know what I'm doing—all I'm doing is wasting time."

"Indeed. What is your goal?"

"Am I supposed to know that? Because I don't. I don't know a thing about it."

"That is a beginning, at least. Do you recall our discussion the other night? I asked you what the aim in schooling a horse was. You gave an acceptable answer. Have you forgotten it so soon?"

Michael sighed and stared for a moment at the rafters. "What's in the Collective Marks—impulsion, relaxation, submission," he said shortly.

"Well?"

"Well, how do I start? The horse is as tight as a wire. He won't move forward. He does what I say, but he's scared to death. What am I supposed to *do*?"

"You are supposed to remember what you have been told."

"*Which* thing I've been told?"

"What did I tell you the other night?"

Michael was silent for a moment before he answered. "You said I had to stop thinking of myself and listen to the horse."

"And now you are attempting to do so. What you have said is correct, the horse is very tense. Where do you look for the reason?"

"I don't know. He's scared of something that happened to him."

"That *happened* to him?"

Michael made an impatient gesture, and Tango shied violently. He leaped away in a succession of bounds and Michael, unprepared, lost his seat and did a flying dismount. He landed off balance on his feet and watched the horse gallop past him with stirrups and reins flapping. The whites of his eyes showed. Automatically, Michael started toward the rail to intercept him. "Whoa—whoa," he said soothingly, but he hated himself. He was ready to give up.

He caught Tango finally and led him back to Erik. The horse was trembling and had broken a sweat. "God damn it," Michael muttered under his breath. When Erik said nothing, he said aloud, "Now what?"

"Now you explain to yourself what happened."

"I *know* what happened. I scared him."

"How?"

"I moved, and it startled him."

"Correct. And in doing so he has told you something important and given you an answer to your question."

"Oh, Christ," Michael said. "I can't even remember the question—"

Erik laughed. "Yes, that is your problem. You leap away like the horse without thought. The horse has responded to an action of the rider. Perhaps that may help you discover why he is, as you point out, tense and hesitant. You may notice that he is far more generous than you are, for he at least listens to you. You do not do him the same favor."

"You mean he's tense because I'm tense?"

Erik bowed formally. He was still smiling. "Very insightful."

Michael remounted. Tango was shaking, and he felt an immediate sense of shame. He stroked him on the neck. "It's OK," he said under his breath, and aloud, "How can I relax after that?"

"One of you must to affect the other. I doubt the horse is able to."

"Well, how do *I?*"

"You are unfamiliar with suppling exercises after all these weeks?"

Michael stared at him. "That's crazy—I'd scare him out of his mind."

"I suspect," Erik said dryly, "you have already done that. I have yet to see a horse whose ambition is to train a man, so if you wait for him to do so, you will wait a long time."

"Tell me what to do," Michael said finally.

"I thought you had an aversion to my telling you what to do. Have you changed your mind?"

"Yes."

"Very well. At the halt, remove your foot from the stirrup and rotate the ankle. Then do the same with the other foot. Put your feet back in the stirrups and repeat the exercise. Do so repeatedly until the horse takes no notice. Then work on the leg. Stretch it down, bring it away from the horse's side and replace it. When he accepts that, bring the leg back from the hip, place it on the horse's side and draw it forward into place. Reassure the horse with your voice and hand when he stands.

"Continue, quietly, to move in the saddle, turning the torso, moving the shoulders and the head and, finally, the arms. You must persuade the horse that nothing you do will hurt him and that consequently he must accept what you do without fear. You must, however, be patient, so that you do *not* hurt him and therefore have not lied to him. In the midst of the exercises dismount and mount again. Why?"

"Because he's used to that and knows he's doing the right thing?"

Erik nodded. "It is always useful to present the horse with a task he has learned is correct to allow him to be successful and thus to be reassured. It gives the rider an opportunity to reward the animal when he is unable to otherwise. When you are able to move freely in the saddle without upsetting the horse, you may find yourself relaxing without effort."

Michael did as he was told. It took a very long time, but as Erik had predicted, it was as reassuring to him as it was to the horse. When he concentrated less on staying immobile, he was able to relax and begin to watch Tango. Still he had not moved from the halt.

"Why didn't you tell me that before?" he asked Erik.

"One does not learn by being told," Erik said. "One learns by understanding what the horse tells him, by the consequences of his own actions. You will learn when you take the time to use your intelligence. I will tell you this, however: in almost every case where the horse presents a problem, it is the rider's fault. The sooner you accept that simple lesson, the sooner you'll be able to influence the horse. One must listen to the horse first, and only then to himself."

Michael faced for the hundredth time a paradox about Erik that always defeated him. He had seen himself always as a loner whom no weakness or depravity could surprise or make helpless. He had tried ever since he had arrived to fit Erik's despotism to that mold and to resist it. Yet he sat now on Tango, wholly dependent on the man who stood before him, and still he couldn't bear to acknowledge it.

"Dismount," he heard Erik say. He did as he was told, patted Tango and prepared to remount. "No," Erik said. "Put the horse away."

Michael turned to face him. "Why?"

"I have other business to attend to, as do you, I believe."

"Can't I even try walking him?"

"No."

"Why not?" He stepped voluntarily into the trap Erik had set for him.

"You have learned a lesson. Now practice it."

"*Practice*? Practice what?"

Erik regarded him with amusement for several more seconds. "Submission," he said and walked away.

CHAPTER 20

▼

The Show Secretary's tent was on a knoll at the lower end of the fairgrounds. In front of it the ground dropped sharply away to the level field where the dressage arenas were laid out, three large rectangles outlined by lengths of white boards raised only twelve or fourteen inches from the ground. At the far end of each arena stood a horse trailer, the ramp down, where the judge would sit with his scribe during the riding of the tests.

Michael was standing just in front of the tent. It was still very early. There was a chill in the air, and the shadows cast by the arenas and the large white lettered signs around them were long and sharply etched.

Michael wore only a cotton shirt with the sleeves rolled up, but he didn't notice the cold or the fact that his sneakers were wet from the dew. From where he stood, he could look to his left and see Ivan riding Orion in the warm-up ring and beyond a part of the racetrack and the bleachers along the far side. Still farther away were the shed rows, which the racehorses shared this week with show horses. Behind him the skeletal structures of the midway loomed in silhouette, and two paved walkways sloped gently upward, bordered by rows of barns and judging pavilions. Pennants and flags flew everywhere. The entrance road was lined with parked trucks, vans and stock trailers, and still more were arriving.

Michael watched the showgrounds slowly come to life around him. Riders in formal attire, grooms and spectators walked to and from the stables and stood in groups near the refreshment tent, drinking coffee. Reluctantly he started back to the barn where he had left Calypso half an hour before. On the way he overtook Pat Bartlett.

"Seen your horse yet?"

"I was just on my way to find him. Is Mr. Sarmento riding now?"

"He's not here yet. Rides sometime around noon, I think. Ivan rides at eight-thirty—" He waved vaguely toward the warm-up ring. Pat shaded her eyes and followed the direction of the gesture.

"On the bay?"

"Yeah." He was caught between a sense of pride at his connection with a competitor and a sudden need to become the center of her attention. "Come see your horse."

He led her toward the barn. "Bet you wish you were riding him."

"In a way I do. But it's been so long since I've ridden seriously, I know I couldn't do him justice. Still, I'm dying to watch him go. Do you think he's doing well?"

"Looks good to me." He watched her surreptitiously from the corner of his eye.

"—extensions," he was suddenly aware of her saying.

"What?"

"I was wondering about the extensions."

"You'll see."

"You're as bad as your boss," she said smiling.

"Don't say that", Michael said wryly and made a face.

Calypso was looking expectantly over the stall door as they approached. Pat went up to him and put her hands on either side of his face. "He looks marvelous," she said to Michael, and to the horse, "You're going to win, aren't you?" She regarded Michael thoughtfully and added, "My coach is going to be here. He's been away all summer competing in Europe. When I told him I'd sent Calypso to Mr. Sarmento for the summer, he was furious at me."

Michael grinned. He leaned back against the door of an empty stall and propped his elbows behind him on its rim.

"Yeah?"

"He said Mr. Sarmento's a circus trainer, rode in circuses as a child. I hadn't known that. And he said Mr. Sarmento never rode in competitions, and he thinks he may have ruined Calypso."

She looked uncertainly at Michael.

"Oh, for Christ's sake," Michael said. "The horse was rearing and carrying on—who taught him to do that?"

"I guess I did."

"Well, why did he let you do it if he's your coach?"

"I don't think I can blame it all on him. Calypso did pretty well for quite a while. It was when we began to work on collection—"

"I'd like to hear what he says today."

"I'm not looking forward to it," Pat said. "He asked me outright to let him ride instead of Mr. Sarmento."

"You're kidding! What'd you say?"

"It was very awkward. I have to work with John."

"Why?"

"What did you say?"

"Why do you have to work with him?"

She stared at him and gave an embarrassed laugh. "He's my coach," she said reasonably.

"What'd you tell him?"

"I told him Mr. Sarmento had had Calypso for almost three months and that since he was riding at my request, I thought he should have the chance to do so. John accepted that, but he's really mad at me. He thinks an awful lot of Calypso." She put her hand on the horse's nose and toyed with his forelock. "John's long-listed for the Olympics," she added.

"Big deal," Michael said. "Did he win in Europe?"

"I don't think he did that well, but that doesn't mean much. Americans never do very well over there."

"Is he riding today?"

"I don't think so. His horses are still in quarantine. But Calypso's original trainer is one of the judges here. I think he may be judging one of Mr. Sarmento's rides. Calypso's entered in three classes. I had him entered in two Third Level tests, but Mr. Sarmento—"

"Will you stop calling him that?" He was unreasonably irritated by her tone of respect. "His name's Erik."

She laughed. "I can't call him Erik, I hardly know him. Do *you* call him Erik?"

"I don't call him anything, except 'sir' when he makes me," Michael said wryly.

She laughed again. "Anyway, I see he's entered one of the fourth-level tests, too. That means he must have worked out the flying change. John and I had started working on that when all this other thing happened. It used to upset Calypso a lot, for some reason. We may have pushed him too fast."

They were still standing there when Peter drove in with the trailer. He greeted Pat and asked if Ivan had ridden.

"I don't know," Michael said. He had forgotten all about Ivan. "I guess he's in there now."

He helped Peter take the horses off the trailer. Lyrik was nervous. She stepped around, lifting her legs high, hampered by the shipping bandages. Her head and neck were raised so that she appeared even taller than she actually was. She gave a ringing neigh and stopped for a few seconds to listen. From somewhere in the distance another horse answered, and she started moving around Michael again. "Whoa," he said firmly and tugged on the leadshank. Peter squatted to remove the bandages.

"What a lovely horse!" Pat said. "You don't often see a truly black horse. Is she Mr. Sarmento's or does she belong to one of his students?"

"His," Michael said. "I don't know why he had her brought down today, she's not going till tomorrow."

From his position on his heels at Lyrik's feet, Peter said, "Erik bought her off the track. I'm sure she thinks she's headed for the starting gate right now. He wants to get her calmed down."

Peter moved methodically around the horse, removing the wraps with a deft hand-to-hand motion. "Walk her around a bit before we put her away," he said to Michael. "Let her graze around the barns and see if she'll settle."

As he started away with Lyrik, Michael passed Ivan on foot, leading Orion. He was wearing a black riding jacket with a white stock and a hunt cap made of rigid plastic covered with black velveteen. He seemed a different person from the one Michael had struggled with all summer, and Michael felt subdued.

"How'd it go?" he heard Peter ask and slowed to hear the answer. Lyrik moved impatiently around him, and he could hear only snatches of Ivan's reply.

"—trouble at the beginning. He was a bit uncertain about the flowers—blew her whistle when I was right about to pass the judge's trailer—go up in smoke, I could feel his heart pounding. He wouldn't stand for the first salute—got better and better—I thought it was OK for his first time out—better in the next ride, and my First Level test isn't 'til tomorrow—" Michael watched him run his hand through his damp hair and toss his hat carelessly into the empty stall they used for a tack room.

Beside him Lyrik pulled urgently on the leadshank and started walking down the grassy aisle. Michael yanked on the shank and elbowed her in the shoulder. "Shape up," he muttered as she jogged lightly beside him, tossing her head gently against the shank. He shifted the leadshank to his left hand and put his right hand on her neck. He had watched Erik ride out on her many times but had never seen her perform. It seemed to him now that he had never really looked at her: the elegant, fine-boned head and glossy, gleaming coat. Her neck beneath his hand was hard and warm. He was proud to have her in his care.

Erik had already arrived when he got back. He was clad in jeans and a faded work shirt and looked just like another groom. Michael felt faintly ashamed that Erik didn't look more like a proper riding master in front of Pat.

He heard her say timidly, "Do you think he'll do well?" There was no answer. "I was telling Michael," she went on, "that John Henderson is here. He wanted to ride Calypso—"

Still Erik said nothing.

"I asked him to come down here to talk to you. You ride at eleven-thirty and again at three or so, don't you?"

"The ride times are in the program," Erik said.

Ivan, who had just finished braiding Tangent's mane, came to her rescue. "That's right," he said, as if Erik hadn't spoken, "and he goes again tomorrow around ten. Want to go with me to watch Peter ride when we've got him ready?"

Suddenly Michael was caught up in a contest for Pat's attention. His heart began to race, and he felt a burning anger at Ivan, and yet he knew that Erik had already isolated her from all of them. He saw with misgiving that Erik had already turned around to face him. "I would suggest," Erik said, "that anything you may be tempted to say remain unsaid." Michael took a half step back and kept his silence. "And you," Erik said to Ivan, "will concentrate your energies on the horses, which is your job, and not on my client." He turned to Pat with a wintry smile and dismissed her with a wave.

And so Pat turned and walked away. Michael would have followed her, had he dared. From the corner of his eye he could see Ivan standing rigidly beside Tangent. Neither of them moved as Erik let his gaze move over them. "I have better things to do than to protect young women from the advances of my stable hands," he said. "I will remind you that it is not Miss Bartlett who requires your attention, it is her horse. Michael, take the mare from Peter and allow him to change his clothes. Then pick up the stalls and make sure the horses have water."

"Jesus!" Michael said later to Ivan when Peter had ridden Tangent away, "I thought this was supposed to be a kind of holiday, but he's going to have all our asses in a sling before it's over."

Ivan didn't answer. He started braiding Calypso's mane.

"He's sure as hell going to lose her as a client," Michael went on. "She'll probably let her hotshot coach ride the horse after all."

"Don't bet on it." Ivan said.

Michael pulled a rub rag from the grooming box and began to run it over Calypso's back and sides. The horse's coat was a rich, dark chestnut, and it shone with metallic, coppery highlights. "When's your next ride?" he asked.

"Not 'til three something."

"Think we could go and watch the rides for a while?"

"Not unless you want to be out of a job. Peter's rides are close together—he goes again before lunch. Erik rides around noon and then again in the middle of the afternoon, almost the same time I do. We've got to get the horses ready, put them away, and clean the tack between rides. I wouldn't be surprised if Erik wants to ride Lyrik, too." As he spoke, Erik came back to the barn. He disappeared into the tack room and Ivan started saddling Calypso.

Michael asked, "How was Orion this morning?"

"I thought he did OK considering it was his first time out. I've gotten really fond of him this summer; he tries so hard. He can jump, too, and he's fast. I keep thinking he'd make a good event horse." He lapsed into silence.

Erik appeared from the tack stall dressed in white britches, black boots with blunt, rounded spurs, a black jacket and a white stock, perfectly tied. He held his hat under his arm and a pair of white gloves in one hand. His face was expressionless. Michael stared at him from Calypso's stall, his mouth open, and Ivan turned away to hide his smile.

Erik pulled the stirrup iron down with a snap and mounted Calypso. "My whip," he said to Ivan, received it without comment and rode away.

"My God, I wouldn't have recognized him," Michael said, staring after him until he disappeared from sight. "Come on, let's go watch. No one'll care if we're gone for a couple of minutes."

Trailers were still arriving and horses were being moved into stalls in all the barns around them. They picked their way around piles of gear and parked vehicles. Bales of hay and straw, tack trunks, shovels and manure forks, rubber buckets and an assortment of tack and clothing lay in piles on the grassy strips between the barns, and there seemed to be people everywhere, holding horses, walking them, moving in and out of stalls.

They found a place on the hillside by the Secretary's tent with the other spectators. The announcer's voice came intermittently over the loudspeaker system to recite the rider's numbers as each entered the arena and occasionally to page competitors. "You have one minute, twenty-three," it intoned now, "fourteen on deck." A rider trotted rapidly toward them from the warm-up ring.

"There's Peter going—" Michael pointed to the center arena. The previous rider's horse ambled slowly toward the gate on a loose rein, and Peter had started to ride around the outside.

"Damn, Tangent's nervous as hell," Ivan said as they watched the horse balk at passing the judge's trailer and then bolt past at Peter's gentle urging. When the judge blew her whistle, Peter made another circuit of the ring, dropped his whip on the ground in the collecting area and made his entrance into the arena. A steward drew a board across the gate after him and leaned over to pick up the whip.

Michael saw nothing extraordinary in the test. Tangent performed the figures obediently as she did at home. But Ivan watched raptly from beside him. "Peter's got one hell of a knack with nervous horses," he commented at one point, and when Peter rode from the arena, he ran down the hill to meet him.

Michael was suddenly aware of Calypso strolling unhurriedly toward them from the hillside at the far end of the grounds. Erik rode over to the sidelines and dismounted to watch the ride that was being performed in the farthest arena.

He heard someone speak his name and turned to see Pat Bartlett coming up the hill with a young man who looked only a few years older than she. Michael turned to her. "I'm sorry about what happened."

"I guess I should have stayed away," Pat smiled at him. "I should know enough by now to stay away from competitors before they ride. John, this is Michael, one of Mr. Sarmento's grooms. Michael, I'd like you to meet my coach, John Henderson."

Michael gave a minimal wave and nodded to Henderson who gave an acknowledging smile. He heard him say in an undertone to Pat, "He has a peculiar way of warming up. Not smart to let the horse stand around like that before a test."

Michael appraised him critically. "He knows what he's doing," he said.

"I hope so," Henderson said and then to Pat, "The horse looks well, anyway."

"Yes, doesn't he? I think you'll be pleased, John."

Michael, watching Peter dismount and lead Tangent away toward the barn, realized he had hardly been aware of Peter's test. Ivan climbed slowly back up the hill to where they stood and shook hands with Henderson.

"Look!" Pat said suddenly. "Calypso goes now!"

Erik did not ride around the outside of the arena as the other riders had done but mounted Calypso unhurriedly and rode a figure eight outside the gate. When the bell rang, he gathered the horse, and Calypso entered the ring at an elevated, springy trot. He moved straight and energetically down the centerline, halted directly from the trot in the center of the arena and stood motionless.

"Oh!" Pat said, her hand on Henderson's arm. "Look, John—isn't he beautiful?"

"Yes, he is," Henderson said. "I'll give him that. The guy has a real classical seat—I'm surprised." He watched as the horse came in half-pass across the diagonal. "Wait 'til the extensions," he said knowingly.

But Calypso moved into extension and collection without incident. Even Michael, unable to evaluate what he was watching, saw that the horse performed effortlessly, as if everything required was easy for him. When Erik stopped for the final salute, the judge stood to acknowledge it and, instead of sitting again, waited until Erik approached him at the walk and stopped the horse just in front of the trailer.

"What do you think he's saying?" Pat asked.

"Who knows?" Henderson said. "Probably 'Nice ride!' It was, you know. Very nice."

Michael could feel Pat's relief. Henderson seemed genuinely pleased with the performance. "I'd like to meet him," he said to Pat.

Erik was riding toward the gate on a loose rein.

"We've got to go," Michael said abruptly and started back to the barn at a jog.

When Erik arrived with Calypso, Peter was setting out again on Tangent, and Ivan was sponging off Lyrik in her stall. Michael took the horse from Erik and watched him disappear into the tack stall to remove his coat and stock. When he reappeared, Michael said, "There are some people who want to talk to you—" Against all reason, he was nursing an optimistic hope that Erik would relent and allow him to stay for the evening.

"Attend to Calypso."

"Yes, sir."

Pat and John Henderson were standing outside Calypso's stall as Michael removed the tack. The reins were slippery with the horse's sweat, and the stirrup leathers and girth had areas of soapy, grey film where he had lathered.

"Mr. Sarmento?" Pat said as Erik walked past, "I'd like you to meet John Henderson."

Michael saw Erik stop and turn an appraising eye on Henderson. "How do you do?" he said and made as if to walk past him.

"I wanted to compliment you on your test," Henderson said. "The horse performed brilliantly."

Erik studied him. "Yes," he said. "He will go to the top—if he is allowed to."

"I agree with you. It's been a rare treat working with him and Pat."

"For whom?"

"I beg your pardon?"

"I said, for whom? The horse does not appear to have shared your pleasure."

Henderson gave an embarrassed laugh. "Pat's told me you had some reservations about his training, and I confess I had some about you, too. Tell me, what did you do with the horse? I understand you have some unique ideas on schooling."

"There is nothing unique in adjusting a horse's attitude. Miss Bartlett's horse in intelligent, and he tries to please. I merely did him the same favor."

Henderson regarded him quizzically. "Well, I suppose I can't expect you to give away your secrets," he said. "As a matter of fact, although I did want to congratulate you on your ride, I came by partly to ask if one of your horses is for sale." He waved toward Orion's stall. "The big bay there. I watched his test this morning—very nice horse. I asked the young man who rode him if he were for sale. He indicated he probably was and directed me to you. May I try him?"

"No," Erik said, "you may not. The horse will perform another test this afternoon."

"I see. Perhaps after the show is over, then? What are you asking for him?"

"He is already sold."

"Oh? May I ask what the general price range was?"

"I fail to see how that is any of your business."

"I'll grant you that. I've been out of the country for a while, and I was just curious. Will you at least tell me his new owner?"

Ivan led Lyrik over to Erik. She was still tense, her attention divided. Erik took the rein and checked the girth. Henderson watched him mount the horse, take the whip from Ivan and ride away, leaving his question unanswered. He turned to Ivan, "Who bought the horse?" he asked.

"I don't know. He didn't tell me he'd sold him." Ivan felt a melancholy sense of loss, although he knew that all the horses he rode and trained were eventually sold. It was one of the hard realities of Erik's business that horses came and went, and those he was assigned were his only on borrowed time.

When Peter returned from his second ride, leading Tangent, he told them wryly, "You should have seen that one! The midway rides have started, and you could hear the music off and on when the wind changed. That gigantic double Ferris wheel kept looming up over the secretary's tent and Tangent thought it was after her. Some clown had left the wrappings of his lunch on the hillside, and they were blowing around all over. She worked herself into a real state. She hadn't wanted to leave the others here anyway, and she seemed to be looking for them the whole time she was out there. She called almost nonstop. Didn't you hear her? When I'd finished the judge made some comment about my musical ride!" He grinned. "Can't win 'em all."

During the course of the afternoon they received a stream of visitors. A number of Erik's clients came by as well as some of Ivan and Peter's students. Some were riding in the show; others had come to watch. Even some of the racetrack grooms, bored, wandered down the grassy aisles for diversion.

When Erik returned with Lyrik, scarcely half an hour before Calypso's next test, Michael had him bridled and waiting and quickly changed Erik's saddle from one horse to the other. He saw Erik recognize his forethought with a slight smile, but once he had changed into his formal clothing, he mounted and rode off without a word.

It was after Ivan's second ride, which Erik had watched from the sidelines, that he astonished them all with a casual announcement. Back at the barn Ivan was attending to Orion in his stall. On the spur of the moment, he put his hands up to the horse's neck, laid his face against him and closed his eyes for a few seconds.

"You may well thank the horse for such a performance," came Erik's voice. He was standing in the doorway of the stall, and Ivan started and turned guiltily to face him.

Ivan made an embarrassed sound. "I was very proud of him," he said simply. "It's the best I've ever gotten from him—that much consistency."

"Yes," Erik said. "It was well done."

Michael, listening, envied Ivan bitterly for the compliment and tried to repress his selfishness.

"I understand you've sold him," he heard Ivan say. "I didn't know."

"He isn't sold."

"What?"

"I said, he isn't sold. I have given him away."

"*Given* him away? Why? He must be worth a lot—he's young, he's never had a lame day in his life, he's a lovely mover, and his attitude is—"

"True," Erik interrupted him. "I trust his new owner will value him for all those reasons."

Ivan shook his head. "Who'd you give him to?"

"To you."

Michael saw the color drain from Ivan's face. He looked suddenly frozen in place beside the horse, who was eating his hay unconcernedly. Michael glanced over at Peter, so recently bereaved himself. But Peter's face was lit with surprise and pleasure. None of them spoke, and finally Erik said, "There is tack to be cleaned and stalls to be taken care of. It is time for the horses to be fed. See that each of them is walked in hand this evening for half an hour and again early tomorrow before they are fed. Michael, get the truck. We will go back to the farm now."

CHAPTER 21

▼

Michael was still absorbed by the events of the day before as he stood by the dressage arenas on Sunday morning. It was noontime, and behind him on the hill groups of spectators sat on the grass eating the hot dogs and cold drinks they had carried from the refreshment tent. Others had brought aluminum lawn chairs, picnic baskets, and an elaborate assortment of food.

He didn't notice Annie Trowbridge seated with Bill Freeman at the top of the hill, but from her vantage point she had seen him and pointed him out to Bill. She stood up, waved and called to him.

Michael heard her and turned to look up the slope. For a moment he stood in what seemed to Annie a posture of indecision, his hand shading his eyes against the sun. His image was framed by the geometric angles of the dressage arenas. As she watched him start up the slope toward them, she was relieved, although she wasn't sure why. She greeted him with delight. "Are you riding in the show?"

"Fat chance!" he said. "What're you doing here?"

"You wrote me about the show—I hoped I'd see you. Do you remember Dr. Freeman? Bill, you remember Michael."

Bill reached up to shake Michael's hand. "Nice to see you again, Michael."

"Hi," Michael said.

Annie asked, "Will you join us?"

"For a couple of minutes. Erik's about to ride, and I'm supposed to take the horse when he's finished. He's warming up somewhere—" He looked around vaguely.

"Are Ivan and Peter riding?"

"Yeah, they're both finished." He sat down on the grass. "You remember that horse the girl was riding when we went up there last spring?"

"Yes—"

"We've got him down here. He's won all his classes."

"I wish I'd seen them."

Michael was silent for a moment, and then he said suddenly, "Erik *gave* Ivan a horse yesterday."

Annie didn't know how to respond. She could feel the pressure of his envy and beneath it the current of yearning.

"How nice," she said uncertainly.

"Yeah? A lot of good it'll do him. No way he can afford a horse unless he works for Erik forever. Maybe that was the idea." He pointed off to the right. "There's Erik now. What time is it?"

"One twenty-five," Bill said.

"Right. What ring's he riding in—three, I think. Fourth Level, Test One."

"Doesn't he look elegant!" Annie said, but Michael didn't answer.

Lyrik was restless. She flattened her ears at every horse that came near her, and once she started to neigh and abruptly broke off. It was an odd sound, almost a squeal.

"Erik stopped her," Michael said. "He doesn't let them sound off like that."

When the bell rang, Lyrik began her entry into the arena. She gave the impression of traveling almost on her toes with dainty, short and hurried steps, but when she reached the center she wouldn't stand still for the salute. Michael could see that she was wound up, resistant, and fighting Erik's direction. She danced impatiently, ears canted back to where Erik sat, and her tail lashed. From the halt she burst forward, started the curving turn at the letter C by the judge's trailer, then shied without warning and tried to canter. Less than half way past the next letter, she began to fight in earnest. She leapt forward and sideways, shook her head violently and tried to buck.

"Jesus Christ!" Michael said. There was a mixture of wonder, concern and admiration in his voice. "What the hell's going on? She never does that—" He was aware of Annie's polite attention to the ride and he wanted her to be impressed, as if it were he who was on trial for her approval.

"She's in season, it's not supposed to be like that," he muttered and willed some sudden heroic action of Erik's to put it right. Lyrik plunged and fought for her head, and against the background of hushed anticipation that followed, he heard a woman seated near them laugh.

"Yes," she said to her companion, "I'm not surprised. He's an absolute laughingstock. I wonder he's willing to put his circus tricks on display at a show like this."

Abruptly Michael turned around. "What the hell do you know?" he said. "Have you ridden the horse?"

"Michael!" Annie said. "For heaven's sake!"

Bill Freeman interceded. "Everyone's entitled to a bad day," he commented mildly as the woman turned at Michael's words and was about to answer.

The woman eyed him coolly and glanced at Michael. "Yes," she said, "but this is a dressage show, not a rodeo. If he can't ride his horse, he should know better than to waste the judge's time."

Annie put her hand out in an instinctive attempt to prevent what she knew would be Michael's reaction. His attention was no longer on their neighbor, however, but on the scene being played out in front of them in the arena. Erik had turned Lyrik and now rode her down the centerline toward the judge. A few feet from the trailer he stopped, removed his hat and saluted. Beneath him Lyrik stepped in place, pulling stubbornly at the rein. Michael saw the judge nod, and Erik replaced his hat and rode directly toward the gate. Lyrik's tail still lashed angrily, and Michael could see the whites of her eyes. He rose quickly to his feet and started down the hill.

"Michael—" Annie started and turned in confusion to Bill. "What's going on, do you suppose?"

"He's excused himself, as well he should," their neighbor said crisply.

Michael had reached the collecting area outside the ring and stood looking up at Erik. Lyrik was still restless and wouldn't stand. She stepped fretfully sideways. Her haunches described an arc around her forehand and her croup lowered as if she might leap from the ground. Erik did not dismount, but Annie saw Michael stoop, pick up a dressage whip from the ground and hand it to him. He rode away in the direction of the horse trailers, far on the other side of the grounds.

Michael watched Erik ride away and then climbed slowly back to where Annie sat.

"What's up?" Bill asked him.

"She blew up for some reason. I didn't ask. He just told me to hand him his stick—they can't carry whips in the ring—and when I asked if I should take the horse back, he said no, he was going to have a few words with her!" He laughed.

Annie changed the subject. "What's been happening with you, Michael? How's the riding going? You are still riding, aren't you? And getting along all right?"

"I'm training a horse, a Thoroughbred some idiot mishandled on the track. Gurney, as a matter of fact." There was an edge of pride in his voice, but Annie couldn't tell if it was his own achievement that motivated it or Gurney's error.

"Really? You must be doing very well."

"Yeah, well, I don't really know what I'm doing." He waved vaguely in the direction Erik had ridden. "He makes me do everything."

It was an extraordinary admission for Michael, and as Annie tried to read his expression, he seemed to realize it himself.

"Good way to break your neck," he added.

"Good teacher?" Bill asked in a neutral tone. He smiled guilelessly at Michael's suspicious look. "Tough, eh?"

"Yeah," Michael agreed. "He knows a hell of a lot, but he won't tell you a damned thing. He made me go back last night to ride. I had to break a date I had and everything. And then when we got there, he made me ride on a longeline with no stirrups like a beginner, and we worked on nothing but my position. I've been working on my position all summer long. Now I have to think about whether one shoulder is half an inch higher than the other, or whether I'm advancing one seat bone in the saddle, or giving the aid with the wrong part of my leg, or tilting my foot or one hand, or sticking my elbow out, or looking down—it's endless. It's worse than going to school."

Bill leaned back on his elbows. "But you chose it, right? So you must like it."

Michael glanced sharply at him and then at Annie. She met his eye and smiled.

"Depends on what you're talking about," he said evenly. "I like horses. They don't put you down. If they try to push you around, you can deal with it. The rest of it—" he cast about for words, "—you can have. You'd have to be some kind of nut case to like working that hard for nothing."

They sat in silence for several seconds. Annie watched Michael as he, in turn, watched the rider and horse in the arena. A familiar doubt lingered in the back of her mind, and she wondered again if she had left Michael defenseless against Sarmento's tyranny. She heard Bill ask Michael to explain the rides being performed and tried to concentrate on his answer.

"Michael—" she said finally, and as if on cue Bill stood up, stretched, and tactfully excused himself. "Tell me the truth, how's it going up there?"

"I told you, it's OK. You know me, I don't like to be pushed around much."

"You don't have to push back, you know," she responded automatically and was surprised to hear him agree with her.

"That's true with horses. You push back and you lose," he said thoughtfully and stared out over the show grounds in the direction Erik had ridden.

She straightened and said directly, "I'm getting some contradictory signals here, Michael. I promised you when you first went up there that I'd try to find something better for you. I really have tried, although I haven't been very successful. Do you want me to keep looking?"

"Never mind. I'm going to hang in there for a while."

"Good for you," Annie said. "Maybe I—"

"There he is—I have to go. See you later." She watched him descend the hill in a series of bounds.

"In some ways he's better than I've seen him in a long time," she said to Bill later. "He seems to be relating this whole horse business to himself. You know, I was so anxious to find someone who'd adapt himself to Michael that it never occurred to me that it might be he who'd do the adapting. He's never been very good at that."

"I told you his kind was tough."

"There was never any question that Michael needed discipline," Annie said thoughtfully. "But he also has this chip on his shoulder—the thing you said once about people needing to fight. It always seemed to me that there was little point getting into confrontations where I ended up being an enforcer, winning by sheer strength or authority. I could have done that, you know. But somehow I felt that he needed an advocate, someone who was on his side, no matter how antisocial that side might be. And to this day I still feel that way."

Bill said, "The fact is, of course, that he needed you as much as he needed authority. Everyone needs an advocate. Funny, isn't it, you break your neck trying to help people, and then you come across someone like Sarmento who doesn't care whether he helps anyone or hurts them. He just does what he does and lets other people swallow it or go elsewhere. That kind of attitude isn't all bad—at least it's honest. But he's lucky he's found a lifestyle where he can do that. Otherwise he'd be Andy Nordstrom's problem instead of Michael's."

She didn't see Michael again until an hour after Bill had left and the show was ending. The ground crew was taking down two of the arenas, and only the central one remained intact. A pickup truck stood in the field, half-filled with white boards, and in the area they had once delineated was a design of dirt paths where the grass had been trampled.

He was standing alone by the letter K near the corner of the collecting area. She waved at him, but either he didn't see her or didn't want to acknowledge the gesture. The hillside was becoming more crowded as riders and grooms joined the spectators, and she made her way down the slope to join him where he stood. Several people followed her example, so that soon there was a scattering of spectators on both sides of the arena. Michael paid no attention to them, but it was while she was watching the activity that she noticed the solitary figure of Kristen standing across the arena from them by the letter B.

The announcer's voice came abruptly over the public address system. "Ladies and gentlemen, we present at this time as a special treat for you, an unusual exhibition of the art of dressage, a musical Kur. A Kur is a freestyle ride to the accompaniment of music and can be ridden to include the movements of any level. In competition with other musical rides, it is scored both on its artistic merit and on the technical performance. Since this is an exhibition and not a competition, it will not be scored, but Mr. Karyl Svenson has agreed to serve as honorary judge.

"Most Americans have had little opportunity to see a Kur performed, and it is with pleasure that we are able to show you today what many consider the true goal of dressage, an art which may be compared to ballet in its—"

Annie saw Ivan and Peter lounging on the slope. Beside her, Michael was starting to look around for the rider.

"The music selected for this ride is the Canon in D by the seventeenth century composer, Johann Pachelbel—" the announcer went on.

Michael said, "Where the hell is he, anyway?" He turned his head, and following his gaze, Annie saw Erik ride into the collecting area.

"With great pleasure, we present to you Mr. Erik Sarmento of Northwood riding the Thoroughbred mare, Lyrik, owned and trained by Miss Kristen Karras."

Erik sat motionless on Lyrik and stared straight ahead. He was wearing white breeches, a formal black coat with tails and a top hat. He held the double reins in white-gloved hands. His boots shone, spurs their only decoration.

Lyrik, jet-black, wore white exercise bandages, which were permitted in exhibitions, although they were forbidden in the riding of tests. Along her crest from her ears to her withers her mane had been done up in tiny braids secured with white tape. Her tail, left unbraided, reached well below her hocks and was brushed so that each hair stood free. There was no hint of color in the picture they made. The saddle and double bridle, dark brown, were almost black, and the saddle was set off by an immaculate white saddlecloth. Against the ebony gloss of Lyrik's coat, the metal bits and buckles gleamed like the highlights on her neck and haunches. Her head held high, she looked around her with nostrils wide, ears strained forward, and a hint of white in the corners of her eyes.

The music over the loudspeaker started, and the mare, impelled by an invisible signal, began her airy entrance. The audience on the hillside fell silent. Standing and sitting, scattered on the grassy slope, they were a patchwork of random color.

Erik sat the trot easily and appeared motionless. The music seemed extraordinarily appropriate to the classical roots of his riding style and to his horse's light and fluid movement. Lyrik performed unerringly, the complete antithesis of the restless, irritated test she had started earlier. Her delicate precision, which grew more energetic as the music did, was totally consistent, obedient and showed a gaiety and elan that made Annie swallow, moved beyond her own understanding.

Michael stood hypnotized by the controlled rhythm and swing of Lyrik's movement. The short tense steps of the earlier test were gone, and she moved in long, relaxed and measured strides, her haunches dropping alternately left and right as she trotted down the long side of the arena. Her gait was almost dainty. She sprang lightly from the ground, and at every stride the grass sprang back from the cadenced touch of her hooves.

Against the swell of the music, Michael heard the clink and jingle of the bits and curb chain, saw the horse's lips drawn back as she chewed and the froth that gathered and spun in flecks from her jaws when she passed only a few feet from where he stood. He could see the light tracing of veins on her shoulder and barrel and feel the heat from her body on his face.

Lyrik flowed effortlessly through the corner and began a half-pass across the diagonal. Without changing the tempo of her trot, she crossed her legs at every stride as she moved both forward and sideways from one corner to the other. Her neck was bent gracefully at the poll, her body lightly curved, and she mouthed the bits gently, her face almost vertical. Her dark eyes were bright and alert.

The hair stood up on Michael's arms and he shivered in the sunlight. Lyrik had moved quietly into canter, and the music, louder now, seemed to drive her forward. Twice on either side of the arena, she moved in a half circle, never varying her stride, and as again she approached the corner she seemed to shorten herself as if she were compressed, still in canter but slow, so slow it appeared she must break her gait or canter in place. But as she reached the long side, her frame lengthened in long, thundering strides, and Michael could imagine her leaping the confines of the ring and moving ever longer and faster across the racetrack and out of sight.

Annie watched the ride with pleasure and glanced at Michael to see his reaction. His face was pale under his tan, and his attention was locked on the performance. She didn't think he remembered she was there. She looked across the ring at Kristen, equally absorbed in the performance, and then at the other spectators. With the exception of Lyrik nothing moved. The music swelled around them.

Through the length of the arena Lyrik was cantering a serpentine. Each time she crossed the centerline she changed her leading leg, and Annie had the impression she was skipping. Her silken tail flicked upward in the change, a gay accompaniment to her dancing stride.

Rounding the turn, Lyrik started down the centerline toward the judge's stand, and as she did so, Erik took the reins in his left hand and dropped his right arm down by his side. At each three strides Lyrik performed a flying change of leg and traveled straight down the centerline to halt directly from canter only a few feet from the judge.

The music ended. Annie saw the judge stand and respond to Erik's final salute with a bow. Moments passed in dead silence, and then a wave of applause rose from the hillside. Annie joined in with enthusiasm. She could see that those seated on the grass had risen to their feet, but from the corner of her eye she noticed that Michael was not applauding. He seemed to be unaware that the ride had ended.

Erik didn't acknowledge the applause. Lyrik pivoted neatly on her forehand and started down the long side of the arena at an active walk. Erik was staring straight ahead. A distance from them he turned his head, and Annie saw his gaze slide over her and meet Michael's. There was no change in his expression, but Lyrik checked her stride for a second, and Annie heard Michael draw a deep breath. Impulsively she reached out, put her hand on his arm and found it rigid. She thought there were tears in his eyes, but his gaze never wavered. It was Erik who looked away. He turned the horse abruptly left and rode her at collected trot straight across the center of the ring to where Kristen stood. He halted the horse and looking straight at her, he repeated his salute.

Kristen stepped over the edge of the arena. She could hear the announcer, taking his cue from Erik's action, identify her again as Lyrik's owner and trainer. She was thinking that in the years she had worked with Lyrik, no one but she had ever ridden her until now. Even when she had had problems that seemed insoluble and had pleaded with Erik to ride the horse, he had refused, and in the end with his help she had done it all herself.

She reached up and put her arms around Lyrik's neck, and then with an ecstatic smile looked up at Erik. "Thank you," she said almost soundlessly. "—so beautiful—I'll never, never forget it."

"It was my pleasure," he answered and smiled at her. "And if it is your wish, I will keep the horse, provided only that you will continue her training."

From across the ring, Annie watched the short exchange and saw Kristen step back and Erik turn the horse and ride toward the gate. A number of people were drifting down the slope to the collecting ring to wait for him. Just beyond her, Michael gave a long sigh and turned from Annie without a word. In silence she watched him trudge back across the grassy field and around the end of the oval track toward the barns.

Annie stood where she was for a long time, thinking over what she had seen. In this unlikely setting, one of her cases seemed to have resolved itself. She felt divided by a combined sense of optimism and loss, for she recognized that Michael was changed. It was the end of her usefulness to him, she thought, and the beginning of some other allegiance, which, until today, she had only dimly apprehended.

In the midst of her reverie she became aware that the judge had left the trailer and was making his way slowly back to the secretary's tent. When he drew abreast of where she stood, the solitary spectator still on the field, he stopped, smiled and made a curious formal bow to her.

"How do you do?" he said.

"How do you do?" Annie answered, flustered.

"You enjoyed the exhibition?"

"Very much indeed—quite extraordinary—"

His smile broadened. "We have both been privileged to see such a performance. My name is Karyl Swenson, and you are—?"

"Annie Trowbridge."

"You are a friend of Erik's?"

It was a natural mistake, she supposed, since she stood alone by the side of the ring.

"No, a friend of a young man who works for him."

"I see. Your young friend is most fortunate, and he will learn a great deal. Erik has genius, you know. I have watched him for years, since he was a boy. I knew his father, you see. He was a talented trainer but—" he put his hand on his chest for a moment and shook his head, "without a heart. You understand? Without a heart."

His words resonated in Annie's mind. She was still thinking of Michael.

"The son has that which the father did not," Svenson went on. "And so he exceeds his father's talent." He bowed to her once again and continued on his way without waiting for an answer.

Partly from curiosity and partly to say goodbye to Michael, Annie made her way to the stable area. She was unprepared for the scene of confusion she found there. All around her horses were being taken from their stalls, walked up and down the aisleways, held while their legs were bandaged for shipping, and led up the ramps of waiting vans and trailers. Piles of equipment lay haphazardly around the shed rows, and cars, trucks, and trailers had been driven into the aisles and left there, some blocking others.

She had trouble finding Erik's stalls and was beginning to fear that Michael might have already left for home when she saw Peter in the distance, walking Lyrik unhurriedly in the unoccupied space at the end of one of the shed rows. The horse's bridle had been replaced with a halter, but she still wore her saddle, the stirrups neatly run up on the leathers. She walked slowly beside Peter, her head down and the lead rope slack.

With Peter's help, Annie found the right barn. Erik was standing just outside the tackroom stall, apparently unconcerned with the activity, which surrounded him. He had shed his formal black coat and stock and stood in his shirtsleeves, his collar unbuttoned. Nearby Ivan stood talking with someone and a distance away Michael was disappearing around a corner with a wheelbarrow full of soiled bedding.

Annie saw Erik watching her as she approached. She remembered her first impression of him in the dim light of the barn aisle at the farm, a dark man with a distant, dark scowl. He wasn't scowling now, and she thought ironically that he looked more like a hero than a villain, dressed as he was completely in white except for his black boots.

"Mrs. Trowbridge," Erik said to her in a voice that held neither curiosity nor enthusiasm. She was surprised that he remembered her at all.

"I wanted to tell you how much I enjoyed the exhibition," Annie said.

"Thank you," he said to her surprise, and she found herself suddenly inarticulate and turned away to find Michael. But when she said goodbye to him he was abstracted and paid her little attention. He seemed eager to get on with his work.

On her way back to her car she stopped for a moment on the deserted hillside by the secretary's tent. The wide field lay below her, the rings gone, the judges' trailers closed and deserted. No elegant horses paraded by now with their manes braided and their riders neatly attired. The only sound was the rise and fall of the wind in the skeletal structures of the midway. Erik's ride seemed only an illusion, and as she stood there confronted by an abandoned landscape, she wondered if she would hear from Michael again.

CHAPTER 22

▼

Annie did hear from Michael, but his letters were short and infrequent. She sent him cards on his birthday and at Christmas and an occasional note or clipping when she came across something she thought would interest him. He never acknowledged them, and sometimes a month or two would pass before he wrote, but she was no longer alarmed by his silence, only sorry that she had no news of him. She was delighted, therefore, when, as he had before, he appeared at the clinic unannounced in early summer of the following year.

She hardly recognized him. She had the impression he had grown taller, although he denied it, and he appeared genuinely glad to see her. He took a seat in her office without urging, and after a few moments of companionable silence pointed to the clay horse, rearing on the windowsill.

"I wish you'd get rid of that."

"Get rid of it!" Annie said. "I wouldn't think of it. Why would you want me to?"

"It reminds me of Tango," Michael said. "Scared out of his mind and ready to fight."

"Tango?"

"A horse I've been riding. Didn't I tell you I was training a horse?"

"Yes, I think you did."

"When I first rode him he was so freaked out I was sure he was going to kill me, and I was sort of walking on eggs around him so as not to set him off. But when I finally took charge, put my legs on him and stopped waiting for him to *do* something, he seemed much more relaxed. And it made sense, somehow. I think he's a lot like me, and I always had that trouble with you."

"Me? What trouble?"

"You never would meet me head on—it was scary as hell." He laughed, "And Erik—he always does, and I always lose."

Annie looked at him in surprise. It was as near as he had ever come to confiding in her. "Scary?" she repeated. "I'd have thought it would be a lot more scary for you if I had."

Michael leaned back in his chair and considered the comment. "Well, I don't know how to describe it, but it's just a lot easier if you know you can't hurt anyone, and I always felt I was going to do the wrong thing. Hell, I *did* do the wrong thing, often as not. But I really didn't *want* to let you down—you know that? I guess I wanted you to stop me."

He glanced at her and looked away again. Then abruptly he got to his feet, walked over to the table by the window and stared out. "When I was in jail that time," he started and turned around to face her, "I was mad as hell at Gurney, the cops, the bartender, that idiot girl I was with. But I didn't mind being in that cell. I'd like to have stayed there even longer, if you can believe that. I mean, there were bars and all and I couldn't get out, but I could relax. There wasn't anyone around I had to deal with—I could just relax. It was kind of peaceful."

"Yes," Annie said, "I do understand that. Do you feel that way up there? At the farm?"

"Sometimes. Particularly when Erik leaves me alone, which isn't often. But I'm even getting better at that, I think. Horses make a lot of demands on you, so you're really locked into a lot of routine. Some of it's pretty obvious—feed, water, stuff like that. Other things take a lot of experience and awareness to figure out."

Annie looked thoughtfully at him. "Like what?" she asked, genuinely curious.

"Oh—," he cast about for examples, "when they're sick or lame or something. I was thinking about this a couple of days ago. If you step on a dog's foot he yelps or cries, and so do cats. Even cows raise a ruckus when they're in trouble, but horses don't make noise like that. You have to be able to recognize when they're acting different. Sometimes it's just that they *look* different, depressed or something. Peter quoted something to me once: he said, 'The eye of the master maketh the horse fat.' It's true."

"You make it sound a little like social work," Annie said, smiling. "Tell me, whatever became of the horse Erik rode in the exhibition?"

"Lyrik? She's still there. She doesn't belong to Erik, you know—"

"Yes, I remember that. He was riding for her owner."

"Right. Kristen, that's the owner, still comes up to ride almost every day after work. Erik helps her."

Annie didn't pursue the subject. Instead she asked, "What about you, Michael? How are you doing?"

"Well, let's see," Michael said. "Nothing's changed really, except that Peter's leaving soon. His parents are helping him set up his own barn." Annie smiled.

There was a long silence, and then Michael said, "It was a long winter. We were snowed in a lot. The county plows that road, but they leave it to last since Erik's the only one up there." He spoke of the cold, the silent mornings when they went out in darkness, leaning against the wind and struggling through drifts to reach the barn. The horses' routine had been changed with the season. They had been kept in at night and turned out for part of each day, regardless of the weather.

He mentioned that he rode more horses now. In winter, because of the difficulty of access, there had been fewer lessons and more horses in for training. Erik bought horses in the autumn and sold them in the spring and summer. Michael commented that he might soon be teaching a few lessons, but his mind was on Blue Tango. He told Annie in detail about his slow progress with the horse and about his frustrations.

A few days before, he said casually, Gurney had come for the horse. The first Michael had known of his arrival was when Ivan came into the tackroom where he was working. "Gurney's here," he said. "I think he's come for Tango."

Michael said nothing, but his heart turned. He washed his hands in the sink and went out into the aisle. He had rehearsed this moment in his daydreams. The scene varied from an angry confrontation with Gurney to a romantic vision in which Erik bought the horse for a song and gave him to Michael as he had done for Ivan.

Erik was already in the doorway of the barn. He didn't seem surprised at Gurney's arrival. "Hope you're right about not needing the trailer rig," Michael heard Gurney say, and it dawned on him slowly that Erik had known Gurney was coming for the horse and hadn't bothered to tell him. He half turned to catch a glimpse of Tango walking in his stall.

"Saddle the horse," Erik said to his surprise.

Gurney entered the barn. His eye fell on Michael, and he smiled. "Still here, eh?" he asked. "Still moving manure piles?"

Michael flushed and turned away. Are you still running lame horses? He said in his mind, and for one long, terrible second wondered if he'd said it aloud. He brought Tango into the aisle and cross-tied him.

Gurney raised his eyebrows. "Put on a little flesh," he commented. "Developed his front end a bit." He glanced at Erik. "Not bad at all."

Michael ran a brush over Tango, picked out his feet and bridled and saddled him. His hands lingered on the horse's face. The dark eyes watched him from under the pale lashes. He looked to Erik and saw him gesture to the back of the barn, and he led the horse out the door to the riding ring. Peter was using the indoor arena.

"Ride the horse," Erik said and opened the gate to let him enter.

When he had closed it, Gurney leaned his elbows on it and watched with a half smile.

"You let the kid ride that horse?" he said mildly to Erik and received no answer.

Michael shortened the rein, pulled the stirrups down and mounted. He walked the horse around the ring on a loose rein and then took up the contact and moved him into a rapid trot. Tango gazed alertly around him.

"Explain what you are doing," Erik said, and Michael spoke to Gurney over his shoulder.

"Right now I'm just warming up," Michael said, "He's a bit hesitant in the beginning, and I've found he always starts out short. So I encourage him to move on out, to get the idea of moving forward. He'll settle in a bit, you'll see."

He turned back to the track and changed direction. When Tango's strides became longer and less hurried, Michael began to sit the trot and then to do a series of transitions from walk to trot and back to walk. At length he asked for the canter. Tango raised his tail and cantered around the ring, snorting rhythmically at every stride. Once he shied into the center of the ring, and Gurney frowned.

"Still at it, eh?" he said.

"Doesn't mean a thing," Michael said as he brought the horse to a walk. "Just feeling good. He won't do that once he starts to work."

"Change the rein and put the horse on the bit," Erik said. "At trot shoulder-in F to M, change rein H to F at working trot and shoulder-in K to H."

Tango moved confidently through the schooling movements. Naturally balanced, his movements were supple and rhythmic. Michael counted silently to himself, keeping the rhythm with his seat and legs. The horse's power seemed to flow up and forward from his hind legs through Michael's own body and he could feel it in his hands. Closing them slightly, he felt the horse come together under him, and he heard Erik say, "Lengthen stride K to M and again H to F."

Rounding the turn past the letter A, he turned across the diagonal at K and opened his hand fractionally, leaning back slightly. Tango's neck lowered, and he lengthened his stride. Michael was in a trance. He hardly knew he was following Erik's directions. The movements flowed together as if he was the center and the source of Tango's energy. When Tango cantered, he felt motionless, the horse rocking beneath him in perfect balance.

He came to a halt at last with a sense of astonishment, almost disoriented. Mechanically he jumped off, loosened the girth and noseband of the bridle and ran the stirrups up.

"Damnedest thing I ever saw!" Gurney said, absently. He removed his cap and ran his hand through his hair. "Wouldn't know it was the same horse! He had you off at all?"

"Couple of times," Michael admitted.

"Gone up with you?"

"No," Michael said, "he never has." He patted Tango's neck.

Gurney eyed the horse for a long moment and shook his head slowly. "Damn," he said. "I don't believe it." He put his hand up slowly and rubbed the back of his neck. "What do you think?" he said to Erik. "Think he'd get much further with this stuff? Be worth more, maybe?"

"He has three good gaits," Erik said. "He's sound. He should progress if he is handled correctly."

"Well, hell, I'm not set up to fool with him. Want to keep him for a while and sell him for me? I'll go halves with you. Can't be fairer than that."

"So he's still there," Michael told Annie with a grin. "I don't know for how long. I felt pretty bad when I thought I was going to lose him, but I think I can take it OK. He's taught me a lot, and I think he's doing well enough that at least he won't end up in a glue factory." He glanced at his watch. "I'd better go. I have some errands to do before I start back."

On his way to the truck, Michael turned around and looked up at Annie's window. He saw her wave and gave an answering wave. He drove down the street with his right hand on the wheel and his left elbow on the sill of the open window. He drummed his fingers on the side of the truck, and thought of what he had not told Annie.

After Gurney had left, Erik appeared in the doorway of the tackroom where Michael was putting away Tango's tack. "Now," he said, "I will hear your evaluation of that ride."

Michael looked up. There was a time when these words from Erik would have made his heart sink, and he couldn't help remembering the time when Erik had imprisoned him in this room with his same stance in the doorway.

"I thought it was OK," he said. "He's still a little stiffer on the right than the left—but I was happy with his transitions."

"And the canter?"

"The canter's gotten much better, more forward and less up and down, and he doesn't lean on me like he used to. I messed up on the circles, particularly to the right, but I thought both of the lengthenings were good. It seems to me that he's getting real rhythm in his trot and canter, and his walk has always been pretty good. All in all, I thought he did well."

Erik had said nothing for a moment. He regarded Michael with a half smile, and then slowly he nodded.

"Yes," he said finally. "It was well done. Very well done."

END

978-0-595-37547-9
0-595-37547-2